THE AFTERMATH: LUNAR

BRADLEY JAMES

BRADLEY BLOOMAN

CONTENTS

Published by Bradley Blooman

https://bradleyjamesauthor.com/

First Edition: May 2024

Second Edition: June 2024 (Trim size change)

Trade Paperback ISBN: 978-1-7385307-2-4

eBook ISBN: 978-1-7385307-0-0

For the dreamers who dare to make their dream a reality.

About the Author

Bradley James published his debut novel, *The Aftermath: Lunar*, in early 2024, realizing a long-held dream. Since then, he has been irreversibly bitten by the writing bug, immediately embarking on his next literary adventure without looking back. When not immersed in crafting narratives, Bradley can be found indulging in long runs, losing himself in books, consuming copious amounts of coffee, or passionately cheering on his favorite football team. Though born in London, he now resides in Southwest England, where the lush landscapes often serve as a backdrop for his creativity.

https://bradleyjamesauthor.com/

CHAPTER 1

A STREAK OF LIGHT tore through the inky blackness, cutting across the stark silence of space. The celestial object, emerging as if from the void, soared across the sky, stopping the two men in their tracks. Instinctively, they raised their hands to shield their heads as a meteor the size of a Volkswagen blazed across the sky, like a projectile from an unseen catapult. They watched in awe and trepidation as it plummeted toward the lunar surface, impacting just feet from the rover they had arrived in. The collision dislodged a plume of lunar dust that slowly fanned out in the low gravity before the meteor skimmed off, mirroring a stone skipping across a lake's surface. It repeated this destructive dance several times, leaving behind a trail of devastation before finally coming to rest.

The two men exchanged horrified glances. Before a word could escape their lips, a second meteor struck to their right. It smashed into modules from the lunar base construction site, then skipped onwards, sowing further chaos. Two more impacts, perilously close, forced them to dive to the ground.

"Meteor shower!" Astronaut Franklin Lewis yelled, pushing off the ground to rise to his feet. "We need to get to the rover and get out of here!"

"Too risky," fellow Astronaut Elliot Adams countered, his voice cutting through the din of relentless impacts, which seemed to be intensifying. "We need to find shelter and wait it out." Straining to assess the chaos, Elliot watched as meteors of all sizes rained down. Though no sound could reach them, the sight of the meteors silently colliding with the surface seemed even more ominous.

"To the entrance!" he shouted, pointing towards a hill they had descended to enter the site. "They're coming from that direction. The hill might offer some protection. We're sitting ducks out here!"

"Let's move!" Franklin responded, giving a thumbs-up and taking long, gliding strides toward the hill. They moved with careful haste, occasionally diving for cover as the meteors continued their relentless assault, each impact a stark reminder of the danger they were in.

Bounding towards the hill's relative cover, Elliot and Franklin found themselves in the direct path of the meteor shower. Elliot's heart raced—it felt like a cosmic game of chicken against the universe. Meteors, large and small, hurtled towards them, their silent trajectory as threatening as any roar.

Mostly, the meteors soared harmlessly over or whisked past them. But not always. Several times during their frantic retreat towards the hill, a meteor would crash into the lunar surface in their path, ricocheting dangerously close. Each time, they found themselves diving to the ground, hearts hammering with fear. Yet, as each meteor careened away, leaving chaos in its wake, they would rise once more, shake off the dust, and push forward again, their movements driven by a fierce determination to survive.

Luck, however, was a mercurial companion. For Elliot and Franklin, its treacherous turn came in an instant. They were level with a stack of conduit pipes when fortune abruptly deserted them.

A meteor struck the side of the pyramid-shaped pile of conduit, a mere thirty feet to their right, just as they passed by. The violent impact sent the pipes hurtling towards them. Caught off guard, both men were swept off their feet by the onslaught, flung twenty feet to their left, and harshly deposited amid a maelstrom of rocks and pipes.

Elliot's back hit the lunar surface with a jarring thud, his breath violently expelled. A high-pitched ringing filled his ears, drowning out the immediate chaos. Pinned beneath the debris, he squinted upwards, seeing the sky ablaze with meteors. Amidst this turmoil, the true nightmare unfurled.

A vast shadow raced across the sky, its speed astonishing. Trapped under the debris, Elliot watched, dread escalating, as the immense asteroid hurtled towards Earth. The impact was cataclysmic, an event scientists would deem extinction-level. A blinding, ferocious explosion of light consumed the entire sky. Earth's atmosphere rippled and tore, the effects visible even from the Moon's surface.

As the blinding light finally dimmed, Elliot stood paralyzed, his eyes wide with disbelief at the catastrophic scene before him. The sight of his home planet in ruins was surreal, like a horrific dream he yearned to escape. This trance was violently broken by a sharp impact against his helmet. Shocked, he reeled from the force of a rock striking him. On instinct, he raised his arms, desperately trying to protect himself from further impacts.

As though his movement had angered the heavens themselves, a ferocious barrage of lunar debris descended upon Elliot. Each impact carried the savage force of a heavyweight boxer's punch—ruthless and unyielding. In desperation, Elliot curled into a tight ball, attempting to shield himself as best as he could. The oppressive weight of surrounding lunar debris bore down on him with a crushing, inexorable force. It was his suit's advanced exoskeleton design that was his thin line between survival and oblivion.

The meteor impacts became relentless, striking from all directions, hammering the lunar surface like a blacksmith furiously working an anvil. Each blow reverberated through the ground beneath Elliot, the vibrations conveying the force of the assault. In those moments, he envisioned his end: buried beneath the lunar rock, pummeled by meteors, his body never to be recovered, or if so, not in one piece. The bombardment intensified, the strikes growing more frequent and fierce. This is it, he thought grimly. Breathing turned into a struggle under the oppressive weight on his chest; the world seemed to constrict around him, the ground eager to tear itself apart to reach him. And then, it seemed to do just that.

The lunar surface beneath him fractured, tearing open as if pulled apart by unseen hands. The ground that had been solid beneath Elliot a moment ago vanished, plunging him into darkness. The first impact sent him spiraling, a sharp jolt that resonated through his body. The second collision came quickly, more disorienting than painful, a harsh rebound that flipped his orientation. By the third crash against the rugged lunar rock, his senses were a maelstrom of confusion, each impact melding into a hazy whirl in his fading awareness.

In those final moments before darkness enveloped him, his thoughts drifted to Earth, shattered and dying, and then to Franklin. I hope Franklin made it out, he thought, a flicker of concern for his friend piercing through the encroaching void. Then, consumed by darkness, his mind surrendered to the silent embrace of unconsciousness.

Chapter 2

Specks of dust floated in the beam of his head torch, drifting in the low gravity, their movements almost unnatural. Elliot watched them with a distant fascination, his mind struggling towards consciousness. A small rock, just outside the light's reach, caught his attention. It tumbled slowly in the low gravity, expanding in his vision as it approached. When it grew to the size of a tennis ball, it softly tapped the top of his helmet. The impact, muted yet startling, snapped Elliot wide awake.

As he became aware that he was lying flat on his back, Elliot tried to sit up, only to find his movement hindered by an unfamiliar weight against his chest. The effort sent a wave of pain through his head, a sensation that seemed at odds with the gentle touch of the rock. His head began to swim, and he felt himself slipping back into unconsciousness. He reminded himself to stay still and calm, focusing solely on his breathing. Slowly, the throbbing in his head subsided. Feeling more in control, he cautiously reopened his eyes to assess his surroundings. Where was he? What had happened? He attempted to use the comms built into his space suit, but a feeble rasp of air was all that emerged from his lips, the pain returning swiftly. He berated himself for trying to speak too soon.

Once more, Elliot opened his eyes and slowly surveyed his surroundings, sending signals throughout his body, awaiting their response. All he received in return was pain, but pain was good. Pain meant sensation; pain wasn't numbness. It indicated he probably wasn't paralyzed. He reasoned that since his face mask wasn't smeared with blood and there were no alarms from his suit's bio-monitors, he likely had no serious internal injuries. However, confirming the absence of broken bones would require attempting to move, something he had to defer for a bit longer. Right now, his eyes were relaying crucial information.

He appeared to be trapped under a substantial amount of debris, which pinned him down, but he could still gaze up at what looked like a vast cliffside wall. Strangely, there were no stars in sight, nor any light from the sun or Earth. Only a towering rock face, which he must have descended—no, fallen. That was right, he remembered now: he had fallen.

Elliot's mind felt like it was shrouded in a dense fog, memories surfacing in fragmented bursts. He closed his eyes, concentrating, trying to piece together the events that led him here. But the attempt was like grasping at smoke: elusive, fleeting. All he could discern was the relentless pounding that resonated through his body, in sync with the throbbing in his head.

In this darkness behind his eyelids, brief flashes of memory flickered. He remembered the sensation of falling, a terrifying, uncontrolled tumble. He could almost feel it again—the disorienting spin, end over end, the jarring impacts as he bounced off unseen walls. Each collision was a sharp jolt, a moment of pain quickly swallowed by the next wave of disorientation.

And then, there was the final crushing impact at the bottom. A force that drove the breath from his lungs and cloaked his world in darkness. After that, there was nothing—just a void where his memories should be.

Elliot opened his eyes again, the sparse details he had managed to recollect doing little to comfort him. He was still trapped, still alone, with only his pain and these fragmented memories for company. The pressing questions remained—how did he end up here, and where was here exactly? These thoughts circled in his mind, but answers remained frustratingly out of reach.

Trapped under the weight of lunar debris, Elliot wrestled with the fragments of his memory. Just as frustration began to mount, something shifted—not in his physical environment, but within his mind. It was as if a dam had broken, unleashing a flood of memories that had been held back.

The trigger was surprisingly mundane, a small detail that would normally go unnoticed. As he shifted slightly, trying to ease the pressure on his body, his hand brushed against a piece of the debris pinning him down. The texture of the conduit, smooth and familiar under the gloves of his space suit, sparked a flash of recognition. It was more than a random piece of debris: it was part of the lunar base's construction material. This connection set off a chain reaction in his brain.

Suddenly, the events leading up to his current situation started replaying in his mind with vivid clarity. He and Franklin had successfully landed on the Moon, their space-craft settling onto the dusty surface with a gentle thud. Together, they journeyed across the barren lunar landscape in a rover, a journey marked by anticipation and a sense of purpose. Upon reaching their destination, they disembarked, stepping out into the vast, silent expanse to survey the site destined to become humanity's first lunar base. It was a moment filled with triumph, the culmination of countless hours of training and preparation. They were in the midst of assessing the site, checking off equipment, when the sky above them suddenly turned traitorous.

Without forewarning, the tranquility of the lunar surface had been disrupted by a meteor shower. It was a violent and spectacular display, with celestial debris streaking across the lunar sky, each one a blazing trail of light. The meteors bombarded the surface, hurling building materials and plant machinery in disarray, transforming the site into a scene of chaos. Each impact sent plumes of moon dust slowly billowing in the low gravity, obscuring the stark lunar landscape. Elliot and Franklin, caught off guard, scrambled for any semblance of cover, but the relentless bombardment was overwhelming.

Amidst the chaos, a haunting vision resurfaced in Elliot's mind, overshadowing even the terror of the meteor shower. This disturbing memory cast a dark shadow over his current plight, trapped and pinned beneath debris in a cave deep beneath the Moon's surface.

The asteroid. Earth. Tears welled in Elliot's eyes as the full magnitude of the disaster came flooding back to him.

His home planet, along with everyone he had ever known, had been wiped out in an instant. He couldn't help but despairingly wonder, How could we not have seen it coming?

A sense of hopelessness began to seep into his mind. Where could he possibly go even if he managed to escape? It was in this dark moment that a name broke through his desolation: Franklin. The possibility that Franklin might still be alive ignited a small but vital spark of purpose amid his overwhelming despair. Clinging to this thought, Elliot allowed it to anchor him. It was all he had left, the solitary beacon in his sea of hopelessness.

Chapter 3

Franklin, Elliot thought, his mind grappling with the uncertainty of his friend's fate. Did he survive the meteor shower? Could he be trapped down here with me? He scanned his surroundings once more, straining to see beyond the confines of his limited view. He shifted, craning his neck to peer along the line of his body, only to be met with an unyielding darkness beyond his feet.

He paused, taking stock of the rocks and dust blanketing him, before lying back to gather his breath, allowing the pounding in his head to ebb. Eyes closed, he visualized his predicament. His body, particularly his right side, was pinned beneath a considerable mass of rubble and debris. His first effort to sit up had confirmed the substantial weight pressing down on him. Were it not for the robustness of his space suit, he may well have been crushed.

Fortunately, his left arm was free from below the elbow, and his legs could move slightly from just below the knees, but these were the only resources at his disposal to tackle his dire situation.

Elliot began by cautiously testing the range of motion in his left arm. He flexed his fingers, relieved to feel each digit respond, albeit with a slight stiffness. Gradually, he extended his arm, wincing as the movement sent a dull ache up his forearm. The space was cramped, and his movements were hampered by the unyielding debris, but his elbow and wrist seemed to have retained their flexibility.

Next, he shifted his focus to his legs. With a grimace, he attempted to bend his knees. The right leg moved only slightly, hindered by the weight above it, while the left responded more freely, though the sensation of the suit pressing against his skin reminded him of the constraints. He tried to wriggle his toes, a small victory as he felt them move inside his boots, albeit awkwardly.

The real challenge lay with his right arm, trapped and immobile under the heavy mass. He tried to wiggle his fingers, but the response was minimal, a faint twitch that ignited a glimmer of hope. With each minuscule movement, a twinge of pain shot through his arm, a stark reminder of his precarious situation.

Resigned to the slow, painstaking process ahead, Elliot began the laborious task of shifting the debris. Using his free left hand, he carefully grasped at the smaller rocks and dust, moving them aside inch by agonizing inch. Each movement was deliberate, mindful of the potential for causing further collapse or injury.

As the minutes stretched into what seemed like hours, Elliot's progress in clearing the debris was painstakingly slow. To keep his mind occupied, he focused on his next immediate challenge: speaking. His initial attempt had been rough, a stark reminder of his harsh landing under the lunar surface. The absence of the taste of blood in his mouth suggested his raspy voice was due more to the impact than injury. Saliva had gradually returned to his mouth during his mobility tests, easing the dryness and soreness in his throat.

He tried speaking again. "Fran-klin," he whispered hoarsely, the words barely audible. A small cough to clear his throat helped slightly. "Franklin," he repeated, a bit stronger this time, though his voice was still faint to his ears. He swallowed, then spoke again. "Franklin." It sounded better to him. Gathering his strength, he continued. "This is Elliot, do you copy?" His voice was raspy but improving. He paused, both to catch his breath and to give Franklin a chance to respond. Silence. He persisted, hoping for a reply.

"Franklin, come in. This is Elliot. Talk to me, buddy." His urgent call transmitted into the void, met only by the oppressive silence. Buried at the bottom of a lunar crater, surrounded by rubble, Elliot considered the likelihood of signal issues. Protocol dictated that his next step should be to try to contact mission control on Earth. They could provide him with guidance on Franklin's vitals and whereabouts. However, given the recent catastrophic events on Earth he'd just witnessed, if anyone had survived, their situation would undoubtedly be more dire than his own. Resolutely, he pushed away these thoughts. Giving in to despair was not an option; he had to stay focused.

Elliot knew mission control had the means to reach out to him. They would be monitoring his suit's telemetry, and in cases of an emergency, which this unequivocally was, it was standard protocol for them to override all communication channels to establish contact. The fact that they hadn't only confirmed to him that either they were gone and he was on his own or he was unable to receive a signal down here. Until he could confirm otherwise, he had to assume both.

Establishing contact with Franklin remained his main priority, but to check his signal status, he needed to clear the dust obscuring his Computer Display Unit (CDU) located on his left arm, a task made impossible with his right arm currently pinned beneath the debris.

As he lay there, a troubling thought crossed his mind. If he had no signal and Franklin was attempting to contact him, Franklin might conclude that he had died. In such a scenario, Franklin would likely scour the site in search of him. But after a fruitless search, rational thinking would dictate that Franklin return to the spacecraft to try and establish contact with mission control. The grim reality of their situation dawned on Elliot: if mission control was no more and Franklin believed him to be dead, his friend's next course of action was unpredictable. The uncertainty of Franklin's decisions, compounded by their dire circumstances, added to the gravity of Elliot's isolation.

Elliot redoubled his efforts, focusing intently on the task of excavating himself from the lunar debris. Minute by minute, he slowly made progress. Finally, after what felt like an age, he had cleared enough rocks to hatch a new plan—employing his legs to aid his escape.

He positioned his heels firmly against the ground, having created a stable platform to push from. His strategy was clear: a coordinated effort of pushing with his legs while twisting his body, aiming to maneuver his right side into the space his left currently occupied, and hopefully roll out to freedom.

Despite the grueling nature of the task and the heavy emotional burden of Franklin's unbroken silence, Elliot's determination remained unshaken. Drawing a deep, steadying breath, he braced himself for the strenuous physical effort that lay ahead. Counting down with resolve, he launched into action, exerting every bit of his strength in a push-and-twist maneuver.

Though the attempt was exhausting and seemed to yield little immediate success, it marked a significant stride toward his goal. He had managed to shift his position slightly, a minor yet crucial movement. This small victory bolstered his spirit. Fueled by this progress, Elliot steeled himself for the next attempt, fortified by the knowledge that he was inching closer to freedom. For him, giving up was not an option. He was resolute: he would free himself, no matter how many attempts it took.

Elliot, filled with a renewed sense of urgency, inhaled deeply, mentally counting down before each new attempt. He persisted time and again, pushing and twisting with relentless determination. On his seventh try, something shifted dramatically. His left side suddenly broke free, the movement abrupt and forceful. His right side quickly slid into the space previously occupied by his left, causing the rocks and dust that had ensnared him to shift into the void below, a small cloud of dust slowly dispersing around him in the low gravity.

Buoyed by this breakthrough, Elliot continued with several more twists and turns. Each movement was labored but purposeful, until finally, he managed to extricate himself completely from the lunar trap. The sense of relief and triumph was overwhelming as he emerged, a free man once again.

Elliot dragged himself into a seated stance, pausing to regain his breath. Once collected, he brushed the dust from the CDU on his arm, inspecting his suit's condition. The Oxygen Regenerative System flashed a reassuring Normal—one less worry; his next breath was secure. Turning his attention to the suit's power supply, Elliot checked the batteries, relieved to find them intact. They hovered just below eighty-percent capacity, sufficient for now. Ingeniously designed, the suit was equipped to recharge using both solar and kinetic energy. The moment he moved, it would start converting his kinetic energy, guaranteeing enough power until he could access sunlight on the Moon's surface.

Upon navigating to the communications menu, he was met with a stark message: No Signal. This at least explained the unnerving silence. Glancing at the CDU's clock, Elliot realized that roughly two and a half hours had passed since he last checked in with Franklin on the surface. He surmised that he must have been unconscious for at least thirty minutes, possibly longer. The time he spent freeing himself was unclear, but two and a half hours without contact would undoubtedly have led Franklin to believe the worst. Feeling a surge of urgency, Elliot realized he had to act fast. His goal was clear: reach the surface or locate a spot where his communications equipment could catch a signal.

Chapter 4

ELLIOT SLOWLY PULLED HIMSELF to his feet, feeling a perverse pleasure as he relished the pain shooting through his muscles while he stretched. He hoisted his arm high, the CDU on his arm pointed upwards, resembling a man desperately seeking a phone signal atop a remote mountain. The No Signal status remained obstinately present. He was much deeper than initially thought. It was a miracle he hadn't killed himself from the fall, he considered for the first time. He peered upwards, his head torch casting stark, elongated shadows against the crater walls, illuminating nothing but the oppressive darkness above.

"Goddamn it!" he exclaimed, his voice swallowed by the vast emptiness. From his vantage point, the crater walls loomed, insurmountable and cold. The vast distance between them mocked his feeble attempts to brace his body and climb. Even with the Moon's reduced gravity, his efforts to leap upwards, superhero-style, in search of a signal proved equal parts comical and futile.

He paused, taking a deep breath that resonated within his helmet, the sound a stark reminder of his solitude. "Okay, enough messing around, Elliot," he chided himself, his voice steady yet tinged with a hint of urgency. "You need to find a way out of here!"

Elliot began scrutinizing his surroundings. The area in which he had awoken stretched about twenty feet across, forming a bowl-like depression in the lunar landscape. Glancing left, his torch's beam showed the space narrowing to a mere ten to fifteen feet in some parts. To his right, it remained consistently wide. He paused to consider. Heading left might bring him to a narrower section, potentially narrow enough to brace against both walls and climb out. It seemed as viable a plan as any.

Before embarking, he meticulously arranged a collection of rocks into an E and an A, his initials, and fashioned a crude arrow pointing left. This marker served a dual purpose: it would guide Franklin, should he descend into this lunar abyss, and it would serve as a point of reference for Elliot himself in case he needed to backtrack.

With the marker set, Elliot began his careful journey. His steps were shaky, hampered by a persistent bruise or strain on his left side, a reminder of his fall. Despite this, he kept his focus sharply on maneuvering through the unfamiliar terrain. The path to the left snaked amidst a clutter of fallen rocks, with the walls slowly closing in and eventually merging overhead, creating a cave-like passage. Within just twenty meters, the cave's ceiling descended alarmingly low, forcing Elliot to significantly stoop as he proceeded.

A few steps further the beam of his head torch was suddenly thrown back by an unyielding rock wall—a dead end.

"Shit!" he cursed aloud, his gloved fist thumping against the cave's roof in frustration. With this route blocked and his choices dwindling, Elliot faced the looming possibility that the opposite direction might lead to a similar impasse. Although there remained a faint hope it might ascend to the surface, Elliot wasn't feeling that lucky.

Head bowed under the low ceiling, he took a deep, steadying breath, eyes closed, and exhaled slowly, banishing the creeping despair. With a renewed, albeit grim, determination, he opened his eyes and turned back. The return journey to the marker and the exploration of the uncharted path beyond awaited him.

Upon his return, Elliot swiftly reoriented the stone arrow to the right and proceeded down the uncharted path. He hadn't gone far when the sinking feeling returned: above him, the walls began to converge while the ground remained wide, no less than fifteen feet across. As he moved forward, the walls above united into a solid ceiling, enveloping him once again in a cave-like tunnel.

Halting momentarily, frustration etched across his face, he lifted his gaze. His head torch swept across the cave ceiling, tracing its contours. A realization dawned on him—could it be that he had plunged through a solitary opening into a cave? This would explain the absence of stars or external light and the lack of a signal on his CDU, which he checked once more, only to be met with disappointment.

If he truly was stuck in a cave, then the hole through which he had fallen might be his only escape. The daunting prospect of reaching this potential exit, whose height was unknown, weighed heavily on him. Yet, there remained a sliver of hope—perhaps this path would lead to a surface exit. If not, his only recourse would be a perilous free-climb ascent of the crater walls at his initial fall site, praying that an exit still existed there.

Resolute in his quest, Elliot pressed on. The light from his head torch cast eerie shadows against the rocky walls, their contours highlighted as he navigated the cave. He noted that the ceiling had stabilized at a height of about fifteen feet, a consistency maintained for the past several minutes. The terrain underfoot had transformed too, from a rugged, rock-strewn path to a smoother surface, dusted lightly with lunar soil. The cave's architecture now resembled an arch, akin to a long-forgotten subterranean railway tunnel. For a moment, Elliot paused, his immediate predicaments momentarily eclipsed by the marvel of his surroundings.

"The guys back on Earth would have loved this place," he mused softly." The cave, with its natural protection, seemed an ideal alternative for a lunar base, far more shielded than the exposed structures above, a thought that brought a stark reminder of the meteor shower.

His mind wandered to Franklin, hoping against hope that his friend had weathered the celestial storm. The likelihood of Franklin being on the surface seemed much higher now, given the absence of any sign of him in the caves. Elliot clung to the hope that Franklin's resourcefulness had kept him safe. With a deep breath, he refocused on the path ahead, the dual objectives of finding an exit and reuniting with his friend fueling his determination.

Elliot proceeded along the tunnel, his head torch casting beams of light that danced across the cave walls, revealing their unusual, almost-artificial structure. The arch-like formations seemed too symmetrical, too deliberate to be natural formations. Could these be man-made? he wondered.

As he shifted his gaze from one side of the cave to the other, a distant glint snagged his attention. Focusing his light ahead, he discerned a reflection shimmering about a hundred meters away, a ghostly presence in the darkness. Is that ice? he wondered, his mind flickering back to briefings about lunar ice deposits. Yet, certainty would only dawn upon a closer examination.

Approaching the source of the reflections, his sense of wonder was gradually replaced by a familiar dread. Flanking the glimmering spots were the unmistakable cave walls, signaling another impending dead end.

"No, not again," he muttered in frustration. He quickened his pace as if trying to outrun the inevitable conclusion. But with each step, the stark reality sharpened into focus. When he was merely ten meters away, Elliot came to an abrupt halt, struck by a wave of disbelief. What lay before him transcended his comprehension, defying not only his expectations but also the very boundaries of what he had deemed possible on the Moon.

Elliot resumed his approach, this time with a cautious, measured pace. The tunnel's end was indeed near, but the source of the reflections was not what he had anticipated. Not ice, but something metallic? No, more than that—a substantial presence of metal. His gloved hand reached out, brushing against a hard, flat surface veiled under a thick layer of dust. The object was substantial, roughly ten feet high and fifteen feet wide, seamlessly integrated into the cave walls like a colossal safe, yet wholly different.

As Elliot swept away the dust in broad, sweeping arcs, a cascade of lunar dust tumbled to the ground. The surface beneath was sleek, a deep black hue with subtle green speckles, smooth and oddly warm to the touch. He rapped on it with a gloved fist, but the impact felt absorbed, solid yet somehow cushioned.

With each sweep of his hand, more of the object revealed itself, challenging his understanding of what should exist in this lunar cave. Its design was paradoxically familiar and alien, igniting a blend of recognition and disbelief within him. As he brushed away the last vestiges of dust, Elliot stepped back, the weight of the implications hitting him hard. There, standing starkly before him, was an undeniable yet inexplicable truth. It was an airlock.

CHAPTER 5

STEPPING BACK, ELLIOT WAS engulfed by a whirlwind of thoughts, each more pressing than the one before. "How is this possible?" he muttered. "An airlock, here, under the Moon's surface?"

His mind darted between theories, dismissing each as quickly as it arose. The logistics of secretly building a lunar base were staggering; such an undertaking couldn't possibly have eluded global notice. Yet, the thought of it being a recent addition, perhaps related to their project, lingered in his mind. It was plausible, considering the proximity to their construction site and the available machinery. However, the secrecy puzzled him. Why here, in a cave only revealed by a meteor's violent intrusion?

The notion that this airlock might be an undiscovered part of their lunar project flickered in Elliot's mind, igniting a frail beacon of hope. Conceivably, there could be another exit on the opposite side, or perhaps, just beyond this barrier lay a communications hub. The prospect of re-establishing contact with Franklin, maybe even reaching out to Earth, sent a surge of excitement through him.

However, as his optimism reached its peak, it was tempered by an undercurrent of doubt. The airlock's secluded location and its mysterious design raised questions that gnawed at the edges of his hope. Was it merely wishful thinking to assume this was part of their project, or was he standing on the threshold of an entirely different revelation? Either way, the site of this airlock caused his heart to beat heavier in his chest.

Elliot studied the airlock intently, his eyes tracing its contours. Something about its design felt out of place with his knowledge of space technology. It was as if it belonged to a different time. He hesitated to scrutinize the thought too closely, fearing what he might—or might not—find. This airlock represented his last hope, his only chance of survival. The alternative was a fate he couldn't bear to contemplate: dying alone, entombed in the Moon's silent embrace.

Elliot methodically continued his task, sweeping away layers of dust from the airlock door in search of some means of entry. His hands explored every inch, but the door itself yielded no clues. Undeterred, he extended his search to the frame surrounding it.

As he reached the right side of the airlock, nestled in the shadows cast by the cave walls and jutting rock formations, he found another flat, dust-veiled surface. With deliberate strokes, he cleared it, revealing a small, slightly protruding rectangular panel. His fingers traced its edges, finding a lip at the bottom. With a cautious tug, the panel tilted forward and hinged at the top like the cover of a notepad. It flipped open, unveiling a large lever nestled within, currently in a downward position.

"Bingo," Elliot exclaimed triumphantly. The discovery was a significant breakthrough, yet it brought with it a new set of unknowns. What would happen once he engaged this lever? With a steady hand and a racing heart, he prepared to find out.

He drew in a sharp breath, his hand gripping the lever tightly as he lifted it upwards. A tense silence enveloped him before the ground seemed to respond with a series of vibrations, reverberating through the cave's expanse. When the vibrations ceased, the wall he had meticulously cleared began to ascend, revealing behind it a hidden passage beyond.

Startled, Elliot instinctively stepped back as the wall shifted. Layers of dust dislodged from the moving door and the surrounding walls, cascading to the floor in a dense cloud. The dust swirled around him, obscuring his vision. His head torch did little to penetrate the thick dust cloud, its beam only highlighting the myriad particles still drifting downwards.

Impatience gnawed at him as he crouched, hoping for a clearer view at the bottom of the door. But the visibility was even poorer there, the dust hanging heavy in the air like a dense fog. He stood there, almost holding his breath, waiting for the air to clear. The anticipation was insufferable, each second stretching longer as he yearned to discover what lay beyond the airlock door, on the other side of this lunar enigma.

As the airlock door completed its opening sequence and the dust settled, Elliot peered into a dimly lit room, approximately twice the size of a standard garage. He stepped forward cautiously, his head torch sweeping across the interior. The room seemed sparsely furnished, with only two walls and a second airlock door on the opposite side coming into view.

Crossing the threshold, Elliot noticed a soft, ambient light gently illuminating the space. The walls, about a foot thick as evidenced by the space left by the now-retracted door, felt solid yet slightly cushioned under his touch. They were coated in a light gray hue, speckled with black, mirroring the room's minimalistic aesthetic. The adjacent door blended seamlessly with this color scheme, prompting Elliot to wonder if the exterior door shared the same design.

The room was stark in its emptiness, devoid of any furniture or equipment. However, he couldn't help but notice several vents dotting the ceiling. Approaching the inner door, he examined the panel, which was identical to the exterior one but unobscured by the cave's natural elements. The absence of dust was notable, save for the traces he had inadvertently brought in, a fact that made him feel slightly guilty.

With a growing sense of urgency, Elliot reached for the panel, his fingers deftly finding the familiar lip at the bottom. Lifting the lid, he revealed the lever, predictably in the downward position. "Up to open, down to close," he said to himself, pushing it upwards with a firm hand.

He waited, anticipating the familiar clanking noise that had announced the opening of the previous door, but was met with silence instead. The lever, unlike the previous one, failed to lock in the upward position and slipped back down to its starting point. "Well shit!" he exclaimed, his voice steeped in disappointment. A second attempt proved just as fruitless. "Oh come on!" His frustration reached a boiling point, and he lashed out with a kick at the door. "What use is an airlock door if it won't even open?"

As he paced the room, his mind raced. "Just one job to do," he muttered, halting mid-stride. A realization struck him like a thunderbolt. He chastised himself for overlooking the obvious—an airlock operated on the principle of isolated environments. Its purpose was to prevent the simultaneous opening of both doors to maintain a secure atmosphere.

"Close the damn door, you fool!" he scolded himself, hurrying towards the outer door's inner control panel. With a newfound clarity, he pulled the lever downwards. The outer door began to descend smoothly from the ceiling, its movement almost silent and seamless, blending perfectly with the room's color scheme.

Elliot marveled at the door's effortless motion, despite its size. He reminded himself to remain vigilant; fatigue was setting in, and in this unforgiving lunar environment, a single oversight could be fatal.

As the outer door slid into place, the familiar series of vibrations started up again and signaled its successful closure. Elliot, satisfied with this confirmation, made his way back to the inner door. Just as his hand hovered over the lever, he paused, a crucial realization dawning on him. "Equalize the pressure," he murmured, scanning the airlock for any additional controls.

In any standard airlock procedure, the safety of the astronaut and the integrity of the adjoining environment hinged on stabilizing the pressure. First, the airlock must seal completely, then it must equalize the pressure to match either the outside or inside environment. Yet, as

Elliot surveyed the room, no additional panels or buttons were apparent. The only visible mechanisms were the levers and the vents in the ceiling.

"Maybe it's integrated into the lever system," he speculated aloud. He weighed his options, considering the potential risks. With the outer door firmly sealed, the lever might initiate pressure equalization before granting access, or it might remain inert. Or worse, it could trigger a rapid decompression. But with no other visible means to control the environment, he felt he had no other choice.

Elliot cast a final thorough glance around the room, ensuring he hadn't overlooked anything crucial. He then steeled himself for what was to come. The decision to engage the lever was laden with uncertainties, but it was a gamble he knew he had to take. Taking a deep, steadying breath, he firmly grasped the lever, bracing himself to lift it and face whatever mysteries lay beyond.

The moment Elliot secured the lever at its topmost position, he felt it lock into place with a definitive click. Almost instantly, a rush of air burst from the ceiling vents, filling the room.

"Whoa, what was that?" Elliot exclaimed, his stomach lurching as he instinctively reached out to steady himself against the wall. The sensation was fleeting, reminiscent of the unexpected thrill he'd once felt when his flying instructor had abruptly put their plane into a dive. It was over as quickly as it had begun, but it left him momentarily disoriented.

Within a few seconds, the forceful jets of air ceased. The sound of three distinct clanks emanated from beneath the inner door, signaling the next phase. Elliot watched, heart pounding, as the door smoothly ascended, disappearing into the ceiling.

"Yeah!" he shouted, his voice booming in triumph as he punctuated the moment with an exuberant fist pump. A wide grin unfurled across his face, an amalgam of relief and exhilaration. "Now, let's see what's behind mystery door number two!"

Chapter 6

Elliot took another look at his CDU. Forty-five minutes had passed since he stumbled upon the mysterious airlock, and his communications device remained stubbornly silent. A sudden shift in the environmental indicator caught his attention, prompting him to delve deeper into the CDU's readings. To his astonishment, the device indicated that the environment beyond the airlock contained breathable oxygen, rendering his suit unnecessary. But that wasn't the only anomaly; the gravity had altered as well.

On the Moon's surface, gravity measured 1.625 meters per second squared—roughly one-sixth of Earth's gravity. However, just beyond the airlock, it had intensified, now registering at 6.540 meters per second squared. This was approximately two-thirds of Earth's gravity, a curious discrepancy that left Elliot pondering why not full Earth's gravity? The change was immediately evident, as he experienced a distinct heaviness in his limbs, a sensation of being grounded that was both unfamiliar and strangely reassuring after the weightlessness of the lunar surface.

This revelation of breathable air, coupled with the gravity shift, added layers of mystery to his already-perplexing situation. As he stood there, processing these anomalies, a part of him resisted the urge to remove his suit—a shield that had become his second skin in the lunar expanse. Yet, the possibility of walking unencumbered, breathing unfiltered air, was tantalizing. He hesitated at the threshold of the unknown, grappling with the decision to step forward into the darkness that beckoned him with silent promises of answers.

Amidst his hesitation, Elliot's thoughts turned to the persistent claustrophobia that haunted him within the suit, despite its consistent temperature control. He yearned for even a brief escape from its confines. Tentatively, he unlatched the locks of his helmet, allowing it to come free. As the helmet came off, a rush of air escaped from the suit, and Elliot took a long, liberating breath. The sensation of the air, cool and unfamiliar against his face, was momentarily exhilarating, stirring a deep-seated longing for freedom. As he breathed in, the expected stale, metallic scent of lunar dust, akin to spent gunpowder or the ashes of a snuffed fire, clung to his senses, the only discernible smell in the otherwise sterile environment.

Elliot's moment of liberation was short-lived. His thoughts swiftly returned to his primary mission—finding Franklin. He realized that venturing further without the protection of the suit could be perilous. The base, with its unexplained oxygen and altered gravity, held too many unknowns. With a renewed sense of purpose, he resolved to keep the suit on. It was not merely protective gear now; it symbolized his resolve and readiness for the challenges ahead. Thus, helmet in hand, he stepped forward into the darkness.

As Elliot exited the airlock, ambient lighting gently illuminated the passage ahead, revealing a corridor about fifty meters in length, mirroring the airlock's color scheme of light gray speckled with black. He noticed two sets of indents on either side of the corridor, evenly spaced, suggesting the presence of rooms. At the far end, a door as large as the airlock loomed.

Moving cautiously along the corridor, Elliot was keenly aware of the silence, his footsteps barely making a sound on the smooth floor. The air felt still, untouched, against his bare face. He reached the first set of doors after ten meters. There were no handles, only panels on the left side, sleek and unlike those of the airlock, lacking any lip or protrusion. Elliot speculated about the technology—perhaps a sensor or a fob entry system. He waved his hand in front of the panel; nothing happened. A gentle push produced the same result. A twinge of frustration crept into him as he tried the door on the opposite side, only to be met with the same silent refusal.

As he continued towards the second set of doors, his frustration grew. Each door, with its stubborn access panel, seemed to mock his efforts, amplifying his sense of urgency. It made logical sense to him that certain areas in a base would be secured, but the relentless dead ends were wearing down his resolve. By the time he neared the last door in the corridor, a sense of despair was beginning to gnaw at him. *Why does it always come down to the last option?* he mused bitterly.

Near the end of the corridor, Elliot eyed the final door. It appeared larger than the others, a fact that contributed to the feeling that this door was more significant. Unlike the others, this one was positioned adjacent to the airlock. In Elliot's mind, this suggested it was either another airlock or perhaps an entrance to a more central area of the base.

The panel beside the door mirrored the sensor-pad style prevalent throughout the corridor, extinguishing Elliot's fleeting hope that it might lead to an airlock. His repeated attempts to gain access were as futile here as they had been with the other doors, each failure ratcheting up his frustration. In a moment of sheer exasperation, he struck the door with his fist; the sound resonated dully through the empty corridor. It served as a stark reminder of his isolation and the oppressive nature of his surroundings.

Taking a deep, steadying breath, Elliot leaned his forehead against the cool, immovable surface of the door. Eyes closed, he sought a moment of calm amidst the storm of disappointment. "C'mon, Elliot, think!" he urged himself aloud. Memories of Franklin's problem-solving prowess came to mind, painting a stark contrast to his own approach. *Okay, what would Franklin do?* he pondered, envisioning Franklin's meticulous, sometimes-overzealous methods.

"He'd take you back to the start and check every step again," Elliot said to himself, drawing on his friend's thoroughness. With renewed resolve, he pushed away from the door and retraced his steps towards the airlock. As he neared the first set of doors, a sudden realization struck him. "The door!" he exclaimed, chastising himself for overlooking such a fundamental aspect—the inner airlock door had been left open. "How could I be so stupid?" he scolded himself in disbelief. "Seriously, this is day one of astronaut training!"

Elliot reached the inner airlock doors and swiftly pulled the lever down. The doors began their descent from the ceiling, but he didn't linger to watch them seal shut, his focus already shifting back to the doors in the corridor. With a sense of eagerness and apprehension, he moved to the first door, hoping for a sign of change. But there was none.

After waiting impatiently for the final clank to come, indicating the inner airlock door was closed, Elliot repeated the familiar routine of pushing, tapping, and waving at the sensor panels with a renewed sense of urgency. But, to his dismay, there was no change; the doors remained as unresponsive as before.

Feeling a surge of frustration, Elliot continued down the corridor, methodically attempting to open each door. The silence of the base seemed to amplify with each failed attempt, echoing his growing sense of futility.

Finally, he stood before the last door once more, the weight of his failed attempts heavy on his shoulders. He gave it a final half-hearted wave, a tap, but nothing changed. Slumping to the floor, his back against the door and his head buried in his hands, Elliot was engulfed in despair. It felt as if every effort, every shred of hope, was being methodically extinguished by the unrelenting silence of the base.

Sitting there, the idea of using brute force momentarily flickered through Elliot's mind. He contemplated smashing the door with his foot or ramming it with his shoulder. But he quickly dismissed these notions, knowing the doors were too robust, built to withstand forces far greater than human strength could muster. "What I need is an access card," he muttered, his voice a faint echo in the stillness of the corridor.

As he sat there, his gaze inadvertently drifted upwards. That was when he noticed it, igniting a spark of hope within him. "... Or a ladder!" he exclaimed, a surge of energy revitalizing his weary frame. There, at the end of the corridor, ingeniously integrated into the now-sealed inner airlock door, was a ladder. It loomed like a solitary beacon of hope, piercing through the shroud of overwhelming despair that had begun to settle around him.

Chapter 7

Elliot sprang to his feet, his eyes widening. "What in the...!" he started, but his sentence trailed off. A tinge of regret hit him as he realized that he would have noticed the descending ladder earlier if he had been more observant while the inner airlock door was closing.

He sprinted down the corridor, slowing only as he neared the airlock door. His eyes traced the ladder's rungs to the top, where an access panel, almost perfectly camouflaged against the ceiling, caught his attention. Scanning its outline, he quickly spotted a button at the top of the door. "That must be what opens you," he said, a wave of excitement building as he began his ascent.

Halfway up, Elliot stretched his left hand out to press the button. The panel slid open silently, revealing a dark crawl space above. Peering in, he could discern little in the darkness, except it seemed to run parallel to the corridor below.

Descending once again, he donned his helmet, the head torch illuminating his ascent. Now, with the light piercing the black, he could see further ahead. Although the end remained beyond the light's beam, a renewed sense of hope surged within him. This hidden passage, unnoticed until now, might be the path forward he had been desperately seeking.

Elliot hoisted himself up through the panel. It appeared to be as wide as the corridor below, but its height forced him to navigate on hands and knees, a scant space above his head. Pipes lined the walls on either side, likely conduits for oxygen and power throughout the base. As he crawled forward through the enveloping darkness, a thought crossed his mind: on Earth, such a space would be laden with spiderwebs and dust, but here, it was almost eerily pristine.

As he progressed, more of the passage ahead fell within his head torch's beam. Much to his disappointment, it appeared to offer no access to the adjacent rooms. However, something indistinct at the far end sparked a flicker of hope within him, suggesting a possible way forward. He crawled on, buoyed by the thought. There must be a purpose if access was provided to this area, he reasoned, clinging to his optimism.

Reaching the end, Elliot encountered a hatch blocking his path. A handle protruded from it, allowing him to slide the hatch aside with relative ease. He cautiously poked his head through the opening to survey his surroundings. Walls enclosed the space directly ahead, to his left and his right. However, below him yawned a vast shaft, its depths shrouded in darkness, its bottom invisible to his eyes.

"Down?" he uttered in dismay. "I don't want to go down. I need to go up!" His words echoed in the vast space, reflecting his frustration and the irony of his situation. Despite his reluctance, it seemed that his only path forward was, in fact, downward.

Pulling his head back from the ledge, Elliot carefully maneuvered to position himself for the descent. "Only one way to go, I guess," he murmured. He tentatively extended his feet, feeling for the first rung of the ladder. As he tested it with his weight, the ladder proved sturdy, bolstering his confidence. Gradually, he eased the rest of his body over the edge. "Easy does it, Elliot," he coached himself, starting the slow, deliberate descent.

Surprisingly, the descent was smoother than he'd anticipated. With his face turned towards the wall, he began to pick up the pace, albeit cautiously. The impossibility of peering directly down the shaft led him to a rhythm: descend ten rungs, then pause to glance downwards between his legs. Each time he looked, the view was the same—an unending stretch of darkness, punctuated only by more ladder rungs. His progress was only discernible when looking upward, but soon, even the edge he had started from vanished from sight, leaving him with no reference point.

After five minutes of uninterrupted descent, the bottom of the shaft remained a mystery. Elliot couldn't help but wonder, *Just how deep does this go?* The question echoed in his mind, unanswered, accompanied by another perplexing thought: and why would anyone build something so deep beneath the Moon's surface? The sheer absurdity of his situation dawned on him, prompting a shake of his head in sheer bewilderment. As he descended deeper into the shaft with each passing moment, the mystery seemed to deepen with it.

Another ten minutes passed, and yet the bottom of the shaft remained veiled in darkness. It was then that a new realization struck Elliot: he wasn't feeling fatigued. He mulled over this as he continued downward, remembering that the gravity here was only a fraction of Earth's—about two-thirds. This reduced gravity meant he was lighter, which placed significantly less strain on his muscles. The logic of the situation was familiar to him; after all, he had undergone extensive training under similar conditions on various space stations. In this lighter gravity, managing his body weight should be relatively effortless, even if he had to rely on just one arm. This understanding brought with it an idea.

Bolstered by the confidence instilled from his astronaut training, Elliot firmly grasped the outer pole of the ladder with both hands. He positioned his feet securely against the sides of the ladder, allowing for a stable stance. Carefully, he began to relax his grip, using his hands more as brakes to modulate his speed. "Why didn't I think of this sooner?" he chided himself, a touch of irritation in his tone. Now, he was smoothly gliding down the ladder, each movement more fluid and assured than before, transforming his descent into a more controlled and enjoyable process.

As he grew more confident, Elliot gradually increased his speed, periodically peering down between his legs for any sign of the approaching ground. The descent had transformed from a cautious task into something almost exhilarating. It was another five minutes of this controlled descent before he finally spotted the ground, forty meters below. He immediately tightened his grip to decelerate, finally touching down at the bottom of the shaft with a sense of accomplishment.

Looking up, Elliot marveled at the vast distance he had covered below the Moon's surface. "I hope I get to use the elevator for the way back up," he joked to himself. Turning, he was met with another hatch at waist height. "Makes sense," he said, half expecting another crawl space leading to yet another ladder.

Elliot proceeded through the hatch, and as he had anticipated, found himself in another crawl space. This one, however, was shorter, leading him half the distance of the previous one before terminating at another access panel. Locating the button, he pressed it, and the panel slid open, his head torch illuminating a ladder affixed to a wall—or possibly another door, he considered.

Before descending, Elliot cautiously poked his head through the opening, keen to avoid any unforeseen hazards. The space below resembled another corridor, similar to the one above. The ladder seemed attached to what he suspected was another airlock, judging by the familiar panel on its side.

Gently, Elliot lowered himself from the access panel to the floor below. As his feet made contact with the ground, ambient light softly illuminated the new corridor. It was strikingly similar to the one above, albeit half its length. Moving swiftly, he approached the two halfway along the corridor, which, to his disappointment, remained unresponsive just like the ones above. He then proceeded to the end of the corridor, where he hypothesized an elevator might be, based on the panel's appearance.

Elliot tested the panel but unsurprisingly, it remained inactive. Deep down, he hadn't truly expected it to work, but hope had spurred him on. If it had been functional, it might have offered an easier way back up, a thought he couldn't help but entertain.

As Elliot returned to the ladder, he paused to check his CDU. The display confirmed his expectations: *No Signal*. This was hardly surprising given the depth at which he found himself. The readings showed that the atmosphere remained breathable and the gravity unchanged. He noted that thirty minutes had elapsed during his descent. He encouraged himself to stop watching the clock, as time-checking wouldn't speed up his progress. As long as Franklin wasn't in immediate danger, he reasoned, they could establish contact once he found a way out or stumbled upon a communication room. The possibility of Franklin needing urgent help lingered in his mind, but he pushed it aside. It was beyond his control, and he was already pushing his limits to find a way forward.

Refocused on the task at hand, Elliot understood the importance of maintaining momentum. He approached the panel beside the airlock door, his movements almost automatic. Lifting the panel lid, he flipped the lever upwards. There was a brief, anticipatory pause before the familiar clanking sounds filled the corridor, signaling the start of the airlock door's ascent. The door began its slow retreat into the ceiling, each mechanical sound a reminder of the alien and isolated environment he navigated. Elliot waited, poised for whatever lay beyond, his resolve as steadfast as ever in the face of the unknown.

CHAPTER 8

AS THE DOOR-OPENING SEQUENCE began, Elliot observed the ladder smoothly retract into the ceiling. His attention then shifted to the airlock, strikingly similar to the one he had previously entered. Upon stepping inside, the chamber was instantly flooded with light. He turned, pulling the inner lever downwards, and watched as the door sealed shut behind him, enclosing him within the confines of the airlock.

As the final clanks of the door sealing resonated, Elliot turned towards the outer door, poised to start the pressure-equalization-and-exit sequence. While waiting, his thoughts wandered, musing over the potential destination this airlock might lead to. Generally, an airlock indicated an exit to the outside, but the notion of resurfacing so effortlessly after such a profound descent beneath the Moon's surface struck him as highly unlikely. Yet, if it didn't lead outside, what purpose did the airlock serve? The baffling nature of this lunar base continued to mystify him.

Activating the lever, Elliot felt it lock into place. Simultaneously, the familiar sound of air jets began to fill the small space. A strange sensation stirred in his stomach, prompting a thought—*had the gravity changed once more?* That could signify a return to the surface, but the logistics of such a transition baffled him.

As the outer door gradually ascended, an unexpected sight came into view, interrupting his train of thought. A splash of green caught his eye, starkly contrasting with the metallic and barren surroundings he had become accustomed to.

"What the...?" he uttered in disbelief, crouching down for a closer look. "Is that a plant?" The sight of something so distinctly terrestrial in this alien environment added another layer of mystery, fueling both his curiosity and confusion about the true nature of this lunar base.

As the airlock door continued to rise, Elliot's eyes widened in disbelief. Before him was a dense mesh of ferns, flourishing over the once-closed airlock. "How is this possible? Plants can't grow without oxygen!" he exclaimed, quickly consulting his CDU for answers. His surprise deepened as the device confirmed a breathable atmosphere still surrounded him. "What the...?!" he repeated, trying to reconcile this information with his surroundings.

The realization struck him with sudden clarity: he was still within the confines of the base. Considering he had only descended since his entry, resurfacing was logically out of the question. But then, the puzzling change in gravity gnawed at his mind. He quickly checked the gravity readings on his CDU, which confirmed his suspicions: the gravity was now at 3.270 meters per second squared, roughly a third of Earth's gravity. This shift raised a flurry of questions in Elliot's mind. *Why has the gravity altered again? If I'm still inside the base, why isn't the grav-*

ity uniform throughout? What sets this section apart? His thoughts spiraled in a whirlwind of confusion and curiosity, each question adding to the complexity of the lunar base's enigmatic nature.

As the door completed its opening sequence, Elliot stood, fixated on the lush ferns that almost completely veiled the doorway. He reached out tentatively, his fingers brushing against the greenery. "It must have taken ages for these to grow so densely," he mused, his touch confirming their reality. The sheer extent of their growth suggested that this airlock hadn't been used for a considerable time, perhaps years. This revelation only deepened the mystery of the base. For the first time, he allowed himself to consider whether the base was even man-made.

To venture further, Elliot realized he would need to clear a way through the dense foliage of ferns. With determination, he reached out and grasped a large clump in each hand, parting them like curtains. Some fronds snapped and tumbled to the ground as he diligently worked to create an opening large enough to peer through.

The airlock's light spilled through the gap he had made, casting beams onto a rocky path that lay directly ahead. Pushing his head through the makeshift opening, Elliot's head torch flickered across the cave-like surroundings. The walls were adorned with a layer of moss, lending the space an almost ethereal quality. The floor glistened under the beam of his torch, the moisture reflecting the light and enhancing the impression of dampness. The scene before him was reminiscent of a botanical garden yet shrouded in darkness. He wondered if the area would illuminate like the rest of the base had, once he stepped outside the airlock.

"Only one way to find out!" Elliot declared, his voice tinged with both apprehension and curiosity. He persisted in tearing away the dense ferns that obscured the airlock entrance, pausing only when he had cleared an opening large enough to pass through. As he stepped forward, he suddenly exclaimed, "Whoa..." his foot meeting empty air instead of solid ground. In a moment of uncontrolled momentum, he tumbled through the gap, inadvertently dislodging more ferns in his descent, and landed in a disheveled heap on the cave floor. A string of curses spilled from his mouth as he rolled onto his back, frustration radiating from him in waves.

Lying there, the light from his head torch cast eerie shadows that danced along the cave's walls and ceiling. The constant shifts in gravity, combined with his lack of rest, were taking their toll, making him increasingly prone to careless mistakes.

Elliot took a moment to gather himself, lying amidst the ferns. The ordeal since the meteor shower had pushed him to his limits, both physically and mentally. He had been relentlessly exerting himself since awakening in the depths of a lunar cave, a constant battle against time and circumstance. The gravity of his responsibility weighed heavily on him: Franklin's life might hinge on his actions. Yet he recognized the peril in his current approach. "I need to be more careful," he admonished himself. A misstep not only endangered his own life but also threatened his ability to assist anyone else. With a deep breath, he prepared to rise, steadying his resolve to continue, albeit with more caution.

After securing the airlock door behind him, Elliot took a moment to disentangle the stray ferns caught in his suit. He flexed his arms and legs, adjusting to the altered weight sensation in the new environment. A thought struck him, prompting a quick check of his CDU. The readings confirmed breathable air and a cave temperature of fifteen degrees Celsius—cool, but tolerable enough for a brief respite from the suit.

Elliot had been encased in his suit for an extended period. Although it regulated his temperature effectively, a more pressing need had arisen—a bathroom break, of which he had been urgently reminded by his recent fall. He saw this as an opportune moment. Although still within the base, this area, with its vegetation and damp floor, felt more akin to an outdoor environment. It might be his only chance for a while to step out of the suit.

Resolved, Elliot began the process of extricating himself from the suit. Modern space suits were far more user-friendly than their predecessors, no longer requiring a team for donning or doffing. He manipulated the exoskeleton's quick-release levers, hidden yet easily accessible. The suit's body section detached from the legs, and seams opened, allowing each part to be removed with ease. Within two minutes, Elliot had successfully shed the suit, a small but significant liberation given his prolonged confinement within it.

As Elliot relieved himself, he was grateful for the light from his suit's headlamp, strategically positioned to illuminate his surroundings. During this necessary break, he became acutely aware of the cave's distinct odors. Alongside the expected damp earthiness typical of a cave, there was an undercurrent of something more pungent and rotten. This unfamiliar and unsettling scent gave him pause, instilling an uneasy feeling of not being alone.

As he finished up, another aspect of the cave demanded his attention: a persistent sound that had gone unnoticed until now. "What is that?" he asked himself, stepping back towards the center of the cave, near his suit. He tilted his head, listening intently in the direction of the cave path.

The sound now resonated with familiarity for Elliot—the distinct echo of water rushing somewhere in the distance. As he stood still, a cool breeze meandered through the cave, offering a fleeting sense of comfort. This breeze, however, carried with it an inexplicable odor, a strong scent of decay permeating the air. It was more than just the dampness of a typical cave; there was something else, something unsettlingly organic about this smell. It hung heavy in the atmosphere, a constant reminder of the unknown factors lurking in the depths of this subterranean labyrinth.

Pulling his attention back to the task at hand, Elliot reached for his suit. The mysterious odor, lingering in the back of his mind, added a sense of urgency to his movements. The distant sound of water not only beckoned him but also reminded him of his intense thirst. His last hydration had been hours ago, back on the rover. Consulting his CDU, he reaffirmed the pressing need to find water. As he equipped himself once more, the possibility of discovering the water source—and perhaps the origin of the mysterious odor—drove him forward. Holding his helmet under his arm to light his way, Elliot stepped cautiously along the cave path, each stride a mix of apprehension and determination to unravel the secrets that lay in the uncharted darkness ahead.

Chapter 9

Elliot progressed along the cave's path, which remained largely straight for nearly a hundred meters. The sound of rushing water grew steadily more pronounced, its presence a constant companion in the otherwise silent expanse. Accompanying this sound was the pungent stench that seemed to intensify with each step, intertwining with the dampness of the cave.

The beam of Elliot's head torch cut through the darkness, unveiling a left turn in the path ahead. He observed the cave floor, now increasingly carpeted with thick patches of moss that lent a surreal quality to the terrain. As he rounded the corner, the path began to curve right once more. His torchlight threw long, ghostly shadows against the cave walls, creating a play of light and darkness that added to the eerie, otherworldly ambiance of the cave.

Suddenly, a sharp *CRACK!* shattered the relative silence. Elliot froze, his heart pounding in his chest. The sound, so jarringly out of place in the monotonous ambiance of the cave, heightened his awareness of the potential danger surrounding him. He stood motionless, trying to calm his racing thoughts.

He looked down at his feet, feeling his heart pounding. "It's just a stick or a branch," he reassured himself, trying to dismiss the surge of panic. Aiming the light of his helmet downwards, he saw a broken stick beneath his foot. He exhaled deeply, chastising himself. "You're gonna give yourself a heart attack." Bending down, he began to brush the moss away from the snapped stick, careful to keep his helmet's light directed on the spot.

But then he paused. "Wait a minute..." he muttered. As more of the stick was revealed, it transformed into something more rounded, more bulbous at one end—disturbingly familiar in shape. With growing apprehension, Elliot cleared away the remaining moss, revealing the unmistakable form of a bone. It was no mere stick; this was something far more significant, a discovery that sent a chill through him.

Elliot scrutinized the bone with practiced ease. It was slender, spanning roughly fifteen to twenty inches, and its shape unmistakably suggested it was a femur, likely from a deer. This recognition came instinctively to him, a skill ingrained during his youth spent in the countryside under his grandfather's tutelage. Together, they had immersed themselves in the natural world, with Elliot absorbing the nuances of tracking and hunting. These expeditions were more than just pastimes; they had equipped him with invaluable skills and helped carve his identity during those pivotal years.

Now, as he held the bone in the dim light of his helmet, Elliot was struck by the sheer absurdity of the situation. Deep beneath the Moon's surface, in a base shrouded in mystery, lay the bone of a deer—or perhaps some other animal. He shifted the light of his helmet, scanning the cave floor. More bone-like shapes, varying in length and partially concealed by moss, became visible. The cave floor was littered with them, a bizarre and unsettling discovery in such a remote and alien location. How and why these remains were here, so far from their natural habitat, was a mystery that deepened the enigma of the base and its purpose.

Elliot cautiously approached another object on the cave floor, initially mistaking it for a rock because of its size and moss-covered surface. Kneeling, he gently brushed off the moss to reveal its true identity: the skull of an adult deer, long deceased. It was devoid of flesh, with only moss adorning its surface—a testament to the time it had lain here. Scanning the cave floor, he realized this was true for all the remains. But what or who had brought them here?

A chilling thought struck him as he stood up. Could he be in the lair of a predator? Or perhaps this was a place where some creature brought its prey to feed? More alarmingly, where was this creature now, and how would it react to his intrusion?

Elliot reasoned that any creature accustomed to this level of darkness might possess night vision superior to his. Turning off his light would only serve to put him at a further disadvantage. Thankfully, the breeze through the cave was flowing towards him, carrying his scent away from anything that might be lurking further ahead.

Moving with heightened caution, Elliot proceeded to the next bend in the passage, careful to avoid any more bones and making unnecessary sounds. His senses were acutely alert, every rustle and shift underfoot sending ripples of apprehension through him.

As he rounded the corner, he was immediately struck by a wave of foul odor, the smell of decay so overpowering it nearly made him gag. He covered his nose, trying to filter out the stench. The passage here had expanded significantly, now twice as wide, a room almost rectangular. There were two exits: the one he had entered through and another leading deeper into the unknown. The floor was no longer littered with bones but was instead covered with a layer of sticks, leaves, and grass. A realization dawned on him—this was a nest. He was standing in the heart of a den, a thought that sent a shiver of fear down his spine as he contemplated the implications of this discovery.

The den, though currently unoccupied, bore the distinct impressions of something large that had once rested there. How long ago, Elliot couldn't ascertain. Amidst the leaves and other nest materials, he spotted dried blood and tattered remnants of meat, a grim explanation for the pervasive stench. Whatever resided here was undoubtedly large and carnivorous.

A wave of urgency washed over Elliot, a primal instinct to be anywhere but in this den. The thought of the creature's possible return sent a pulse of fear through him. He knew he stood little chance of reaching and securing the airlock in time if the den's inhabitant were to suddenly appear. The idea of becoming another discarded remnant in the lair, a late-night snack, was unthinkable.

Moving swiftly, Elliot navigated around the edge of the den, heading towards the adjacent tunnel. He paused briefly at the entrance, ensuring it was clear of any immediate threats. But then, interrupting the silence, an over-whelming roar engulfed the space, its intensity almost paralyzing. He felt the sheer force of it, a presence so powerful it dominated the entirety of the new passageway. A dim, twilight-like light emanated from beyond, casting both terrifying and mesmerizing shadows across the cave's walls and ceiling. A cloud of breath billowed towards him, enveloping the area in a chilling mist. Elliot stood frozen, his mind grappling to comprehend the sight before him.

Chapter 10

At the far end of the passageway, Elliot beheld an astonishing sight: a waterfall cascading down, its water scattering light in all directions. The beams of light penetrated the waterfall's veil from behind, refracting like a kaleidoscope or a disco ball, illuminating the cave with an ethereal glow. Clouds of mist erupted where the water struck the rocky surfaces, darkening the stone with their damp touch. A natural formation of rocks had diverted part of the flow, creating a stone basin brimming with water before it spilled over and rejoined the waterfall's main torrent, disappearing into the unseen depths below.

As the initial shock of finding a waterfall on the Moon subsided, Elliot began to approach it, half expecting the surreal scene to dissolve into a dream at any moment. He imagined waking up under a pile of conduit pipes on the lunar surface, with Franklin's familiar smile greeting him. Yet, as he drew closer and felt the spray of cold water on his face, the dreamlike quality faded into stark reality. Each droplet that landed on his skin was a reminder of the inexplicable truth of his surroundings. This was no dream; the waterfall, with its mesmerizing beauty and chilling touch, was as real as anything could be in this bizarre lunar landscape.

Reminded again of his intense thirst, Elliot acted with caution. He dipped his left arm into the stone basin, allowing the sensors on his suit to analyze the water's composition. After a brief moment, he withdrew his arm and quickly checked the environmental screens on his suit's CDU with his right hand, eagerly awaiting the analysis results.

A sense of relief enveloped him as the data on the screen confirmed the water's safety. It was not only water but also nontoxic and suitable for consumption.

Elliot carefully positioned his helmet to illuminate the basin's edge before he knelt, his movements driven by a primal need. He drank with a fervor that betrayed his desperate thirst, akin to an animal at a watering hole. The water was refreshingly cold, each gulp more satisfying than the last. To an onlooker, Elliot might have appeared as a traveler who had endured an arduous journey through a vast desert.

Having satisfied his intense thirst, Elliot paused to catch his breath, his eyes riveted on the spellbinding waterfall cascading before him. Its existence, deep within the bowels of the Moon, was yet another enigma. He pondered whether this marvel was a product of nature or an extraordinary feat of human engineering. On Earth, creating such a spectacle would be a monumental task, but here, on the Moon, it bordered on fantastical.

The sheer scale of such an endeavor seemed almost beyond the limits of imagination. Yet, the reality of the waterfall, with its mesmerizing flow and ethereal beauty, stood before him, challenging his understanding of what was a possibility. As he absorbed the scene, Elliot was struck by a profound realization: despite the wonders he had already encountered, there were likely even more secrets hidden within the depths of this mysterious lunar base, waiting to be uncovered.

Elliot observed the waterfall's relentless cascade, brief interruptions in the flow granting him fleeting glimpses of what lay beyond. Natural light, reminiscent of the soft glow of early evening, filtered through, casting a mystical radiance. The intermittent flashes revealed tantalizing images of trees and distant land, igniting a spark of excitement within him.

With renewed energy, Elliot stood up, helmet in hand, and began to scrutinize his surroundings more intently. The passage he had followed ended at this waterfall, which impressively spanned twenty meters across the cave's end wall. On the left, the rocky cave wall intersected with the waterfall, diverting part of the flow into the basin from which he had drunk. His eyes traced the waterfall's expanse from left to right, the roar of the water almost overwhelming in its intensity.

As he neared the right corner of the room, Elliot noticed a subtle change. The light filtering through the waterfall there was dimmer, and the flow of water was slightly less dense. Peering through the watery veil, he discerned a passage tucked away in the corner, bending to the right and partially concealed by the cascade. It appeared to be a viable route, a potential path leading towards the source of the natural light and the glimpses of an outside world. The possibility of exploring beyond this waterfall, of stepping into the landscape he had seen in flashes, filled him with a sense of urgency and determination. This hidden passage could be his gateway to uncovering the secrets of this enigmatic lunar base and the surreal world it concealed.

With his helmet securely back on, Elliot pressed his body against the cave's right wall, extending his left arm forward like a blind person's cane. He extended his hand through the waterfall, feeling for the rock wall on the other side. Gently, he inched closer to the cascading water, tentatively extending his left foot to gauge the rocky floor's stability. He discovered that the ground extended about two feet from the wall before giving way to empty space. Carefully, he shifted his weight onto his left leg, positioned about a foot from the wall, and eased his head through the watery curtain.

The sensation was surreal, reminiscent of being in a car wash, watching the world distort through jets of water. It felt like being submerged and yet somehow remaining dry. Once he fully emerged on the other side, his first instinct was to look down. The ledge where he stood was the passage's narrowest point, but it quickly widened to about five meters just around the bend.

Elliot continued his careful progress into the new passageway, each step measured and cautious. Once he was safely past the narrow ledge, he leaned against the far right wall, taking a moment to let the rush of adrenaline subside. He turned to observe the crude entrance he had just navigated. The waterfall had formed a natural curtain across the passage, its continuous flow likely eroding the rock over countless years. The sight of the water sculpting its way through the stone passage was a testament to the power and persistence of natural forces, even in this most unexpected of places.

The passageway extended for about twenty meters, curving gently to the left towards its end. It was bathed in a soft illumination, a blend of the light seeping from behind the waterfall and another source emanating from around the bend. Filled with a sense of hope, Elliot moved steadily towards the light, yearning for the openness of the outside world after his prolonged stay in the confines of the caves.

As he navigated the left-hand bend, the unexpected sight of the sky struck him with profound impact. Ahead, through an archway at the end of the passage, lay a vast expanse of sky, awash in the hues of a dying day. He rushed towards it with a sense of desperate longing, his eyes greedily soaking in the abundance of light and color, a stark contrast to the dimness of the underground.

Reaching the arch of the cave, his view expanded into a breathtaking panorama. The sky was a canvas of oranges, purples, and pinks, painted by the setting sun as if just for him. Below, forests in varying shades of green and brown sprawled across the landscape, dissected by a meandering river that flowed into a vast lake two hundred feet below. The sight was overwhelming, filling him with a mixture of joy and disbelief at the natural wonder that unfolded before his eyes, a stark and beautiful contrast to the darkness of the cave's passageways.

Elliot leaned against the cave wall, his hand seeking support as he grappled with the staggering reality before him. This wasn't just a hidden waterfall or an underground cave: it was an entire world, seemingly impossible and yet undeniably real. With breathable air and a setting sun painting the sky, the scene defied all logic. How could such a place exist miles beneath the Moon's surface? It was inconceivable, yet the evidence was right before his eyes—he had tasted its water and now, he craved to breathe its air.

In a frenzied rush, Elliot fumbled with his helmet, hastily removing it to take in a deep, exhilarating breath of fresh air. It was a glorious sensation, a taste of freedom that surpassed his wildest dreams. For a fleeting moment, he questioned his reality—was this death a coma, or some heavenly construct conjured by his mind? The questions swirled in his head, but they couldn't overshadow the tangible beauty of this place.

The urge to explore was irresistible. He longed to descend to the world below, to touch the trees, swim in the lake, and wander through the forest. The explorer within him, long confined by the boundaries of space and the lunar base, was now unrestrained, eager to experience everything this newfound paradise offered. He felt like a child in a candy store, overwhelmed by the possibilities and unsure of where to begin his adventures in this surreal and magnificent landscape.

"I need to find a way down there," Elliot said to himself, his eyes scanning for a path. His gaze landed on a passage that continued through the arch, morphing into a naturally formed staircase etched into the mountain's side.

The steps wound down the mountain in a zigzag pattern. Eager to immerse himself in the breathtaking landscape below, Elliot began his descent, his eyes captivated by the spectacular vista unfolding with each step. He was so absorbed in the scenery that the first bend in the staircase almost took him by surprise.

But as he prepared to navigate it, doubling back on his path, Elliot came to an abrupt halt. There, just thirty meters below, at the upcoming bend, was the largest brown bear Elliot had ever seen.

CHAPTER 11

IN THE FACE OF danger, the primal response of fight or flight would kick in, an instinctive and automatic physiological reaction that occurred to a perceived threat or stress. Throughout his life, Elliot's default had always been to fight. His military training had honed his combat skills against human adversaries, but now he faced a different kind of opponent—a brown grizzly bear. His grandfather's words echoed in his mind: "If it's black, fight back. If it's brown, stay down." The advice was clear—while black bears might be intimidated, brown bears were a different matter entirely. They were known as grizzlies for a reason, and their reputation for ferocity was well deserved.

The bear hadn't spotted him yet, but it was only a matter of time before she would round the next bend in the zigzagging path. Elliot's options were limited. There was no place to hide on the exposed mountainside, leaving him with a stark choice: confront or escape. But escape seemed futile. He knew the terrain that lay behind him, and he was painfully aware that the bear could easily outpace him before he reached the safety of the airlock.

Confrontation was his only viable option. With a grim resolve, Elliot quickly donned his helmet once more and picked up two sizeable rocks from the path. Clutching them tightly, he readied himself for the impending encounter, his every sense heightened, his mind racing with strategies to face the formidable beast that lay ahead.

The massive brown bear ambled around the bend, her nose to the ground, oblivious to Elliot's presence as she made her way up the path. With the bear closing in, now only twenty-five meters away, Elliot knew he had to act before it was too late. He planned to use rocks and loud noises to drive her back, but time was running out.

In a decisive move, Elliot stood as tall as he could, drawing upon every ounce of his strength and courage. He let out a thunderous roar, aiming squarely at the grizzly. The bear, caught off guard, jerked her head up and instinctively hopped backward. Seizing the moment, Elliot hurled one of the softball-sized rocks in his hand. It struck the ground just in front of the bear, bouncing up to hit her front paws. Without hesitation, Elliot bellowed another roar, gripping a second rock tightly while snatching up a third.

The grizzly, surprisingly unfazed by the rock's impact, glanced down at it with a nonchalant air, as if dismissing it as no more than a falling acorn. However, the expression in her eyes as she turned them back to Elliot was chilling—a look of unadulterated malevolence. This was her territory, her hard-won domain, and she was ready to defend it fiercely. Rising to her full formidable height of ten feet, she let out a deafening roar in response. Her teeth bared menacingly, spittle flying from her jaws, she stood as an embodiment of primal power and defiance, challenging the intruder who dared to encroach upon her mountain home.

"Ah, shit," Elliot blurted out in dismay, realizing his efforts to intimidate the bear were failing. Yet, he couldn't afford to show any hesitation. He hurled the second rock with all his might, aiming for the bear's massive belly. The rock hit its target, forcing the bear momentarily back onto all fours. But this action only fueled her fury, provoking an even-more-thunderous roar as she began her charge.

"Ah, shit," Elliot muttered again, a sense of dread washing over him. He hastily threw his last rock at the oncoming beast before pivoting to flee up the steps. The sounds of grunting, growling, and dislodged rocks echoed behind him as he sprinted with all his strength, bounding up the staircase several steps at a time. He made quick progress, but a backward glance as he dashed through the archway confirmed his fears. The bear was already rounding the bend where he had thrown his final rock, closing the distance between them with terrifying speed.

As Elliot raced towards the waterfall, he knew there was no room for hesitation. The methodical approach he had previously taken was a luxury he no longer had. His only option was to rely on his memory of the chamber's layout and make a daring leap through the waterfall. His heart thundered in his chest with every stride as he sprinted down the passageway, with the roar of the waterfall intensifying with each step.

A guttural, nightmarish roar echoed from behind, indicating the bear had reached the archway. He realized with grim certainty that reaching the airlock was an impossibility. Even retreating to the bear's nest was too far for safety.

Elliot's mind raced as he sprinted towards the waterfall. His strategy was clear: dive through to the chamber and swiftly move to the right, near the stone basin. He hoped the bear, fueled by fury, would barrel past him toward her den. If not, he'd have to make a split-second decision to leap back, a desperate gamble for his life. Maybe, just maybe, he'd survive the dash down the path if the bear lost interest once he distanced himself from her den.

The waterfall's prismatic light danced before his eyes as he closed in. He mentally counted his steps, timing his leap perfectly. "Jump on three," he coached himself. One... There was no room for fear of the rocky ledge below. Two... The bear's hot breath seemed to graze his back. Three! With a primal yell, Elliot launched himself into the waterfall's curtain.

As he plunged through, a colossal thud hammered into his back—a powerful swipe from the bear's paw, catapulting him further than intended. He hurtled through the air, crashing and skidding to a halt in the center of the chamber. Behind him the bear emerged with fluid grace, landing deftly on all fours, her gaze locked on Elliot, a low growl rumbling in her throat.

Rolling onto his back, Elliot found himself face-to-face with the drenched grizzly. She reared up on her hind legs, water cascading off her sleek brown fur, her massive frame nearly eclipsing the dwindling light from the waterfall. She towered over him, making herself as large as possible—a formidable, almost-mythical figure. Then, with her massive jaws agape, revealing a row of razor-sharp teeth, she let out a roar that resonated with primal fury.

CHAPTER 12

IN THE WAKE OF the bear's thunderous roar, Elliot lay on the ground, momentarily stunned by the ferocity and sheer magnitude of the creature looming over him. The grizzly, drenched and formidable, stood like a sentinel of the wild, her figure casting a vast shadow across the cave. Her eyes, reflecting a raw, untamed strength, were fixed intently on Elliot. In that moment, suspended between awe and terror, he fully comprehended the enormity of his predicament. It was a call to action, a signal that he needed to move, and fast.

Following this moment of realization, Elliot scrambled to get back on his feet, but the grizzly was upon him with astonishing speed. She knocked him down with her massive body, pinning him to the ground. Her colossal head lunged towards his chest, her teeth gnashing at his suit in a frenzied attempt to tear through it. As her powerful front paws dragged him backward, she sought a firm grip on his chest armor.

In sheer desperation, Elliot pummeled her head with both fists, fighting for his life, hoping she wouldn't crush him with her full weight. The suit's exoskeleton was incredibly robust, a lifesaver during the meteor shower and his fall into the cave. However, it was not designed to endure the relentless onslaught of a grizzly bear. It held together, shielding him from the worst of the bear's fury, but the repeated impacts were jarring, threatening the limits of both the suit and his endurance.

The bear's frustration mounted as her efforts to tear Elliot apart proved futile. In a swift maneuver, she flipped him onto his stomach. Seizing what he thought was a chance to escape, Elliot tried to scramble away, only to be slammed back to the ground by a heavy paw. The bear's jaws clamped onto his suit's backpack, trying a different tactic in her relentless assault.

The adage from his grandfather echoed in Elliot's mind: "If it's brown, stay down." It contradicted every instinct he had to fight back, but his efforts to escape had been futile. Physically overpowered, he realized the futility of resisting. With great effort, Elliot forced his body to go limp, stifling his screams as the bear's formidable claws continued their assault. His exoskeleton suit, the thin line between life and death, was holding up, but he couldn't help but wonder how long it would last under such a relentless attack.

Time seemed to stretch endlessly as the bear's blows gradually lessened in frequency. Eventually, she pressed her snout against the back of his helmet, sniffing intently, searching for any sign of life or resistance. Elliot remained as motionless as possible, barely daring to breathe. The bear delivered a couple more exploratory strikes, then paused to observe him. After another intimidating roar and a cautious nudge, she seemed to be waiting for a reaction, but Elliot gave none.

The bear started to pace, her heavy footsteps echoing in the chamber. She seemed to be allowing her adrenaline to dissipate, all the while keeping a watchful eye on Elliot's motionless form. After a couple of tense minutes, she ambled over to the stone basin for a drink, the sound of water echoing softly in the cave. Then, with a final sniff and a series of snorts, she slowly made her way toward her nest, leaving Elliot lying still, relieved yet exhausted as the imminent threat receded.

From his position on the floor, Elliot watched warily as the bear's massive silhouette disappeared toward her nest. He waited, every second stretching into an eternity, before attempting to rise. As he cautiously pulled himself up, a sharp jolt of pain shot through his back, nearly drawing a scream from his lips. With great effort, he stood, turning towards the waterfall. Tears welled in his eyes from the intense pain that racked his body. Assessing his injuries would have to wait; his immediate focus was on escaping, silently and swiftly.

Just as he took his first tentative step toward the hidden passage, a guttural roar erupted from the direction of the bear's den. "Oh no!" he gasped, turning to see the bear standing at the entrance to her den, her eyes filled with a terrifying resolve. Panic surged through him as he realized there would be no surviving a second confrontation. He bolted, fueled by adrenaline and fear.

The bear charged after him, rapidly closing the distance. In her domain, she was the unchallenged predator, and Elliot was the unwelcome intruder. She was convinced she would catch him before he could reach safety. This time, she was determined there would be no escape.

Elliot pushed his body to its limits, sprinting with a speed born of sheer desperation. Yet, deep down, he knew he was merely postponing the inevitable. He couldn't outrun the bear, nor could he hope to overpower her. His eyes locked on the waterfall—his only chance, a gambit hinged on perfect timing and a bit of luck.

As he neared the passage, acutely aware of his surroundings, he prepared for the critical moment. Just as the bear readied herself to pounce, shifting her weight onto her hind legs, Elliot made his move. He leaped with every bit of strength remaining in his battered body—a body that had been pummeled by raining pipes and crushed by falling rocks. A body deprived of rest and nourishment for countless hours. A body that had been brutally battered, nearly to the point of death, by the relentless assault of a ferocious brown bear.

But Elliot's dive was a feint. In a daring twist, he veered sharply to the left at the last second. The bear, caught off guard, lunged forward towards the passage, her claws outstretched, narrowly missing his trailing leg by mere inches. She landed at the water's edge, turning in fury to finish her prey, only to catch a fleeting glimpse of him. Elliot, propelled by a last burst of energy, shot through the waterfall like a torpedo, his body disappearing into the cascade, plunging with the rushing water to an uncertain fate two hundred feet below.

Chapter 13

The lone deer grazed peacefully among the ferns and wildflowers, beneath the protective canopy of the towering trees of the forest. Her russet coat glowed in the dappled sunlight of the fading sun. A snapping sound rang out. She froze, head raised, assessing the situation for potential danger nearby. Sniffing the air, her ears perked forward and swiveled towards the sound, trying to pinpoint its source. After a moment, she settled, content there was no immediate danger, and resumed grazing, but remained, as always, on high alert.

SNAP! The sound came again, from the same direction. Taking no chances, she bolted, using her powerful legs to propel her away at incredible speed, seeking safer ground, and only stopping once hidden amongst denser vegetation.

Moments after the second snap, an arrow buried itself into the ground where the deer had once grazed. "Damn it," Bella muttered, pushing her ponytail back over her shoulder. Her long black hair came to rest halfway down her back as she slumped her shoulders in defeat.

"I told you, you have to be patient," Ava said calmly, standing up from her kneeling position behind Bella.

"I was patient, Mama," Bella retorted, turning to face her. "I waited for twenty minutes before I took that shot."

Ava chuckled. "You've been here for five minutes, Bella." She sheathed the hunting knife she had been holding, ready to quickly put the deer out of its misery if the arrow had found its target. "But being patient is about more than just the time you wait," she added.

Bella furrowed her brow, tilting her head slightly. "Huh?" she said.

"It's also about the care you take in doing something," Ava explained. "When you lined up to take the shot, you placed your left foot in front of you."

"Yeah, so? That's how you taught me to shoot," Bella interrupted defiantly.

"And that was correct," Ava agreed. "But in doing so, you weren't paying attention to your surroundings and you stepped on a twig," she said, pointing to the ground in front of Bella.

"But..." Bella started.

"Then, when you positioned your right foot for support," Ava continued, "you broke another twig," and she again indicated the ground.

"That's not my fault!" Bella exclaimed, dropping her head towards her chest.

"Hey," Ava said, gently lifting Bella's face to meet hers; she knelt so they were at eye level. "We're all responsible for our actions in life, no matter how unfair they may seem," she took the bow from Bella's hand. "If we want to learn, we must first accept we might be wrong; otherwise, we can never be taught. Do you understand?"

Bella looked away, chewing her lower lip, then returned her gaze to Ava. "Yes, Mama," she finally replied. "Show me!" she added with a smile.

Ava returned her daughter's smile. "Okay, darling, watch me closely." She stood up straight, taking a step to the side so Bella had a clear view. "Your body position was correct when you took your shot, but your movements were clumsy." Ava demonstrated by exaggeratedly placing her left foot down loudly.

"When you move, you need to do so with control..." Ava reset to her starting position. "And with patience." She lifted her left leg slowly, moved it forward, and then gently placed it on the ground, making no sound.

"How did you do that without looking where to place it?" Bella asked.

"But I did look," Ava responded, turning to face Bella.

"I watched you. You were looking forward the whole time," Bella observed. "You never stopped to look down!"

"Your eyes can see more than what you're directly looking at, darling," Ava explained. "You just need to open your mind to perceive everything your eyes capture."

"But how do I do that?" Bella asked.

"With practice and patience," Ava replied, smiling warmly. "Now, why don't you give it a go?"

Bella moved into the same position as her mother and lifted her left leg. "Hold on," Ava interjected. She took an arrow from Bella's quiver and handed it to her. "I want you to aim at that tree over there," she said, pointing to a thin-looking reddish tree fifteen meters away.

"Okay, Mama," Bella replied, standing side-on to the tree, fixing her aim on the target. She held an arrow pointed towards the ground in her right hand and slowly lifted her left leg.

"Okay, freeze there," Ava instructed just as Bella was about to place her foot back down. Bella stood still, her left foot hovering several inches above the ground. "Can you see the ground?" Ava asked.

Bella glanced down. "No, I want you to keep looking at the target," Ava quickly said.

Refocusing on the tree, Bella replied, "No, I'm looking at the tree. I can't see it."

Ava moved around to Bella's left side, raising her hand in the air. "Can you see my hand?" she asked.

"Yes, Mama," Bella replied.

"That's good," Ava encouraged. "Now stay focussed on the target, but follow my hand as I move it." Ava slowly lowered her hand towards the ground. "Can you still see my hand?"

"Yes, Mama," Bella replied, her voice tinged with excitement.

"That's really good, darling. Stay with it." Ava said, pausing inches above the ground. "Can you still see it?"

"Yes, Mama."

"And the target?" Ava asked.

"I can still see it, Mama," Bella affirmed.

"Now, tell me what else you see near my hand," Ava instructed.

"I see green and brown," Bella observed, her interest growing.

"Try to look a little closer. Focus on my fingers. Can you see them moving?"

"I can see them!" Bella exclaimed with a smile. "And I can see the grass, and there's a brown stick there too," she added, her voice filled with pride.

"You're doing brilliantly, darling," Ava praised. "Now, carefully place your feet, being mindful of all the things around that could make noise."

Bella adjusted her left foot, gently placing it on the ground. She then rearranged her right foot with equal care, ensuring her stance was shoulder-width apart. With the bow angled towards the ground, she nocked the arrow by feel, drew back steadily, and anchored the bowstring at the corner of her mouth. Her arm extended, and her back muscles contracted for stability. She inhaled slowly through her nose, held her breath, and then relaxed her fingers, letting the arrow fly.

"Perfect, Bella!" Ava exclaimed, eyes following the arrow as it buried itself in the center of the target tree.

Bella's face lit up with a wide grin. "I did it!" she exclaimed, jumping with excitement.

"You certainly did, darling," Ava affirmed. "With practice, you'll be able to do this every time, effortlessly."

Ava retrieved the two arrows, placing them back in Bella's quiver. "What do you say we find another deer and try again?" she suggested. "I saw the herd moving towards the Great Falls earlier," she added, pointing off to her right.

As they started to walk, Bella asked, "Mama, why do none of the other girls have to hunt?"

"Because they believe there will always be a man to do it for them," Ava responded, stepping over a log. "But you shouldn't rely on always having someone else to do things for you, whether a man or a woman. If you can do things for yourself, like hunting, you'll always be able to support yourself and help others."

Bella ducked under a low branch, which her mother held up for her. "Would you have learned to hunt if Daddy was still around?" she asked.

"It was your father who taught me how to hunt properly," Ava said.

"It was?" Bella asked.

"Yes. That's how we met," Ava said, pointing towards a hill and nudging Bella to continue walking. "I used to sneak out to hunt when I was your age," she revealed.

"You did?" Bella's voice carried a tone of amazement. She had never heard this story about her mother before.

"Yes," Ava said nonchalantly. "The boys were often mean, excluding me or mocking me for wanting to hunt."

"Some boys can be mean," Bella remarked, a knowing look crossing her face.

"Not all boys are mean," Ava said, a smile touching her lips. "Your daddy was one of the nice ones. He would defend me from the others, telling them to leave me alone."

"So, was Daddy kind of like your hero?" Bella asked.

"Yes, he certainly was. He used to take me out to the forest after his lessons, just the two of us. He'd teach me everything he learned that day, just like we are doing now."

"Really?" Bella said softly. "I miss Daddy!"

"I do too, darling," Ava replied, her voice softening. She put her arm around Bella's shoulder, and together they continued up the hill.

Chapter 14

As afternoon gave way to early evening, the first streaks of fiery orange began to fuse with the azure blue of the evening sky. The deer drank from the river's edge, quenching her thirst and cooling herself from the day's activity, unaware of the danger she was in.

Ava and Bella knelt quietly in the tall grass halfway down the hill, watching. The sounds of the nearby river carried on the wind like musical notes to their ears. With her bow in hand and an arrow nocked, Bella was ready. Ava, her hunter's knife in hand, was just behind her.

There was no snap of twigs or rustle of leaves this time; the blow came without warning. A single flash of gray crossed the deer's vision, leaving her no time to react before the warm bite to her neck; the deer hit the ground a second later, her muzzle still glistening with the river's water.

Ava and Bella, motionless in their hideout, had watched the pack's stealthy approach from the hill's summit. Wolves rarely ventured this close to human territory, usually cautious to avoid encroaching on the lands of man. Occasionally, a rogue pack, perhaps driven out by their own kind, dared to cross the boundary.

Ava watched the wolves intently, knowing they posed a potential danger to her village. If unchecked, they might soon turn their predatory instincts towards the villagers. She needed to track their movements, especially since they would likely transport the deer's remains to their den. Identifying the location of their lair was crucial for organizing a future hunting party.

The wolves displayed remarkable organization. While the alpha and another wolf fed, the rest stood guard, marking their territory around the kill. Their heightened alertness soon became evident: a low growling filled the air, signaling the pack's awareness of an approaching threat.

Across the river, the underbrush rustled, drawing the wolves' attention. Ava knew immediately it could only be Savage-Heart, a formidable predator known in these parts. Being so close to her den at this hour, no other creature could elicit such a reaction from the wolves. The pack, recognizing the presence of a larger, more dangerous animal, quickly formed a defensive circle around their kill. They crouched low, bared their teeth, and growled towards the unseen threat, a clear warning not to come any closer.

Ava, with a cautious hand, signaled Bella to start retracing their steps, moving deeper into the forest and back up the hill. If the wolves decided to retreat in their direction, she wanted to ensure they remained undetected. Bella, understanding the gravity of the situation, had already swapped her bow for a spear. Despite being only thirteen, she had learned to respect both the beauty and the savagery of nature. She was as proficient with a spear as she was with a bow and was prepared to use either if necessary.

Across the river, the tall grass parted like a green curtain, revealing the imposing figure of a massive brown bear. Her face was twisted in a menacing snarl. "Savage-Heart," Bella whispered to her mother as they maintained a slow, cautious retreat up the hill, their eyes still fixed on the unfolding drama below.

"She must be returning to her den for the evening," Ava murmured. "She's always more irritable when she comes back without her cub."

"I don't think she's ever going to find her cub, Mama," Bella replied, a note of sadness in her voice. "I think her cub is with the gods now."

"You're probably right, darling," Ava agreed softly. "It's been many days since he disappeared. She searches every day, and each night she returns alone and angrier."

Bella glanced back at the scene. "We may not need a hunting party for the wolves," she observed. "If Savage-Heart catches them first, there might not be much left for us to chase away." Just then, the bear reared onto her hind legs, issuing a thunderous roar at the wolves.

"I think she believes they killed her cub!" Bella exclaimed, stopping to watch the bear's display of fury.

"They might have," Ava acknowledged. "Let's continue up the hill and keep a safe distance," she advised, gently tugging at Bella's arm to encourage her onward.

The bear, Savage-Heart, lumbered into the river, her substantial weight rendering the current inconsequential. With deliberate, powerful strides, she began to cross towards the snarling wolf pack, who held their defensive stance, visibly torn between protecting their prize and avoiding a direct clash with the formidable predator.

Upon reaching the opposite bank, Savage-Heart was met by a pair of anxious wolves, darting forward with snarls and snaps. They hoped their aggressive display would deter her, but the bear, seemingly incensed by their audacity, advanced up the bank unflinchingly.

From the rear, a sudden flash of gray signaled a tactical move from the pack. Two wolves had stealthily flanked the front line, now launching themselves at the bear. Savage-Heart, with a swift, powerful swipe of her right paw, struck one wolf mid-leap, the impact emitting a sickening crunch as the wolf crumpled lifelessly to the ground.

The second wolf managed to land on her shoulder, snapping ferociously at her thick fur. However, it struggled to secure a firm grip with its teeth. Reacting instinctively, Savage-Heart reared up, dislodging the wolf with a forceful shake. She then spun, bringing her entire weight crashing down onto the first wolf she had struck, ensuring its demise.

The front two wolves, seizing their moment, lunged at Savage-Heart, biting at her massive rear. In a display of startling agility, the bear whirled around, her mighty paw striking one wolf in the side, sending it crashing into its companion. She then lunged forward, barely missing the wolf on the right with a glancing blow as it dodged away in the nick of time.

Sensing the tide of battle turning against them, two of the more forward wolves began a hasty retreat towards their pack. Savage-Heart, undeterred, reared up on her hind legs, unleashing a thunderous roar that echoed across the river. She then descended upon one of the downed wolves that attempted to stir, her massive form mauling it mercilessly.

The alpha wolf, recognizing the direness of their situation, signaled for a retreat. He darted along the river's edge, followed by the remaining members of his pack, one visibly struggling to keep pace. Savage-Heart gave chase, her grunts and growls punctuating the air.

From their vantage point atop the hill, Ava and Bella observed the scene with awe. They had often heard tales of Savage-Heart's fury, but witnessing it firsthand was a starkly different experience. "Quickly," Ava urged. "We need to follow them from the hill and see where they're headed." Without hesitation, she broke into a sprint, Bella closely on her heels, both keeping a keen eye on the direction of the retreating wolves.

Rounding the second bend in the river, Ava and Bella arrived just in time to witness Savage-Heart's relentless pursuit. The wounded wolf, desperately trying to escape at the river's edge, was beset by another brutal blow from the bear. Despite the efforts of the remaining wolves to distract her, Savage-Heart was undeterred. The pack, realizing the futility of their efforts, scrambled across the river, seeking refuge in the dense forest on the other side.

Unyielding, Savage-Heart delivered a final precise swipe to the hind legs of the wounded wolf, sending it tumbling to the ground. She then clamped down on its neck, shaking it violently until it went limp in her jaws. The remaining wolves, after a brief hesitation to assist their fallen comrade, continued their retreat. Savage-Heart, triumphant, gave chase to the remaining pack.

Ava and Bella continued their pursuit for another five minutes, guided by the distant echoes of the chase. As they finally regained sight of Savage-Heart, the remaining wolves had vanished.

"They must have retreated deeper into the woods," Ava conjectured, gesturing towards a disturbed area across the river.

Bella watched the bear's impressive form as she ascended the natural stone steps of the Great Falls. "Savage-Heart seems to be returning to her den," she remarked, her attention captivated by the bear's powerful strides. "It looks like she was triumphant, Mama."

"Indeed, she has proven herself once again," Ava commented, observing the bear's progress. "And, without intending to, she's helped us as well."

"What do you mean, Mama?" Bella asked curiously.

Ava handed Bella a canteen from her backpack, watching as her daughter drank deeply. "Savage-Heart has driven off three wolves from their pack. Now we have fewer to worry about." After taking a sip herself, Ava continued. "That is, if they even consider coming back after today's events." She repacked the canteen, slinging her backpack over her shoulders with a contemplative look.

A sudden guttural roar shattered the evening calm, drawing Ava's and Bella's attention abruptly to the top of the Great Falls. There, against the backdrop of the fiery setting sun, stood a solitary white figure, his howl echoing across the water.

"What's that, Mama?" Bella asked, squinting at the distant shape.

Ava frowned, her eyes narrowing as she tried to make sense of the scene. "I'm not sure, darling," she replied. "It looks like a man," she observed, her hand shielding her eyes from the glare of the sun. "A very foolish man!" she added as she watched the figure hurl a rock at Savage-Heart.

"Yep!" Bella agreed as the deafening roar of the now-standing Savage-Heart returned his challenge.

CHAPTER 15

AVA AND BELLA WATCHED in disbelief as the man recklessly hurled a second stone at Savage-Heart. Panic seemed to grip him as the bear, now provoked and enraged, began her pursuit. In a frantic attempt to escape, the man committed another potentially fatal error: he sprinted directly towards the bear's den, situated within the Great Falls, effectively cornering himself.

"Why would he go up to her den?" Bella asked. "No one has ever dared approach it and lived to tell the tale."

"I wish I knew, darling," Ava replied, her gaze intensely focused on the dramatic scene unfolding. "But it doesn't look like we'll have the chance to ask him," she added as the bear chased the man up the steps of the mountain and they both disappeared into the den behind the Great Falls.

A few moments later, a thunderous roar reverberated from within the depths of the mountain, its intensity echoing off the rocky cave walls. "She sounds even more furious than when she fought the wolves," Bella remarked.

"I don't think she likes unwanted guests in her home," Ava commented, a hint of worry in her voice as another muffled roar echoed, softened by the cascade of the Great Falls.

"What was he wearing, Mama?" Bella asked. "I've never seen clothing like that before."

"Nor have I," Ava responded thoughtfully. "It might be some sort of new armor," she mused, just as the sounds of growling and a series of thuds reached their ears.

A look of sadness crossed Bella's face. "I think she's caught him now, Mama."

Ava nodded, wrapping her arm around her daughter in a comforting gesture. "Yes, I'm afraid so. Let's hope it's over quickly for him."

Ava and Bella stood in silent contemplation, the sounds of the struggle fading into a haunting stillness. The unspoken understanding between them was clear as the silence lingered. "Come on," Ava finally said, motioning towards the river. "Let's check the wolf tracks on the other side before heading home. We shouldn't be out here after dark with them still around."

Halfway down the hill, Bella abruptly stopped, her gaze snapping back to the Great Falls as the roar from Savage-Heart bellowed once more from the mountain. Ava halted beside her, just in time to see the astonishing sight of the man in white flying out of the waterfall. He soared momentarily against the backdrop of the setting sun before gravity abruptly claimed him, sending him plummeting down the two-hundred-foot drop.

Frozen in shock, Ava and Bella watched as the man descended in a surreal slow-motion tumble, his arms flailing wildly. The final moments of his descent were obscured by the river's bends, but the sound of him hitting the water below was unmistakable.

Without a word, Bella raced down the hill towards the river, Ava calling out after her. She veered right, following the river's course towards its convergence with the Great Falls, her mind racing with questions about the bizarre man and the tragic turn of events they had just witnessed.

Chapter 16

Elliot recalled the fall in three distinct parts. The first, he was engulfed in absolute fear. As he leaped through the waterfall into the abyss, he half expected to feel the claws of Savage-Heart grasping at him, trying to drag him back to her den. The second part was a fleeting sense of peace. At the peak of his dive, before gravity's inexorable pull took over, Elliot experienced a moment of weightlessness. The view was breathtaking: miles of horizon stretched before him, with a luscious green forest sprawling beneath a vast sky. However, this serene moment was short-lived.

The final part of his fall was marked by helplessness. Elliot tumbled through the air, flapping and somersaulting in a futile attempt to control his descent before crashing into the water. His conscious mind retreated once more, leaving him in darkness.

Submerged twenty feet below the water's surface, Elliot's advanced suit sprang into action, detecting its submersion and automatically adjusting to provide buoyancy. He surfaced, face down, as the current from the Great Falls nudged him towards the far shore.

Even with the suit's life support system providing essential oxygen, Elliot remained unconscious, bobbing in the waves on the pebbly shore. Unknown to him, figures moved cautiously through the underbrush towards his prone form. Their silhouettes were vague and indistinct, blending with the twilight shadows. The low, measured sounds of their approach suggested a predatory grace, hinting at a danger far different from the one he had just escaped.

From the forest's edge, two wolves cautiously emerged, their alpha watching intently from a distance. Drawn by the commotion at the Great Falls, they had arrived just in time to witness the man plummeting from the sky and washing up on the shore.

The wolves circled Elliot's motionless form, sniffing at his outstretched arms with wary curiosity. They recoiled once, only to return with bolder intent. One wolf tentatively bit at his arm, but its teeth found no purchase on the strange material. Frustrated, it opened its jaws wider, clamped down on his wrist, and tugged fiercely, causing Elliot's body to jerk towards the shore. Startled, both wolves retreated a few steps.

Emboldened by their initial success, the pair returned, each seizing the same wrist. Together, they dragged Elliot out of the water, onto the pebbly bank. The alpha joined them, nosing around the body, trying to bite into the bicep, but it too struggled to find a grip on the suit.

As the wolves gnawed at the narrower sections of his limbs, Elliot's consciousness surged back with a jolt. He awoke to a nightmare—three wolves attempting to tear at his arms and legs. Panic and instinct merged as he thrashed wildly, trying to shake off their relentless hold. Though his mind was still foggy, Elliot managed to free one arm and delivered a desperate, powerful hammer blow to the nearest wolf's head, instantly incapacitating it.

The suddenness of Elliot's counterattack momentarily stunned the other wolves, offering him a few brief seconds of relief amidst the heated struggle.

The remaining wolves, incensed by the fall of their alpha, redoubled their assault with savage ferocity, their teeth gnashing at Elliot's legs, dragging him across the pebbled beach. Elliot, fueled by adrenaline and survival instinct, bucked wildly, trying to draw the wolves within range of his arms. His first few swings were frantic, connecting with a wolf but failing to loosen its grip.

With a surge of effort, Elliot violently bucked his body, finally shaking one wolf off. He then lashed out with a desperate, powerful kick, connecting squarely with the head of the other wolf, forcing it to release its hold. This momentary victory allowed him to scramble backward, gaining precious distance from his attackers.

Scrambling to his feet, Elliot barely had time to orient himself before the two wolves, undeterred, charged towards him again. To his right, the alpha was still dazed, struggling to rise after the blow it had received. Elliot clenched his fists together, channeling every ounce of his strength. As the wolves lunged, he swung with all his might, mimicking a batter at Yankee Stadium swinging for the fences. His timing was impeccable—his fists connected with a resounding crunch against the skull of one wolf, the force of the blow propelling it into its companion.

After his forceful swing, Elliot's momentum sent him crashing to the ground. He quickly scrambled to his feet, adrenaline coursing through him, and adopted a defensive stance. His mind raced, noting the position of each wolf. The one he had struck lay motionless, its eyes glazed over, blood oozing from its mouth—clearly out of the fight. To his right, the alpha he had hit earlier was staggering, struggling to find its footing like a drunkard. Elliot deemed it no immediate threat. His attention then snapped to the last wolf, which had regained its footing after being struck by its fallen pack member. It was now crouched, growling menacingly, clearly poised for attack.

Elliot could sense the charge was imminent. The wolf's body was tensed, like a coiled spring, ready to unleash its pent-up aggression. In a sudden burst of speed, the wolf charged, rapidly closing the distance between them. It then launched itself into the air, teeth bared, aimed directly at Elliot.

Anticipating the wolf's attack, Elliot was as ready as he could be. As the wolf lunged through the air towards him, he instinctively reacted. Falling backward, he thrust his feet upward into the wolf's underbelly with all the force he could muster. Capitalizing on the wolf's momentum, Elliot propelled the animal over him, sending it crashing onto the rocky shore behind him.

Elliot didn't allow himself a moment's respite. He sprang back to his feet, turning to confront the wolf, which was now struggling to rise after its hard landing. His body screamed in protest, battered from the relentless assault and drained of energy. Elliot knew he couldn't prolong this fight. He had to finish it now.

Digging deep into his dwindling reserves, Elliot summoned what little strength remained. Lowering his head, he released a primal roar, the sound emanating from deep within. It was a roar of defiance, a declaration of his unwillingness to succumb despite the overwhelming odds.

"Let's finish this!" Elliot seethed through clenched teeth, his body trembling with pent-up rage. Taking a deep, steadying breath, he unleashed a fierce battle cry. "C'mon!" he screamed, charging headlong towards the wolf.

The wolf, its survival instincts fully ignited, charged with ferocious determination towards Elliot. They both leaped into the air, the wolf with bared teeth and outstretched paws, Elliot with his body rigid, headfirst, like a human spear. Each knew this was the endgame.

Their collision was catastrophic. Elliot's helmet, reinforced by the suit's durability, struck the wolf's face with the force of a battering ram. His superior weight and the suit's power allowed him to plow through the wolf as though it were made of straw. They hit the ground with a bone-jarring thud, the wolf twitching helplessly, incapacitated by the brutal impact.

Summoning his last reserves of strength, Elliot staggered to his feet, his breaths ragged and labored. He grabbed the largest rock within reach and with a final exertion of force, brought it crashing down onto the wolf's head. His energy spent, Elliot collapsed onto his back, gasping for air, every fiber of his being aching from the ordeal.

As darkness began to encroach upon his vision, Elliot fumbled with the locks of his helmet, managing only to partially turn it before his strength gave out. His mind slowly slipped away, dragging him back into the inky depths of unconsciousness.

Chapter 17

From his position to the right of the fray, the alpha, still reeling from the blow he had received, watched the battle intensify with mounting fury. His head cleared with each passing second, sharpening his focus. He had expected a swift victory, his pack overwhelming the man, then feasting triumphantly. Then later, once they had regained their strength, they would devise a plan to confront the devil bear that had long haunted them.

Yet, as he watched the man defeat another of his pack, a surge of rage coursed through the alpha. He struggled to rise, to join the fray, but his body betrayed him. His balance was off, and his limbs refused to cooperate, forcing him to remain a spectator to the grim spectacle.

The man's resilience and strength were unlike anything the alpha had ever encountered. In all his years, never had he seen a human display such formidable strength. By all rights, their numbers should have granted them an easy victory. However, there the man stood, a roaring force of nature, hurling one of the pack through the air with a strength that mirrored their most feared adversary, the bear.

In a fleeting moment of clarity, the alpha attempted to signal a retreat. But it was too late—the final charge was already in motion. As the man and the last wolf lunged toward each other, the alpha realized the grim truth: this encounter would end in death, either for the pack or the man. If the pack fell, the alpha would be forced to flee alone, his leadership and strength questioned by nature's unforgiving law. If the pack won, they would feast.

However, in the aftermath of the brutal clash, the alpha stood alone, his thoughts a tumultuous mix of grief and rage. Today had indeed been cursed, he reflected bitterly. He had watched helplessly as his pack fell, one by one, until none remained. Now, in solitude, survival became his sole imperative, with thoughts of revenge simmering in the back of his mind.

As he turned to retreat into the sanctuary of the forest, he noticed the man collapsing to the ground. The man lay motionless, a sign that perhaps the day's trials were not yet concluded. A flicker of opportunity sparked in the alpha's mind.

He approached the fallen man with cautious steps, his keen senses detecting a new scent emanating from him. It was the scent of vulnerability, of injury—likely inflicted during the struggle with his pack. This realization fueled the alpha's resolve. He would avenge his pack and claim this man as his prize.

Driven by his bloodlust and the need to honor his fallen comrades, the alpha quickened his pace towards the motionless figure, each stride a calculated risk born out of desperate need, his primal instincts fully awakened. Today had brought loss, but it might yet end with the satisfaction of revenge and survival.

Chapter 18

Bella raced towards the river's bend, her mind swirling with questions. The haunting image of the man plummeting from the Great Falls lingered vividly in her thoughts—was survival even possible? Logic argued against it, yet his inexplicable escape from Savage-Heart's den suggested that the impossible might just be plausible. Driven by a need for answers, she hastened along the path. As she rounded the bend, her view was partially veiled by tall grass and dense bushes, yet she pushed through, the rustling of the foliage punctuating her urgency.

Ava's heart raced as she hurried after Bella, twenty yards ahead. Each step Bella took fueled Ava's growing worry. Though Savage-Heart was likely in her den, the wolves' location was still alarmingly unknown. The fresh paw prints she discovered at the river's bend made this all the more ominous. Ava cast a wary eye at the forest to her right, alert for lurking wolves. Despite wanting to call out, she knew it risked drawing their attention. Instead, she quickened her pace, determined to bridge the distance to Bella. Her every sense was heightened, ready for any threat as she pushed toward the Great Falls' distant shore, driven by the need to reach her daughter before danger did.

Bella stumbled onto the rocky beach from the tall grass, her steps halting abruptly in shock. In front of her, the man in strange white armor grappled with three wolves, one visibly injured. Weaponless, he fought with only his suit and sheer strength.

Ava appeared behind Bella, heart pounding in alarm. She quickly scanned Bella, relieved yet fixated on the battle across the beach.

"Mama, look!" Bella's voice was sharp with urgency, pointing as the man landed a powerful blow on a wolf, mirroring Savage-Heart's intensity.

Ava gasped. "What the—" she started, but her words faded as the chaotic scene captured her full attention.

"We need to help him, Mama!" Bella tugged at Ava's arm, her eyes burning with resolve.

"We can't." Ava held her back firmly. "Taking on three wolves is too risky." She surveyed the fight; now, only one wolf actively engaged with the man.

"I have my bow!" Bella insisted. "We could scare them off."

"It's too risky from this distance. You might hit him instead," Ava said, eyes locked on the relentless battle.

Bella's urgency surged. "We need to get closer!" She tugged at Ava's arm again, fixated as the man sent the last wolf hurtling through the air.

"How is he doing that?" Ava whispered in disbelief, watching the man and wolf. "Wait, he might not need our help."

Side by side, they witnessed the final showdown. Both winced at the brutal crunch of bone as the man delivered a decisive blow with a rock. "Is he a god, Mama?" Bella asked quietly, awestruck and fearful, her hand over her mouth.

"I... don't know," Ava murmured, transfixed as the man collapsed. "I've never seen anyone fight like that."

"He's not moving," Bella noted, her voice tinged with urgency. "We should check on him."

Nodding, Ava allowed Bella toward the fallen man, her mind abuzz with questions. Her eyes briefly flickered to the Great Falls, a reminder of the man's miraculous survival from the fall.

"Mama, the wolf!" Bella's alarmed voice snapped Ava back to the present. Breaking free, she ran toward the man, bow in hand.

"Bella, no!" Ava's sense of alarm spiked, her focus shifting to the new threat—the injured alpha wolf, now stealthily approaching the vulnerable man.

Events unfolded in rapid succession, each moment a flurry of swift reactions. Ava, with a surge of protective instinct, grabbed her spear and dashed after Bella. The wolf, ignited by a sudden burst of energy, charged towards the fallen man, its eyes locked on its prey. Bella, recognizing the peril, dropped into a ready stance, her arrow nocked and aimed in one fluid motion. Her focus was laser-sharp on the advancing wolf. Breathing deeply to steady herself, she released the arrow with practiced precision.

The arrow sliced through the air, narrowly missing its mark but grazing the wolf's back, drawing a sharp yelp and a line of blood. The wolf faltered, then quickly regrouped.

As it turned, eyes meeting Bella's determined stare, it growled threateningly. It stepped forward, intent on attacking. But Ava's sudden appearance, spear in hand and war cry echoing, halted its advance. Surprised and out-numbered, the wolf retreated into the forest. Bella's second arrow followed in quick succession, just missing the wolf and embedding into the rock where the creature had stood moments before.

Ava's charge didn't falter, her screams reverberating across the beach. These cries served a dual purpose: to disorient and intimidate the wolf. Her mind was sharply focused on the necessity of her actions, particularly since the wolf had seen Bella. She maintained her relentless advance until she reached the still man, her heart a tumult of fear and relief.

As Bella neared, Ava spun around, her voice laced with anger and concern. "You shouldn't have run!" she said. Yet, her stern tone quickly softened. Without waiting for Bella's response, Ava drew her in close, scanning for any harm. "I was so worried," she confessed, her voice trembling, eyes glistening with unshed tears.

"Mama, I'm okay," Bella said, trying to comfort her mother as she saw the worry in Ava's eyes.

Ava's voice was thick with emotion. "I can't lose you too, Bella," she whispered, pulling Bella close and kissing her hair.

"You won't lose me, Mama." Bella's voice was soft against Ava's chest. "But you're going to have to stop squeezing so tight; I can't breathe."

Ava's laughter broke through, tinged with a sniffle, as she stepped back and wiped her tears. She held Bella's shoulders, looking into her eyes. "You were amazing back there, Bella. I'm so proud of you."

Bella's face brightened, her brown eyes still moist. "Thanks, Mama, but I missed. The wolf escaped," her smile faltered into disappointment.

"You didn't miss," Ava corrected gently. "You struck the wolf. And thanks to you, this man might make it." She nodded towards the motionless figure on the ground.

Bella glanced at the man, her curiosity piqued by his unusual attire. "Mama, what do we do with him?" she inquired, stepping closer to inspect his strange clothing and mask.

Ava knelt beside him, pressing her hand lightly against his chest. After a moment, she let out a small sigh of relief. "He's breathing," she announced, standing up. She scanned their surroundings—the looming forest where the wolf had vanished and the sky, now darkening. "We need to move fast," she said urgently. "Night's coming, and that wolf might still be close. We can't make it back to the village before dark, especially with him," she nodded at the man. "He's too heavy for us to carry."

"So, what do we do, Mama?" Bella asked with a hint of concern in her voice.

Ava pointed towards the river. "There's a shelter nearby we can use for the night. It's not far, but moving him won't be easy."

Bella's expression brightened with an idea. "We could make a stretcher," she suggested, pointing to a pile of broken branches by the forest. "I have rope in my pack."

"That's a great idea, Bella," Ava said, nodding in agreement. "I'll collect the branches. You stay here and cut the rope into lengths we can use."

"Will do, Mama," Bella responded, reaching for her pack with purpose.

Ava took a step, then paused, turning back with a stern look. "Keep your eyes on the forest edge for that wolf," she instructed firmly.

"I will, Mama," Bella promised.

"And don't forget to watch for Savage-Heart near the Falls," Ava added, gesturing towards the waterfall.

"I won't. Be quick, Mama," Bella urged, her gaze already sweeping their surroundings vigilantly as Ava hurried off to gather the branches.

Chapter 19

Within minutes, Ava was back, arms full of sturdy branches, each two to three inches thick and complemented by smaller branches for additional support. Bella had efficiently cut the rope into various lengths, prepared for the task ahead. Together, they quickly set to work, piecing together the makeshift stretcher with a sense of urgency and focus.

They laid the long branches parallel to each other on the ground. Across these, they placed the smaller branches horizontally, securing everything tightly with the rope. "It will have to do," Ava remarked, casting a wary eye at the sun now dipping behind the mountain.

"I'm going to roll him onto his side," she stated, tone resolute. "Slide the stretcher underneath as far as you can when I do."

"Okay, Mama," Bella replied, positioning herself beside the stretcher, her face a mask of concentration.

"We need him secure," Ava added, moving to the man's left. "We can't risk him falling off en route."

Bella nodded and said, "I'm ready," aligning the stretcher with precision.

Ava bent the man's right leg and gently lifted his shoulder, rolling him to his side. "Now, Bella."

Bella slid the stretcher under him with meticulous care. "Done," she announced. "You can lower him back."

Ava eased the man onto the stretcher, noting his left side overhanging the edge. "We need to shift him," she said, her voice laced with concern. "Help me with this, Bella."

Ava and Bella carefully nudged the man towards the center of the stretcher. "That should do," Ava said, satisfied. "Now, let's secure him." They used the remaining rope lengths, tying them around him to prevent him from slipping and falling.

"All set, Mama," Bella declared, finishing the last knot around his ankles.

Ava eyed the man's size. "He's too heavy for you to lift alone," she observed. "Let's both lift from this end," she suggested, pointing to the head of the stretcher. "We'll drag him together."

Joining Ava at the front, Bella readied herself. "I'm set, Mama. We should move quickly, it's nearly dark."

Ava nodded. "On three. One... Two..."

Their count was interrupted by a distant howl, a sinister echo across the quiet beach. Their eyes met, sharing a moment of fear. "We've got this," Ava reassured Bella, her voice steady. Bella nodded, her courage reignited.

"Three!" Ava said with resolve.

Ava and Bella lifted together, hoisting one end of the stretcher up to their waists, taken aback by the man's unexpected weight. The branches groaned under the strain, yet held firm.

"Are you okay, darling?" Ava checked, seeing Bella's strained expression.

"He's heavier than a bear, Mama!" Bella replied, her hands gripping the ropes firmly.

A brief laugh escaped Ava, a moment of lightness amidst the seriousness of their situation. "He certainly is," she agreed. "Let's get moving. Ensure your grip is solid and the ropes tight. We can't afford to drop him."

Laboriously, they trudged across the rocky beach, the terrain unforgiving, their progress slow. Several times they nearly lost balance due to uneven footing, but each time, they regained control just in time. Their determination, coupled with a stroke of luck, kept them going.

Approaching the river's entrance, the sun was nearly hidden behind the mountains. The fading light cast long, eerie shadows, barely illuminating their path. Both were soaked in sweat, backs aching from the burden. Ava couldn't shake the thought of the man's weight; it was as if he were made of stone, further deepening the mystery surrounding their silent companion.

"We're almost there," Ava assured, her voice heavy with fatigue, yet underscored by determination. She gestured towards a large tree ahead, its expansive branches reaching towards the river. "Just twenty more meters to that tree. We can do this."

Suddenly, another howl shattered the quiet, closer this time. Bella's voice quivered. "That sounded like it came from the beach."

"We've got to pick up the pace," Ava urged. She lowered her head, pushing onward with a burst of resolve, steering them towards the tree.

Exhausted from the rocky beach's challenges, their energy reserves dwindling, they welcomed the relief offered by the easier grassy terrain. Their muscles strained and hands ached from the coarse ropes, but the looming threat of the alpha spurred them on, their focus locked on the tree's sheltering branches.

"Mama, where are we going?" Bella's panic was evident as they neared the tree, though no clear refuge was visible.

"Just behind this tree," Ava panted, her voice strained with effort. "Almost there. Keep going!" As they rounded the tree, Ava gestured to set down the stretcher. She immediately began scouring the grass, her hands moving swiftly, searching with purpose.

"Mama, what are you looking for?" Bella's confusion mingled with her rising fear as she observed Ava's urgent search.

Ava's hands combed through the grass with intent, as if seeking something crucial, a hidden key to their safety.

Another howl pierced the night, the alpha's eerie call echoing from the beach. Bella instinctively turned towards the sound, her eyes searching the dim landscape, but their recent path through the grass obscured the beach from view.

Unfazed by the encroaching danger, Ava continued her frantic search. "It's here somewhere," she murmured, her fingers sweeping through the grass.

The distinct sound of paws on stone echoed through the forest, growing steadily louder.

"Mama, hurry!" Bella pleaded, her voice laced with fear.

Suddenly, Ava's fingers found their target. "Here!" she exclaimed, grasping a rope handle hidden in the ground.

With a firm pull, she revealed a camouflaged hatch, a dark opening beneath now exposed. Ingeniously disguised with soil and grass, the hatch swung open.

"Quickly, inside," Ava directed, her tone urgent but steady as she motioned towards the concealed shelter.

Confronted with the stark choice between an unknown dark abyss and the looming threat of a predatory wolf, Bella didn't hesitate. She jumped into the hole, landing on a solid surface barely three feet below. The blackness around her seemed to stretch infinitely, veiling any clue of what lay ahead.

Ava acted with swift urgency, positioning the stretcher's foot end over the hatch. As she pushed it forward, ensuring the man's feet dangled into the opening, she lifted her end, carefully easing the stretcher down. Bella, quickly catching on to her mother's plan, helped guide the head end, lowering it gently onto the unseen floor.

The sound of paws thudding on the ground was now dangerously near. The alpha had reached the grassy area, his heavy breaths adding a haunting cadence to his approaching steps. He was probably only twenty meters away when Ava made her decisive leap. Seizing the rope handle inside the hatch, she pulled it shut and jumped down after Bella. The hatch landed with a muffled thud, plunging them into complete darkness.

In the pitch black, Ava's hands fumbled upwards, searching for the bolt. Finding it, she slid it into place with a swift motion, locking the hatch just as the thud of paws passed overhead, their proximity chillingly close.

<h1 align="center">CHAPTER 20</h1>

"MAMA, IT'S SO DARK in here," Bella whispered, cutting through the pitch-black void.

"I'm here, darling," Ava replied, her voice a reassuring presence in the darkness. She reached out, her fingers finding Bella's, drawing her close for comfort. "We're safe for now."

"Will we stay here all night, in the dark?" Bella's voice wavered, betraying her unease.

"No, not in complete darkness," Ava responded, her tone steady and calming. "There's a fire pit here. We'll light it soon. For now, let's find some kindling. Stay close to me." Hand in hand, they cautiously began to crawl.

The floor sloped gently from the hatch, transitioning to a flat expanse. The feel of the cool, damp earth was a vivid contrast to the sleek, unusual material of the man's clothing they had encountered above. As they edged towards the center, Bella's hand brushed against the rough stone rim of the fire pit. Carefully maneuvering around it, they continued their blind journey across the room.

Reaching the room's far side, Bella's hands traced its textures—the coarse stone wall with the jagged wood edges stacked against it. In the darkness, her senses intensified.

She deeply inhaled the earthy, woody scents, the forest's aroma lingering. Outside, a river's gentle murmur flowed soothingly, while a cool breeze hinted at another opening in the room.

Ava, upon reaching the opposite end, skillfully searched for fire-making supplies. Her fingers found tinder, kindling, and flint, each item distinct in shape and texture. "Bella, gather some logs for the fire," she instructed.

"Okay, Mama," Bella replied, eagerness in her voice. She collected logs, feeling the bark's roughness against her skin. "Got them!"

"Good job," Ava said. "Let's head back to the fire pit."

Together, they felt their way to the pit's stone edge. Ava meticulously cleared the pit of old leaves and debris. She then carefully laid the tinder and arranged the kindling in a teepee formation, ensuring proper airflow for the fire.

"I'm going to light it now," Ava announced, her voice steady with focus yet tinged with anticipation. She held the flint in one hand and her knife in the other. With skilled, precise movements, she struck the knife's sharp edge against the flint, sending a shower of sparks toward the tinder. On the third strike, a small flame caught. Ava leaned in, her breath gently coaxing the flame, nurturing it with careful attention. Once the tinder was lit, she carefully added the kindling, watching as the fire began to grow, casting flickering shadows around the hidden room.

In the growing light, Bella's face became visible, her eyes wide with wonder yet shadowed by recent anxieties. Noticing this, Ava decided to engage her in the task of tending the fire.

"Bella, can you watch the fire for me?" Ava's voice carried softly across the flickering light. "Add the logs when it's ready."

"Of course, Mama," Bella responded, her features brightening with a sense of purpose as she moved closer to the fire. The warmth and responsibility seemed to ease her anxiety, infusing her with quiet determination. "Where are you going, Mama?" she asked, a hint of concern in her voice.

"I need to check on our friend over there," Ava said, nodding towards the hatch where the man still lay silently.

As the fire grew, its warm glow brought the room to life. The room, ten meters long and five meters wide, was lined with walls of variously sized and colored rocks, standing seven feet high. Dark, sturdy trunks of fallen trees formed a rustic ceiling above. A solitary clay pipe punctured the ceiling over the fire pit, allowing smoke to escape.

Bella's gaze swept across the room. At the far end, shelves held an array of tools and supplies, suggesting past habitation. Beneath them, piles of chopped wood ensured a continued source of warmth. Straw cots with blankets, undisturbed and dust-covered, lay on either side of the room. In the far-right corner, something peculiar caught Bella's eye: a clay pipe, sealed with a wooden cork, extended from the wall above a shallow hole in the floor.

At the hatch end of the room, Ava was carefully dragging the stretcher down the slope. Bella, having just added a log to the brightly burning fire, watched her mother. "How long has this place been here, Mama?" she asked, her voice soft in the well-lit room.

"Since before I was a little girl," Ava replied, with a touch of nostalgia in her voice. Dragging the man was easier here than on the stony beach. Pausing at the bottom, she wiped her brow. "I'm not sure when it was built, but there are more like it across the land."

"Why's that?" Bella asked.

"They were built as safe havens for times when people couldn't get back to the village at night," Ava explained, pulling the stretcher further into the room. Positioning it near the fire, she continued. "They also served as hideouts in the early days, during village attacks."

Ava grabbed a clay cup from the shelf and held it under the pipe, uncorking it to let cold water flow in. She first rinsed, discarding the water in the hole beneath, then filled the cup again and stopped the flow with the cork. After a deep drink, she refilled the cup and brought it to the man, setting it next to his head. Her eyes lingered on his still form, reflecting both concern and curiosity.

"You should drink some water too, Bella," Ava said. "It's been a tough journey."

Bella, now aware of her thirst, took her canteen and filled it at the water pipe, following her mother's example. She drank deeply, refilled the canteen, and returned to the fire.

"Add another log to the fire, Bella," Ava directed, her focus still on their guest. "Then help me remove his armor so we can check his injuries."

While Bella added logs to the fire, Ava closely examined the man's unusual helmet. It was made of a smooth, durable material she hadn't seen before. The helmet's transparent face section revealed a white male beneath. His face, showing the start of a beard flecked with white, contrasted with his thick brown hair. He seemed in his late thirties, ruggedly handsome, and definitely not from their village.

Bella, sitting across from her mother, gazed at the unconscious man with curiosity. "Who is he, Mama?" she asked, studying his unfamiliar face.

"I don't know," Ava admitted, her voice tinged with concern. She gently touched the helmet's clear section, feeling its texture. "His clothes are like nothing I've seen. Let's try to remove this," she suggested, indicating the helmet.

Ava and Bella carefully gripped either side of the helmet, lifting it gently. As they moved it, a gap formed between the helmet and the suit. "Let's try pulling it up over his head," Ava suggested.

Together, they raised the helmet, revealing the man's face. They placed the helmet on the floor and leaned in to examine him under the fire's flickering light.

"He smells a bit strange, Mama," Bella observed, wrinkling her nose at the unfamiliar scent.

Ava chuckled. "He's probably been in there a long time," she said, eyeing the white suit. "How do we get him out of this?" she wondered aloud.

To their surprise, a groggy voice answered. "You can start by telling me your name first," the man said, his eyes fluttering open. He offered a weak, warm smile. "I don't usually take this off for every pretty girl I meet," he joked, a glint of humor in his green eyes.

CHAPTER 21

At the unexpected sound of the man's voice, Bella and Ava instinctively recoiled, springing to their feet in unison. In one fluid motion, they both drew their knives, with their eyes fixed on the stranger. Ava moved to Bella's side, her knife aimed steadily at him.

"Whoa, easy. I mean you no harm," the man said, his voice calm. He attempted to sit up, but the ropes binding him to the stretcher restrained his movement, forcing him to settle back down. "Easy," he repeated, his tone reassuring. He looked around, noting the stone walls, log ceiling, and the fire pit's warm light. "Where am I?" he asked.

"You're somewhere safe," Ava answered, her grip tight on her knife.

"Who are you?" Bella asked, stepping out from behind her mother, knife now at her side.

"Stay back, Bella," Ava cautioned, grabbing her daughter's arm.

"Bella, that's a lovely name," the man remarked with a gentle smile playing on his lips. "Is that your mother, Bella?"

Bella's face lit up at the compliment. "Yes, that's my mama. Her name is Ava," she said proudly, then saw Ava's stern look.

"It's okay, Ava. I'm not here to hurt anyone," the man said. "My name is Elliot. Can you tell me where I am?"

After a moment of scrutiny, Ava lowered her knife and gestured for Bella to sit beside her. They sat about five feet from Elliot, cautious, but not openly hostile.

"Why were you in Savage-Heart's den?" Bella blurted, her curiosity overcoming her.

Elliot looked puzzled. "Savage-Heart?" Then understanding hit. "The bear!" he realized.

"Yes, her name is Savage-Heart," Bella said. "Mama says only fools approach her den."

"Bella!" Ava chided.

Elliot laughed. "She's right," he conceded, a glimmer of humor in his eyes. "But I didn't go up to the den. I came out of it."

Bella and Ava exchanged a look of confusion. "Came out of it?" Bella repeated, puzzled.

"I didn't know it was a bear's den when I did!" Elliot quickly added. "I'm not that foolish," he added with a smile, which Bella returned.

"Wait, how did you come out there? The only way in or out is via the stairs of the Great Falls," Ava said.

"That's exactly what I did, Ava," Elliot explained. "I came through a big door into the cave. I followed the cave and stumbled upon the den. Realizing where I was, I decided to make a quick exit, and that's when I ended up outside by the waterfall, right in the path of the bear." Recollecting the encounter with the massive bear, he winced, the pain from his injuries starting to reassert itself.

"A door?" Ava echoed.

"So the bear threw you from the Great Falls?" Bella asked, captivated.

"Well, actually I jumped," Elliot confessed, with a mix of embarrassment and pride.

"You jumped!" Bella exclaimed, her eyes wide.

"I thought you weren't foolish," Ava said with a playful glance at Elliot.

"Fair point." Elliot grinned, his green eyes shining in the firelight. "But it was either the waterfall or the bear; after a rough encounter with Savage-Heart, the waterfall seemed like the lesser evil."

"You fought Savage-Heart and survived?" Bella asked, awestruck. "Are you some kind of god?"

Elliot laughed. "No god, just lucky. This suit made the difference," he said, indicating his outfit.

Ava looked at his suit curiously. "Is that a suit? It looks more like armor," she inquired.

Elliot nodded. "It's more protective gear than armor," he explained. "Back where I'm from, we call it a suit."

Ava leaned in. "And where might that be? You're not from around here. Are you from the Forbidden Mountain?" Her questions reflected the growing mystery around Elliot.

"I don't know what the Forbidden Mountain is!" Elliot said.

"Ava," Elliot continued, his voice strained but gentle, "I'm happy to answer all your questions, but I think I might have some broken ribs under here that need tending to, and my throat feels like it's full of sand." He gestured weakly towards the cup on the floor next to his head. "Can you cut me loose and let me have some of that water, please?"

Ava hesitated, her gaze moving between Elliot's pained expression and the cup of water. Her instincts as a caregiver were at odds with her protective nature as a mother. As she hesitated, Bella reached for the cup.

"Bella!" Ava warned, her voice tinged with caution.

"He's not a threat, Mama," Bella reassured her, moving to hold the cup for Elliot to drink. As he gratefully sipped the water, his relief was apparent, easing some of Ava's apprehensions.

"Thank you, Bella," Elliot said, his voice growing a bit stronger, "But you should listen to your mother. She's only trying to keep you safe."

"I know," Bella replied with a playful eye roll. "Mama's always looking out for me."

"That's because she loves you," Elliot remarked, a hint of sadness in his voice. "You'd miss it if she wasn't around. Trust me."

"Do you not have a family?" she asked softly, sitting down beside him.

"No," Elliot admitted. "My parents passed when I was younger than you. I lived with my grandfather until I was eighteen, but he's gone too."

Ava, who had joined her daughter, gently touched Elliot's forearm, her wariness replaced by empathy. "I'm sorry, Elliot. It's tough losing loved ones," she said, her voice resonating with shared loss.

Bella looked down. "The gods took Daddy when I was little," she whispered.

"I'm sorry, Bella. But you've got a loving Mama, right?" he said, smiling warmly.

Bella's face lit up as she looked at Ava. "Yeah!" she beamed. Ava then wrapped Bella in a hug, a tender moment of motherly love.

After pulling away, Ava drew her knife. "Bella, can you help me with these ropes?" She looked back at Elliot, empathy replaced with seriousness once more. "I'm going to trust you, Elliot, but I'm staying alert. If you make me regret that, I won't hesitate to use this. Understand?"

Elliot nodded, a genuine appreciation in his eyes. "Thank you, Ava," he said earnestly. He found himself admiring Ava, struck by how she could be tender and loving one moment and tough and decisive the next. "Don't worry about me," he assured her with a lighthearted smile. "I've used up my quota of foolishness for today."

Bella, cutting through the ropes at his feet, teased, "Speaking of being foolish... you picked a fight with Savage-Heart, somehow survived jumping out of the Great Falls, and then you decide to take on three wolves without any weapons?" She looked up at him, her eyes sparkling with amusement.

Ava laughed as she untied the ropes around his chest. "She's got a point," she agreed, grinning. "You do have a talent for finding trouble."

"Mama, I'm starting to think we might have rescued a madman," Bella joked, giving Elliot a playful smile, which he returned, laughter lines crinkling around his eyes.

Chapter 22

Ava carefully cut through the last of the ropes. "There!" she announced. "You should be able to move now."

Elliot tried to sit up, but a sharp pain on his right side made him fall back, grimacing.

"You okay?" Ava leaned in, her eyes reflecting genuine concern.

"I'm fine," Elliot said through gritted teeth, the pain subsiding to a dull ache. "I guess 'getting up too quickly' is another addition to today's list of foolish acts," he added, smiling between clenched teeth.

"Would you mind helping me get out of this suit?" he asked Ava, his voice strained.

"Of course," Ava said, rising to her feet. "But how does it come off? I couldn't find any zippers or buttons while you were out."

"There's a lever here," he said, lifting a Velcro flap and pulling. Suddenly, the suit, rigid before, began to part at the waist. A seam appeared, running down its center, and the two sections separated smoothly. The fabric softened and loosened, leaving Ava and Bella amazed.

"What is this?" Ava asked, touching the suit's now-soft surface.

"It's amazing!" Bella joined in, fascinated. "Is it magic?"

Elliot laughed. "No, just advanced technology. It hardens for protection and softens for comfort," he explained. "I don't know how; it's made by people much smarter than me."

"So, anyone could have made it, huh?" Ava quipped.

"Ava, that hurts more than the bear attack," he said, then turned to Bella. "Is your mom always this tough?"

Bella thought for a moment. "No, it seems like it's just with you."

Ava, feeling slightly embarrassed, quickly refocused. "So... um, what's the next step?" she inquired, her voice faltering slightly. "With the suit, I mean."

Elliot pressed a button under the Velcro flap, further widening the suit's seams. "Could you help me take this top off?" he asked Ava.

As Ava leaned in to assist Elliot, the flickering firelight cast a warm glow on her face and revealed her striking features: her complexion was a radiant light brown, complemented by high cheekbones, a trait she shared with Bella. Her eyes, deep and expressive, were a rich dark brown, almond-shaped and captivating. Elliot noted her height, just under six feet, which lent her an air of athletic grace. She seemed to embody a unique blend of strength and elegance.

"It should come apart now," Elliot refocused. "If you could help me sit up, it would be easier to get this off."

Ava paused, then said to Bella, "Can you assist, please?"

"Sure, Mama," Bella said eagerly.

"Get behind his head. I'll pull from the front while you lift," Ava instructed.

Bella positioned herself as directed. Ava squatted down in front of Elliot, hands outstretched. "Ready?" she asked Elliot.

"As I'll ever be," he replied, taking hold of Ava's hands.

Ava pulled firmly, her muscles tensing with effort. Elliot, heavy but trying to minimize his pain, assisted as much as he could. Bella slid her arms under his shoulders, gently pushing to help raise him. With concerted effort and some struggle, Elliot finally sat up.

Working together, they removed the suit. Elliot opened the top part, and Ava and Bella carefully eased it over his arms and shoulders.

The boots, now softer, slipped off easily with the trousers still attached. With Bella's help, Elliot eased out of the trousers. He then folded them neatly, aligning the boots, and placed them beside the rest of the suit.

Beneath the suit, Elliot was dressed in a plain navy blue shirt, paired with olive green cargo trousers and sturdy black combat boots. Ava couldn't help but notice how his frame appeared slimmer without the suit, yet still strong. Standing at six-foot, three-inches tall and weighing around one hundred and eighty-five pounds, his physique was lean and toned, a testament to years of rigorous physical activity. To Ava, Elliot appeared to be of average height for a man in her village, yet his build was noticeably more muscular. His shoulders were broader and his chest more expansive than most men she knew, giving him a distinctive presence.

"I'm going to check for any injuries," Ava declared, rising to her feet. She moved behind Elliot and knelt, her fingers gently probing his back for any signs of trauma.

As Ava carefully lifted Elliot's shirt to check his back, he flinched. "No need to be a baby," she joked with a smile. "You've got some serious bruises, but nothing's broken." Her fingers were gentle yet thorough over his skin. "Did Savage-Heart give you all of these?" she inquired.

"Most of them," Elliot replied, wincing as she touched a tender spot. "I also fell down a hole and hit a few walls on the way down. I woke up at the bottom, so I don't know how far I fell, but I'm guessing some bruises came from that too."

"You fell down a hole as well?" Bella asked, laughing, her amusement filling the room. "You might be Lunar's most unlucky man!" Her giggles softened the serious moment.

"Lunar?" Elliot repeated, confused.

"Yes, Lunar," Bella said, her tone playful but concerned. "Don't you know where you are? You must have hit your head pretty hard!"

"Lunar," Elliot repeated, the name rolling off his tongue as he tried to make sense of it. "So, that's what this place is called?"

"Not just here, but our whole world."

Ava, meanwhile, fetched a small leather pouch and a mortar and pestle. Handing them to Bella, she asked, "Can you grind these for me?"

"Of course, Mama," Bella responded, taking them and starting the task.

Ava turned her attention back to Elliot. "It seems we both have many questions. Let me tend to your injuries first, then we can talk more. This way, you won't be screaming like a baby every few minutes," she smiled teasingly.

Elliot smiled back, amused by her playful yet stern demeanor. He looked at Bella, still smiling, and shrugged in mock resignation. "She's not wrong," he admitted. "I do scream like a baby."

"Go ahead, Ava, I'm ready," he said playfully, biting his fist and closing his eyes dramatically, causing Bella to burst into laughter.

Chapter 23

Ava's meticulous examination of Elliot revealed several cracked ribs and an expanse of bruising across his back and chest. After preparing a poultice from ground leaves steeped in boiling water, she let it cool before gently applying the soothing mixture to Elliot's tender areas. Despite his best efforts to remain stoic, Elliot winced and shifted under Ava's careful application, amusing Bella.

Midway through Ava's attentive treatment, Bella's voice cut through the room, declaring her hunger. Ava suggested she prepare a stew with vegetables and cured meat from her pack. Bella set to work with enthusiasm, and by the time Ava had finished with the ointment, a warm, inviting aroma filled the room.

Gathered around the fire pit, Ava unwrapped some bread, giving pieces to Bella and Elliot before taking one for herself. Elliot tasted his share of the stew, visibly impressed. "This is great, Bella. Is it rabbit?"

"Yes," Bella said proudly. "I caught it myself."

"You're quite the hunter!" Elliot praised.

"Mama's been teaching me."

"My grandfather taught me to hunt when I was young, too," Elliot shared, his voice tinged with nostalgia. "How did you catch the rabbit?"

"With a bow," Bella answered. "I practice every chance I get."

"That's impressive! Hitting a rabbit is no small feat," Elliot praised with evident admiration.

As they continued to eat, the conversation flowed easily, filled with laughter and shared stories. Ava observed Bella and Elliot's interaction, touched by Bella's pride and Elliot's genuine interest. Despite the warmth of the moment, she felt a twinge of sadness for Bella's years without such companionship.

After the meal, Ava cleaned up and brought back boiled water to drink. As the fire crackled softly, Elliot, sensing the time was right, thanked them for the meal, then shifted the conversation to a more earnest topic.

"I believe I owe you both a thank you," Elliot began, his tone sincere.

"You don't need to keep thanking us for the food, Elliot," Ava replied.

"No, it's not just about the meal," Elliot clarified. "I mean for saving my life. As I've been sitting here, replaying the events of the day, two things became clear to me." He paused, sipping his drink before continuing. "Firstly, the incredible effort you both made to carry me here on that stretcher."

"We dragged you actually," Bella interjected. "You were far too heavy to carry," she added, her eyes twinkling with humor.

Elliot chuckled. "Then I'm doubly grateful to both of you for dragging my enormous unconscious body to safety." The laughter from both Bella and Ava echoed in the room.

Elliot's expression sobered. "Reflecting on my encounter with the wolves," he said, "I realized something."

"How foolish it was?" Bella asked, grinning sheepishly.

"It certainly was!" Elliot agreed, smiling briefly. "But what I meant was, I remembered that I only killed two of the wolves. One was still alive when I passed out." He looked at them intently. "That means... someone else must have dealt with the last wolf."

A silent exchange passed between Ava and Bella. Elliot nodded, understanding. "That must have been frightening," he said warmly, his voice conveying gratitude. "I can't thank you enough. I owe you both my life."

"It was Bella," Ava said. "She didn't hesitate, even though I tried to stop her. She shot the wolf with her bow."

"I only grazed it, Mama," Bella interjected modestly. "You were the one who scared it off."

Elliot watched them argue over their bravery with a smile. "All I know is that I owe my life to two of the bravest people I've ever met," he said earnestly.

Their faces brightened at his words. "Thank you, Elliot. That's very kind of you to say," Ava responded. As she spoke, her eyes fleetingly met his, before she quickly redirected her gaze.

"I think it's time we talked about where you came from," Ava said, smoothly steering the conversation in a new direction.

"Yes," Elliot agreed, his expression turning thoughtful. "But be prepared, it's going to sound unbelievable." He hesitated, searching for the right words. "There's no easy way to say this, but..." He paused, uncertain. "I believe you're living inside the Moon."

Ava and Bella exchanged glances, a flicker of amusement quickly turning into uncontrolled laughter. They both started laughing so hard that they were nearly doubling over, tears forming in the corners of their eyes.

Elliot watched, bewildered, as their laughter grew. He tried to assert the seriousness of his statement, but this only seemed to fuel their amusement.

Finally, Ava, managing to regain some composure, said, "I thought you were starting a serious conversation!"

"I am serious," Elliot insisted, his voice firm. "You really are inside the Moon."

Ava, still smiling slightly, replied, "Elliot, we know we're inside the Moon. Where else would we be?"

Now it was Elliot who was taken aback, his confusion evident. "I'm lost," he admitted. "Maybe you should start explaining because I feel like I've just tumbled down a rabbit hole."

"I'm not sure I understand what you mean by that," Ava responded, her expression reflecting his confusion.

"It's like I've landed in a strange world where nothing is as it seems," Elliot explained. "Can you start from the beginning, as if this is my first day on Lunar?"

Ava and Bella shared a confused look. "Alright, Elliot," Ava said, her tone becoming serious once more, "we'll start from the beginning, but let's stick to the truth, okay?"

Elliot nodded, his expression solemn. "I promise. Just tell me everything," he urged.

"Okay. So we live in Lunar, our home inside the Moon," Ava began.

"But how does this place exist?" Elliot asked, then seeing Ava's puzzled look, he quickly added, "I'm being serious. I really don't know any of this."

"The gods built it for us," Bella said.

"What do you mean by 'the gods,' Bella?"

"The gods!" she repeated, as if it were the most obvious thing in the world. "They created Lunar for us after a massive rock from space hit Earth. They saved us!" she explained.

Elliot's mind was a whirlwind of questions, each more perplexing than the last. "But Earth hasn't experienced a catastrophic impact for millions of years," he said. "That is, until today," he added, his words hanging heavy in the air.

"No, Earth was struck by a massive rock from space nearly a hundred years ago," Ava responded. "It was a catastrophe that nearly wiped out all humanity. The gods, seeing potential in our species, saved a select group, now known as the Lunari. They were brought here to the Moon so humanity could survive until Earth became habitable again. We've been here for almost a century now. But you're suggesting Earth was healthy and only struck by a large rock today? That seems hard to believe. You must be mistaken, Elliot."

"Ava, I'm certain of it. Until today, Earth hasn't faced an asteroid impact of that magnitude for sixty-five million years," Elliot insisted. "Before this catastrophe, Earth was bustling with life, billions of people, of which I was one. But now..." His voice trailed off, the enormity of his realization dawning upon him. "I might be the only one left," he said. A heavy silence followed, underscoring the magnitude of his loss.

"I was there just four days ago," he continued, his voice a mere whisper. "My friends... my home... everything was there." He glanced down at the space suit beside him. "That suit..." He pointed to the white garment and helmet. "That's what I wore to travel here from Earth."

Ava and Bella looked at the suit, their faces showing uncertainty. "Why would you say such things, Elliot?" Ava asked, her voice reflecting a hint of hurt. She had begun to trust, and maybe even like, this man. Now, his words appeared as improbable tales, leaving her bewildered and questioning why he would fabricate such a story.

"Ava, I'm not lying to you," Elliot insisted, frustration creeping in. He thought hard about how to validate his story but quickly realized the difficulty of doing so without the option of going back to the Moon's surface.

"Wait!" Elliot suddenly exclaimed, inspiration lighting his face. He dug into his trouser pockets and produced a sleek black rectangular object. "This is a smartphone," he explained, activating the device. It glowed softly, drawing Ava and Bella closer in curiosity.

"What does it do?" Bella asked, her eyes fixed on the screen.

"It can do almost everything," Elliot said as he held the smartphone. "But here, its uses are limited. However, there's something I can show you." He navigated to his photo album, selecting a special picture. Gently, he turned the phone towards Ava and Bella. "Look at this," he said softly. "This is a picture of me as a young boy with my grandfather. It's old, but what's in the background isn't Lunar; it's Earth. Do you see the mountains? The trees?"

Ava and Bella leaned in, their eyes widening at the sight. The image was a vivid glimpse into a world they had only known from stories. The realization that Elliot's story might be true began to dawn on them, as the Earth's landscapes were so different from anything in Lunar. A hushed awe filled the room as they absorbed the implications.

Breaking the silence, Elliot asked, "In your people's time on Earth, before you came here, did humans ever travel in space? Like, to the Moon or beyond?"

Ava, still mesmerized by the photo, shook her head. "No, space travel wasn't possible in our time. The first time a human traveled in space was one hundred years ago when we were brought here."

Elliot nodded. "My journey here isn't from a past era; it's from an Earth that was alive and thriving just days ago. A time when space travel is possible," he clarified.

The room fell into a profound silence as the magnitude of Elliot's revelation settled in. Ava and Bella exchanged a look, their expressions reflecting a newfound understanding of Elliot's extraordinary situation. The air was thick with a mix of awe and uncertainty as they both grappled with the implications of a thriving Earth.

Chapter 24

"What's all that white stuff?" Bella asked, her gaze returning to the picture on Elliot's phone.

"That's snow," Elliot explained. "It's what happens to rain when it gets really cold. Do you have snow here in Lunar?"

"No," Ava replied, with Bella nodding in agreement. "The weather in Lunar doesn't change much."

"I've got more I can show you," Elliot said enthusiastically. He turned the phone back towards himself, selecting a video. Flipping it around again, he hit play. The video showed someone skiing down a slope, quickly approaching the camera. Just as the skier neared, they executed a swift turn, spraying snow at the lens. Ava and Bella instinctively flinched, then laughed.

"This is Earth?" Ava asked, her voice filled with awe.

"Yes," Elliot confirmed, placing the phone before them. "Earth was a world full of life... until today, that is," he said.

After a moment lost in thought, Elliot finally said, "On Earth, we had a defense system, DART, which was designed to divert any large space rocks on a collision course. It must have failed somehow." He slowly shook his head.

"But what's baffling is the complete lack of warning. Even if we couldn't stop it, we should have still seen it coming!"

Bella, still intrigued, pointed at the phone. "Do you have more videos like this?"

Elliot nodded, a faint smile returning. "Yes, plenty."

Taking a moment, he showed Bella how to use his smartphone, guiding her through swiping photos and playing, pausing, and rewinding videos. She caught on quickly, her fascination clear with each swipe. As Bella explored Elliot's collection, absorbed in the images and videos, Elliot turned back to Ava, ready to continue their conversation.

"You mentioned your people have been living here for nearly a hundred years?" Elliot asked.

"Yes, almost a century now," Ava confirmed, tearing her gaze away from the captivating screen to face Elliot.

"And you said these 'gods' constructed this place and brought your ancestors here?" he continued, piecing the story together.

"That's right," Ava nodded. "They built everything we know and brought people and animals for us to care for."

"But what about the sun and the sky I saw earlier? How are they possible?"

"They're not real. They're just images, like your smartphone," Ava replied, nodding towards the device still enchanting Bella. "But the light from our sun is vital for our plants to grow."

"This place is incredible," Elliot said. "Our technology on Earth wasn't capable of anything like this, especially not inside the Moon."

He paused, awestruck by the technological marvels of these "gods." The thought of such an advanced habitat hidden inside the Moon, and constructed a century ago, was almost beyond belief.

A new question formed in Elliot's mind, surprising him with its delayed emergence. "Ava, why do you call them 'gods'? What can you tell me about them?"

Ava looked puzzled at his question. "They are gods! They watched over us from above, saved us from extinction, and promised to one day return us to Earth."

"Do they expect anything in return?"

"We abide by their rules," she said, with a hint of unease creeping in.

"And if someone doesn't?" Elliot pressed further.

"Then there would be consequences," Ava replied, her eyes avoiding his. "I'd rather not talk about the gods anymore," she added quickly. "Tell me more about Earth and your journey to Lunar."

Elliot sensed he had reached a boundary with Ava on this topic. There was evident unease in her voice when discussing these "gods." Who were they, and from where did they originate? The possibility that they still might be overseeing Lunar lingered in his mind. They were clearly an advanced civilization if they were capable of creating a world like Lunar. But why had they misled Ava's ancestors about the fate of humanity, especially when the cataclysm had only occurred today? The reasons for bringing them to the Moon were shrouded in mystery. Despite his burning curiosity, Elliot realized these questions would have to remain unanswered for the moment. For now, it was his turn to answer some questions.

Elliot began his story with the moment he'd landed on the Moon. As he began, Bella set the smartphone aside and scooted closer to Ava, her attention wholly fixed on his every word. He detailed the meteor shower, the catastrophic strike on Earth, and his subsequent plunge into the cave. Bella clung to her mother's arm, her grip tightening as the story unfolded.

He recounted the ordeal of waking up trapped under rubble and debris from the site, his struggle for freedom, and his eventual discovery of the airlock. Ava leaned in, particularly engrossed as he described navigating from one airlock to another, emerging behind the waterfall in the cave.

The suspense built as Elliot spoke of his trek through the dark cave and the chilling moment he stumbled upon bones strewn across the den floor. Both Ava and Bella seemed to hang on every word, visibly on the edges of their seats. Elliot's description of stepping outside into a breathtaking world, only to face the terror of encountering Savage-Heart, heightened the drama of his tale.

Bella couldn't resist interjecting at this point. "That's when we first saw you, screaming like a fool at Savage-Heart," she said, her smile breaking through the tension.

Once he recovered from laughing, Elliot continued with his harrowing recount of the chase back to the cave's entrance and the grueling fight with Savage-Heart that had led to his desperate leap through the Great Falls. He spoke of his fragmented memories of awakening to wolves gnawing at his suit, the ensuing battle, and finally losing consciousness. Bella eagerly jumped in to fill the gaps in Elliot's story, animatedly reenacting the parts he'd missed.

Her enthusiasm was infectious, and Elliot responded with delighted applause.

After Elliot had finished his story, Bella bombarded him with questions about Earth. Her curiosity was insatiable—she wanted to know about the weather, the fashion, the cuisine, and particularly, the experience of touching snow.

Elliot responded to each of Bella's questions, but Ava couldn't help noticing the tinge of sorrow that shadowed his face during his recollections, particularly when he mentioned his friend, Franklin.

The weight of uncertainty regarding Franklin's fate hung heavily on Elliot. His resolve to return to the surface and uncover the truth remained firm, even as he acknowledged the slim chances of finding his friend alive. To embark on this journey, he knew he would have to navigate past the daunting presence of Savage-Heart, the bear, as well as acquire suitable climbing gear so he could make his way back to the surface. In his heart, Elliot was certain: only by uncovering the truth about Franklin's fate could he truly find peace.

Touched by his poignant story, Ava and Bella offered their support for his mission. They suggested taking him to their village to meet their chief, confident he could assist Elliot and welcome him into their community upon his return. They reassured him that, though Lunar was different from Earth, he might find a new sense of belonging with them in time.

As the evening unfolded and their conversation meandered, the fire's glow softened. Eventually, Bella succumbed to sleep, her head resting gently in Ava's lap. Ava's fingers lovingly stroked her hair.

"She's an incredible girl," Elliot remarked, smiling warmly as he looked at Bella. "You've done an amazing job raising her, Ava."

Ava met his gaze, a sense of gratitude and a flicker of something else—perhaps recognition of a long-forgotten feeling—in her eyes. "Thank you," she murmured. It had been ages since she had simply sat and talked with a man, being heard and understood. The experience stirred something within her, a memory of a connection she once cherished.

"Do you have children, Elliot?" Ava inquired. "You have a natural way with Bella."

A shadow of sadness briefly crossed Elliot's face. "I had a son, but I lost him and his mother in an accident while I was away, serving as a soldier," he revealed, his voice laden with deep, lingering grief.

"I'm so sorry, Elliot," Ava said softly, reaching out to gently take his hand in hers. "You've endured so much loss in your life. More than anyone should have to bear."

Elliot responded by covering her hand with his other one, a silent gesture expressing his gratitude. "Thank you, Ava," he said. "It's been a while since I've talked about them. Sharing this... it feels good, so thank you for asking."

After a brief moment, Elliot carefully withdrew his hand, conscious of the shared sleeping arrangements and not wishing to make Ava uncomfortable. "I think it's time we all got some rest," he suggested, glancing at the peacefully sleeping Bella. "Tomorrow seems like it'll be another eventful day."

"You have no idea!" Ava replied, a hint of excitement in her smile. "Tomorrow, you'll meet everyone in our village."

Ava tenderly lifted Bella into one of the cots, then returned to help Elliot settle into another. Although he moved with less difficulty than earlier, his pain was still apparent. "You'll feel stronger tomorrow," Ava assured him. "Strong enough for our journey to the village."

The room was quiet as they settled down, but then Ava's voice softly pierced the silence. "What was his name? Your son?"

Elliot paused. His voice was soft when he spoke again. "Kurt. His name was Kurt Adams."

Ava's response was heartfelt. "Kurt would be proud of his father. You're a good man, Elliot," she said warmly. "Good night."

"Good night, Ava," Elliot replied, his eyes closing. As he drifted into sleep, memories of Kurt enveloped him, offering a sense of solace and comfort.

CHAPTER 25

ELLIOT AWOKE TO THE soothing sounds of Ava and Bella deep in conversation. For a moment, he lay still, soaking in his surroundings and observing them quietly. Then, with a soft tone, he interrupted. "Good morning," he greeted.

"Good morning," they replied in chorus, turning towards him with matching smiles as Elliot stretched out on his cot.

"Sorry for sleeping in so late," he apologized, sitting up. "What time is it?"

"Around mid-morning," Ava replied, handing him a steaming cup. "This is maté," she explained, noticing his puzzled glance at the unfamiliar drink.

Curious, Elliot took a tentative sip, then immediately spat it out, wiping his tongue of the leafy bits that clung to it.

Bella and Ava couldn't contain their laughter. "You have to use this, silly," Bella said, handing him a straw-like object with amusement. "It keeps the bits out."

Elliot took the straw, placed it into his cup among the leaves, and gave it another try. This time, he nodded in approval. "Much better, thanks! And sorry about the spitting," he added with a mischievous grin towards Bella.

Surveying the shelter, Elliot noticed the tidy space—the dinnerware neatly stored away and the fire pit cleaned. He then spotted the source of the bright daylight illuminating the room without a fire—a sun tunnel in the center of the ceiling.

"That's clever," he remarked, admiring the mirrored dome at its end, scattering sunlight throughout the shelter.

"Yes," Ava agreed. "It saves us from building a fire during the day too."

Bella, who was busy organizing her pack, finished and placed it by the hatch door, signaling readiness.

Catching the cue, Elliot said, "I guess it's time for us to get moving, right?"

"Yes, we can head to the village when you're ready," Ava responded. "It's a few hours' walk, and you might need breaks along the way."

Elliot stood up, subtly masking the pain that momentarily crossed his face. "Don't worry about me," he assured her.

"We'll take breaks," Bella remarked. "I'm not dragging you again!"

"What, not even if I pretend to be unconscious again?" Elliot responded, his grin widening.

"Try it and you'll get a little poke with my knife to check!" she warned, her eyes alight with mischief.

Elliot and Ava laughed. "You walked right into that one, Elliot," Ava said, amused.

"Fair point. I deserved that," Elliot said, raising his hands in mock surrender.

As Ava began organizing her pack near the hatch, her gaze shifted to Elliot's space suit. "You know, it might be best to leave your suit here," she suggested thoughtfully. "The villagers might be unsettled if they see you in that."

"They'll think he looks odd in those clothes too, Mama," Bella commented, eyeing his combat trousers and T-shirt.

"What's wrong with my clothes?" Elliot asked, looking down at himself.

Bella gestured towards herself and Ava. "Just look at us, then at you. You look weird."

Elliot turned his attention to Ava. She was clad in a simply patterned dark brown dress, its material durable as well as functional. The dress ended just above her knees, adorned with tassels along the hem. Its sleeveless V-neck cut was accented with tassels along the neckline, and a beige waist belt cinched the fabric, accentuating her hourglass physique. Her feet were ensconced in black moccasin-style ankle boots, also with tassels.

Bella's attire was a lighter brown version of Ava's dress, with a contrasting dark brown belt. It was clear that Elliot, in his current attire, would stick out like a sore thumb. "I see your point," he admitted.

"You look like, uh... Mama, what's a nicer way of saying 'weird'?" Bella asked, her tone lighthearted. Elliot couldn't help but smile at her directness.

"Erm... unique?" Ava offered with a smile.

"This"-—

*Elliot gestured to his clothes—"is pretty standard back on Earth."

"Really?" Bella's eyes widened in mock disbelief.

"Well, not exactly mainstream," Elliot clarified. "But it's common among, well, certain groups."

Bella's skeptical look remained.

"Okay, okay," Elliot chuckled, "it's mostly just unique, weirdo, ex-army guys like me."

Bella nodded. "I thought as much."

"But this is all I've got," Elliot said. "I wasn't exactly planning a visit to see any secret moon people."

"Lunari," Ava corrected. "Although your clothes might make your story more credible."

As Elliot reached for his space suit, Ava quickly added, "However, that suit might be a bit too much. It could cause fear or misunderstanding with the people in my village."

"I was just going to get this," Elliot said, retrieving a small device from the suit's arm.

"What is it?' Ava asked, looking at the device.

"It's called a CDU," Elliot said. "It monitors air quality and temperature, and it also helps me communicate with my team," he explained, holding up the gadget.

"Like the smartphone?" Bella asked, recalling their earlier conversation.

"Exactly," Elliot confirmed, showing them the display. "But without a signal, like now, it's just a fancy monitor."

"What's a signal?" Ava asked.

Elliot pondered how to simplify the concept. "It's a bit complex but think of signals as invisible waves that carry messages through the air. They're everywhere, but can't pass through solid things, like rock. They help us send and receive information over long distances," he explained, slipping the CDU into his pocket.

"That sounds like magic," Bella said, her eyes wide with wonder.

Elliot smiled. "In some ways, it is," he admitted. "But here, deep inside the Moon, I can't get any signal."

"So, you can't contact Franklin or anyone else because of that?" Ava surmised.

"That's right," Elliot confirmed, his face clouding over briefly with concern.

Ava stood up, her voice firm. "Then we should get moving to the village. Our chief might have some ideas on how to help you get back to the surface."

She approached the hatch, unbolting and cautiously opening it just a crack, her knife at the ready. After a quick survey of the area, she pushed the hatch fully open and climbed out. Moments later, her voice called down reassuringly, "It's safe. Come on up."

Chapter 26

THE LUNAR MORNING WAS breathtaking, with the sun casting a warm glow against a sky of deep ocean blue, accompanied by a soft breeze that rustled through the trees. The melody of birdsong intertwined with the gentle murmur of the nearby river, creating a tranquil symphony.

Bella, emerging next from the hatch, climbed the ladder with the agility and ease of someone accustomed to this environment. Upon reaching the top, she stood poised and vigilant, her bow at the ready. She glanced down the hatch and called out to Elliot, "Come on up, it's a beautiful day."

Inside, Elliot had been cautiously testing his legs, expecting discomfort. To his relief, they felt surprisingly strong, despite the persistent ache in his back and ribs. Motivated by Bella's call, he approached the ladder. As he took his first step, he paused in astonishment. There was no pain, no hint of difficulty in his movements. Instead, he felt an unusual lightness, almost as if his body was on the brink of floating.

"Everything okay down there?" Ava's voice floated down to him.

"Uh, yeah," Elliot called back, still adjusting to his new-found agility.

"What's taking so long?" Ava inquired.

"I'm just... getting the hang of walking again!" Elliot replied with a chuckle.

A moment later, he emerged from the hatch, almost soaring into the air before landing gracefully on the grass with a triumphant grin. Ava and Bella exchanged amused glances at his exuberant entrance.

"What on Lunar was that?" Bella exclaimed, her eyes wide with astonishment.

"It seems I might be experiencing some... interesting side effects here," Elliot replied, his grin widening. "Looks like I have superpowers," he joked, giving a casual shrug.

"Superpowers?" Ava echoed.

"What do you know about gravity?" Elliot asked.

Ava and Bella shared puzzled glances.

"Gravity is the force that keeps us anchored to the ground instead of floating away," Elliot explained. He picked up a small rock and let it drop to the ground. "Like this. Gravity pulls it down."

Ava nodded slowly. "And how does this relate to you having superpowers?"

Elliot chuckled. "Well, it's not actual superpowers. Gravity here on Lunar is about a third of what it is on Earth. That means my muscles find it easier to move here."

Bella tilted her head. "So?"

Grinning, Elliot demonstrated his point. He leaped into the air, soaring over six feet high, before landing lightly back on the ground. "Here, I can jump much higher because I have greater strength."

Bella's eyes sparkled with excitement. "Woah! What else can you do?"

"That's about it," Elliot said. "I'm just stronger and more agile here than I am on Earth."

Ava nodded, a realization dawning. "That explains how you managed to fight off those wolves, almost like you were Savage-Heart."

"Well, maybe not quite that strong," Elliot conceded with a smile.

"Speaking of wolves, Mama," Bella cut in, her tone turning serious, "shouldn't we move away from here? This was where the wolf last saw us."

"You're right, darling, we should start moving," Ava agreed. Then, turning to Elliot with a playful glint in her eye, she teased, "Are you ready to walk with us, or do your superpowers include flying now?"

"Ha-ha, very funny," Elliot replied, starting to walk towards them.

However, his second step turned into a clumsy hop, followed by an unintended leap that sent him tumbling to the ground. Ava and Bella couldn't help but laugh at the sight.

From the ground, Elliot grinned up at them. "Looks like I need a bit more practice with this new gravity!"

For the next twenty minutes, Ava offered her arm to Elliot, her weight helping him stay more grounded. To her, it felt like an awkward dance, but gradually, Elliot's movements became more controlled. By the time they veered away from the river and began ascending a hill into the forest, he was walking on his own, albeit with an occasional spring in his step.

An hour and a half into their journey, they emerged from the dense woods into a sprawling grassland. Ava proposed a break, and Elliot, feeling a familiar ache in his chest, readily agreed. He found a fallen tree at the forest's edge and sat down, welcoming the chance to rest his tired muscles.

"How far is it to your village from here?" Elliot inquired, looking towards the horizon.

"We're about halfway there," Ava replied. "It's another walk similar to what we've already covered but it should be pretty flat now. How are your ribs holding up?"

"Better than expected, considering my encounters with Savage-Heart and the wolves," Elliot joked. "I don't think I've ever seen a bear that furious, or that large!"

"She's been restless since her cub disappeared," Bella explained solemnly. "She searches every day but never finds him."

Elliot nodded. "That explains why she's so angry. But who would be silly enough to take her cub?"

As they continued to talk, Ava retrieved her water from her pack and shared it with Elliot.

"Thank you," Elliot said gratefully, taking a sip before passing the bottle back. He then turned to Ava. "Why were you and Bella hunting so far from your village?"

Ava sighed. "The village doesn't approve of women hunting."

"That's ridiculous," Elliot exclaimed. "There's nothing you can't do as well as any man."

Bella's eyes lit up hearing this. "Do women hunt on Earth?" she asked.

"Absolutely," Elliot affirmed. "On Earth, women hunt, fight, and do everything men do. I've served alongside many incredible female soldiers."

"Female soldiers," Ava mused, her eyes sparkling with wonder.

Bella looked at her mother. "Imagine that, Mama!"

"It's not something that would happen here," Ava said.

Elliot nodded. "Change takes time. On Earth, it started with just a few people who dared to challenge the norms. Over time, their voices grew, and as a result, change followed."

He stood up, surveying the landscape ahead before his gaze returned to Bella, who was absentmindedly fiddling with her bow. "It seems to me that there are already two people here ready to be the catalyst for change."

As they resumed their journey, they stepped out from the cool shade of the forest into the warm embrace of the late morning sun. The vast grassland stretched before them, dotted with herds of grazing animals. In the distance, the silhouette of another forest marked their destination.

"Our village is just beyond that forest," Bella said, pointing ahead.

"How many people live there?" Elliot inquired.

"Around one to two hundred," Ava answered.

"That's quite a lot," Elliot remarked as his attention was briefly captured by a passing herd of sheep. "And what about animals? What kinds do you have here?"

Bella's face lit up. "We have sheep, cows, chickens, horses, pigs, buffalo, fish—and you've already met the wolves and bears," she added with a playful grin.

Elliot chuckled. "Yeah, unforgettable meeting, that one."

As they walked, Bella spoke up. "Mama, can I grab something to eat from my pack? I'm hungry."

"Sure, just be quick and catch up," Ava said.

As Bella stopped to rummage through her pack, Ava and Elliot continued towards the forest, now just a short distance away. Elliot pondered how to approach the subject of the "gods" with the villagers. Turning to Ava, he decided to broach the topic.

"Ava, can I ask about the gods you mentioned? Do you see them?" he ventured cautiously.

"Yes, they appear quite often," Ava replied, her voice taking on a somber note.

"I don't mean to upset you," Elliot said, sensing her discomfort. "I was just wondering, what do they look like?"

Ava hesitated before answering. "Their appearance is similar to how you looked in your suit," she began. "But their suits have stripes, and their helmets aren't transparent like yours."

"Do they look like us? Physically, I mean," Elliot asked.

"They have two arms, two legs, and a head; if that's what you mean, then yes," Ava confirmed. "But no one has ever seen their faces or what lies beneath their suits."

"So how can you be sure they're not just men in suits, pretending to be gods?" Elliot pressed further.

"We've considered that possibility. But, as you've pointed out, Earth humans lack the technology to create a world like this. And we, the Lunari, certainly don't possess such capabilities either. So how could they just be men in suits pretending?" Ava responded.

"You have a point," Elliot conceded reluctantly. A nagging question persisted in his mind, though. Why would these "gods" deceive them about Earth? This thought gave way to another. "How do your people feel about these gods, Ava?" he asked.

"We're grateful to them for saving us," Ava replied, after a brief pause.

"But do your people have any affection for them? Do they worship them?"

"We just do as they say," Ava replied curtly.

Perplexed by her response, Elliot asked, "Ava, do your people fear these gods?"

Ava halted and turned to face Elliot, her expression serious. "You must understand something, Elliot," she began earnestly. "The gods are our lifeline. Without their technology, we couldn't survive here. They have the power to end this world at any moment. Our continued existence, the faint hope we hold of one day returning to Earth, it all depends on them. We have no choice but to do as they ask."

"And what do they ask of you?" Elliot probed further.

Ava's response was measured. "They occasionally select someone to go with them."

"For what purpose?"

"We don't know," Ava admitted.

Elliot's concern deepened. "Do they kill those they take?"

"No, the taken are usually returned within a day or two, but with no memories of their time away," she explained.

"So, does that make people fear the gods?" Elliot asked.

Ava paused, searching for the right words. "Partially, but also, the fear comes from what happens if someone resists or tries to prevent a taking. Then... people get hurt."

Elliot felt a chill at her words. "Has that ever happened to you?"

"I don't want to talk about it," Ava said, her voice noticeably lower.

Elliot tilted his head, noticing a new sound. "Ava, listen—"

Ava began to object but halted as she too heard it. A low rumble, like distant thunder, but coming from the ground. Her face morphed from confusion to dread. "It's a stampede!" she gasped, her voice edged with panic.

She spun around, searching the horizon, her dread swiftly turning to sheer terror. "Bella!" she cried out, her voice filled with fear.

Chapter 27

A herd of over a hundred buffalo thundered relentlessly up the gentle hill, their advance towards the flat grasslands at the top a breathtaking spectacle. Bathed in the morning light, their dark shaggy coats radiated with a warm glow, accentuating the power of their massive frames. Each ground-shaking step echoed rhythmically through the air.

Upon reaching the hill's crest, the herd executed a dramatic, almost-choreographed turn onto the grassy expanse between the two forests. Their movement was astonishingly coordinated, reminiscent of a ballet troupe in perfect unison.

Their raw power was mesmerizing. Muscular bodies surged forward, effortlessly propelling the beasts as a swirl of dust and grass enveloped them, veiling the earth beneath their hooves. Nearby, other animals grazing in tranquility moments earlier were now swept up in the urgency. Sheep, cows, and various birds scattered in a frenzy, adding to the dynamic chaos of the scene.

Before Ava's warning had escaped her lips, Bella had slung her pack over her shoulder and was already sprinting toward them. Growing up in the wilds of Lunar had sharpened her instincts; despite her young age, she wasn't one to be paralyzed by fear.

Bella had fallen a full football field's length behind Elliot and Ava while rummaging through her pack. The buffalo, just three times that distance away, thundered across the flat grasslands, closing the gap at an incredible rate. Their sight, a formidable mass rapidly gaining ground, was both awe-inspiring and terrifying.

Ava sprinted forward, driven by a mother's instinct that overshadowed any fear. Initially a few steps behind, Elliot quickly realized the advantage his Lunar-enhanced muscles gave him. He surged ahead, his effortless long strides devouring the ground.

"I'll get her!" he called out to Ava as he surged ahead. "Head for the forest!"

Ava, momentarily stunned by Elliot's astonishing speed, stood frozen, watching him race away. His words echoed in her mind as she turned and dashed toward the safety of the forest, still two hundred meters distant.

Moving at an incredible speed, Elliot estimated that he was nearing forty miles per hour. He could have pushed for even greater speed, but he began to decelerate as he neared Bella. Coming to a skidding halt, he watched Bella rush past him, her face etched with fear. "Keep running!" he urged her.

As he turned to start running back, Elliot saw that the buffalo had drastically closed the gap on them. At their current speed, the herd would overtake them well before they could reach the safety of the forest. He needed a plan, and fast. The image of them being trampled under the hooves of a relentless stampede spurred him into action.

Ava, torn between maternal instincts and rational thought, placed her trust in Elliot and his extraordinary abilities. She recognized that her presence could impede Bella's chances of survival, so with a heavy heart but a clear mind, she bolted toward the forest, seeking refuge among the towering trees. Despite her focus, she couldn't help but steal a glance back, a surge of relief washing over her as she witnessed Elliot catching up to Bella. She knew he would do everything in his power to protect her daughter. With no other option, Ava pressed on, her strides fueled by hope.

Elliot, having rapidly closed the distance to Bella, assessed Ava's progress toward the forest. She was almost there. But at their current speed, he and Bella wouldn't make it.

"Bella!" he shouted. "Jump on my back!"

"Are you crazy?" Bella shouted back in disbelief.

"Just trust me!" Elliot responded, matching her pace with ease. "Superpowers!" he added almost gleefully.

Elliot surged ahead effortlessly and paused five meters in front of Bella, then turned back to her. "Jump on!" he urged.

The herd was closing in, now only twenty meters behind Bella when she made a leap of faith onto Elliot's back, her face a mask of terror. Without hesitation, Elliot immediately accelerated, his strides gaining momentum even with the added weight.

The buffalo began to charge past them, their pace relentless. Bella looked over her shoulder, her heart pounding at the sight of the endless herd and the thunderous sound they created. They were on the brink of being engulfed and trampled. But then, slowly, the tide began to turn. Elliot's speed was increasing, and they were gradually closing the gap with the leading buffalo.

Elliot had taken more time than he'd liked to regain his full speed with Bella on his back. He'd quickly calculated that even with the extra burden, his enhanced speed on Lunar should be sufficient. His physical fitness on Earth allowed him to sprint to nearly twenty-five miles per hour. With the reduced gravity of Lunar, his rough estimation was that he could potentially triple that speed, a theory his initial sprint had somewhat validated.

Elliot's strategy hinged on the assumption that carrying Bella would reduce his running speed by about fifty percent. If his calculations were correct, he should still be able to reach a velocity between thirty to forty miles per hour. It was a significant improvement over Bella's top speed, offering them the best chance at escape.

As Elliot adjusted to the feel of Bella's weight on his back, he gradually extended his stride. She felt surprisingly light, a realization he attributed to Lunar's gravity affecting her body mass. His speed increased steadily, and soon he was not only catching up to the leading buffalo but also overtaking them. Confidence surged as they closed in on the forest's edge with a substantial lead.

Ava, having reached the relative safety of the forest, spun around anxiously to locate her daughter. The sight that met her was terrifying: Elliot, in the midst of the thunderous stampede, carrying Bella on his back, seemingly inches from disaster. She clapped a hand over her mouth, stifling a scream, her eyes locked on the unfolding scene.

Then, as if defying reality, Elliot began to distance himself from the raging buffalo. Despite his seemingly leisurely pace, each of his strides covered an astonishing distance. It was a surreal and breathtaking display of agility.

With the forest's edge barely a hundred meters away, Elliot had widened the gap to twenty-five meters between them and the stampeding herd. The safety of the trees was tantalizingly close.

"Hold on tight!" he shouted to Bella, his mind racing with plans for their imminent arrival at the forest.

From her vantage point, Ava watched on, her heart pounding as Elliot and Bella rapidly approached the forest. The mass of buffalo bore down relentlessly behind them. Ava had already picked out a large tree for cover, but she was concerned: would Elliot be able to slow down quickly enough to find cover?

As the crucial moment neared and Ava's eyes searched for Bella, what she saw took her breath away. Clinging to Elliot like a jockey in a thrilling race, Bella's face was alight with exhilaration. This unexpected display of joy eased Ava's fears, replacing them with a sense of awe.

In the final stretch, Elliot began to moderate his speed, expertly eyeing a gap between the trees. As they reached the forest's edge, still moving at a significant pace, Elliot skillfully executed a controlled slide into the underbrush, reminiscent of a baseball player sliding into home base; a cloud of dust billowed around him as he decelerated, spraying debris in all directions.

They came to a halt fifteen meters inside the forest, and Elliot quickly sought shelter behind the thickest tree he could find.

"You okay back there?" he called out to Bella, peering around the massive trunk.

"That was amazing!" Bella replied, her voice filled with excitement.

"You're crazy!" Elliot responded, grinning back at her. "But hold on, it's not over yet!"

The buffalo charged relentlessly across the grassy flat landscape toward the forest's edge. As the herd surged forward, their collective energy seemed unstoppable. However, as they neared the dense forest marking the end of the open terrain, a sudden shift occurred. At the very precipice of the forest, where tall trees loomed like guardians of the wilderness, the lead buffalo veered abruptly to the right.

The sudden change in direction rippled through the herd like a shock wave. The ground trembled beneath their pounding hooves as the buffalo adjusted their course in unison. Their massive bodies leaned into the turn, displaying remarkable agility for creatures of such size.

From their vantage point within the forest, Ava, Elliot, and Bella watched in awe as the herd veered off to the right, disappearing over a nearby hill. The once-deafening sound of their hooves gradually faded, leaving behind only a profound silence in its wake.

Chapter 28

Bella sprinted to the forest's edge where Ava stood, her eyes filled with excitement. "Did you see that?" she exclaimed.

Ava, however, was more concerned with her daughter's safety. "Are you okay, darling?" she asked, inspecting Bella for any injuries.

"I'm fine, Mama," Bella said reassuringly, gently pushing Ava's hands away. "But did you see how fast we went? I've never seen anyone run that fast before!"

"I've never run that fast before!" Elliot admitted as he emerged from behind a tree, brushing dust off his clothes.

"How did you do that?" Bella asked.

"It's the gravity here," Elliot explained. "My muscles are just used to a lot more force."

"That was too close. You could have been seriously hurt, Bella," Ava stated.

"But I wasn't, Mama. Elliot saved me," said Bella, trying to soothe her mother.

Ava's gaze shifted to Elliot, her expression softening. "I'm sorry, Elliot, I should have thanked you sooner. Bella's right though, that was incredible."

Elliot offered a modest smile. "No need to apologize, Ava. I'm just relieved she's safe," he said, then added playfully, "Besides, I heard all the good snacks were in Bella's pack." He turned to Bella. "Come on then, hand it over!" he said, his tone teasing.

Bella chuckled and produced a small leaf-wrapped package. "I suppose you've earned a share as your rescue fee," she said, handing it over.

Bella then impulsively hugged Elliot. "Thank you for saving my life," she said sincerely.

Elliot returned the hug warmly. "Anytime, Bella. And let's not forget, I owed you one for the wolves."

"Yeah, you did!" Bella agreed, her voice carrying a hint of playful smugness.

After Bella released him, Elliot unwrapped the leaf parcel to find a handful of nuts. Popping one into his mouth, he quipped, "Is it always this eventful around here?"

"Actually, it's usually quite peaceful," Ava responded, accepting a nut from Elliot. "But ever since you arrived, things have taken a more... lively turn!"

"She means it's been more exciting!" Bella added.

"I have a feeling the excitement isn't over yet," Elliot observed, gesturing towards the grasslands.

Ava turned to see a group of fifteen horse riders galloping toward them. Recognizing them as part of the village's hunting party, her heart sank. This wasn't the introduction to Elliot she had envisioned. She had hoped to present him directly to the village chief, a man known for his fairness and thoughtful judgment. Now, they would face Mayto, the chief's son, a man renowned for his impatience and volatility.

sat astride a striking black stallion that shimmered in the sunlight, contrasted sharply with the other riders on their brown horses. He reined in his horse with a show of skill, circling in front of Elliot without dismounting.

Mayto regarded Elliot with immediate suspicion, his brown eyes narrowing as he inspected him. The stranger's unfamiliar attire and robust physique marked him as a potential threat. Mayto, a towering figure himself at six feet, eight inches, carried a broad chest and a muscular build reminiscent of Samoan warriors. His formidable appearance was enhanced by his shaved head and light brown skin. In the village, he epitomized physical dominance, matched only by his father, the chief. His authority stemmed not only from his lineage but also from being the community's most skilled hunter and warrior. Elliot's unfamiliar presence, coupled with his equally solid, if somewhat-slimmer build, represented a disruption to the established order, challenging the hierarchy Mayto had always known.

Mayto's immediate distaste for Elliot had a deeper root than mere suspicion. His eyes had caught the moment Bella embraced Elliot, a gesture she hadn't shared with any man since her father's death. Mayto had long harbored desires for Ava, aspiring to claim her as his wife once he ascended as chief. He firmly believed any woman, especially a widow with a child, would consider herself fortunate to be chosen by him.

Mayto grunted. "Who are you?" he demanded of Elliot, his voice bristling with authority.

Elliot, unfazed, casually popped another nut into his mouth. "Nice to meet you too," he replied, extending his hand with nuts towards Mayto. "Want one?"

Ava, keenly aware of Mayto's short fuse, quickly intervened. "This is Elliot," she said. "Elliot, meet Mayto, the chief's son."

"A pleasure," remarked Elliot with a nod, maintaining a calm demeanor.

Mayto's gaze remained fixed on Elliot, his expression unyielding. "And where did this Elliot come from?"

Ava stepped forward. "That's a long story, one that is best told to the chief first," she suggested diplomatically.

"He's not from our village, therefore, he should be considered dangerous," Mayto retorted. "I'll take him to the chief myself."

"There's no need," Ava countered firmly. "He's not dangerous. He just saved Bella from a stampeding herd of buffalo. They just came from the direction you rode in from. You wouldn't know why they were stampeding this way, would you?" she asked, her tone laced with suspicion.

Mayto, momentarily unsettled by Ava's direct accusation, swiftly regained his composure. "We saw the buffalo were agitated and came to ensure they weren't a threat to the village," he explained. Then, his tone shifting, he added, "You and Bella didn't return last night. We were out searching for you. Where were you?" he asked Ava, but glared at Elliot.

"That's another long story," Ava responded calmly. "But as you can see, we're both safe. We were just heading back to the village."

As Ava began to walk away, Mayto's commanding voice stopped her. "Wait! We'll escort you back," he ordered. He then pointed at two of his men. "Tie up this stranger. Use force if he resists."

"No one is tying me up today, Mayto." Elliot's response was icy yet composed. "Why don't we keep this friendly, there's no need for any trouble. As you can see, I'm unarmed, so why don't we all just walk to the village as Ava suggested."

Mayto, unaccustomed to being defied, paused to consider Elliot's challenge. Then he nodded to his men and ordered, "Tie him up. My orders stand."

The two men dismounted, their tall, lean figures in stark contrast to Elliot's more solid build. Their wiry frames were typical of Lunari men, except for Mayto, whose muscular physique was more pronounced.

Elliot, unfazed, called up to Mayto. "Why don't you come down here and try it yourself? Or are all those muscles just for show?"

Elliot had been in a lot of fights growing up. Being an orphan gave him unwanted attention from bullies. After returning home from school one day, tear-streaked from a bully's torment, his grandfather had taught him a valuable lesson: always stand up for yourself. More importantly, he advised Elliot to target the ringleader first. That strategy had served him well, warding off bullies throughout his childhood.

However, life had shown Elliot that bullies lurked at every corner, from high school and college to his time in the army. His grandfather's advice had evolved into a refined skill set. Now, Elliot wasn't just a fighter; he was trained and experienced.

Mayto, weighing Elliot's challenge, flashed a wicked smile. "No, I don't think you're worth my time," he responded dismissively, signaling his men to proceed.

Elliot recalled his grandfather's words about bullies who hid behind others. He'd learned the hard way as a young boy that sometimes you had to face more than one opponent. That early experience had been tough, but it taught him resilience. Now, with his training and experience, he felt confident in handling the situation.

Nashoba, the taller of the two men, dismounted first. He sized up Elliot, his judgment clouded by Elliot's unfamiliar attire and seemingly unimposing stature. It was a critical miscalculation.

Nashoba charged at Elliot, who swiftly countered. Elliot deftly stepped inside Nashoba's reach, driving his forearm into Nashoba's face with enough force to potentially break his nose. Nashoba's eyes welled with tears from the sudden pain. Elliot then twisted Nashoba's arm behind his back, forcing him into a doubled-over position before hurling him through the air. Nashoba landed in the dirt five feet away, a crumpled heap. Elliot had quickly neutralized the threat.

He then turned to Onada, the second man. "You sure about this? You'll end up just like him, maybe worse," Elliot cautioned, nodding toward Nashoba's fallen form.

Onada hesitated, glancing between his injured companion and Mayto, whose face was now a deep shade of crimson. Mayto's impatience erupted. "What are you waiting for? Get him, you fool!" he shouted.

Faced with a dilemma, Onada chose to avoid Mayto's wrath, albeit cautiously. He retrieved a spear from his horse and advanced towards Elliot.

Elliot eyed the weapon warily. "If you bring a weapon into this, I won't go as easy on you," he warned.

Onada's resolve wavered, torn between fear and obedience.

It was then that Ava intervened, her voice cutting through the tension. "Enough of this nonsense!"

But Mayto was relentless, his fury boiling over. "Get him!" he roared. "And if I have to step in, you'll answer to me next!"

Resigned to his fate, Onada steeled himself and faced Elliot once more, spear in hand. "Lie down, face down, now!" he commanded, pointing the weapon threateningly.

Elliot remained calm, yet firm. "This won't end how you expect. Last chance," he warned.

Undeterred, Onada advanced a step closer, jabbing his spear forward for emphasis.

Elliot's response was measured. "Don't say I didn't warn you," he cautioned.

As Onada lunged forward, wielding his spear like a club aimed at Elliot's head, Elliot deftly stepped back, evading the strike. Then, seizing the moment, he closed in just as Onada's swing lost momentum. Elliot struck swiftly, landing a precise punch to Onada's throat.

Stunned and gasping for air, Onada was defenseless as Elliot seized the spear and swept his legs from beneath him. Elliot discarded the spear to the side, watching as Onada staggered back to his feet, still wheezing for breath.

The battle was essentially over, yet Onada, driven by desperation, swung a clumsy punch at Elliot. It was effortlessly deflected, and in a fluid motion, Elliot maneuvered behind him, securing him in a chokehold. Within moments, Onada slumped to the ground, unconscious.

During the early stages of the encounter, Elliot rapidly assessed the significant difference in strength between himself and his opponents. Recognizing his physical advantage, he quickly adapted his fighting style, consciously avoiding causing serious injuries. Normally, an assailant with a weapon would face severe consequences in Elliot's hands, potentially leading to lengthy hospital stays.

However, on Lunar, he was unsure of their medical capabilities, if any. Understanding the importance of first impressions in his quest for acceptance within the village, he knew that inflicting grievous harm could jeopardize his chances. With this in mind, Elliot exercised restraint, using just enough force to defend himself effectively without causing lasting damage to his attackers.

Elliot's gaze, now icy and challenging, locked onto Mayto. "Do I need to go through all your men before you face me yourself?" he demanded.

Mayto, observing from atop his horse, couldn't help but admire Elliot's fearlessness and combat skills. Yet, he knew the importance of asserting his authority. To let such defiance go unanswered would undermine his standing, especially in front of Ava. Regretfully, he prepared to confront Elliot personally.

"No, I'll handle this myself," Mayto declared, dismounting with a sense of purpose.

Ava, alarmed by the escalating situation, hurried over to Mayto. "That's enough, Mayto," she said. "This is not how your father would treat our guests."

Mayto grunted. "I am not my father, and he is not a guest," he retorted, signaling two of his men to assist him.

Elliot, noticing the additional men, raised an eyebrow at Mayto, "I thought you were handling this alone?"

"I am," Mayto replied dismissively, then instructed his men, "Keep her safe and out of the way."

Before Ava could protest, the men grabbed her arms. Bella, reacting swiftly, charged in with her spear, striking one man's shin and forcing him to release Ava. Simultaneously, Ava drove her knee into the groin of the other man, then landed a second knee strike to his head, sending him to the ground in agony.

Ava spun around just in time to see Bella delivering a second strike to the first man's forehead with her spear, incapacitating him as well. A wave of laughter erupted from the remaining members of Mayto's party, witnessing the unexpected prowess of Ava and her young daughter.

Standing tall amidst the chaos, Ava issued a bold challenge to the onlookers. "Anyone else want to try and lay hands on me or my daughter?"

The laughter from Mayto's men quickly subsided under Ava's stern gaze. "No one else then? Good!" she declared firmly. "We're taking Elliot to see the chief. Anyone who has a problem with that will have to contend with all three of us," she stated defiantly, her eyes locked on Mayto. Bella, standing beside her mother, mirrored the sentiment with a fierce stare of her own at Mayto.

A tense silence hung in the air as everyone awaited Mayto's reaction. The injured men slowly began to rise, while Elliot stood there with a look of admiration and amusement on his face. Ava and Bella were quite incredible, he thought.

Mayto's eyes swept over his men, lingering on Ava and Bella, before settling on Elliot. His authority had been challenged, and his pride was at stake. He was about to speak when an unexpected, deep, resonant sound echoed through the forest, silencing everything in its wake.

In an instant, Mayto's priorities shifted. He turned to his men with a sense of urgency. "To the village, now!" he commanded.

Elliot, puzzled by the sudden change in atmosphere, moved closer to Ava and Bella. "What was that sound?" he inquired.

"We must hurry to the village," Ava urged as she guided them towards the horses. "That was the horn."

"What does the horn mean?" Elliot asked, confused.

"It means... the gods are coming!" Bella whispered.

CHAPTER 29

As the reality of the gods' impending arrival sank in, Elliot found himself grappling with a flurry of questions. How many gods were there? Would they choose someone to take from the village this time? This unexpected turn of events gave him a rare chance to seek answers to the questions clouding his mind.

With a sense of urgency, Elliot quickly secured Nashoba's and Onada's horses, guiding them towards Ava and Bella. Handing Ava the reins of Nashoba's horse, he said, "You and Bella take this one. I'll follow on the other." He indicated Onada's horse as he spoke.

"But what about them?" Ava asked with concern, gesturing towards the fallen men.

"They should have thought about that before they picked a fight," Elliot replied, devoid of any compassion for them. "Perhaps some of their friends over there will give them a ride back," Elliot added, mounting Onada's horse.

Ava and Bella exchanged a brief look, shrugged, then climbed onto their horses, with Bella sitting in front of her mother. Ava gently spurred her horse into a trot, leading them through the dense forest, with Elliot following close-ly behind.

Twenty minutes later, they emerged from the forest into a wide clearing. Before them stood a large palisade, span-ning the width of a football field. Its formidable structure was broken only by a single entry point in the middle. With purpose, they directed their horses towards this gateway, joining the stream of villagers converging on the village in response to the ominous call of the horn.

As they passed through the entry point and entered the village proper, Elliot observed its layout: a sprawling settle-ment extending twice as long as it was wide, with a central path leading to a square. Wooden houses with thatched roofs lined the path, transitioning into a bustling market area with butchers, fishmongers, stables, and various stalls. Reaching the village square, they found it teeming with a restless crowd of over a hundred villagers.

Mayto, arriving first, tied his horse to a hitching post in the square. Without hesitation, he strode towards a large wooden building, far grander than any others Elliot had seen in the village. He climbed the steps to the veranda and disappeared through the doors.

As Ava and Elliot followed suit, tying their horses near-by, Elliot's presence seemed to heighten the crowd's un-ease. He queried, "What now?" looking around at the anxious faces.

"We need to see the chief... and quickly!" Ava replied urgently. "The gods will be here soon!"

Before Elliot could put a voice to his burgeoning ques-tions, Ava cut in. "Not now, Elliot. There will be time for questions after the gods leave."

With a playful mime of zipping his lips, Elliot followed closely behind Ava, who was leading Bella by the hand and adeptly navigating through the bustling crowd. They were heading towards the large shack at the heart of the village, the same one Mayto had entered. Elliot deduced it must be the residence of the chief.

Reaching the veranda steps, they were momentarily halted by two guards blocking the entrance. Ava, her impatience clear, addressed them with assertive urgency. "Move aside," she commanded. "We need to see the chief immediately. It's urgent." She then gestured towards Elliot. "He must make a decision about him before the gods arrive."

The guards exchanged hesitant glances, each reluctant to make a call. Ava's patience wore thin. "Now!" she commanded authoritatively.

At that moment, a deep voice echoed from within the shack. "Ava, is that you?"

"Yes, chief," she responded promptly.

"Then come in," the voice replied, warm yet commanding.

Ava shot a stern look at the guards, who sheepishly stepped aside. "They're with me!" she insisted, gesturing to Elliot and Bella.

Upon entering the chief's home, Elliot was struck by the modernity of its interior. The floors and walls were made of polished wood beams, and each room, including the entry hall and a spacious living room, was adorned with elegant rugs. The walls were decorated with an array of weapons and intricate woven tapestries. In the center of the living room, a large rug was surrounded by various colored cushions, creating an inviting seating area.

At the far end of the room, two imposing figures were deep in conversation. As Elliot entered, Mayto turned with a look of disdain. In contrast, the other man, sharing Mayto's size and bearing a familial resemblance, greeted Elliot with a welcoming smile.

"Ava, Bella, it's a relief to see you both," the chief greeted warmly, his concern evident. "The village was worried when you didn't return last night."

Ava approached the chief with a smile. "Hello, Chief," she greeted, kneeling before him in a gesture of respect.

The chief gently cradled Ava's head, touching their foreheads and noses together in a traditional greeting. "I'm just glad you're safe," he said softly.

"I'm sorry for the worry," Ava replied. "We encountered some unexpected drama last night."

"So I see," the chief said, his eyes shifting to Elliot with the hint of a smile. "And who might this be?"

Elliot introduced himself respectfully. "My name's Elliot Adams. It's an honor to meet you, Chief. I apologize for the timing of my arrival."

After Ava rose, Bella took her place before the chief, receiving the same affectionate greeting. She beamed a smile, then rejoined her mother.

The chief, turning his attention back to Elliot, remarked, "Your arrival certainly wasn't uneventful. I understand there was a confrontation with some of Mayto's men?" He glanced at his son, whose expression had visibly hardened.

Elliot nodded. "The reception was less than friendly, but I assure you, I did not intend to offend."

"Elliot saved Bella's life this morning," Ava broke in.

The chief raised his eyebrows in interest. "Is that so?"

Elliot nodded humbly. "Yes, but Bella and Ava saved mine first. I owe them both a great deal."

The chief looked from Bella to Ava, who appeared slightly bashful at the praise, and then back at Elliot, pondering the implications of this unexpected turn of events.

"There's clearly a story behind all this," the chief said, his gaze fixed on Elliot. "And you, you're not from around here, are you?" His tone indicated it was more a statement than a question.

"That's correct, Chief," Elliot confirmed.

The chief nodded knowingly. "I can see that. Another long story, I presume?" he said with the hint of a smile.

At that moment, one of the guards from the doorway stepped into the room. "Apologies, Chief, but they're only a few minutes away now."

"Understood," the chief responded, rising to his feet. He was a large man, comparable in height to Mayto but wider around the middle. Age had softened his once-muscular physique, but he still carried the air of someone not to be trifled with, even in his sixties.

"With our visitors soon to arrive," the chief began, "it would be best if you stayed out of sight for now."

Elliot nodded in agreement. "I'll follow your lead, Chief. I don't want to cause any problems."

"Then you'll stay here," the chief decided, approaching Elliot. "Once they've left, we'll have time for your story."

Elliot extended his hand in a gesture of gratitude. "Thank you, Chief," he said.

The chief paused, looking quizzically at the offered hand. Mayto, interpreting the gesture as a threat, stepped forward protectively.

Elliot quickly clarified his gesture. "It's just a custom from where I come from. Shaking hands is a sign of respect and thanks."

The chief, understanding the gesture, gently signaled Mayto to step back. "My apologies. My son can be a bit overprotective at times," he explained, then turned and shook Elliot's hand.

Mayto, visibly annoyed and muttering under his breath, stormed out of the room, leaving Elliot standing with the chief.

"He can also be a bit short-tempered, especially on the days the gods visit," the chief remarked, watching Mayto's departure. "Now, about that greeting of yours. Shall we try it? I'll show you our traditional greeting when I return."

"Absolutely," Elliot agreed, extending his hand once more. "You simply grasp my hand like this."

The chief's massive hand enveloped Elliot's, dwarfing it in comparison. "Like this?" he inquired.

"Exactly," Elliot confirmed. "Then we give a firm squeeze and shake lightly a couple of times."

Bella observed them with curiosity, attempting to mimic the handshake with her mother, but with less success. Elliot and the chief chuckled at their playful attempt, finishing their own handshake.

The chief then turned to Ava and Bella. "Now, would you ladies assist an old man to the door?"

"You're not old, Chief," Bella responded, grasping his large hand. Ava took his other hand, and together they escorted him towards the door.

Pausing at the threshold, the chief's expression turned solemn as he addressed Elliot. "I need you to promise to stay hidden, no matter what. Your presence, especially in those clothes, could bring unforeseen consequences upon my people. Their safety is my utmost priority. Do you understand?"

Elliot nodded, his expression serious. "I understand, Chief. You have my word—I'll stay out of sight until you return."

The chief nodded appreciatively. "Thank you, Elliot." With that, he stepped through the doorway, accompanied by Ava and Bella, leaving Elliot alone in the house.

Chapter 30

Elliot found himself alone in the spacious main room of the chief's house, with two windows providing views of the outside world. The first window provided a view of the bustling main square, and the second overlooked the northern main road, an area Elliot had not yet explored. Thin wooden slats served as blinds, partially obscuring the view while allowing glimpses of the outside.

Approaching the window facing the main square, Elliot watched as the chief, accompanied by Ava and Bella, crossed the road towards the expansive grassy area traditionally used for festivals and gatherings. The village square had transformed into a hub of activity since the sound of the horn. Villagers, drawn by the summons, were congregating towards the back, facing the chief's home in anticipation of the impending event.

Nearing the assembly area, Ava and Bella gently released the chief's hands and mingled with the other villagers. The chief, standing before the assembled crowd of over a hundred Lunari, paused, allowing a hush to fall over the square. He then spoke, his voice deep and resonant, effortlessly reaching the ears of his attentive audience.

"My fellow Lunari," he started, his tone steady and commanding. "It has been thirty-seven days since we last heard the horn. Thirty-seven days since Jacob was taken from our midst, and thirty-five since his return." He gestured towards Jacob, who stood amongst the crowd, his arms wrapped around his wife, a silent testament to the community's shared experiences.

The chief's voice resonated with a somber weight as he continued his address to the villagers. "Many of you have witnessed numerous takings, and you have seen them returned. I could easily stand here and urge calmness, to not resist, to accept being chosen, or to refrain from intervening. Yet, I can only imagine the agony of watching a loved one being taken away," he said, his gaze sweeping over the crowd, acknowledging their shared anguish.

"The unknown is daunting, and the urge to act is powerful. However, I implore you, for the sake of your safety, for the well-being of those taken, and for the protection of all our people, to stand back and do nothing.

"History has shown us that those taken are returned. Let this give you strength and courage in these trying moments," he urged, his voice managing to be both empathetic and authoritative.

A bell tolled from the village's outskirts, sending a ripple of murmurs through the crowd. The chief exchanged a solemn glance with Mayto; the pivotal moment had arrived.

"They are here," the chief announced, his tone firm yet reassuring. "Please, heed my words and let this pass peacefully."

From his vantage point at the window, Elliot watched as a wave of fear and anticipation swept over the crowd. Their attention shifted from the chief to the northern road, their murmurs fading into a hushed silence.

Feeling his heart rate quicken, Elliot moved to the window overlooking the northern approach. Carefully adjusting the blinds to ensure he remained unseen, he prepared to witness the arrival of the beings referred to as "gods."

The first hint of their approach was the steady thud of hooves against the ground. *They're using horses*, Elliot noted with curiosity, a detail that piqued his interest. He couldn't discern their number yet, but the multitude of hoof-beats suggested a significant contingent.

As the first horse entered his line of sight, Elliot observed that it bore no extraordinary armor or insignia, just a lone rider. The rider's form was unmistakably human, which aligned with Ava's earlier description of these beings. Two arms, two legs, a torso, and a head—all the hallmarks of a human figure.

However, any further details were obscured by the rider's attire—a full-body suit with an integrated helmet, remarkably similar to his own. The helmet's design featured a visor-like slot across the face, sheathed in black glass-like material, allowing visibility from the inside but concealing any facial features from onlookers.

The rider's suit was an understated off-white color, strikingly contrasted by golden stripes that adorned the length of the arms and legs. In one hand, the rider wielded a staff-like object. Its black form, lacking any sharp edges, seemed more symbolic than functional, suggesting a role in ceremony rather than combat. Elliot observed these details intently, piecing together the puzzle before him. They appeared human in form and carried weapons, yet their identities remained shrouded by their enigmatic suits.

As the procession of riders continued to file into view, Elliot noted a distinct uniformity in their attire, save for one striking difference: the color of the stripes adorning their suits. The lead rider, distinguished by a gold stripe, was followed by a majority wearing suits with blue stripes. Interspersed among these were a few with black stripes. Elliot surmised that the colors signified rank, with the gold-striped leader presumably commanding the group, followed by those with black stripes.

Elliot counted the riders as they made their ominous approach, encircling the village square. His count reached twenty-six, including the gold-striped leader. The initial ten, taking cues from the gold-striped leader, dismounted their horses and secured them to a hitching post. The rest of the riders positioned themselves strategically around the perimeter of the square, remaining mounted, a clear display of vigilance. Elliot interpreted this formation as a tactic, likely intended to assert dominance and instill a sense of intimidation among the Lunari villagers.

During their dismount, Elliot observed that these "gods" shared a physical resemblance to the Lunari he had encountered so far. The Lunari generally possessed a slender build, taller than average humans, a trait Elliot attributed to the effects of Lunar's reduced gravity on human development. The chief and Mayto, with their more muscular and towering statures, were exceptions in this community. While the gods' suits could potentially obscure their true physiques, Elliot concluded that they were not significantly different in size or stature from the average Lunari.

Switching his attention back to the main window, Elliot watched Gold Stripe, along with nine others, take their positions in the square. Gold Stripe assumed a place beside the chief, both of them facing the gathering of villagers. The others formed a line behind their leader, each holding a black staff in a display of silent authority.

Focused on the unfolding scene, Elliot's gaze was fixed intently on Gold Stripe as he prepared to address the crowd. The possibility that these so-called "gods" could communicate in a language understood by the Lunari piqued his interest. It supported his growing suspicion that these beings might be mere mortals masquerading as deities. History was replete with examples of men assuming divine status for power—Egyptian pharaohs and Roman and Chinese emperors had all done it. Were it not for the extraordinary setting of Lunar, a world nestled within the Moon, Elliot would have confidently wagered that these "gods" were simply men hungry for control and power.

Chapter 31

Gold Stripe theatrically extended his arms above him, as if drawing the crowd's awe directly from the air. His voice, a male-synthesized tone, resonated across the square. "Children of Lunar," he began, his words echoing with an eerie, artificial quality.

"Today, your gods bring forth a divine revelation from the heavens. For nearly a century, you have lived safely under our guardianship on the Moon, longing for the day of return to Earth." He pronounced "Earth" with a discernible hint of disdain. "That day... is now closer than ever."

A collective gasp rippled through the villagers, mirroring their astonishment and confusion.

"Silence!" Gold Stripe's command thundered, silencing the crowd instantly. "Remember your place," he admonished sternly. "In a mere year, you will be leaving Lunar for Earth, where we will establish a new utopia, ruled by your gods!" Gold Stripe's proclamation was grandiose, filled with an unsettling promise.

Despite their underlying fear, the villagers exchanged looks of shock and muted excitement. Gold Stripe's words carried the weight of a profound, yet foreboding, promise.

"As we prepare for this momentous transition, the frequency of takings will increase... starting today!" The initial excitement in the crowd quickly morphed back into fear.

The black-striped men advanced in unison, planting their staffs into the ground with a coordinated thud. The familiar ritual, despite its regular occurrence, never failed to evoke a deep-seated dread among the villagers.

Gold Stripe's command was clear and decisive. "Prepare for scanning immediately," he ordered, his tone brooking no argument. Turning towards the chief, he continued. "As is customary, we will commence with your chief. The rest of you, form an orderly line." With these curt instructions given, Gold Stripe returned to his men.

From his hidden vantage point, Elliot wrestled with the unfolding scenario. The declaration of returning the villagers to Earth within a year was baffling, especially considering the recent asteroid impact on Earth. For a century, these "gods" had barred the Lunari from Earth, claiming it was unsafe. Now, in the wake of a real catastrophe, they were preparing for a return. Was this merely a coincidence, or something more calculated?

Elliot watched intently as the scanning process began. The chief stepped forward, presenting his arm to one of the blue-striped figures. Intriguingly, the man used a device integrated into the forearm of his suit, not unlike Elliot's CDU, to scan the chief. After a brief moment, he consulted a readout on his forearm, then nodded to the chief, indicating he was cleared to move on.

The villagers, following the chief's lead, lined up in front of the blue-striped men. One by one, they extended their arms, each undergoing a similar scanning process. Relief washed over their faces as they were allowed to pass, though their eyes often darted back anxiously, hoping their loved ones would also receive the same clearance.

As Ava and Bella successfully passed their scans, Elliot exhaled a breath of relief he hadn't realized he'd been holding. Despite his promise to the chief, he had been fraught with tension, uncertain of his reaction if either of them had been detained.

The process was halfway complete when the calm was shattered. A blue-striped figure halted one of the villagers, signaling Gold Stripe with a raised hand. The rhythm of scanning ceased, and a hush fell over the crowd, punctuated only by the faint, desperate pleas of a teenage girl, aged between thirteen and sixteen. She was the focal point of the unexpected interruption.

Gold Stripe approached, conducting his own scan on the girl's arm. After a brief consultation with his forearm device, he declared: "This is the one. Take her aside and continue with the others!"

The girl's cry of "NO!" was heart-wrenching as she struggled futilely against the firm grip of the blue-striped figure. "Come quietly," he commanded, his voice synthetically cold. "Do not defy your gods."

In that tense moment, a man pushed through the crowd, desperately making his way towards the girl. "There must be a mistake," he refuted, his voice laced with panic. "Take me instead! Please, just let her be!"

The moment the man, who seemed to be the girl's father, reached the front of the line, Gold Stripe intervened with brutal efficiency. Brandishing his staff, he thrust it into the man's abdomen. The resulting *THWUMP* echoed across the square, propelling the man through the air. He landed hard among the villagers in the adjacent line, scattering them like tumbled dominoes.

The fallen villagers hastened to their feet, distancing themselves in fear of attracting Gold Stripe's wrath. The man lay writhing on the ground, struggling to rise. Gold Stripe advanced and effortlessly hoisted him up with one hand, then flung him further across the square.

"Daddy!" The girl's plaintive cry was heartrending. "Please, stop! I'll go, just don't hurt him anymore!"

Gold Stripe loomed over the incapacitated father once more, lifting him with ominous intent. The chief's voice broke through, pleading, "Enough, please. She will go quietly, and there will be no further resistance."

Gold Stripe's icy gaze fixed on the chief. "Ensure that there is not!" he commanded. "Or you will bear the consequences!"

The chief nodded, a silent vow of compliance. Satisfied with the impact of his actions, Gold Stripe callously dropped the father to the ground and then strode towards the tearful girl. "Continue the scanning," he ordered the others, his voice void of empathy.

The chief addressed the assembled villagers with solemn authority. "Everyone, please do as the gods command," he urged. His tone softened as he turned to the young girl. "Evelyn, be strong, my dear. You will return to us. We will look after your father for you," he said. "Please, for your father, be strong," he encouraged gently.

Tears streamed down Evelyn's cheeks as she nodded, resigning herself to her fate. Gold Stripe led her away, her reluctant steps heavy with dread.

The scanning resumed, proceeding without further disruptions. Elliot speculated that the thoroughness of the process, despite having already identified their chosen person, might be a method to account for every villager.

After the completion of the final scans, Gold Stripe led Evelyn to one of the waiting horses. With a cold efficiency, he handed her over to another figure clad in a similar suit, this one distinguished by a blue stripe. The chosen escort helped Evelyn onto the horse before mounting it himself, ready to lead her away.

One by one, the gods vacated the square on horseback, proceeding slowly down the northern road from which they had arrived. The villagers, left in their wake, experienced a mixed sense of relief and guilt. There was relief that the ordeal was over, and they had been spared. Yet, this relief was shadowed by a profound sense of guilt over the young girl's fate—a distressing reminder of the price they paid for their own safety.

Chapter 32

Elliot watched from the chief's window, his gaze following the slow revival of the village. People, dazed and grief-stricken, gathered around the father who had been brutally cast aside by Gold Stripe. The stark pain of losing his daughter was etched on his face, eclipsing the physical agony of the assault he'd endured. Elliot shuddered; the sheer power Gold Stripe wielded was unnerving. He'd tossed the man as if he were weightless, a feat that made Elliot wonder whether it was due to an enhancement from the suit or the Moon's lesser gravity. Their strength, not unlike his own, was formidable.

The gods' weapons, impressive shock sticks, had caught Elliot's attention next. A single blast had hurled Evelyn's father across the square as if he had just been hit by a bus. He had survived, but Elliot was left pondering the potential long-term effects of such a force.

Their suits, though not overly complex, shared a curious similarity with his own—a fact that intrigued Elliot. The helmets, with their opaque visors, were the most striking difference. The embedded scanning devices and computers on their arms mirrored the technology in his suit, raising questions about their functions and origins. This first encounter with the gods left Elliot with a whirlwind of thoughts and far more questions than answers, his mind racing to make sense of this bewildering display of power and technology.

Though the "taking" had finished, an uneasy stillness hung over the square. Elliot observed the crowd, noting their reluctance to disperse. He later realized they were waiting for the chief's address, which came moments later.

"My fellow Lunari," the chief began, his voice carrying a solemn weight. "It is always a heartrending sight to witness one of our own taken, especially one so young. Let our thoughts and prayers be with Evelyn and her family. In these trying times, we must unite and extend our support to them until her safe return."

The villagers listened in somber silence, their expressions mirroring the grief and uncertainty that the chief's words evoked.

"This would usually be the time I would ask you all to resume as normal, but today is undeniably different," he continued, pausing as nods of agreement rippled through the crowd.

"I'm sure you all have many questions after today's revelations from the gods. I am no exception," the chief stated. "For nearly a hundred years, we've clung to the promise of returning to Earth, a promise that, until today, never had a timeline." He paused, allowing the murmurs and whispers of the crowd to ebb away.

"Within a year, they have promised, our journey back to Earth will begin. Never did I imagine this day would come in my lifetime, and I believe many of you shared that sentiment," he remarked as his gaze swept over the villagers whose faces reflected hope and disbelief.

"Just like you, I have many questions, but right now we do not have the answers. We need time to reflect on this. Not just me, but all of you too. Tomorrow night, we will reconvene here and share our thoughts on this news and plan for our future.

"For now, I encourage you to return to your families and resume your daily routines. We have much to reflect upon, but rest assured, we will reconvene to discuss this further. Until then, keep Evelyn and her family in your hearts and minds." With these final words, the chief, assisted by Mayto, slowly turned and retreated from the gathering crowd.

As the chief paused at the entrance of the square, his eyes sought out Ava. She soon approached, with Bella's smaller hand firmly clasped in hers, a silent testament to the day's unsettling events. Together, the four of them—the chief, Ava, Bella, and Mayto—began their solemn procession back across the road. Their steps were measured, mirroring the heavy atmosphere that lingered in the aftermath of the chief's announcement and the earlier ordeal.

Still clinging to her mother, Bella cast occasional glances around, her young mind trying to make sense of the day's occurrences. With a protective arm around her daughter, Ava wore an expression of quiet resilience. The chief, leading them, exuded a sense of weary determination, embodying the responsibility he carried for his people.

Hidden yet watchful from his concealed spot, Elliot was engulfed in a storm of conflicting emotions. The Lunari's belief in an Earth devastated a century ago, which he knew had only suffered an asteroid impact the previous day, formed a complex puzzle in his mind. This contradiction was perplexing, but the gods' recent announcement of their intent to bring the Lunari back to Earth within a year added an entirely new and baffling layer to the mystery.

The timing of this promise seemed oddly coincidental and suspicious to Elliot, considering the recent asteroid strike on Earth. Was it a calculated move by the gods, or merely a strange twist of fate? The deceit at play, spanning over a century, was staggering, and Elliot wrestled with the enormity of its implications.

His eyes scanned the crowd, absorbing the varied expressions of hope and bewilderment. They clung to a dream based on a falsehood, an intricate tapestry of lies woven by their so-called saviors. This revelation stirred a profound sense of responsibility in Elliot. How could he unravel this web of deception without shattering the hopes of an entire civilization? The complexity of this quandary weighed on him as he contemplated his role in this alien yet familiar world, where the line between myth and reality delicately blurred.

Elliot's thoughts were abruptly interrupted by the familiar sound of a horn, which this time was followed immediately by a second blast. He looked around, half expecting the return of the gods, but instead, he saw a wave of sadness wash over the villagers. Their expressions, previously etched with fear, now bore the weight of sorrow. Elliot deduced that while a single blast heralded a taking, two blasts might signify that someone had indeed been taken. He pondered if a third blast would announce Evelyn's return. As he observed the villagers' solemn acceptance of this ritual, he felt a growing resolve to uncover the truth.

CHAPTER 33

As Ava and Bella stepped into the main room of the chief's home, Elliot moved towards them, his relief evident. Embracing them both, he realized the depth of his concern during the taking. The comfort of holding them safe in his arms was almost overwhelming, a stark contrast to the helplessness he had felt watching from afar.

"I'm sorry," he said, aware that his display of emotion might be unfamiliar to them. "Seeing you two being scanned was more distressing than facing that bear. I felt so powerless hiding here."

Ava responded with a tighter embrace, feeling a sense of gratitude yet vulnerability. It had been a long while since she had allowed herself to be comforted, and the sensation was both reassuring and unsettling.

As Elliot gently released them, he turned to the chief, acutely aware of Mayto's scowling presence. "Is it always this intense?" he asked.

"Only when there's resistance, which is unfortunately common," the chief responded. "It's one thing to ask someone to comply; it's entirely another to expect them to watch their child being taken without protest."

"So why do you not fight back?" Elliot asked. "I counted twenty-six of them, and there must be at least a hundred villagers here."

Mayto grunted. "Do you think we are too scared to fight back?" he retorted. "We are not! Their strength and weapons are superior, but to fight is to accept death."

The chief, with a calming presence, placed a hand on Mayto's shoulder. "Son," he said gently, "I'm sure Elliot did not mean any disrespect."

"How could he not!" he snapped, his frustration evident. "Has he been living under a rock his whole life? Everyone knows the consequences of starting a war with them."

The chief turned to Elliot. "Though my son's anger is misplaced, his words bear truth," he explained. "If we rebel against the gods, they have the power to cut off our life support. We would suffocate and die in the darkness."

"Father, there's no way he doesn't know this," Mayto said contemptuously. "Every man, woman, and child understands the reality we live in."

Elliot met Mayto's gaze. "I can assure you, this is all new to me, Mayto. The reason I'm not on their list is because I'm not from here," Elliot said. "I'm from Earth."

The chief's expression shifted to one of shock and disbelief. "But how can that be?" he asked.

Mayto grunted. "More lies!" he said with contempt.

"He's telling the truth, Chief," Ava confirmed. "I was as disbelieving as Mayto when I first met Elliot. But the things I have seen him do, and what he has shown me, convince me he tells the truth. Why would he lie? Remember, there was no one missing when the gods completed their scans. He isn't on their list because they don't know he exists."

"What things have you seen?" Mayto spat out.

"His strength and speed are unlike anything the Lunari are capable of," she stated firmly, holding her ground.

Mayto's eyes narrowed. "The gods are also strong. Perhaps he is one of them!"

"No, I don't think so," Ava countered. "I've never seen the gods run as he does. He was faster than the buffalo, even with Bella on his back."

"How do we know how fast the gods are? We've never seen them run; they always ride horses. This proves nothing."

"But we saw him emerge from Savage-Heart's den, not from the Forbidden Mountain where the gods come from," she insisted.

"That doesn't prove anything!"

Ava continued, undeterred. "He came from the Great Falls disoriented, like someone completely unfamiliar with our world. He didn't even know Bella and I were watching him."

The chief, intrigued, leaned forward. "What do you mean, Ava? How did he act?"

"He ran into Savage-Heart's den after encountering her on the mountain steps, where he fought her and survived. Then he jumped from the Great Falls," Ava recounted, her voice firm. "What Lunari or god would ever dare to do that?"

Mayto scoffed. "No one would survive that fall. That's ridiculous!"

"It was a close call—I nearly didn't make it," Elliot remarked.

"He was then attacked by three wolves on the beach, and he killed two of them with his bare hands," Bella added, eager to support Elliot's case.

"Stop talking nonsense, child," Mayto dismissed, his tone harsh.

Ava's voice hardened. "She's not talking nonsense, Mayto. I was there. I saw it, too!" she asserted, frustration coloring her words.

The chief, sensing the escalating tension, quickly intervened. "Okay, there's no need for us to fight amongst ourselves," he said, his voice calm.

Ava nodded. "I'm sorry, Chief," she apologized. "My point is, these aren't the actions of someone familiar with Lunar. Neither a Lunari nor a god would act this way."

Mayto grunted, his doubt still apparent but momentarily silenced.

The chief then turned to Elliot, his expression one of genuine interest. "I think it would be best if you tell me your story from the beginning, Elliot," he suggested, settling himself on a cushion.

Turning to Bella, he added, "Bella, would you be so kind as to bring us all something to drink and eat? I'm sure we could all use some refreshments after hearing of such adventures."

"Of course, Chief," Bella replied, her smile brightening the room as she left to fulfill the chief's request.

"Everyone, please sit and relax. We will allow Elliot to tell us his story, and then I will make my decision afterward," the chief announced, his tone commanding yet open.

"Thank you, Chief," Elliot replied, with a hint of humility in his voice.

"Okay, Elliot, please begin when you're ready," the chief said, settling himself comfortably.

Over the next two hours, the room was enveloped in an attentive silence as Elliot narrated his extraordinary tale. Although Ava and Bella had heard his story before, they listened with rapt attention, particularly as he recounted his journey from the Moon's surface to the waterfall. Their faces reflected a mix of wonder and familiarity, especially during the parts they had witnessed themselves.

Elliot started with his landing on the Moon, weaving his narrative through the series of unexpected events that led to his arrival at the Lunari village. As he spoke, his voice was steady, filled with the awe and bewilderment of his experiences. Ava and Bella joined in occasionally, adding details from their perspective, especially during the moments when Elliot was unconscious. Their contributions painted a fuller picture, bridging the gaps in Elliot's memory.

Throughout the storytelling, the chief remained a silent, contemplative figure, absorbing every word. Mayto, despite his earlier skepticism, refrained from interrupting, a sign of respect for his father, though he occasionally let out a disbelieving grunt.

As Ava or Bella took over parts of the narrative, Elliot took the opportunity to sample the food and drink that Bella had prepared. He found himself amazed by the richness of the flavors, a stark contrast to the comparatively bland astronaut food he had become accustomed to recently.

When Elliot finished recounting his story, he fielded questions from the chief and shared the photos on his phone and the CDU he had brought, just as he had with Ava and Bella.

The chief, after a long contemplative pause, his eyes closed as if to weigh every word he had heard, finally spoke. "Your story, Elliot, initially seemed like a tall tale," he began. "Had it not been for Ava and Bella corroborating parts of it, I would struggle to believe a word, despite the sincerity in your voice."

He raised his hand gently, signaling Ava to hold her thoughts, and she reluctantly settled back. "As chief, I must be cautious," he continued. "I accept the parts witnessed by Ava and Bella. However, your claim of coming from Earth just days ago needs more than just words for me to believe it, especially when it so starkly contradicts what the gods have told us."

Elliot nodded in understanding. "I can appreciate that, Chief," he said.

The chief's posture shifted, leaning forward with a deeply pensive expression etching his face. "If what you say is true, that Earth was hit by an asteroid only yesterday, then it presents a troubling reality. Neither of our people would have a home on Earth right now. More disturbingly, it would imply that the gods have been lying to us for a long time."

"It would appear that way," Elliot agreed, his voice low. He hadn't fully allowed himself to process the magnitude of what had happened to Earth yet. The implications were too vast, too overwhelming to fully accept at the moment.

"What my son, Mayto, is saying could also be true. If you possess the same strengths as our gods, how can we be sure you're not one of them, here to spy on us?" the chief inquired, his eyes narrowing slightly as he studied Elliot.

"Exactly!" Mayto affirmed, his delight evident.

The chief, however, tempered his son's accusation with a more diplomatic tone. "But, if he is indeed one of the gods, my son, it would not be wise to mistreat him either," he cautioned.

Mayto responded with a noncommittal grunt.

"I can only offer you my word that I am not one of these gods and that everything I've told you is true," Elliot said earnestly. "But I understand your duty to protect your people, and that my mere word may not suffice, especially since I have yet to earn your trust."

"And therein lies our predicament," the chief concurred.

Elliot, sensing an opportunity, ventured a suggestion. "May I make a proposal?"

"Of course, please do," the chief encouraged.

"I wish to return to the surface to search for my friend, Franklin. If you could assist me in this endeavor, I could bring back proof of my claims," Elliot proposed. "And if I were one of the gods, then I would have no reason to expose them as liars by bringing back proof."

"What kind of proof could you bring?" the chief asked.

"I'm not entirely sure yet," Elliot admitted. "Perhaps something from my spacecraft, if it's still intact. Or maybe a video from the surface?"

The chief, though contemplative, remained doubtful. "I must admit, I'm wary of trusting your photos and videos,

Elliot. As you can see from our sky, things that do not exist can be made to look very real."

Elliot paused, taking in the chief's words. He understood the challenge at hand: finding a way to prove his truth in a world built on illusions was not going to be easy.

"I'll go with him," Ava declared, her voice firm. The room fell into a hushed silence as everyone turned to look at her. "If he's telling the truth, then I can be the one to confirm it."

"Definitely not," Mayto said immediately, his tone laced with authority. "I forbid it!"

"I do not require your permission, Mayto," she retorted, her eyes flashing with defiance.

"But you do require mine, Ava," the chief remarked, his voice calm yet carrying an undeniable weight.

Ava inhaled deeply, her resolve unwavering. "Chief, there is no other way for us to verify his claims," she began, her voice softening. She reached out, gently taking the chief's hands in hers. "I ask for your blessing out of respect, but know that if you forbid me, I will still go."

"Ava..." the chief murmured, his gaze softening. He enveloped her hands in his, a gesture of paternal affection. "The fire in you has always been strong and has only grown since you lost your husband." A shadow of sadness crossed Ava's face, her eyes briefly flickering away.

He offered her a warm, affectionate smile. "Ava, you have been like a daughter to me, long before you lost your parents."

Ava's voice trembled slightly. "Then please, give me your blessing, Chief."

The chief was silent for a moment, his eyes moving from Ava to Elliot. "Do I have your word, Elliot, that you will protect Ava, even at the cost of your own life?" he asked, his tone serious.

Elliot met his gaze squarely. "You have my word, Chief," he affirmed, then turned to look deeply into Ava's eyes. "I will protect Ava with my life."

The chief nodded solemnly. "In that case, you have my blessing, Ava. But Elliot, if your word proves false, god or not, I will hold you accountable myself," he added, his voice carrying a stern warning.

Elliot nodded. "Understood," he replied, accepting the responsibility of the chief's words.

"This is foolish!" Mayto exclaimed, frustration etched on his face as he abruptly stood up and stormed out of the room.

The chief watched as his son left the room, saying nothing. Turning back to Elliot, he said, "My son carries a lot of anger and frustration. When I was younger, I too suffered as he does."

"You seem so composed now," Elliot said. "What changed for you?"

"Don't be fooled, Elliot," he responded. "Beneath the surface, I too boil with the same frustrations as he does. You see, to be so strong, and yet feel so helpless, is a difficult burden to carry. I pray my son will learn to deal with this, as I once did, for I am not a young man any longer and he will need to take my place one day."

"You're not going anywhere for a long time, Chief," Bella said.

The chief smiled at her affectionately. "Not if I can help it, Bella."

His attention then returned to Elliot. "Now, tell me, how do you plan to return to the surface?"

Elliot pondered for a moment before answering. "The only way I know is through the waterfall, the same path I took to get here. But I'll need some climbing gear, and a way to get past the bear."

The chief's face lit up with the hint of a smile. "I believe I can assist with both. Tell me, Elliot, how do you feel about going on a bear hunt tomorrow?"

Chapter 34

THE REMAINDER OF ELLIOT'S day unfolded amidst the unique backdrop of the Lunari village, a place that seemed to defy time itself. Encircled by an imposing palisade, its perimeter was a testament to both the community's craftsmanship and their need for protection.

A central path, reminiscent of a main street, led through the heart of the village, culminating in a bustling square. Wooden houses with thatched roofs flanked the path throughout the village, their simple yet sturdy structures exuding a sense of warmth and homeliness. Progressing towards the center of the village, the residential calm gradually gave way to the lively hum of the market area.

Here, the air was rich with the aromas of fresh produce and the sounds of daily commerce. Butchers and fishmongers proudly showcased their goods, while stable hands carefully tended to their animals. Various stalls dotted the area, each offering an array of goods that spoke of the Lunari people's skills and resources.

Elliot's presence in the Lunari village, an entirely unfamiliar face, sparked a profound curiosity among the villagers. His strange attire and foreign demeanor marked him as an anomaly in this close-knit community, where every face was known, and every story shared. Yet, despite the palpable intrigue his appearance generated, the Lunari people welcomed him with a warmth and openness that surprised him.

The air in the village still held a subtle undercurrent of sadness, a lingering echo of the recent painful events. However, the Lunari's resilient spirit shone brightly, their inherent friendliness remaining undimmed. The only exception to this warm reception was Mayto, whose distant, wary gaze followed Elliot with a mix of suspicion and guarded curiosity.

After their discussion, the chief had outlined a straightforward plan to safely bypass Savage-Heart. Recently, the Lunari had begun closely monitoring her movements due to her increased aggression after losing her cub. She had been observed leaving her den just after sunrise and returning shortly before sunset, but her daytime activities remained a mystery.

The plan for the next morning involved Elliot, Ava, and Bella shadowing Savage-Heart from a secure distance, gathering crucial information on her movements. They would then report their findings to the chief, who planned to assign some of his men to monitor the bear the following day. While the chief's men maintained surveillance, Elliot and Ava planned to stealthily enter Savage-Heart's den and proceed toward the lunar surface. Elliot estimated that their expedition might take a full day. To ensure their safe return, they planned to use Elliot's watch to gauge the best time to head back. The chief's men were instructed to deter Savage-Heart from returning to her den until sunset or until Elliot and Ava safely returned, whichever occurred first.

Initially, the chief had offered to have his men track Savage-Heart's location the next day, but Elliot was keen on exploring more of Lunar himself. Bella, too, was thrilled at the prospect of joining in another day's adventure with Elliot.

Elliot, accompanied by Ava and Bella, ventured into the village market to gather supplies for their impending climb to the Lunar surface. His mind was a whirl of plans and precautions, each detail meticulously considered. Procuring rope and grappling hooks was straightforward, but Elliot was keen on bolstering their safety measures for the ascent.

He took the time to explain the concept of natural anchors, pointing out rock features and formations where climbers could secure their ropes. He also instructed them to look for shorter lengths of rope or webbing, ideal for creating these anchors. Elliot's description of climbing axes, which could be attached securely to their wrists, sparked particular interest. The chief, understanding the importance of these tools, promised that all necessary items would be ready for their journey in two days.

However, amidst these preparations, Elliot harbored a significant concern he had not yet disclosed to anyone. Ava's enthusiastic insistence on accompanying him to the Lunar surface had overshadowed a crucial detail—he had only one space suit. This limitation meant Ava couldn't exit the airlock, making it impossible for her to verify his claims about Earth. Elliot had withheld this information, not wanting to jeopardize the chief's support, yet he could not bear the thought of deceiving Ava. Resolving to address this dilemma, he planned to share this critical issue with her in private later that evening.

As the sun began its descent, casting a warm golden hue over the veranda, Elliot, Ava, and the chief found themselves immersed in a profound conversation. The day had been eventful, with Elliot getting acquainted with the entire Lunari village and its inhabitants. They had successfully gathered all the necessary supplies for their journey, except for the climbing axes, which were to be provided the following evening.

Sitting together, they watched the sun dip below the horizon, the simulated sky of Lunar painting a breathtaking scene. "I know you say it's just an image, but it is a truly remarkable one," Elliot commented, his eyes lingering on the vibrant colors.

The chief, deep in thought, responded softly. "It has always been my fondest wish to see a real sunrise and sunset. If the gods are right, then perhaps I soon will. But if you are right, Elliot, then I fear that dream may never come true. Which option I prefer, I cannot answer." His smile was tinged with a bittersweet sentiment.

Elliot shifted, a thoughtful expression crossing his face. "The question that haunts me the most is, why?" he said.

Ava, intrigued, leaned in. "What do you mean?"

"Why have you all been here for a hundred years under the pretense of a lie?" Elliot asked. "And why were you told today, just one day after Earth was struck by an asteroid, that you would soon be returned home?" He straightened his posture, his muscles feeling rejuvenated after a day of rest.

"I know what we'll find on the Lunar surface," he continued. "But what that means for you, Chief, for your people, and even for myself, that's what truly concerns me. Living under the rule of those who harm, intimidate, and control lives through the mere threat of extinguishing others... that is a terror unlike any other I have known."

"You carry the weight of the world with you, Elliot," the chief observed, his voice gentle. He placed a large, reassuring hand on Elliot's shoulder. "Sometimes, we must allow ourselves a moment to forget our burdens and appreciate the blessings we have." His gaze then shifted downward towards Bella, who had peacefully fallen asleep with her head resting in Elliot's lap.

Elliot's eyes softened as he looked down at Bella, feeling a warmth in his heart at the sight. In the mere span of twenty-four hours, this remarkable young girl had intertwined herself into his life, becoming a presence he couldn't fathom being without. He accepted a blanket from the chief and tenderly draped it over her, his fingers brushing gently through her hair.

As he looked up, his gaze met Ava's, and in that moment, the world around them seemed to pause. A silent, magnetic pull drew them closer in spirit, though physically they remained still. The backdrop of the village, the fading light, everything else blurred into insignificance. All that remained was the profound connection in Ava's eyes, reflecting back at him. In that instant, Elliot felt a profound sense of belonging, a certainty that there was no place he'd rather be than here with her.

"Perhaps it's time you took Bella home to bed," the chief suggested.

Caught off guard by the interruption, Ava, still locked in Elliot's gaze, responded with a surprised, "Huh?"

"I was saying, maybe it's best if Bella gets some rest. You three have an early start tomorrow," the chief clarified gently.

"Erm, yeah, that's a good idea," Ava agreed, her gaze shifting from Elliot to the chief, and then resting on Bella.

"I assume Elliot will be staying at your place tonight?" the chief asked.

Ava, a little flustered, replied too quickly. "Why do you assume that?"

With a knowing smile hidden in the dim light, the chief responded. "Because the three of you will be leaving together very early."

"Oh, yes, right. That was the plan!" Ava said, recovering her composure.

"I wouldn't want to impose on you and Bella," Elliot said.

Once again, Ava's eyes locked with his. "No, you wouldn't be imposing at all. Besides, I could use your help to carry Bella over, if that's okay?"

"It would be my pleasure," Elliot replied warmly, smoothly lifting Bella into his arms and standing. "It's been a pleasure talking with you again, Chief. Thank you again for your hospitality."

"You're welcome, Elliot. Let's do this again tomorrow evening when you return," the chief said, rising to his feet. Ava approached him, and they shared a traditional farewell, their foreheads and noses touching in a sign of affection and respect. "Good night, Ava."

"Good night, Chief," she replied softly.

As Ava and Elliot made their way back to her home, a cocoon of silence enveloped them, charged with an unspoken energy neither knew how to address. Ava entered her home first, the soft glow of the fire lamp casting a warm light in the room. She quietly shut the door behind Elliot, who carefully carried the still-sleeping Bella in his arms. Guiding him to a small room at the back, she watched as he gently placed Bella in her bed, his movements tender and attentive.

Elliot returned to the main room to find Ava setting up a bed for him. The small gestures of hospitality—offering a drink, complimenting her home—filled the space between them, yet an unspoken tension lingered in the air.

They both took their seats on the cushions around the unlit fire pit. The silence stretched, becoming almost charged, until Ava, unable to bear it any longer, blurted out, "You see, I told you it was going to be another exciting day!"

"It seems every day I'm around you is," he responded without thinking, his words slipping out. He hadn't intended to reveal so much so soon.

Ava's cheeks flushed with a mix of surprise and perhaps something deeper, a realization that maybe there was more to her feelings than she had admitted to herself. She wrestled with a whirlwind of thoughts. Was it possible to feel so drawn to someone she'd just met? The connection they shared was undeniable, the moment they'd had earlier unmistakable in its intensity. He had a way with Bella, a natural kindness, and the way he looked at her—Ava felt seen, truly seen.

But it was all happening too fast, amidst a storm of events that demanded their attention. She needed to slow down, to process these unexpected emotions. Yet here they were, alone in her home, the night stretching out before them, filled with unspoken possibilities.

"Hey," Elliot said softly, breaking the silence. "I think I lost you there for a moment."

"I'm sorry," Ava replied, snapping back to the present. "It's just been such a long day."

"And the next couple aren't looking much shorter either, are they?" he said with a gentle smile, trying to lighten the mood.

"No, they're not," Ava agreed. "We should probably head to bed soon... to sleep! I mean... we should probably head to bed soon to get some sleep!" she corrected hastily, a flush starting to show on her cheeks. "Sorry, I think I'm just really tired."

Elliot moved closer, taking Ava's hand in his. "I think we're both exhausted," he said, his eyes meeting hers. "And to be completely honest, there's nothing I'd rather do right now than... 'go to sleep,'" he said, echoing her words, a twinkle in his eye.

A small smile tugged at the corners of Ava's lips. Elliot gently brushed a strand of hair behind her ear, and she closed her eyes at his touch. In a whisper barely above a breath, she said, "I don't think I would stop you if you wanted to... 'go to sleep.'" Her eyes locked on his.

This time, it was Elliot who smiled, the moment feeling surreal yet perfectly right. "I'm getting to the point where I won't be able to... 'stay awake'... in a minute," he admitted, and they both erupted into a shared laughter, dispelling the remaining tension in the air.

As their laughter faded, Elliot spoke again, his voice tender. "Let's focus on the next two days. And after that, if we're still this... 'tired,' we can sleep for a lifetime."

Ava's reply was playful yet sincere. "That sounds like an awful lot of sleeping." Suddenly, she leaned in and kissed him passionately, then pulled back with a devilish grin. "I'll see you in the morning, Elliot."

As she retreated from the room, Elliot sat there, a mix of astonishment and elation washing over him. He marveled at how he had traveled across the stars, finding a world inside the Moon, and had somehow found the only person who could take his breath away.

CHAPTER 35

"Hey sleepyhead," Bella said, her voice piercing the quiet of the early morning darkness.

Elliot slowly opened his eyes, adjusting to the light from the recently reignited lamp. Ava and Bella were already up and bustling about, efficiently packing supplies around the small room.

"Seems like every day I wake up to your face I'm whisked off into another crazy adventure," Elliot said jokingly to Bella, stretching out his limbs. A pleasant surprise greeted him as he moved; the lingering aches and pains from his recent exertions had almost entirely vanished, leaving him feeling surprisingly rejuvenated and ready for the day's challenges ahead.

"Since I've known you, it's been one animal chase after another," Bella retorted playfully. "Maybe they don't like how you smell," she teased, her smile brightening the room.

Elliot feigned a wounded expression. "How can such a pretty girl be so mean?" he joked.

Bella's smile widened at the compliment, even as it was delivered with a hint of sarcasm. "Actually, it wouldn't be such a bad idea if I freshened up a bit," Elliot mused, giving himself a quick sniff.

"I left a bucket of warm water for you next door," Ava remarked. "We're planning to leave in about fifteen minutes."

Elliot got up, mock-grumbling as he headed next door. "You're in on this too, Ava! Why is it always the pretty ones who are so mean?" he said with a playful grin.

From the other room, Ava's voice followed him, still laced with amusement. "There's a cloth for washing in there too."

Ten minutes later, Elliot returned, feeling invigorated and noticeably fresher. Ava handed him a hot drink and gestured towards a spear propped in the corner. "This one's yours," she said. "Bella and I will take ours as well, along with our hunting knives. But ideally, we won't need them if we keep our distance," she added.

Elliot grasped the spear, familiarizing himself with its weight and balance. "Better safe than sorry!" he agreed.

Within moments, they were ready to depart. Stepping out of Ava's home, the trio made their way towards the village's east entrance, the early morning air crisp and expectant with the day's impending adventure.

"If we follow the hill down to the river, one of the chief's men should be waiting for us," Ava explained as they prepared to depart.

"Is he joining us on the trail?" Elliot inquired, adjusting his pack.

"No, he's stationed there to observe the area. After Savage-Heart passes, he'll spend his day fishing the river," she responded.

"And in this darkness, how will we locate him?" Elliot asked, peering into the forest shrouded in shadows.

"He'll find us when we arrive," Ava assured him.

Their hike through the dense forest took about forty minutes. The first hints of dawn were just beginning to illuminate the sky as they reached the river's edge. True to Ava's word, the chief's man emerged from his concealed spot among the trees to greet them, guiding them to his hidden campsite on a slight elevation.

They settled in, their eyes scanning the opposite riverbank, awaiting the first sighting of Savage-Heart. The air thrummed with anticipation, tinged with both excitement and caution.

Nearly an hour passed before the telltale rustling from the other side of the river announced the bear's arrival. Savage-Heart emerged, her massive form moving with a purposeful grace. She strode along the river's edge, pausing occasionally to sniff the air and ground. Her path led her northward, away from the Great Falls.

On Lunar, the wind predominantly flowed from north to south, which worked in their favor. As long as Savage-Heart didn't double back, they could follow her downwind without detection. Ava decided to keep to the west side of the river, mirroring Savage-Heart's path on the east side. The higher ground of the surrounding forest offered them an added layer of safety and an advantageous viewpoint.

For an hour, they shadowed Savage-Heart, trailing her as she relentlessly navigated the river's course northward, then gradually veered west. As they moved, Elliot learned about the unique geography of the Lunar world—the river flowed counterclockwise, encircling the landscape. Their current path would eventually lead the river to vanish within the foreboding northeast mountains, only to reemerge at the summit of the Great Falls. Elliot pondered the engineering marvels required to achieve such a feat, his mind awash with images of colossal pumps hidden within the mountains, a testament to the gods' architectural prowess.

Periodically, Savage-Heart paused to quench her thirst from the river. During these moments, they too would stop, seizing the opportunity for a quick refreshment. Twice, the bear halted abruptly, her gaze and growls directed towards them. Each time, their hearts skipped a beat, frozen in place, fearing detection. Relief washed over them when it became apparent that her attention was aimed at other nearby animals, warning them to keep their distance.

As they neared the Forbidden Mountain in the northeast of Lunar, Ava's confidence in their destination grew. Elliot's earlier assumption was confirmed: these mountains were deemed "forbidden" as they were the abode of the "gods." Probing for more details, he learned from Ava that this was also where the taken were believed to be brought, a place inaccessible to anyone but the gods, hidden behind a passage that only they could open.

Bella and Ava had theorized that Savage-Heart's cub might have been taken by the gods, leading the mother bear to search for her lost offspring. They were surprised to learn that her daily journey led to the Forbidden Mountain. They watched with a mix of awe and empathy as Savage-Heart paced back and forth at the juncture where the river ended and the mountain began, a poignant display of a mother's relentless quest. "Is this the place where the gods come from?" Elliot asked as he scanned the horizon.

"Yes," Ava replied, her eyes fixed on the distant tree line. "That must be why she's here. It's the last place she can smell her cub's scent."

"But why would the gods take her cub?" Elliot's brow furrowed in confusion.

"I don't know. Perhaps for the same mysterious reasons they take us?" Ava suggested, her gaze distant.

"But her cub has been missing for nearly seven days now, Mama," Bella added, her voice small. "Anyone who's been there more than three days… they've never returned."

"Has someone been taken and never returned?" Elliot's question hung in the air, heavy with implication.

"Only once," Ava answered, her voice suddenly brisk. "But we should move up into the forest to get ahead of her," she added quickly. "She always travels home along the river. We can't risk being caught in her path."

They moved south, their steps muffled by the thick carpet of fallen leaves, ascending deeper into the forest. The canopy above whispered secrets in the wind, a chorus of leaves and branches. Once they were out of sight of Savage-Heart, they veered west, hoping to outpace her.

From the peak of the hill, Elliot surveyed the vast expanse before him. The mountain arced majestically from north to west, its immense form stretching endlessly toward the southern horizon.

"How far does that mountain range go?" Elliot asked, his eyes tracing the majestic sweep of the terrain.

"All the way to the Great Falls in the south," Ava replied.

"That's impressive!" Elliot exclaimed. The mountain stood as a monumental barrier, encompassing their entire Lunar world, a stark reminder that this was not Earth.

As his gaze traced the mountain line back to its origin, a sudden flash of white caught his attention. Instinctively, he gestured for Ava and Bella to crouch lower.

"Get down!" Elliot's voice was a sharp whisper, slicing through the stillness of the forest. He crouched low, his eyes fixed intently on something in the distance.

"What is it?" Ava's voice was a hushed murmur, barely audible above the gentle rustling of leaves.

Elliot extended a hand, pointing northwest, where the dense canopy parted slightly to reveal glimpses of the world beyond. "Over there," he whispered, his gaze locked on a distant movement. There, two figures, draped in the unmistakable white uniforms of the gods, moved with a deliberate purpose.

Ava's gaze shifted to follow Elliot's outstretched hand, her eyes widening with a mix of recognition and dread. In the distance, the Forbidden Mountain loomed large, its formidable silhouette casting a deep, elongated shadow over the forest, adding a layer of ominous foreboding to the scene.

"They're heading towards the Forbidden Mountain," Ava murmured. The distant figures, reduced to mere specks against the vast landscape, moved with purposeful stealth, their intentions veiled yet unmistakably sinister.

Bella's whisper, frail yet charged with alarm, cut through the tension-laden air. "Blue Stripes!" she said, her words heavy with a fear that seemed to echo the very danger they faced.

Chapter 36

Ava and Bella instinctively froze, their eyes scanning the forest below from their concealed spot. Perched high, they were almost invisible, safely observing the two gods navigating through the underbrush. Despite the dense foliage, the stark white of their suits betrayed their presence, making them conspicuous against the natural backdrop.

"If they keep heading that way, they'll encounter Savage-Heart," Bella said.

"Good!" Ava's response was laced with a cold resolve. "Let them get a taste of their own medicine for a change."

Elliot turned to look at Ava, noticing a shift in her demeanor. A steely edge had crept into her voice, a hardness that seemed to surface whenever she spoke of the gods.

"Regardless, we should stay out of sight," Ava added. "We don't want to get caught here."

Elliot's eyes narrowed in contemplation, weighing the risk against the necessity of gathering information. "I need to see where they're headed," he finally said, his tone decisive. "Understanding could be crucial."

"You two stay here," Elliot instructed, already strategizing his approach. "I'm going to get a closer look, find out what they're up to."

Ava's face was a portrait of anxiety, her eyes wide with apprehension. "That's incredibly risky, Elliot. What if you're seen... or worse, caught?" The fear in her voice was noticeable, mirroring her deep concern for the danger she feared Elliot might encounter.

Elliot offered a reassuring smile. "Don't worry, they won't catch me. And even if they do, there's no way they can connect me back to your village. I'm untraceable."

Seeing Bella's anxious expression, Elliot added, "Besides, if things get too close for comfort, I'll just use my superpowers to make a quick getaway. They won't stand a chance at catching me." His wink elicited a small, brave smile from Bella.

"Be careful, Elliot," Ava implored.

"I will," he assured her, giving Ava's shoulder a gentle squeeze. With a nod of quiet determination, Elliot turned and slipped away into the forest. Each step was calculated, blending seamlessly with the rustling of leaves and the natural sounds of the woodland.

He moved cautiously toward the northwest peak, weaving through the forest. This vantage point was critical for his mission. It offered an unobstructed view of both the Forbidden Mountain, where Savage-Heart prowled, and the path taken by the gods. Upon reaching his destination, Elliot crouched low, satisfaction mingling with anticipation as he realized his chosen spot provided the perfect vantage he had hoped for.

Perched high, Elliot had a clear view of the unfolding drama. The Blue Stripe gods, still a short distance from the mountain, moved with purpose, their black shock sticks in hand, a stark contrast against the natural hues of the forest. To his far right, Savage-Heart was a poignant figure, pacing the northern flank of the mountain. Her movements were restless, filled with maternal anxiety as she searched for her cub.

"This should be interesting!" Elliot murmured to himself.

Upon exiting the forest, the Blue Stripe gods faced an open expanse of grass before reaching the mountain's base. They advanced, oblivious to the looming presence of the bear. Meanwhile, Savage-Heart began retracing her steps, edging closer to the front of the mountain. Elliot held his breath, knowing it was only a matter of seconds before their paths crossed.

Elliot wondered about Savage-Heart's reaction. Having been raised amongst these gods, would she exhibit the same wariness as the Lunari? He suspected that such caution might be cast aside by a mother's fierce instinct to protect her offspring.

He didn't have to speculate for long. As Savage-Heart rounded the corner, she instantly locked sights on the two men. Only fifty meters away and still at a distance from the mountain, her reaction was visceral. She reared up on her hind legs, unleashing a roar that resonated through the forest and sent shivers down Elliot's spine, reviving memories of his harrowing encounter with the bear.

The men, initially oblivious to Savage-Heart's presence, continued their march until her thunderous roar halted them abruptly, one of them even dropping his weapon in surprise. They quickly regained their composure, thrusting their shock sticks forward defensively as they began to spread out, widening the gap between them. This tactical shift made Savage-Heart pause her charge, reassessing her approach even as she continued to inch closer, steadily narrowing the distance.

Elliot watched perplexed as the men maneuvered into positions at four and seven o'clock relative to Savage-Heart. It seemed counterintuitive to him; a twelve and six o'clock approach would have left her constantly blind to one of them.

But as the gap shrank to a mere ten meters, Elliot's confusion cleared. The men were ensuring that neither was in the other's line of fire. His realization came just as Savage-Heart rose again on her hind legs, her roar a defiant challenge. Then, the air was pierced by two *THWUMP* sounds in quick succession, followed immediately by two muffled thuds.

Elliot observed two reactions: a noticeable recoil from the men's blasts coinciding with the sound, and then, a split second later, Savage-Heart was jolted backward twice, in perfect sync with the thudding impacts.

Elliot concluded that the weapons were effective at range, albeit limited. He reasoned that the men had waited to fire until Savage-Heart was close, suggesting that they were most effective at short range, like a shotgun. Against a threat as formidable as Savage-Heart, one would not risk her getting too close unless absolutely necessary.

Elliot had initially assumed that their weapons were akin to oversized tasers, but witnessing their ranged capabilities had altered his perception. They seemed to harness a form of kinetic energy, judging by the forceful thuds that resonated upon striking Savage-Heart's body.

The bear, having been jolted backward by the unseen forces, was visibly stunned. It was an unprecedented experience for her, to be repelled with such force. Yet, driven by a fierce maternal instinct, she quickly shook off the disorientation and regained her footing, undeterred.

However, as she advanced once more, the air was split by the now-familiar *THWUMP THWUMP*. The subsequent impacts were immediate and brutal, one hitting her left shoulder and the other her head. The force knocked her to the ground, leaving her dazed. It was a moment of realization for Savage-Heart: she was outmatched. With a newfound sense of vulnerability, she turned and lumbered towards the safety of the northern forest.

Elliot watched the scene unfold, awestruck and concerned. The bear's retreat was unsteady, almost desperate. As she staggered away, five more *THWUMP* sounds echoed, but this time, there were no accompanying thuds of impact. Elliot's observations seemed to confirm his theory: the efficiency of their weapons diminished with distance.

Elliot, concealed by the foliage, watched as the brown bear vanished into the dense underbrush. The forest air, momentarily filled with the gods' synthetic laughter, seemed to echo their cruel amusement. They lingered, eyes fixed on the spot where the bear had disappeared, clearly hoping for her return. After a couple of fruitless minutes, their attention waned, and they resumed their journey toward the Forbidden Mountain, heading for its northwest corner.

From his hidden perch, Elliot observed the men's approach to the mountain wall. The god on the left performed a subtle gesture with his forearm, and in response, a section of the wall silently receded before rising smoothly, reminiscent of the airlock doors Elliot had encountered before. The door, sliding into the mountain's structure, revealed an entrance wide enough for a vehicle as large as a school bus.

From his position, Elliot strained to see into the passage. Details eluded him, except for the glow of ambient light and a glimpse of a light gray wall. As the gods stepped inside, one lingered momentarily to manipulate a control on the wall, setting the massive door in motion once again. Within seconds, the mountain facade was restored, leaving no trace of the doorway's existence.

Compelled by an overwhelming curiosity, Elliot began his cautious descent from the forest hill. His senses remained sharply attuned to any hint of movement, whether from the concealed doorway or a possible return of Savage-Heart. Confident in his newfound swift reflexes, he edged closer to the forest's boundary.

As he neared the grassy clearing at the forest's edge, a sudden, chilling sound abruptly stopped Elliot in his tracks. The calm of the forest was shattered by a terrified scream, echoing starkly and hauntingly among the trees and disrupting the natural harmony. Elliot froze, his heart pounding, as the sound—unmistakably that of a terrified young girl—reverberated through the air.

CHAPTER 37

As Elliot disappeared into the dense foliage of the forest, a wave of familiar unease swept over Ava. The mere mention of the gods always triggered such feelings, deeply ingrained over the past five years since that life-altering day. She often thought of her preference: a lifetime on Lunar without the gods, rather than a single day on Earth in their presence.

"What do you think is going to happen, Mama?" Bella's question shattered the heavy silence.

"I don't know, darling," Ava replied, her gaze lost in the trees. "But I certainly wouldn't want to be in the path of Savage-Heart right now."

"I hope she tears them up," Bella stated with a hint of defiance.

Ava turned to face Bella. "You mustn't talk that way, darling," she said.

"But why?" Bella said. "You feel the same way too. Don't you?" she asked, her fingers absently playing with fallen leaves.

Ava hesitated, torn between honesty and the need for caution. "Yes, but we must never speak ill of the gods where others might hear. It's too risky."

"I won't, Mama," Bella promised, then paused, pondering. "What about Elliot? Can I say what I think about them in front of him? I trust him."

Ava considered for a moment before nodding. "Yes, you can. I trust him too," she said.

"Will Elliot come live with us if he can't go back home?" Bella asked, catching Ava off guard with the sudden change of subject. "I'd like him to."

"I'm not sure, darling," Ava responded. "It's not something I can decide alone. We also need to think about what Elliot wants. He might not want to live with us."

"Oh, he will. He likes you. I can tell," Bella said with a mischievous glint in her eye. "And you like him too!" she added, her smile broadening.

"What do you mean you can tell?" Ava asked, feeling a blush warm her cheeks. "How do you know I like him?"

"Because you just admitted it!" Bella exclaimed, her giggles filling the air.

"Stop it, you," Ava said playfully, pulling Bella in to squeeze her, which naturally evolved into a heartfelt hug.

As they sat embraced, Bella said softly, "You know it's okay if you like someone else, don't you, Mama?"

Ava sighed. "I do now, darling. Thank you," she said, hugging her a little tighter.

"Just make sure it's not Mayto." Bella wrinkled her nose in mock disgust. "'My name's Mayto! I'm so big and angry!'" she imitated, causing Ava to laugh.

"No, definitely not Mayto," Ava assured her, suppressing a laugh.

Their moment of levity was abruptly broken by the distant roar of Savage-Heart, causing them both to look towards the sound, as if trying to see through the dense forest.

The sudden snap of a branch behind them made Ava and Bella whirl around in unison. Confronting them was a god, his white suit adorned with blue stripes and his shock stick aimed menacingly in their direction. Fear clutched at Ava's heart as she instinctively drew Bella closer. She briefly considered reaching for her spear, but the notion vanished as quickly as it had come when a second god emerged from the trees, joining the first.

"Get to your feet!" the first god commanded, his voice synthetic and devoid of empathy.

Rising slowly, Ava positioned herself protectively in front of Bella.

"You, get in front where we can see you," the second god ordered Bella coldly.

"Please," Ava said, her voice quivering with fear, "we were just out hunting."

"You know you're not allowed to hunt on this side of the forest!" snapped the second god, his gaze drifting ominously towards Bella.

"We didn't mean to! We were trying to avoid the bear!" Ava rushed out. Noticing his unsettling attention on her daughter, she shielding her once more.

"I think you're lying," the first god stated.

"I'm not," Ava protested, her mind racing with thoughts of escape.

"Stop moving!" the second god barked. "And I told you to get out in front," he said, pointing at Bella.

Tears brimmed in Bella's eyes as she slowly stepped forward, clinging to her mother's arm as if it were her only anchor in a sea of fear.

"I think we need to teach these two a lesson," the first god said to his companion, a sinister edge to his voice. "Help me tie them to the tree."

Ava's protective instincts surged to the forefront as she recognized the imminent threat to Bella. Channeling her fear into action, she unleashed a powerful forward kick, driving her foot squarely into the first god's stomach just as he reached out for her. The force of the blow sent him reeling backward, collapsing hard onto the ground. Without hesitation, Ava ushered Bella back several steps and reached for her spear.

The second god, reacting swiftly, advanced with his shock stick poised. But Ava was ready; as he aimed for her head, she ducked. The *THWUMP* sound of the discharge rang out overhead. Rising swiftly, she thrust the blunt end of her spear with full force. His helmet was the only thing that saved him from a fatal blow, but the impact still sent him stumbling backward, tripping over his comrade who was attempting to rise.

"Run!" Ava's urgent shout snapped Bella out of her shocked paralysis.

Bella hesitated for a split second before turning to flee, her heart pounding. But then, two sounds shattered the air—a *THWUMP* followed by a *THUD*.

A third sound, a heavier thud, sent a chill through Bella. She glanced back in horror and saw her mother, having been hit by the shock stick's blast, collapse to the ground, motionless. Before Bella could even scream, she felt a sharp, agonizing blow from the shock stick on the side of her head. The world around her began to blur and spin, her vision fading in and out as darkness encroached.

Bella's world became a disorienting haze of blurred shapes and muffled noises, lasting what seemed like forever. She vaguely felt herself being moved, yet her body wouldn't respond, offering no resistance. Abruptly, a sharp pain across her chest jolted her back to reality.

Her head throbbed painfully, and her chest felt constricted. Realizing she couldn't move, Bella discovered she had been tied to a tree with her own rope. The surroundings were unfamiliar; she had been relocated to another part of the forest. Panic surged anew. Frantically, she scanned the area for her mother but found only the emptiness of the forest. Her gaze fixed on the god in the white suit with blue stripes. Helmetless now, he was methodically shedding his suit.

"Welcome back," the man said, smiling in a way that sent a chill down her spine. He was no god. With his helmet off, his human features were starkly evident: angular, with black hair contrasting his pale skin. His smile, disarmingly genuine, deepened Bella's sense of dread. His voice, now free of any synthetic distortion, retained a chilling tone, further intensifying the menacing air around him.

Bella's terror burst forth in a scream, but the man only smiled more unnervingly. "There's no point in screaming," he said calmly. "No one can hear you here."

"I want my mama," Bella sobbed desperately.

"Your mama can't help you now. She's... otherwise occupied!" he taunted, taking pleasure in Bella's distress.

"But don't worry, I'll make sure you forget all about this," he laughed cruelly.

"MAMA!" Bella's scream was fraught with desperation, her cries echoing unanswered into the forest's emptiness.

"If you don't stop screaming, I'm going to have to shut that pretty little mouth of yours myself!" the man said, his tone laced with a menacing edge.

Tears streamed down Bella's cheeks, born of a fear more profound than she had ever known. The absence of her mother, her lifelong protector, left her feeling more isolated than ever. Tied and immobile, she couldn't shake the terrifying thought that her mother might be similarly restrained somewhere nearby.

Drawing on the courage her mother had always nurtured in her, Bella fought to steady her thoughts. "If you can't be stronger than a man, then you better be smarter than one," her mother's words echoed in her mind.

Frantically, she tried to formulate a plan. Escape was impossible on her own, and with her mother potentially incapacitated, she felt utterly helpless. But then, a flicker of hope ignited within her. There was still one person who could come to their aid.

With all the strength she could muster, she let out a piercing scream:

"ELLIOT!"

Almost instantly, a harsh slap struck her face, snapping her head to the side, followed swiftly by a gag being forced into her mouth.

CHAPTER 38

A PIERCING SCREAM SHATTERED the tranquility of the forest, its echoes resonating sharply against the previous stillness. The sound, laden with fear and desperation, cut through the air, immediately capturing Elliot's attention. His heart leapt into his throat when he recognized it as Bella's voice. Instinctively, he surged into action, his feet pounding against the forest floor as he dashed toward the source of her distress. Any thoughts of the concealed doorway faded into irrelevance.

The forest became a blur as Elliot raced through it, his speed remarkable. The raw urgency in Bella's scream propelled him forward, but frustration at his inability to quickly locate her began to gnaw at him. The forest, dense and disorienting, seemed to mislead him. Returning to where he had left Ava and Bella, he found only their abandoned packs and spears, no sign of them. With each second that ticked by, his anxiety intensified.

Another scream tore through the silence—a desperate cry. "MAMA!" It was more than a cry for help; it was a plea steeped in fear and urgency. Bella's terror echoed in every syllable, pushing Elliot to move even faster. Amidst his concern for Bella, worry for Ava's safety also lingered in his mind. Why hadn't he heard anything from her?

As he sprinted, darting through the underbrush, the forest seemed to thwart his efforts, obscuring Bella's whereabouts. Frustration mounted with every stride, and just as despair threatened to overwhelm him, one final, desperate scream filled the air: "ELLIOT!"

Elliot's name rang through the trees like a beacon of hope in the darkness. His heart was pounding, more from the fear of not getting there in time than the exertion of the pursuit. He adjusted his course, heading towards Bella's voice. It sounded closer than ever. She couldn't be far from here, he thought.

He frantically searched ahead for any sign of her. Then, amidst the trees to his left, a lone figure in a white suit with a blue stripe stood out, a ghostly apparition against the greens and browns. The ominous figure had removed his helmet and partially undone his suit. The scene unfolding made Elliot's jaw clench and body fill with rage. As he charged, the last images burned into the back of his brain was the hand over Bella's mouth and the tears that were streaming down her face.

Elliot was a blur of motion, weaving through the trees and bounding over the terrain with astonishing agility, his focus resolute. As he closed the gap, the man heard his approach. He turned towards Elliot with an arrogant smile playing on his lips and wielding his shock stick with overconfident assurance.

But he continued to charge relentlessly, undeterred by the threat of the weapon. His only focus was the hand cruelly clamped over Bella's mouth, driving him forward with an unstoppable fury.

As the man poised to unleash the energy blast from his shock stick at Elliot, his face abruptly contorted in agony. Bella, despite her bindings, had deftly maneuvered enough to reach the hunting knife tucked in her belt. Taking advantage of the man's proximity as he clamped a hand over her mouth, she drove the blade deep into his side. His reaction was cut short by Elliot's rapid approach, his arms wrapping around the man's midsection in a viselike grip. The impact of their collision was intense, echoing the force of a quarterback getting blindsided by an unstoppable defender.

The momentum lifted the man off his feet, expelling the air from his lungs before Elliot slammed him back down to the forest floor. The ground met him with a harsh thud, scattering leaves and debris in a chaotic flurry.

Rising swiftly, Elliot moved with clear intent. The man lay sprawled on the ground, disoriented from the abrupt takedown, bleeding from the wound inflicted by Bella's knife.

Elliot, with a steely resolve, picked up the shock stick next to the man. He quickly assessed its mechanism: a simple power indicator, a dial for adjusting the intensity, and a larger button to fire. Without hesitation, he directed the charged end at the man's head. His eyes were steady, his decision final. He pressed the button, delivering a point-blank shot at full power. The *THWUMP* of the discharge was followed immediately by a resounding *THUD* as the blast hit the man's head. The lethal discharge left an imprint on his face—a haunting amalgamation of pain and life extinguished.

Elliot stood amidst the aftermath, his emotions a tempest of relief and anguish. The sight of Bella, tied and tear-streaked, was a haunting image of vulnerability and courage. He hurried to her side, his hands shaking yet gentle as he reached out, a silent promise of protection resonating in his actions.

"Hey," he said softly, his voice tinged with urgency, cutting through Bella's sobs. "It's over, Bella. You're safe now!" he added. "Can you be brave for me just a little bit longer? I need to know where your mother is. Can you tell me?" he asked tenderly.

Carefully, Elliot loosened Bella's hand from the knife's grip and used it to sever her bonds.

After spitting out her gag, Bella took a shuddering breath, her young face streaked with tears. "He said... the other man took her to the mountain," she managed to say, her voice broken by sobs.

"How many more men are there, Bella?" Elliot inquired, his tone steady.

"Just... one more," she stammered, "He... he shot her in the back. She wasn't moving!" Bella's gaze flicked fearfully towards the man on the ground. "What if she's dead?" Tears began streaming from her brown eyes, breaking Elliot's heart, but now wasn't the time, he needed to stay focused if he was going to save Ava.

"She's not dead, Bella," he said with unwavering conviction. "The blast would have knocked her out, nothing more. They don't kill at half power, and his shock stick was only at half power when I took it from him." He showed her the shock stick as if to prove his point. "We'll find her, I promise."

Elliot maintained his gaze on Bella. "Listen carefully, Bella. I need you to be strong. I need to go to find your mother now," he said firmly yet gently. "But I need to leave you here so I can move faster," he continued, cutting off any chance for Bella to object. "I want you to go back to where I left you earlier and wait for me there, okay? Your spear and packs are still where we left them." He gestured northward, indicating the direction she should head.

Bella's eyes flicked anxiously to the man on the ground. "What if he gets up again?"

Elliot met her gaze squarely, his voice unwavering. "He's not going to get up, Bella. He's dead. I made sure of it."

"But how can you be so sure?" she said, her voice tinged with fear.

Elliot responded with a decisive action. He walked over to the motionless figure and aimed the shock stick at the man's head, triggering it twice in quick succession, each discharge a confirmation of the man's conclusive fate. The sounds echoed, final and irrefutable.

"Positive," Elliot affirmed, his gaze locking onto Bella's, instilling a silent promise of return. Urgency pulsed through his veins. "I have to go now, Bella."

Bella's eyes, wide and gleaming with a mix of terror and bravery, watched Elliot. Every cell in his body resisted leaving her, yet the urgency of Ava's safety compelled him forward with equal force.

He kissed Bella lightly on the forehead—a tender moment amidst the chaos. "Remember, head to where the packs are. Stay hidden, stay safe. I'll be back for you. I promise!" The words were an unbreakable vow. They lingered in the air as Elliot sprinted away, shock stick in hand, each stride fueled by a mix of dread and determination.

Bella, left amidst the silent rustling of the trees, clutched the hunting knife close. She was alone, but not powerless. The forest, having silently observed Bella's ordeal, now stood as a testament to the unspoken strength taking hold within her.

Chapter 39

As he dashed through the dense forest, his chest rising and falling rapidly, Elliot felt the gravity of his task weighing heavily on him. The shock stick he clutched was a tangible reminder of the violent encounter he had just left behind. The memory of Bella's screams, still echoing in his mind, fueled his growing sense of urgency and dread.

The scenery around him melded into a blur, a whirlwind of green and brown, as he pushed his speed to its limits. His mind raced as fast as his feet, grappling with the unsettling situation. Thoughts of Ava in danger vied with the disturbing image of Bella, tied to a tree with a man ominously discarding his suit nearby.

Upon reaching the northwest peak, Elliot halted, taking a moment to scan the route he had seen the men use last. The area showed no signs of recent passage, no clues to indicate they had come this way. His eyes traced the path leading to the hidden mountain entrance, now closed and seemingly untouched. A wave of self-doubt washed over him. Could he have been too late? Had Ava already been taken inside, beyond his reach?

A sudden glimpse of white at the edge of his vision instantly redirected Elliot's focus to the far right. There she was—the man hadn't taken Ava into the mountain. Instead, he was navigating along the mountain's right side, heading north. A cold realization dawned on Elliot: the man had deliberately chosen this hidden route for whatever heinous act he intended to commit next.

As soon as Elliot spotted them, he sprang into action. His speed was unmatched, and his resolve resolute, but a persistent doubt gnawed at him: could he reach them in time to prevent an irreversible act? With unwavering determination, he descended the hill, cutting through the forest at an angle designed to intercept them. A solemn vow echoed within him, reinforcing his determination—he would not allow harm to befall those he had sworn to protect.

Closing in, a wave of fury overwhelmed Elliot at the sight of Ava's unconscious body draped over the man's shoulder. Her long black ponytail swung in time with the man's strides. Finally reaching his destination, the man callously dropped Ava onto the ground, looming over her, a disturbing sense of satisfaction in his posture as he ominously admired his trophy.

As the man moved to kick Ava's feet apart, she showed faint signs of regaining consciousness, stirring slightly. He seemed visibly disappointed by her awakening. Lifting his shock stick, he adjusted the power settings to a lower level—his intent was not to kill her, but merely to send her back to sleep with a minor shock.

From his hidden vantage point in the forest, Elliot could see the man tampering with the controls on his shock stick. Frustratingly, he was still too far away to intervene, a river separating them. In a desperate bid to distract the man, Elliot let out a thunderous roar. The man's head whipped up in startled confusion, his attention momentarily diverted from Ava.

But in that critical moment of distraction, another presence emerged from the forest: Savage-Heart had returned. The bear burst forth in a blur of brown fury. Caught off guard, the man spun around, raising his shock stick. He fired instinctively, a swift, fluid motion. *THWUMP. THUD.*

The shock stick's blast struck Savage-Heart directly on the head, fired from a mere three meters away. However, its low power setting rendered the impact feeble. The bear, undeterred by the weak blow, maintained her relentless momentum. With her massive neck and sheer force, she drove her head into the man, propelling him with a violent thrust against the mountain wall. The sudden impact sent a reverberating thud through the forest.

Savage-Heart, utterly unfazed by the blast's ineffective attempt to stop her, unleashed her full fury on the man. She tore into his suit with ferocious power, her claws ripping through the fabric. The man's synthetic screams of agony pierced the air, echoing hauntingly across the river to where Elliot stood, witnessing the brutal scene.

Seizing the moment, Elliot burst from the forest cover, his speed increasing as he approached the river's edge. Confidence surged within him, bolstered by his enhanced abilities and Lunar's lower gravity. With a powerful leap, Elliot effortlessly cleared the river, landing smoothly on the other side.

Elliot then dashed the remaining distance to Ava, his eyes darting cautiously towards Savage-Heart. The bear was now ferociously mauling the man, who lay motionless under her wrath. Upon reaching Ava, Elliot gently shook her, a wave of relief washing over him as he detected faint signs of movement. Despite this relief, the urgency of the situation remained paramount. They were perilously close to the raging bear, and their safety was far from assured.

With careful haste, Elliot gently lifted Ava onto his shoulder, ensuring her safety was his foremost priority. As he adjusted her weight, Savage-Heart, catching sight of him for the first time, began to growl menacingly. The sound was deep and resonant, filled with primal threat. Elliot, recognizing the imminent danger, quickly raised his weapon, extending it defensively in front of him. His eyes locked on the bear, prepared for any sudden movement.

The air was heavy with tension when suddenly, Savage-Heart unleashed a terrifying display of raw power. With one swift, brutal motion, she dismembered the man, tearing his arm from its socket. The limb was flung towards Elliot, landing with a heavy thud near his feet. It served as a grisly and stark warning from the bear, a demonstration of her lethal strength and ferocity.

Elliot stood his ground as the severed limb landed ominously nearby. Gripping the shock stick with determined resolve, he unleashed two powerful blasts into the man's lifeless body, sending a clear message of his own. The bear paused, her growls reverberating through the air, but she gradually began to retreat, slowly melting back into the depths of the forest.

With the shock stick still raised and ready for any sudden threats, Elliot cautiously backed away towards the river, Ava securely positioned on his shoulder. His movements were measured, every sense alert to the dangers around him. Reaching the river's edge, he took a moment to orient himself before turning to navigate along the mountain's base. Having determined his route, Elliot set off to reunite with Bella, driven by the singular focus of ensuring their safety.

Casting one final vigilant look over his shoulder, Elliot stepped into the forest. The trees seemed to embrace their presence, offering a temporary shield from the peril they had just escaped. With Ava safely in his care, he moved with renewed purpose, each step bringing him closer to Bella and the reunion that lay ahead.

CHAPTER 40

ELLIOT PUSHED HIS WAY through the dense undergrowth, his lungs aching from the intense exertion of the past twenty minutes. His familiarity with the forest's layout guided him. Its recognizable landmarks assured him that he was closing in on where he had left Bella. As he broke into the clearing, he immediately spotted Bella. She held a spear in hand and was poised in a stance that spoke of alert readiness.

"Bella!" he called out. "It's me, Elliot. I have your mother."

At the sound of his voice, Bella's tense posture relaxed slightly, and she lowered her spear. Her face, etched with concern and relief, turned towards her mother, who was draped over Elliot's shoulder, unconscious but alive.

"Mama!" Bella's voice was laced with worry. She studied her for any sign of response. "Is she okay?" she asked, her voice trembling.

"She's going to be fine," Elliot reassured as he carefully laid Ava down on the forest floor. "But we need to help her wake up."

Kneeling beside her mother, Bella gently grasped her hand, while Elliot cautiously shook Ava's shoulders.

"Mama, wake up!" Bella urged, her voice filled with concern. After a tense moment, Ava let out a faint moan, her eyelids fluttering open to reveal a confused but conscious gaze, first fixing on Elliot, then on Bella.

Ava's expression shifted as if piecing together fragmented memories. She attempted to sit up, but Elliot gently pressed her back down.

"It's okay," he reassured her softly. "You're safe now. We're all safe."

Ava's eyes, still wide with lingering fear, focused intently on Elliot. "The gods!" she exclaimed.

Bella, holding her mother's hand firmly, reassured her. "It's okay, Mama. They're gone now. Elliot saved us."

"Bella was incredibly brave today," Elliot added. "You'd be so proud of her."

Ava pulled Bella into a tight embrace, her emotions brimming over. She then looked up at Elliot, her eyes filled with tearful gratitude. "Thank you, Elliot."

The distant sound of the horn pierced the air three times before Elliot could respond. "That must mean Evelyn has been returned," Ava said, recognizing the signal immediately. "That would explain why the gods were out today," she added, trying to sit up.

"Would they have taken her to the village?" Elliot asked, assisting her up.

Ava shook her head. "No, they usually just leave them in the forest to find their own way back," she explained.

Suddenly, Elliot stood up, a sense of urgency about him. "I need to go back to do something," he declared. "I'll be back in ten minutes, at most. Be ready to leave when I return; we can't risk being found here if more of those gods show up."

Bella, her anxiety resurfacing, looked up at him. "What are you going to do?" she asked, her voice tinged with worry.

Elliot avoided her gaze, his expression firm yet troubled. "Something that needs to be done," he stated. "Just be ready!" With that, he turned and disappeared into the forest, leaving Ava and Bella with a growing sense of unease and anticipation.

Moving swiftly, Elliot made his way back to the site where Bella had been tied up, his mind racing with the events of the last twenty minutes. Two gods lay dead, a fact that could not lead back to the Lunari for the sake of the village's safety. The repercussions of such a discovery would be disastrous. With this in mind, Elliot formulated a plan: he would move the body of the man who had attacked Bella and place it alongside the one taken down by Savage-Heart. He was uncertain how long he had before the gods went looking for their missing men, but he knew Savage-Heart roamed this area until sunset. He hoped she might return and further disrupt the scene. If not, he had to ensure the staging was convincing enough.

Upon reaching the first body, Elliot felt a wave of anger at the memory of the man's intentions towards Bella. Pushing his emotions aside, he focused on the task at hand, aware of the limited time available. Taking out his phone, he began to record a video, capturing the man's face and the details of his suit. This evidence would be crucial to show the village chief that the "gods" were, in fact, human. More than that, he intended to examine the suit more thoroughly later when time allowed. With steady hands, he completed his recording and prepared to enact the rest of his plan.

Elliot meticulously redressed the man, ensuring that his helmet was properly secured to maintain the appearance of a sudden, violent attack. With the body prepared, Elliot hoisted it over his shoulder. He chose a route back to the mountain that would avoid crossing paths with Ava and Bella, ensuring to keep clear of the mountain entrance.

Upon reaching the site near the mountain, he carefully placed the body beside the other, arranging them to convincingly appear as victims of a single brutal animal attack. Satisfied with the staging, Elliot was about to head back when a sudden thought halted him.

He turned back, his gaze landing on the severed arm, specifically noticing the CDU that was still attached to it. After a moment's consideration, he picked up the arm and placed it securely in his backpack. The absence of the arm at the scene would undoubtedly reinforce the narrative of a savage animal attack. With this final adjustment complete, Elliot set off once again, heading back through the forest to reunite with Ava and Bella.

He stepped out of the forest's shadow, finding Bella and a now fully awake Ava hurriedly packing their gear. As he drew nearer, their faces shifted from worry to visible relief, their eyes lighting up at his return.

"Is everything okay?" Ava asked, her eyes searching his face for any hint of concern.

"Better now!" he assured her. "I just needed to make sure they wouldn't come asking any questions of the Lunari later," he added, gratefully accepting a canteen of water from Ava. He took a quick drink, then said, "We need to leave... now."

Their nods indicated agreement, and they promptly started their journey back to the village. Bella took the lead, her steps determined and swift, while Ava, still regaining her strength, relied on Elliot's steady support. As they ventured away from the scene, Elliot cast a final look back. He was aware that each step took them away from immediate danger, but also distanced them from much-needed answers.

Looking ahead at Bella and then across to Ava, he was suddenly struck by how close he had come to losing them. This realization of their importance to him surprised him, but also reaffirmed his resolve: their safety was paramount, and he would do anything to keep them safe. With determination, he focused ahead, guiding them away from the forest's dark embrace and steering them toward the familiar safety of the Lunari village.

Chapter 41

As Elliot, Ava, and Bella stepped into the safety of the village, a sense of profound relief enveloped them. The air buzzed with a fresh sense of hope, invigorated by the news of Evelyn's return. The village, which had been shrouded in unease the day before, now thrummed with a lively energy. Without hesitation, they made their way to the chief's residence, where they found him in deep conversation with Mayto.

Upon their arrival, the chief glanced up. "Ava, what brings you here?" he asked.

"There was an incident with the gods today, Chief," Ava began, her voice indicating urgency. "It's something you need to hear about." Acknowledging her seriousness, the chief motioned for them to sit down, ordering refreshments for them.

Before sitting, Ava turned to Bella, her maternal instinct taking over. "Bella, why don't you go play with your friends," she said. "You've been through a lot today. I think it would do you some good."

Bella paused, hesitating to leave her mother, but she eventually nodded and moved towards the door, clutching some food. "I'll be right here, darling," Ava reassured with a smile. Bella returned it briefly before disappearing through the doorway.

Elliot and Ava found a spot to sit. Ava then began recounting their harrowing encounter in the forest. She detailed their unexpected discovery by the self-proclaimed "gods," their disturbing interest in Bella, and the violent intentions they had openly expressed.

Elliot's gut churned with guilt for leaving them alone, even for a moment. Ava spoke of the brief battle that ensued, leading to her being knocked unconscious by a blast from a shock stick. Elliot listened intently, his concern growing with every detail Ava revealed.

He then took over the storytelling, beginning with the moment he recognized the danger, triggered by Bella's desperate cries for help. He detailed the scene he had stumbled upon: Bella, bound yet defiant, managing to stab her captor with a hidden knife. Ava listened intently, pride swelling in her at the revelation of Bella's bravery, even as a wave of great distress washed over her.

"I then used the man's shock stick to kill him," Elliot continued, his voice carrying a cold edge.

He went on to describe how he had freed Bella and then set off to track down Ava's abductor. Elliot's narrative painted a vivid picture of his grim discovery around the side of the mountain and the timely, albeit brutal, intervention of Savage-Heart that led to the second man's death. He concluded with his cautious extraction of Ava from the vicinity of the bear.

Mayto leaped to his feet, his face contorted with anger. "By killing a god, you've put our entire village at risk!"

"No, he saved my daughter and me from a fate far worse than death!" Ava interjected sharply.

Mayto grunted. "Better two than all!" he responded coldly, his anger prevailing once more as he stormed out of the room.

The chief sighed deeply. "I apologize for my son's outburst," he said. "His words were harsh, but he raised a valid concern. These actions, no matter how noble, have indeed provoked those much more powerful than us. Their response will be severe."

"Chief, there's more to the story you need to hear," Elliot responded. He then told of his efforts to stage the scene of the deaths to implicate a bear attack. Ava and the chief listened intently, their expressions starting with surprise and ending in tentative relief.

"Your quick thinking might just have saved us," the chief acknowledged thoughtfully.

"If it doesn't, I'm prepared to take full responsibility," Elliot responded firmly.

"You can't do that, Elliot!" Ava said, her voice trembling.

"It's the only way to ensure the Lunari aren't blamed," Elliot said. "The consequences would be too severe otherwise."

"But they'll kill you for this!"

"Mayto was right... better one than all!"

"You're a man of honor, Elliot," the chief said, extending his hand in a gesture of respect. "Let's hope your plan works and it doesn't come to this."

Elliot shook the chief's hand and then pulled his phone from his pocket. "There's something else you need to see," he said, and showed them the video he had recorded earlier, revealing the true nature of their so-called "gods." "As you can see, Chief, they're no gods. They're just flesh and blood like you and me. I don't know how they created this world, or why, but I do know one thing: they're human!"

The chief let out a heavy sigh. "I know they're not gods, Elliot. Most of us probably know that deep down. But they did bring us here; they saved us."

Elliot started to object, but the chief raised his hand to stop him. "I know you say humanity wasn't wiped out a hundred years ago, but you can't prove that," he said, his eyes meeting Elliot's. "Do you at least concede that they brought us here?"

Elliot nodded in agreement. "Yes, Chief. Regardless of the discrepancies between their story and mine, it's clear they built this place and brought your people here."

The chief pondered this for a moment. "If we agree on that, then what would you have me do if your version of Earth's story is true?" the chief asked.

Elliot took a moment to reflect. The truth was, he had come to the same question when he turned the problem over in his mind. "Honestly, Chief, I don't know," he said finally. "I feel like there's still a significant part of the puzzle missing; something just doesn't feel right about it all. Can I ask you something?"

"Of course," replied the chief.

"If you were in my position, and believed as I do, what would you do?" Elliot asked.

Leaning forward, the chief responded thoughtfully. "I'd seek more answers, making sure not to endanger others in the process."

Seizing the moment, Elliot said, "Then if I still have your blessing, I'd like to take Ava to the surface in the morning?"

The chief relaxed back again in his cushion. "For what you did today, for Bella and Ava, you have earned that much," he said. "But Elliot, I will need you to keep your promise should the gods not believe what happened today."

"You have my word, Chief," Elliot said with sincerity.

The Chief's warm response and another firm handshake solidified their understanding. Elliot's smile, warm and genuine, conveyed his gratitude. "Thank you, Chief. It's been a long day, and tomorrow will be even more challenging. We should rest."

"Chief, could Bella stay with you while we're away tomorrow?" Ava asked. "After all she's been through today, I can't think of anyone better to look after her than you." She glanced at Elliot. "Well, except maybe him," she added.

The chief's smile mirrored Ava's. "It would be my honor to look after Bella. She'll be safe with me, that's a promise."

Ava expressed her gratitude with a traditional gesture of respect, touching her forehead and nose to the chief's.

"When you bring Bella in the morning, I'll have updates on Savage-Heart's movements from my men. We'll make sure it's safe for your journey," the chief informed them. "And your climbing axes will be ready too."

With heartfelt thanks, they bid the chief farewell and left to collect Bella, who was happily playing in the nearby square. As they crossed the road towards her, Elliot's voice took on a serious tone as he turned to Ava.

"There's something important about our journey tomorrow I need to discuss with you when we get back."

"Is it about us having only one suit?" Ava replied with a sly smile.

"You knew?" Elliot asked, slightly taken aback. "Why didn't you mention it in front of the chief?"

"If I had, he might not have allowed us to go," Ava replied pragmatically. "Besides, I figured you'd have a plan to work around that," she added.

Elliot's smile grew. "I might have a couple of ideas," he admitted, his mind already turning over potential solutions to the challenge that lay ahead.

Chapter 42

Elliot and Ava stepped into the village square, bathed in the fading glow of the evening sun. The scent of fresh bread wafted from nearby, and the laughter of children playing filled the air. Despite the uplift in spirits from Evelyn's return, an undercurrent of tension persisted, a hangover from the previous day's unsettling events. As they moved through the square, the tranquil scene was abruptly disrupted. From behind the lush foliage of a large tree, Mayto emerged, stepping into their path, his presence like a sudden storm cloud darkening the otherwise peaceful setting. His clenched fists and narrowed eyes spoke volumes about his simmering anger.

"What are you doing here, Mayto?" Ava asked, noticing his aggressive stance.

Mayto grunted. "What am I doing here? The better question is, what are you doing here?" he spat out, his voice dripping with contempt. Shifting his focus sharply towards Elliot, he advanced a step, his expression hostile. Mayto's finger pointed accusingly, almost touching Elliot's face. "Because of him," he said, his tone seething with anger, "we're all in danger!"

Elliot remained calm, but his body was alert, ready for any sudden movements. "I understand that you're upset, Mayto," Elliot said. "But you left before hearing everything. You should go and speak with your father. Hear the full story before you decide to do something you'll regret."

Around them, villagers gathered, drawn by the loud voices. Curiosity and concern were etched on their faces. Rumors of Elliot's confrontations with wolves and clashes with Mayto's men were rife. Now, as they watched, speculation mounted. Would this newcomer dare face Mayto's infamous temper? The square held its breath, waiting to see how the standoff would unfold.

Mayto's sneer deepened. "Who are you to tell me what to do?" he said. "Do you think that because you've fought some wolves, that you're my equal?"

"There's no reason for us to fight, Mayto. It solves nothing!" Elliot's response was measured, his voice steady. "And out of respect for your father, I won't beat and humiliate his son in front of the village," he added.

Before Mayto could react, a furious Bella rushed in, attempting to push him back. "Leave him alone, you bully!" she yelled. But her effort had little to no effect on him.

In a thoughtless moment of irritation, Mayto pushed Bella aside, causing her to lose her balance and fall to the ground.

"Bella!" Ava cried out, rushing to her daughter's side.

Rage surged within Elliot. He'd been able to contain himself when the hostility was aimed solely at him, but seeing Bella hurt again reignited the rage he had felt earlier. With a burst of speed, he closed the gap between him and Mayto in an instant. Elliot's hands shot forward, shoving

Mayto squarely in the chest with such force that it was as if a wrecking ball had hit him. Mayto, surprised, was sent sprawling backward, landing hard on the ground several feet away. A collective gasp rippled through the crowd.

Elliot stood firm, his voice resonant and commanding. "That's enough, Mayto! If you want to fight me so bad… you've got me!" The square fell silent, the villagers looking on with a mix of awe and apprehension.

Mayto, fueled by anger, quickly regained his footing and launched himself at Elliot. His fists, clenched tight, cut through the air with the precision of guided missiles. But Elliot, with his sharp reflexes and focused mind, effortlessly parried and dodged each strike. He moved with the grace and skill of a seasoned fighter. At the right moment, he sidestepped a particularly wild swing from Mayto, grabbed the fabric of his shirt, and used his leg to unbalance him. With a firm push, he sent Mayto crashing back to the ground, a cloud of dust billowing around him as he hit the dirt.

Undeterred, Mayto's frustration boiled over into a thunderous barrage against the ground, each strike reverberating like a miniature earthquake. He rose again, charging at Elliot with the single-minded determination of a bull in a rampage. Towering at six feet, eight inches, Mayto was a giant compared to Elliot, his broad shoulders and massive build adding to his imposing presence. But Elliot had faced giants before; his training and innate strength, amplified by the lesser gravity, made him confident that this would never be a contest to begin with. He knew Mayto's charge was more a release of pent-up frustration than of hatred for him. But if it wasn't for Elliot's deep respect for the chief, a figure both men revered, he would have done more than merely bruise Mayto's oversized ego.

As Mayto barreled towards him, Elliot deftly side-stepped, sweeping Mayto's legs out from under him and leaving him face down in the dirt for the third time. Mayto, resilient, was quick to get back up, his spirit unbroken. Elliot could not help but admire the man.

"Enough, Mayto!" Elliot said, his voice steady and controlled. "I don't want to hurt you." His anger had begun to subside, replaced by a desire to prevent the situation from escalating to a point where someone would get seriously injured. The villagers, sensing the shift in Elliot's demeanor, waited to see how Mayto would respond.

"You'll need to do a lot more than that to hurt me!" Mayto bellowed, before launching himself at Elliot once more, his charge fueled by pride and anger.

Elliot frowned; they were at an impasse. Mayto, too proud to yield after just being knocked down, left Elliot with a tough choice. Reluctant to cause serious harm but ready to end this, Elliot steeled himself for the next move. If Mayto wouldn't stand down, he'd have no choice but to put him out cold. Poised, Elliot prepared for a choke hold.

Mayto charged again, his head low and eyes ablaze with anger. Elliot subtly adjusted his stance, intent on keeping his opponent guessing. But in the final split second, Mayto aborted his charge, a ruse to lure Elliot closer. Knowing Elliot would likely opt for a takedown, Mayto had laid a trap. Elliot had just initiated his countermove when he realized he'd been tricked, leaving him vulnerable for a fraction of a second.

Seizing the opportunity, Mayto aimed a crushing blow at Elliot's head. Caught off guard, Elliot had just enough time to roll with the punch, diffusing some of its power. Yet, even the dampened force was enough to send him sprawling towards the ground.

Wasting no time, Mayto advanced towards Elliot, looking to seize the advantage. Anticipating the move, Elliot kicked out, sweeping Mayto's legs out from under him as he closed in. As Mayto crashed down beside him, he swiftly aimed an elbow strike at Elliot's head. Foreseeing the attack, Elliot rolled away just in time.

In an instant, both men were up, surrounded by a cloud of dust. Fists raised, eyes locked, they stood ready to continue their confrontation. The electric tension in the square, however, was abruptly broken by the chief's commanding entrance. His strong, clear voice boomed through the silence. "Enough!"

As the chief strode into the square's center, a hush fell over the crowd. Matching Mayto in size, his presence was formidable, especially with his temper flaring. The crowd parted like the sea, opening a clear path for him to the two men. "This ends now!" he declared, voice firm. "We face greater threats than these petty squabbles."

Mayto, still bristling with anger, looked ready to challenge the command, but a single stern look from the chief shut down any objections. Instead, he took several deep breaths, visibly trying to calm the storm within him.

Elliot, too, relaxed his stance, allowing the tension to drain from his body. The strike of Mayto's last punch had been a close call. Though he was not injured, he was relieved not to have absorbed its full impact.

"Mayto, go to my house and wait for me there," the chief said, his voice now softer but still carrying an undercurrent of seriousness. "We have much to talk about." Mayto stood frozen for a moment, wrestling with his pride. "NOW!" the chief commanded, his voice rising with authority once more.

Mayto hesitated for just a second longer before pulling away, his face a mask of wounded pride. Without another word, he turned and began to make his way towards his father's home.

The chief turned to the onlookers. "I think it's time everyone heads home," he said, his words falling between a command and a request. Gradually, the crowd began to disperse, heading towards their homes, buzzing with excitement to share news of the fight they had just witnessed.

As the villagers began to leave, Elliot turned to Bella. She was a little shaken but appeared to be okay.

"You okay, Bella?" Elliot asked.

"Yeah, I'm fine. It's not the worst fall I've ever had," she said with a little shrug. "What about you?" she asked, pointing to the mark that was beginning to show on his face.

"I'm fine, too," he said. "It's not the worst hit I've ever had!" He gave her a reassuring smile and then put an arm around her shoulder.

Ava, standing on Bella's other side, leaned in towards Elliot. Her voice was soft, but the gratitude in it was unmistakable. "Thank you," she whispered.

Elliot watched as the chief made his way back to his home. He pondered how the forthcoming conversation with Mayto would unfold. There was no denying the anger boiling within Mayto; Elliot couldn't help but wonder if he would ever learn to harness it as effectively as the chief had. One thing was certain: he was grateful Mayto hadn't been born on Earth. Had he been, that punch would have been lethal.

As they headed back to Ava's house, Elliot's thoughts drifted back to the chief's earlier words. If Elliot's story about Earth was true, then what did he expect the chief to do? He still didn't have an answer. But that was primarily because he didn't yet understand the true crux of the matter: if all he had said was indeed true, why were the gods being deceitful? He hoped tomorrow would shed some light on that unsettling question.

CHAPTER 43

IN THE WARM CONFINES of Ava's home, the day's events hung heavily in the air. Ava, Bella, and Elliot, each lost in their own thoughts, sat together in quiet solidarity. Ava's heart was filled with gratitude for Elliot's bravery, but her mind was clouded with worry for Bella. Her daughter had been through a harrowing ordeal, and Ava was acutely aware of the potential long-term impact such trauma could have on her young mind.

Bella seemed somewhat detached, her gaze often distant as she processed the day's events. However, whenever her eyes met Elliot's, a flicker of gratitude shone through her quiet disposition.

As they sat around the fire pit in Ava's home, the atmosphere was thick with the residue of the day's events. The conversation inevitably circled back to the most distressing aspect of their ordeal: both Ava and Bella had been targeted by men with dark, threatening intentions. The gravity of this reality hung over them, a shadow that touched each of their stories. Ava, who had been rendered unconscious by a sudden blast, and Bella, who had faced a traumatic situation while tied to a tree, both had narrowly escaped a fate too grim to fully comprehend.

As they recounted their experiences, a tangible atmosphere of fear, relief, and resilience permeated the air. Bella, young but remarkably brave, listened and contributed, displaying wisdom beyond her years. Elliot, pivotal in their rescue, shared his perspective and actions, though his modesty belied the significance of his role.

It was a conversation marked by cautious words and shared reflections, a first step towards understanding and healing. One Ava knew would not be the last.

As evening deepened, their talk naturally shifted to the next day's plans. Bella, though visibly disappointed at not being able to accompany them to the surface, brightened a little at Elliot's promise to document their journey with his phone. Ava reassured her that she would be in good hands with the chief and could spend time with her friends.

As yawns began to punctuate their conversations, feeling worn out from the day's emotional and physical strains, Bella decided it was time for her to go to bed. Rising, she shared a warm embrace with her mother and Elliot, lingering a bit longer than usual to soak in their comforting presence. Whispering a soft goodnight, she retreated to her room, leaving Ava and Elliot in silent contemplation, quietly anticipating the adventure that the next morning would bring.

In the hushed atmosphere following Bella's departure, Ava's voice gently pierced the stillness. "She adores you, you know."

"I'm pretty fond of her too," Elliot responded with a gentle smile.

"Do you think she'll be okay while we're gone?" Ava asked, her concern evident.

"Yeah, I believe so," Elliot reassured her. "A day with her friends, just being a kid, might be exactly what she needs after today. It would be a lot for anyone. Especially someone so young."

Ava nodded, her gaze drifting as she pondered the day's events. "Do you think they'll buy the bear story?" she finally asked.

Elliot considered her question for a moment. "I think so. Savage-Heart made a mess of that second guy. It's not the kind of damage a human would typically inflict," he explained. "Plus, these 'gods' seemed pretty arrogant."

"How so?" Ava asked, intrigued.

"Well, when they ran into Savage-Heart today, they didn't seem afraid," Elliot recalled. "In fact, they seemed confident and went straight on the attack," he added. "And later, the man who took Bella, when he saw me coming, he just smiled at me like I was nothing. They're confident to the point of arrogance, and I think that will fall in our favor. I think they'll take one look at that scene and think it ridiculous that the Lunari could, or even would, do something like that."

Ava nodded, finding sense in his logic. "Yeah, you could be right. Let's hope so," she said.

A comfortable silence settled between them, occasionally broken by their eyes meeting. Each time, Ava would quickly look away, a subtle dance of glances revealing the unspoken thoughts and emotions they were both navigating. The weight of the day's events hung between them, a shared experience that had drawn them closer yet left so much unsaid.

Elliot finally broke the silence. "How are you feeling after today, Ava?" he asked. "We've been so focused on Bella, but it was a lot for you as well."

Ava's eyes filled with unshed tears. "I don't know," she admitted softly. "Does that sound silly?"

"No, it's not silly at all," Elliot reassured her, moving closer and gently taking her hands. "You've been through a lot, and on top of that, you've had to worry about Bella."

Tears began to flow down Ava's cheeks, her lip trembling with the weight of her emotions. "I haven't had time to process it..." she said with a quavering voice. "I have to be strong for Bella."

Elliot reached up, tenderly cupping her face, his thumb brushing away a tear. "You don't have to be strong all the time," he said. "Not for me. And you're not alone in this. I'm here for you both, and I promise to protect you both, always."

Ava leaned in, her lips finding Elliot's in a soft, lingering kiss. When she drew back, their faces were mere inches apart. "I want you, Elliot, but after today, I feel..." Her words were gently cut off by Elliot's reassuring kiss.

As they parted, Elliot locked eyes with her. "I want you too, Ava," he echoed. "But for now, if it's okay with you, I'd like to just stay here with you until you fall asleep."

In Elliot's eyes, Ava saw a depth of love and compassion that spoke volumes, reassuring her of his sincerity and trustworthiness. "I'd like that," she whispered. Leaning in, she kissed him again, a soft seal on their shared bond.

As night deepened, the stillness of the house wrapped around them. They lay together in Elliot's bed, the external world fading into the background. Ava, exhausted from the day's emotional tumult, had slipped into a peaceful sleep, breathing evenly. Elliot, with gentle care, had covered her with his blanket for comfort. He lay beside her, his arm resting protectively around her, a silent sentinel in the night's quiet.

CHAPTER 44

A CREAKING SOUND WOKE Elliot. His eyes opened instantly and he assessed the room for danger. Instead, what he found was Bella standing in the doorway with a blanket wrapped around her.

"Can I stay here with you for a while?" she said, her voice trembling as the echoes of the nightmares still haunted her.

"Of course you can," he said, creating a space between him and Ava. "Bad dreams?" he asked as she stepped over him and laid down between them.

"Yeah, I keep dreaming I'm tied up and that man is coming for me," Bella said in almost a whisper.

Elliot gently pulled the covers up, enveloping Bella in a warm, comforting embrace. "When I was young I used to have bad dreams about my parents, and being chased by cars," he said, his voice quiet so as not to wake Ava. "My grandfather told me one day that dreams were just my mind trying to make sense of all the things I'd seen or heard. But the important thing to remember is that they're not real. They can be influenced by what happened to us before, but they have no control over what will happen to us next."

"He told me to remember that the next time I went to bed, and do you know what happened that night?" Elliot asked playfully.

"What?" Bella asked eagerly.

"I had a nightmare about getting chased by a car again." He grinned, and Bella's smile mirrored his, lighting up her face.

"So, after having the same nightmare again, I went back to my grandfather the next day," Elliot continued. "And I told him that I followed his advice, but I still had the dream about the car. He chuckled, a twinkle in his eye, and said, 'Ah, I seem to have forgotten the most important part of the trick.'"

Bella leaned in, her eyes wide with curiosity. "What's the most important part?" she asked.

"That's what I asked him," Elliot said. "Have you heard this story before?" he teased.

"No, silly! Keep going!" Bella urged, giving him a playful nudge.

"Yes, keep going!" Ava, now awake, echoed.

"Alright, alright," Elliot said, chuckling. "I asked him about the most important part. He told me, 'To chase away the bad dreams, you need to fill your mind with good ones.'"

"But how do you do that?" Bella asked.

"That's exactly what I asked him! And he said the secret was for us to take a photo together."

Bella looked puzzled. "A photo? How does that help with bad dreams?"

Elliot laughed. "You're asking exactly the same questions as I did! But I took a photo with him anyway. And believe it or not, it worked. I haven't had a bad dream since. Do you want to see the photo?" Elliot asked.

Bella and Ava nodded eagerly.

Elliot retrieved his phone, scrolling to the cherished photo he had shown them before—the one of him as a young boy with his grandfather, the snowy mountains in the background.

Bella's eyes sparkled with recognition at the photo. "I remember this one," she said. "But how does it keep the bad dreams away?"

Elliot's face lit up with a smile. "It's easier to show you than to explain. How about we take a picture together?" he asked.

"Yeah!" Bella exclaimed, her energy infectious as she sprang to her feet.

Ava reached over and turned on the fire lamp, casting a warm glow that brightened the room. "Should I take the photo for you?" she offered.

"No need," Elliot replied. "Actually, it'd be better if you joined us."

"Yeah! Come and join us, Mama," Bella said excitedly.

Elliot arranged the three of them so they were sitting close together. Handing Bella the phone, he showed her how to operate the front-facing camera. "Just make sure we're all in the frame and press the button when you're ready," he instructed.

Bella, filled with excitement, adjusted the phone. "One—two—three!" she counted, pressing the shutter button.

At the count of three, Elliot unexpectedly doused both Bella and Ava with water from cups he'd been holding behind their backs, eliciting a chorus of surprised screams from them. Their initial shock quickly transformed into bursts of laughter. In playful retaliation, Bella scooped up a handful of water, splashing it back at Elliot, their laughter crescendoing into a joyful uproar.

After a few moments of giggling and playful jostling, Elliot gestured for calm. "Let me show you something cool," he said, bringing up the photo on his phone. "It's called a Live Photo."

As they huddled around the phone, the still image of their smiling faces suddenly came alive with the motion of the water splash and their animated reactions. Bella's eyes widened in mock shock, while Ava tried, and failed, to suppress her chuckles. They replayed the video, their laughter echoing again and again, filling the room with the joy of the moment.

A curious expression crossed Bella's face. "Does the photo of you and your grandfather come to life too?" she asked.

Elliot's eyes crinkled with amusement. "Why don't you try it and see for yourself," he encouraged.

With eager fingers, Bella scrolled back to the cherished photo of a younger Elliot with his grandfather. She extended her arm so everyone could see the image, then pressed and held her finger on the screen. To their delight, the static image suddenly animated. A young Elliot could be heard counting to "three" just before his grandfather playfully dumped a mound of snow onto his head. Young Elliot's surprised scream and the clatter of the dropped phone filled the room, sending Bella and Ava into another fit of laughter.

As the echoes of their mirth eventually faded, the room was enveloped in a serene hush once more, the earlier laughter giving way to a more tranquil atmosphere. Elliot gently tucked Bella back into bed, whispering words of reassurance. "Whenever I have a bad day, I remember that photo and I know my dreams will be alright. If you start having a bad dream, just remember, I'm right here... and I might just dump another cup of water on your head," he said with a playful grin.

Bella wrapped her arms around Elliot in a grateful embrace. "Thank you, Elliot. Good night."

"Good night, Bella," he replied softly, planting a gentle kiss on her forehead before laying down beside her. Ava reached across Bella, her hand finding Elliot's, her thumb gently caressing his hand in a soothing rhythm.

From the comfort of her bed, Bella's voice drifted softly, filled with longing. "I wish we had snow."

CHAPTER 45

THE DAWN OF A new day met them with a sense of calm and renewal. Having slept soundly, free from the grip of nightmares, they rose early, greeted by the first light of morning. The packs they had meticulously prepared the night before stood by the door, their poised presence a silent testament to their readiness for the journey ahead. They gathered for a quick breakfast, sharing a quiet camaraderie before setting out for the chief's residence.

At the chief's house, they received the final pieces of their expedition gear. The chief handed Elliot the climbing axes, their custom-made design tailored to his exact specifications. He then briefed them on Savage-Heart's recent movements, noting her path towards the Forbidden Mountain. With a reassuring nod, he promised to keep her occupied until sunset, ensuring their safe passage.

The moment to part ways arrived all too quickly. The chief offered his blessings for a safe journey and conveyed his hopes for Elliot to find his friend in good health. In turn, Elliot reaffirmed his vow to safeguard Ava throughout their expedition.

Ava's goodbye to Bella was tinged with a mother's concern. She studied her daughter, searching for any sign of distress hidden behind Bella's cheerful demeanor. The chief, noticing Ava's concern, offered comforting words. "I'll take care of Bella as if she were my own grandchild," he assured her, giving Bella an encouraging wink.

Comforted by the chief's words, Ava wrapped Bella in a final loving embrace. Elliot, moved by a growing bond with Bella, joined the embrace with a warm, protective hug. As they turned to leave, Bella's voice rang out. "Don't forget my pictures!"

Elliot grinned. "Keep your head dry until I return!" he called back, his hand raised in a parting gesture.

Bella watched them go, a beaming smile on her face. She stood there until their figures blended into the southern path leading out of the village.

Their first goal of the day was clear: to reach the shelter where Elliot had spent his first night. They made good time, reaching it within an hour without stopping for rest.

Once they arrived, Ava was the last to enter, securing the hatch behind them. Inside, everything was just as they had left it. Elliot wasted no time and began suiting up, his movements practiced and efficient. He paused only when it came to donning his helmet, taking a moment to reflect whilst he sat by the fire pit. Momentarily, he got lost in memories of his first night here, bound to a makeshift stretcher. A faint smile touched his lips as he thought about how much had changed since then.

He methodically attached the CDU to his arm and ran a quick diagnostic on his suit. The display indicated everything was in optimal condition: the air supply was abundant, and the power level was nearly at full capacity.

Ava joined him by the fire pit, handing him a drink before sitting down beside him. "So, what's our plan for getting through the caves?" she asked.

"I thought we'd head straight up to the den," Elliot said. "We'll make our way through the cave to the airlock. It'll be dark, so I'll go in front and use my head torch. Just a heads-up, though—there are a lot of bones scattered on the ground up there."

"I'll be alright, I've been in dens before," Ava said confidently.

"That's good," Elliot said. "Once we get to the airlock, the gravity shift might feel a bit like butterflies in your stomach," he continued. "And it'll make moving around more challenging for you, almost twice as hard as usual. If it gets too much, we can always head back, okay?"

Ava nodded, absorbing the information. "And in there, will you lose your superpowers?" she asked, a smile playing across her lips.

He chuckled. "A little. Earth's gravity is about three times Lunar's, but in the airlock, it's only twice as much. So, I'll still be stronger than an average person."

"That's hardly fair!" Ava said.

Elliot shrugged. "It's one of the perks of growing up on Earth," he teased.

"Okay, so it's going to be difficult for me whilst we're inside."

"Yes, but once we're outside again, it will be much easier," Elliot said. "You'll have superpowers then!"

"Yes!" Ava said, giving a little fist pump. "So tell me what I've got to go through before I get them," she asked.

"After we exit the first airlock, there's a short corridor leading to a lift. We'll take that up. Then there's another corridor ending with the airlock to the outside. Pretty straightforward really," Elliot said.

Ava's brow furrowed. "Didn't you say you came down a big hole with a ladder?"

"I did," Elliot confirmed. "But I'm hoping this will make it easier," he said, retrieving a long, wrapped object from his pack.

Curiosity piqued, Ava leaned in. "What's that?" As Elliot unwrapped it, a foul odor wafted through the air, causing Ava to recoil. "What on Lunar is that?" she exclaimed, staring at the gruesome sight of a severed arm still clad in a white suit sleeve.

Her reaction was a mix of horror and disbelief. "Oh my god, that's disgusting! Why do you have that?"

Elliot responded with a sly, almost mischievous smile. "I thought we might need it."

"Why would you need a dead man's arm?" Ava asked, still reeling from the smell.

"It's not the arm I need," Elliot said. "But this." He carefully removed the CDU from the forearm, then promptly rewrapped the limb and stowed it back in his pack.

Ava cautiously tested the air for the lingering stench before asking, "What are you planning to do with that?"

"I noticed those Blue Stripes used this to access the Forbidden Mountain," he said. "I'm hoping it works on all their doors and—"

"The lift!" Ava interjected, her eyes lighting up with realization.

"Exactly," Elliot confirmed with a nod. "I planned to leave the arm in the den to avoid it being discovered."

"Probably a good idea," Ava agreed, still clearly disgusted by the sight of the severed arm. "I can't believe you've been carrying that around all this time."

Elliot gave a half smile. "There hasn't exactly been an opportune moment to bring it out until now."

"No, I guess not," Ava said with a slight grimace.

After finishing their drinks, Ava and Elliot redirected their focus to the task ahead. They thoroughly examined their packs, double-checking each item to ensure they were fully prepared for the next stage of their demanding journey. Looming before them was not just a physical climb but also the challenge of navigating through the dark, mysterious cave.

The ascent up the Great Falls was a daunting two hundred feet. The path, mercifully, was made more manageable by the series of steps carved into the mountain's face. Nevertheless, the climb demanded their strength and endurance. The steep incline tested their resolve, each step a deliberate effort against gravity.

Twice they stopped, allowing their tired muscles a moment of respite, Ava's breaths heavy and labored. These brief pauses also gave them a chance to appreciate the rugged beauty of their surroundings, a fleeting distraction from the task at hand.

Finally, with a mix of relief and accomplishment, they reached the archway crowning the mountain's summit. Standing at the top, they took a moment to catch their breath, their eyes adjusting to the new perspective of the landscape stretching below them.

Elliot paused to take in the sweeping view of Lunar, reminiscent of his first awe-inspiring day within the Moon. Though it had been only a few days, it felt like a lifetime had passed. Ava joined him, sharing in the moment of contemplation.

Looking out over the expanse before them, Ava couldn't help but express her amazement. "Wow," she remarked, absorbing the panoramic view of Lunar. "I don't think I've ever seen my home quite like this."

"It's breathtaking, isn't it?" Elliot said, nodding in agreement. "I felt the same way when I first saw it."

He then pointed down the steps they had climbed, recalling his first encounter on Lunar. "Right down there was where I met Savage-Heart. A bear on the Moon was the last thing I expected!"

Ava laughed, her gaze drifting towards the distant river. "And over there is where Bella and I watched you, shouting at the bear like a madman."

Their laughter subsided as Elliot remembered Bella. Pulling out his phone, he said, "Let's take some photos for her."

They captured the stunning view of Lunar, with the Great Falls providing a majestic backdrop. After securing a few good shots, Elliot put his phone away, giving the waterfall one last lingering look.

"Hard to believe you jumped from that height, huh?" Ava remarked.

Elliot shook his head. "Hard to believe I survived it, more like," he said.

Turning on his head torch and facing the cavernous entrance, Elliot asked, "Ready to head in?"

"As ready as I'll ever be," Ava replied, resolute and determined.

Together, they stepped through the archway, embarking on the next leg of their journey, their path illuminated by the faint beam of Elliot's torch as they ventured into the cave's enveloping darkness.

Chapter 46

Their descent into the cave deepened, the path twisting and turning, drawing them further into a realm of profound darkness. The faint beam of Elliot's torch was their sole guide, cutting through the blackness that enveloped them. After a short distance, the cave's curves obscured any hint of daylight, cloaking them in an otherworldly silence.

Ava's eyes widened as they came upon a waterfall cascading across their path, its waters glinting in the torchlight. "What now?" she asked, her voice tinged with awe, echoing off the cavern walls.

"The path continues through the water into a chamber beyond," Elliot explained. "Stay to the left when you pass through, there's a dangerous drop on the right. Wait a moment, I have an idea."

Elliot cautiously approached the waterfall with his helmet securely fastened. He probed the ground on the other side with careful steps, ensuring it was secure for their passage. Elliot then maneuvered himself strategically, using his body to divert the water and forge a makeshift protective corridor. He gestured to Ava, indicating she should quickly pass under the water.

Elliot watched as Ava passed safely under the makeshift archway to the other side, before he too crossed through, removing his helmet as he entered the chamber.

"Sorry, I should've warned you about getting wet!" Elliot said, noticing Ava's damp clothes.

"It's freezing!" Ava replied, shivering slightly from the chill of the water. "I'll be alright," she added, pulling out a small blanket from her pack to dry off.

While she dabbed at her clothes, Ava's attention shifted to the chamber around them. Initially, she was captivated by the play of light on the walls and ceiling, creating a mesmerizing spectacle. However, as she looked around, she realized the source of the light show: a breathtaking waterfall, cascading majestically down one side of the chamber, its waters creating a symphony of sound and light.

Ava stood transfixed, her voice a whisper of wonder. "Wow, this place is incredible. I think it's the only spot on Lunar I haven't seen," she marveled.

Noticing her awe, Elliot handed her his phone with a warm smile. Ava, her eyes still wide with admiration, eagerly captured the waterfall's magnificence and the serene stone basin beneath it.

"This is where Savage-Heart attacked me," Elliot remarked, his tone turning solemn. "She left me over there, thinking I was dead, right before that final chase and my leap through the waterfall." He gestured towards the roaring water.

"I can't even begin to imagine how terrifying that must have been for you," she said, her hand gently brushing his forearm.

Elliot shook his head, a faint smile on his lips. "Not the best memory I have of Lunar," he said. "But we should keep moving. There's still a lot to explore. Hold on to the camera. You might find more worth capturing."

They made their way to the far end of the chamber, entering the area known as Savage-Heart's den. The space shrank, heavy with an overpowering smell. Elliot swiftly disposed of the severed arm among the den's scattered remains. Behind him, Ava snapped a quick photo of the den from the doorway, then hurried to catch up.

"Watch your step," Elliot warned as they ventured further, his torchlight illuminating the skeletal remains scattered on the ground. "The airlock isn't much further ahead from here."

Guided by his previous experience, Elliot led them with confidence through the twisting passageway. Soon, they reached the airlock door, its once-concealing ferns now tattered and sparse, Elliot's previous exit having left its mark.

Locating the hidden lever on the right, Elliot initiated the door's opening mechanism. The familiar clanking sound resonated through the air as the massive door slowly ascended, unveiling the entrance to the airlock. Ava, her attention unwavering, captured each moment with the camera, documenting their journey into the unknown.

Stepping into the airlock, Elliot vividly remembered his clumsy fall during his exit; a smile creased his lips. Once they were both inside, he pulled the lever, sealing them within the dimly lit chamber.

"What happens next?" Ava asked, her voice tinged with anticipation.

"We're about to experience a gravity shift," Elliot responded. "It might feel a bit odd. You ready?"

Ava moved to stand beside him at the inner airlock door, gripping his arm firmly. "Ready!" she said.

"Here we go!" Elliot announced, initiating the door-opening sequence.

Air hissed from the ceiling vents as the gravity within the airlock intensified. Ava felt a sudden heavy sensation pulling her downwards. "Whoa," she exclaimed, tightening her grip on Elliot. "That felt so strange!"

"You okay?" Elliot asked.

"I'm okay," Ava reassured him, though her voice betrayed a hint of discomfort. She watched in anticipation as the massive door before them slowly ascended, unveiling the dark, foreboding corridor that lay ahead. "I feel so heavy!" she said. "Like I'm carrying a weight on my back."

Elliot checked his CDU. The gravity had indeed shifted; they were now experiencing two-thirds of Earth's gravitational force, but their oxygen levels were still stable.

"Are you ready to try walking?" Elliot asked. "It'll feel much harder now."

Ava's response to the gravity change was a cautious step forward. She paused, feeling the increased weight, then looked back at Elliot. "I think I can manage, but let's take it slow."

Elliot nodded, pointing to the corridor. "The lights will come on as soon as we enter," he said. "Our first stop is those doors up there. I want to see if we can get through them before we head up top."

The moment Elliot stepped forward, the corridor responded, springing to life with a gentle, ambient illumination. The soft light cast an ethereal glow on the walls, creating an almost-otherworldly ambiance. Ava, entranced by the scene, paused to capture the moment with Elliot's phone. "Go ahead, I'll catch up," she said.

As she lingered by the airlock, she called out, "Should I close this?"

Elliot's laughter echoed down the corridor. "Yes, please. I have a bad habit of leaving those open. Just lift that panel and pull the lever inside downwards."

Ava followed the instructions, observing the door as it slid down and locked securely. She began navigating the corridor, leaning on the wall for support. But the overwhelming gravity soon took its toll. After a few steps, she stumbled, her knee striking the ground with a resounding thud.

Hearing the noise, Elliot quickly retraced his steps back to her. "Are you okay?" he asked, extending a hand to help her up.

Dusting herself off, Ava nodded, slightly embarrassed. "Yeah, it's just a bit tougher than I expected."

Elliot crouched in front of her. A solution in mind. "Here, climb on my back. It'll be easier."

With Ava securely on his back, Elliot rose with remarkable ease and set off, effortlessly carrying Ava down the corridor.

"How do you do that so easily?" Ava asked, amazed by his strength.

"Years of practice," Elliot replied with a grin.

Halting midway down the corridor, Elliot gazed at the doors lining the passageway. "Last time I was here, I couldn't get any of these open. I'm hoping the CDU in my pocket will make a difference this time."

Ava, balancing herself on Elliot's back, reached into his pocket and retrieved the CDU. "Got it!"

"Good, now try it on that panel to the left," Elliot suggested, nodding his head in that direction.

Ava extended the device towards the panel, and to their delight, the door slid open, disappearing into the wall. As it opened, a light flickered on, illuminating the interior with the same ambient glow as the corridor.

"I can't believe that actually worked!" Elliot remarked, his surprise evident.

He ventured into the room, and a chuckle escaped him. "It's a restroom!"

Ava looked puzzled. "Why's that amusing?"

"It's not really," Elliot explained, shaking his head. "I spent ages trying to access these rooms, curious about their contents. And now, the first one I open is... a toilet. Ironically, I was desperate earlier and used the cave outside the airlock."

Ava raised an eyebrow. "Should we try the next door?" she asked. "They can't all be restrooms, right?"

Elliot grinned. "I certainly hope not. That would be so disappointing!"

Upon leaving the restroom, Ava and Elliot made their way across the corridor. Ava used the CDU on the panel, and, as before, the door opened with a smooth glide, revealing a well-lit interior. However, unlike the subsequent laughter that followed their earlier discovery, this time their entry was met with an eerie silence. Before them stood an array of figures clad in white suits with blue stripes, motionless and imposing.

273

CHAPTER 47

THE ROOM THEY ENTERED was squarely proportioned, each side measuring approximately ten meters. It was lined with storage racks that bore a striking resemblance to professional sports team lockers, each seemingly designed for individual use.

Intrigued, Elliot moved towards the nearest rack, placing Ava down on a bench opposite it. The centerpiece of each station was a white suit marked with a distinctive blue stripe down each side. A full-face helmet with a narrow visor hung above, and white boots were neatly positioned in a compartment below. To the left of the suit, a large black shock stick spanned the rest of the rack.

Elliot's gaze swept across the room, noting there were approximately thirty such stations in total. "This appears to be an equipment room," he remarked. "I wonder if these suits are still operational."

"Why wouldn't they be?" Ava queried, running her fingers over the fabric of a suit.

"Well, because they may have been here for a long time," Elliot replied. "I suspect these 'gods' no longer use this entry into Lunar. The airlock I found was buried and covered in layers of dust. And the one we just came through was overgrown with ferns on my first visit."

"That does make sense," Ava agreed. "And it explains why Savage-Heart chose this place for her den. It's unlikely she would have settled so close if there were regular visitors."

Intrigued by the equipment, Elliot picked up a shock stick and cautiously set it to its lowest setting. Pointing it at the ground, he pressed the trigger. A soft *THWUMP* sound resonated through the room. "Looks like it's still working to me," he commented, placing the stick back in its slot. Turning to Ava, he suggested, "Why don't you try one of those suits on?"

"Why would I do that?" Ava replied, regarding the suit with disgust.

"Because I think they're space suits," Elliot explained, his tone encouraging. "If they still work, you could use one for our trip to the surface." He selected a suit and held it out to her. "Don't worry, I'm planning to try one out as well."

Elliot swiftly took off his current suit, eager to examine the new one. He scrutinized the CDU of the white suit, ensuring its power levels were optimal. Practicing helmet attachment and detachment on a spare suit, he got the hang of its mechanics quickly. Once confident, he turned to help Ava into hers.

The process was surprisingly straightforward. Like Elliot's, the suit was initially loose, but once the helmet was connected, it conformed snugly to Ava's figure. The helmet clicked into place with a simple twist, securing a tight fit.

Ava, now fully encased in the space suit, stood in front of Elliot. With a touch of flair, she executed a playful twirl, showcasing her new look. "What do you think?" she asked through the helmet, her voice synthetic.

Elliot chuckled at her theatrics. "You manage to be both intimidating and mesmerizing in equal measure," he teased. "Especially with that voice."

Entering into the playful spirit, Ava picked up a shock stick, pointing it at Elliot in jest. "Don't get any ideas, mere mortal!" she bantered.

Elliot raised his hands in mock surrender, playing along. "Terrifying. Absolutely terrifying," he said, his eyes sparkling with amusement.

"Good! Now kneel before your goddess," Ava continued, her tone playful yet commanding.

Elliot obliged, kneeling with dramatic flair. "And suddenly, I find the attraction returns!" he declared, his grin irrepressible, the playfulness in his voice causing them both to chuckle.

Ava's laughter, tinged with the electronic timbre of the helmet's modulator, echoed through the room. She lowered the shock stick, her stance easing into a more relaxed posture. "Wearing this feels weird," she confessed, her voice still carrying the remnants of her amusement.

"Everything okay? Breathing and temperature comfortable?" Elliot asked, concern lacing his voice.

Ava nodded. "Yeah, all good. It just feels weird to be wearing this," she said. "Your turn now," she added. "We need to get moving again."

Slipping into one of the white suits, Elliot immediately noticed its superior comfort compared to his own. As he adjusted the fit, he couldn't help but recall how his suit had withstood Savage-Heart's brutal attack, a testament to its durability. In contrast, he remembered the condition of these blue-striped suits after a similar encounter. Despite this, he recognized that for the task at hand, the sleek design and functionality of these suits would be more than adequate.

"I'll need a moment to familiarize myself with their CDU. I want to ensure we're safe when we're outside," Elliot remarked.

While Elliot acquainted himself with the suit's controls, Ava took the opportunity to explore the room with the camera. She captured images of the equipment room, Elliot in his new suit, and the corridor outside. After a few minutes, Elliot signaled he was ready.

"Right, I think I've got the basics down, but the language here is unfamiliar," Elliot said. "Which further supports that these 'gods' might not be from Earth."

Ava's eyebrows raised. "But you said they looked human," she said.

"Yes, they do," Elliot acknowledged. "But now I'm considering the possibility that they might have originated elsewhere."

"Are you implying there could be humans from other planets?"

Elliot shrugged. "It's a leap, I know, but consider this: humanity's origins had to start somewhere. What if humanity, or beings very similar to us, were seeded across various worlds?"

Ava considered this, her gaze distant. "So, you think these 'gods' might have had a hand in our existence after all?"

Elliot paused, weighing his words. "Possibly. Or they might just have evolved independently on another planet, advancing technologically far beyond us. The universe is enormous, and there's so much we don't understand about it."

"What else can you tell from that device?" Ava asked, pointing to the CDU.

Elliot refocused on the display. "These suits are far more advanced than I initially thought," he said. "They have self-contained oxygen and power systems, similar to mine, but the specifics of how that works are beyond my current understanding. However, it's clear they're both fully operational." He pointed to a full power indicator on Ava's CDU.

"Check this out," he said, pointing excitedly to a specific setting on the CDU screen.

Ava leaned in closer. "What's that?" she asked, her curiosity evident.

"It's a gravity-assist function," Elliot revealed excitedly. "It looks like it can modify the suit's response to external gravity, easing movement."

Ava's brow furrowed. "I'm not sure I understand."

"Try jumping," Elliot suggested, eager to demonstrate.

Obligingly, Ava leaped, reaching a respectable height. Elliot then adjusted a setting on her CDU. "Now, jump again."

This time, when Ava attempted to jump, she struggled to get off the ground. "I didn't even realize it was helping me before!" she remarked.

"That's what I thought," Elliot said, his suspicions confirmed. "When you did that spin earlier, you seemed too agile for the gravity here." He reactivated the gravity assist on Ava's suit. "With the assist on, the suit offsets the external gravity, making you feel lighter, stronger. It's calibrated for Lunar's gravity, I presume."

Ava gave a playful smile. "Guess I won't be getting any more piggyback rides from you then?"

Elliot chuckled. "Only if you ask nicely!" he replied with a teasing smile.

With her curiosity still evident, Ava asked, "So, what does the gravity assist do for you then?"

"If I activate it on my suit, I'd feel as strong here as I do on Lunar," he explained, adjusting the settings on his own CDU.

A moment of realization flickered across Ava's face. "That's why the gods seemed so powerful!"

"Exactly," Elliot nodded in agreement. "Their strength suggests they're adapted to a higher-gravity environment than Lunar's."

"You seem deep in thought," Ava observed. "What's on your mind?"

Elliot pondered the question. "I'm wondering why Lunar's gravity is so much lower if the gods are accustomed to something stronger, like I am," Elliot said.

"That could be intentional," Ava suggested. "Maybe they want to maintain an upper hand over us?"

Elliot nodded slowly, absorbing Ava's words. "That theory holds up," he said. "Especially if you consider they brought the Lunari from Earth, where the gravity is stronger, to Lunar, where the gravity is weaker," he mused. "That may suggest their natural gravity is stronger than Lunar's but weaker than Earth's." The implications of this thought lingered in his mind. Shifting his focus back to their immediate task, he added, "Anyway, we need to keep moving. We've been here long enough. Make sure you grab a shock stick on the way out."

"What about you?" Ava inquired.

"I've got my own from yesterday," Elliot said, pulling out the shock stick from his pack. "I'll leave my suit here for now. We can pick it up on our way back."

Ava selected a shock stick of her own, and together they did a final check of their equipment. At the doorway, Elliot used his suit's CDU to test the door mechanism. Satisfied it worked, he decided to leave the old CDU behind with his suit. With everything in order, he closed the door behind them and led the way toward the lift.

Chapter 48

Elliot swept his CDU across the lift's panel, causing the doors to part smoothly down the middle. "You can't imagine my relief at seeing these doors open," he confessed to Ava. "Without this lift, we'd be facing a daunting climb."

Ava stepped inside. "How high does this go?" she asked.

"Based on my descent, I'd guess it's at least double, if not triple, the height of the Great Falls," Elliot estimated.

Ava gave a skeptical glance at the lift's interior. "And this contraption can take us all the way up?"

Elliot chuckled. "Yeah, that's the plan!"

He moved to the far end of the lift, using his CDU on a panel beside a second set of doors. As the entrance sealed behind them, a gentle upward motion commenced, noticeable but unobtrusive.

In less than a minute, the motion halted, and the doors parted to reveal the corridor Elliot had once been desperate to escape. Stepping out, the corridor lights illuminated, revealing the distant airlock.

"That didn't feel like we just went up two or three Great Falls," Ava said.

"I know," Elliot agreed. "These lifts are not just fast, they're near-silent too."

Ava's gaze followed the corridor's length. "Is that the airlock leading outside?"

"Yeah, just two more doors between us and the outside now," Elliot confirmed. "But first, let's take a look in these rooms. We might find something useful."

As they advanced down the corridor, they slowed their pace at the first set of doors. Elliot brought his CDU to the panel, and with a gentle sigh, the door on the right silently opened, unveiling a kit room that was markedly larger than the one they had seen below. After a brief inspection where nothing caught their interest, they crossed the corridor. Elliot then activated the panel on the left, which revealed a restroom, bearing a striking resemblance to the one they had seen earlier. With a mutual glance confirming their lack of findings, they continued their journey toward the final set of doors.

Opting for the left door first, Elliot watched as it glided silently open, the interior lights flickering to life. This room was unlike any they had encountered: its walls were lined with large screens displaying the operational status of various systems. Dominating the room's center was an impressive oval-shaped table, radiating a soft glow. Hovering above the table was a holographic display, depicting a detailed map of Lunar.

Ava's eyes widened in awe as she absorbed the map's intricate topography and labeled zones. "Is this our home?" she inquired, her finger tracing the contours of the map.

Elliot, equally captivated, nodded. "It seems so," he said. "This room seems to be some sort of observation and monitoring hub," he mused, his attention drawn to the live feeds on the screens encircling the table's edge.

Walking the room, Elliot scrutinized each screen. One showcased the Moon's serene silvery landscape, while others displayed a variety of terrains and locations on Lunar's surface. However, he observed an absence of any imagery from within Lunar itself. One screen in particular captured his attention. Instead of the usual lunar vistas, it portrayed a harrowing scene: a construction site in utter disarray, its machinery strewn around as if tossed aside by a giant hand. Drawn to a specific detail, Elliot's gaze fixed on a lunar rover, overturned and abandoned.

A sharp pang of recognition struck Elliot. "That's the rover!" he said softly. "The one Franklin and I arrived in." Ava placed a reassuring hand on his arm. "If the rover's here, overturned like this... it means Franklin never made it back to the ship," he added, his voice shaky.

"I'm so sorry, Elliot," Ava said.

Elliot's eyes grew distant. "I knew it was a long shot, holding on to hope he'd make it back to the ship. Seeing this, though... it seems he would have been doomed anyway."

Puzzled, Ava inquired, "What do you mean?"

Gently guiding her gaze, Elliot motioned towards another screen. The sight that met Ava's eyes was heart-wrenching: a once-vibrant Earth now marred by a colossal dark blemish. The planet's familiar blues and greens were overshadowed by a looming dust cloud, which cast unsettling silhouettes across its surface.

Elliot's voice broke the heavy silence. "That... that's not how I remember Earth."

"It looks like it's been recently hit," Ava commented.

"The asteroid. It struck the day I got here," Elliot replied, his voice heavy with grief. "This is my first glimpse of the aftermath," he sighed. "It's what we would call an extinction-level event. No one would be expected to survive it."

A profound silence fell over the room. Elliot and Ava stood side by side, confronting the harrowing new reality of their wounded home planet.

Ava broke the silence first, her voice colored with resignation. "This confirms your suspicions, doesn't it? We can't return to Earth anytime soon."

Elliot gave a somber nod. "With an impact of that scale, Earth might be uninhabitable for years, possibly decades."

"So, what do we do now?" Ava asked, overwhelmed. "Is there any point heading to the surface still?"

"I don't see any compelling reason to," Elliot said. "Unless you still want to witness it firsthand?"

Drawing a deep breath, Ava made up her mind. "I think the evidence here is convincing enough," she said. "I'll photograph everything in this room to present to the chief."

Elliot nodded. "While you do that, I'm going to continue looking around. Make sure you capture each screen."

As Ava photographed the room's displays, Elliot returned to the screens, pondering the stark images of Lunar and Earth. Eventually, his attention was drawn to the holographic map on the table. To his astonishment, he found that the map was interactive, responding to his touch much like the photos on his phone.

Quickly becoming familiar with the interface, he started examining key locations, beginning with the village. He noted with interest that the village was absent from the map, leading him to speculate that the map was based on a preloaded design blueprint rather than real-time data.

Elliot rotated the holographic map, bringing the Forbidden Mountain into closer view while pushing the Great Falls into the background. As he delved into the map's intricate details, he discovered the ability to explore inside the mountain's structure. "Ava, come look at this," he called out.

Ava approached, her eyes widening in amazement as Elliot navigated deeper into the Forbidden Mountain, revealing the elaborate blueprints of a vast hidden base spanning three levels. The map was dotted with indecipherable symbols in each chamber, prompting Elliot to concentrate on the architectural layout.

"Make sure you get all this," Elliot urged. "It might prove useful later on."

As he navigated through each level, Elliot surmised that the second tier likely served as a residential quarter, given its series of uniformly sized rooms. But what truly captured his attention was an elongated annex on the ground floor's northwest side. Zooming out, he traced the annex's path, noting it ran parallel to Lunar and extended towards the mountains of the Great Falls.

"What do you suppose that is?" Ava inquired, peering closely.

"It might be a conduit, possibly redirecting the water back here to restart the cycle," Elliot hypothesized.

Continuing his exploration, Elliot discovered that the tunnel did indeed end within the Great Falls. Pulling the perspective further back, he realized its end point was in the corridor, opposite the very room in which they stood.

Chapter 49

Elliot paused for a moment, glancing between the digital map display and the door opposite them in the corridor. "I mean, we could just go in and see what's there," he suggested tentatively.

"It would be silly if we didn't," Ava said, playing along. "It's right in front of us."

He smiled inside his helmet. "Okay, so we'll take a look, but we need to be careful. This isn't just any room; it's directly connected to the Forbidden Mountain."

Nodding in agreement, she said, "The Forbidden Mountain is a long way from here though. Maybe four or five hours' walk. But we'll be cautious."

After leaving the observation room, they stood staring at the door in front of them. The anticipation hung heavily in the air, a weighty silence enveloping them. Finally, Ava reached out, presenting her CDU to the panel. The door slid open silently, revealing an expansive room bathed in a dim blue glow. The hum of machinery echoed throughout.

They cautiously stepped inside, their eyes immediately drawn to a vast pump system. Powerful pistons churned in rhythm, connected to an intricate network of pipes and tanks. It seemed water was drawn from below, then propelled towards the Great Falls, presumably restarting the cycle.

Realizing the enormity of the system before her, Ava's eyes widened. "It's like the heart of the mountain," she said quietly.

Elliot nodded, marveling at the engineering feat. "This must be a pump room, responsible for returning water to the Great Falls."

She took out her phone and snapped pictures of the impressive pump system. A doorway at the room's far end caught her eye. Approaching it, she realized it led to the tunnel depicted on the holographic map. Peering inside, she noticed twin metal tracks stretching into the darkness below. At the tunnel's mouth, a shuttle hovered just above the rails, its sleek design hinting at the remarkable speed it might be able to achieve.

"Elliot, come take a look at this," she beckoned. "This track—it must lead to the Forbidden Mountain... I think we should go take a look!" she said, turning to face him.

"The Forbidden Mountain? Ava, that will be dangerous. We have no idea what we might find there," Elliot said.

"And we never will unless we go," she replied defiantly. "Something's going on there and we're not going to find out unless we take a risk. Why would they claim we're returning to Earth when... well, you saw for yourself! I need to do this, Elliot. I can't protect my daughter if I do nothing."

"You're right, we do need answers," Elliot said gently. "But the risk of being caught... I might not be able to protect you." A contemplative look crossed his face. "Maybe it's safer if I go alone," he added.

"You're not leaving me behind," she replied firmly. "The chief needs to hear it from me too." Elliot paused, considering her words. Seizing the moment, Ava pushed on. "Plus, in these suits, we'd blend right in." She stretched her arms out, showcasing her outfit.

Elliot sighed. "Alright, but we need to be extra careful. We don't know what awaits us there. If I say it's time to leave. We don't hesitate."

"Agreed," Ava replied with a nod.

"Let's leave our packs here," Elliot suggested. "We need to blend in; we shouldn't be carrying anything they wouldn't have."

"We can leave both packs here and retrieve them on our return," she agreed.

Elliot walked over to the shuttle, inspecting it for the first time. Parked at the tunnel's entrance, the shuttle was a marvel of modern engineering. Its sleek, streamlined design spoke of efficiency, designed to cut through air with minimal resistance. The exterior was a smooth, polished metal, reflecting the dim light of the tunnel.

Upon closer investigation, they realized it had the capacity to carry eight passengers. The interior featured four rows of two plush, ergonomic seats, each with a personal display and control panel. A narrow aisle ran between the rows, facilitating movement.

The shuttle hovered a few inches above the metal track, a gentle hum betraying the presence of powerful electromagnets beneath.

Climbing aboard, he scrutinized the controls. "Looks like it's automated with just this one button," he observed.

Ava settled into the seat next to Elliot. "Only one way to find out," she encouraged, nodding towards the control panel.

After a moment's hesitation, Elliot pressed the button, only to find that nothing happened. Ava gave a light chuckle. "Well, that was anticlimactic!" she remarked. "Why don't you try your CDU on the panel?" She gestured towards a small console to the left of the button, where a panel sat, almost invitingly, ready for interaction.

Taking her advice, Elliot placed his CDU over the indicated panel. Instantly, the shuttle's front lights flickered on, projecting a beam down the tunnel.

"That did it," Elliot stated, before turning towards Ava. "Last chance to back out," he said.

Ava leaned forward and pressed the button without hesitation. The shuttle commenced its journey, smoothly pulling away from the station. The displays flickered to life, adorned with strange symbols, possibly indicating speed. A progress bar at the bottom of one screen indicated the distance they had covered and the remaining journey.

As the shuttle accelerated, tunnel lights blurred past them, creating an illusion akin to a starry sky in fast-forward. For Elliot, the ride was an unprecedented experience—seamlessly smooth yet almost surreal. Despite the tranquility of their travel, his mind was a whirlwind of thoughts, preoccupied with what might await them at their destination.

Throughout the journey, Ava, ever the avid documentarian, diligently recorded their progress with the phone, capturing the tunnel's lights, the display screens, and the sensation of their rapid descent—she wanted to capture it all.

The progress bar on the display inched steadily towards completion, mirroring the escalating tension that filled the shuttle. Elliot glanced at Ava. She had put away her camera, her hands subtly betraying her anxiety. In a wordless gesture of support, Elliot reached out, their fingers intertwining in a comforting, reassuring grip.

Doubts began to surface in Elliot's mind. Was embarking on this journey truly a wise decision? What would they find at the end of the track? He shook off the uncertainty, steeling himself for what lay ahead, and readied for the unknown.

The rhythmic hum of the shuttle and the blur of lights outside mirrored their deep, contemplative thoughts. As the progress bar edged to completion, the shuttle began its descent. It leveled off, slowing its pace, smoothly transitioning into a gentle glide, readying for their imminent arrival.

CHAPTER 50

ELLIOT AND AVA STEPPED out of the shuttle, their boots landing with a soft thud on the hard floor of the underground station. As they distanced themselves from the track, the shuttle doors slid shut behind them. Almost instantly, the engines hummed back to life, and the shuttle began its journey back to the Great Falls, operating autonomously without waiting for any passengers or commands.

They watched the shuttle ascend, its mechanical hum fading into a peaceful silence. "Why would it return on its own?" Ava asked.

"Maybe it's programmed to head back, ensuring there's always a shuttle at each end," Elliot speculated.

Ava considered this and then shifted her focus back to the station. She motioned towards a door. "Shall we find out what's inside?"

Crossing the threshold, Elliot and Ava encountered a scene strikingly similar to the one they had left above: another pump room. This one, while almost a mirror image of the first, was bathed in dimmer lighting, casting elongated shadows across the machinery. The rhythmic motion of pistons and the elaborate network of pipes were familiar, yet here, the water flowed in the opposite direction.

Elliot surveyed the room. "The purpose of this room seems to be to pump the water upwards, which makes sense given the steep incline to the Great Falls."

"Makes sense," Ava agreed, her voice blending with the steady hum of the machinery. As they continued their exploration of the second pump room, Ava's gaze fell on an exit. "The map showed only one way forward from here, didn't it?"

Elliot paused, recalling the base's layout. "Yes, we should turn right. To the left is what looked like a lift," he said. "If we go right, we'll be on a corridor leading to a larger area filled with multiple rooms on the left. Staying on the corridor will take us to the airlock that exits the Forbidden Mountain, the one we saw yesterday."

"Then let's head for the larger area on the left," Ava suggested. "We'll more easily blend in there. With these suits, it shouldn't be too hard to appear as if we belong," she added, adjusting her suit. "But, what's our plan if someone approaches us?"

"I'll do the talking unless they speak to you directly," Elliot said. "We haven't encountered any female guards as far as we know, and even though your synthetic voice matches the others, it's best to be cautious."

"Understood," Ava said. "Let's find a private spot for any necessary conversations. I'll signal you with a touch on your arm if I need to speak, and you do the same to me."

"Sounds like a plan. Are you ready?" Elliot asked.

Ava inhaled deeply, then nodded in affirmation.

They exited the pump room to find themselves in a spacious corridor. To their left was a familiar set of double doors: a lift, as they had presumed. People moved with purpose up ahead of them to the right, some in suits like theirs, adorned with blue stripes, while others wore no suits at all, revealing a sea of diverse faces. Men and women of all ethnicities, their expressions ranging from stern to weary, wearing uniforms that seemed to indicate different ranks or functions. A distant chatter could be heard coming from the end of the corridor. The words were familiar, even if they couldn't discern the conversations.

Feeling conspicuously visible, Elliot and Ava cautiously started their journey down the corridor. They had barely taken a few steps when a stern voice called out from behind them, halting them in their tracks.

"Hey, you two!"

Elliot's heart skipped a beat. Turning slowly, he prepared for confrontation. He found himself facing a man in a black uniform, his features visible, annoyance etched on his face. The man had just stepped out from the lift behind them.

"You left the door open!" he reprimanded. "You wouldn't want to get caught breaking protocol, would you? Especially not by the general!"

Reacting swiftly, Elliot stepped forward and used his CDU to close the pump room door. He then turned back just in time to see the man stride off down the corridor without another word. "Thanks," Elliot muttered.

Sharing a quick, relieved look, Elliot and Ava resumed walking, maintaining a safe distance from the man ahead as they absorbed the environment around them.

Upon reaching the corridor's junction, Elliot and Ava hesitated: left towards the main room or straight to the airlock? Choosing left, they entered an expansive mess hall buzzing with life. People chatted at tables and moved with purpose as they went about their work. The aroma of food wafted from stations to their left. Most strikingly, the right wall, starting a few feet above the ground, was transparent, offering a view of stables housing thirty to forty horses. Doors intermittently placed along this wall seemed to provide access to them.

Elliot, intrigued by the presence of the horses, wondered about their means of exit. His question found an answer when his eyes landed on a door connecting the stables to the airlock.

The far end of the hall was dominated by large screens. One displayed unsettling images of Earth's recent asteroid impact, in stark contrast to another showing live feeds of the Moon's barren surface. Amid the bustling hall, Elliot and Ava acutely felt the weight of their presence. Scanning the room, Elliot noticed how other soldiers handled their helmets: those eating had removed theirs, while others, engaged in mere conversation, kept them on. Considering this, he decided it was prudent for them to keep their helmets on, lest their unfamiliar faces stir alarm. They promptly found an unoccupied table, situating themselves among others who were deeply immersed in their discussions.

Once seated, Elliot and Ava hoped to meld with the mess hall's atmosphere. Elliot's gaze wandered across the room, taking in the diverse array of individuals. The hall was a melting pot of ethnicities and genders, all unmistakably human, yet their origins remained a mystery. The variety in uniforms and space suits around them hinted at an established hierarchy.

Elliot studied the individuals in suits similar to his, noting a specific detail: they were the only people equipped with shock sticks. This observation led him to surmise that such suits were exclusively worn by soldiers, a distinction that set them apart within the base's complex hierarchy.

Amongst the uniformed individuals, all wore black trousers and shoes. Their tops, while consistent in style, varied in color: blue, green, or black. Elliot assumed these colors indicated their specific role within the base and made a mental note to find out what those roles were.

Amidst the low hum of conversation and the occasional clink of utensils, a snippet of conversation from a nearby table caught their attention.

"Did you hear about the two men found dead outside?" a woman from the table opposite whispered.

"Lunari?" another inquired.

"No, they were soldiers," came the hushed reply. "Seems like the bear got to them. I heard an arm was torn clean off!"

"How did they get caught in the bear's path?" a third voice asked. "Someone's going to be in big trouble with the general for that. Probably their squad leader."

"They should have known better!" the second speaker added. "That bear's been showing up here every day, I hear."

"Word is she's searching for her cub."

Elliot and Ava's attention shifted, following the gaze of the group, to a large transparent enclosure near the screens at the hall's end. From their position, its contents were unclear, but they mentally bookmarked it for a closer inspection later.

Ava leaned towards Elliot, her voice a whisper. "I set the phone to record while we were on the shuttle," she murmured, subtly adjusting her suit where the concealed device was. "Let me know if it's visible."

Elliot discreetly checked Ava's suit for the hidden phone, then gave a subtle thumbs-up to confirm all was fine. Scanning the room cautiously, he whispered, "This place is bigger than we thought. Let's quietly explore and see what else we find."

As they moved away from their table, they passed along the stable wall. The movement of horses inside drew their gaze. The animals appeared well kept, yet there was a certain anxiousness in their demeanor, perhaps a reflection of their unfamiliar surroundings.

Continuing their counterclockwise journey around the room, Elliot and Ava approached what looked like the last stall. As they neared, the reason for the focused gazes earlier became clear. Inside the stall was, instead of a horse, a bear cub. It paced restlessly, its eyes reflecting a poignant blend of fear and sadness.

Their exploration next led them to the wall adorned with the large screens. Below these screens, a raised platform or stage jutted out, evidently meant for addressing those gathered. Though currently empty, it was easy to envision someone standing there, captivating the audience with their presence.

Beyond the commanding array of screens, in the room's top left corner, a separate area caught their attention. Enclosed by transparent panels, it allowed an unobstructed view inside. The occupants, all dressed in the uniform black trousers and shoes, were busy with various tasks, their tops either blue or green. The space hummed with urgency, echoed by the data flashing across screens and the intermittent beeping of equipment.

Eager to see more of what was happening inside but careful not to attract undue attention, Elliot and Ava continued on their path around the room, passing by the lively serving stations down the left side. Circling back to the entrance of the mess hall, they noticed someone step out from a door opposite them, possibly another equipment room like the one they'd seen before.

Soft murmurs and distant conversations permeated the mess hall, but it was the conversation among a group of women in green tops that captured Elliot's and Ava's attentions. "Did you hear about the prisoner the general is interrogating?" one asked.

"Yes," another replied, visibly pale. "My workstation is so close I could hear the screams. The general really scares me!"

The third woman joined in, her tone laced with apprehension. "I know, right? And with everything supposedly 'going to plan...'" She trailed off, glancing significantly toward the large screens. "You'd think he'd be in a better mood."

Exchanging a glance, Elliot's expression was pensive. What did they mean by "going to plan"? he wondered.

Returning to their table, the snippet about the prisoner lingered in their minds. "If there's a Lunari here," Ava whispered, "we need to find out who it is."

"One of those women said she works near where the prisoner is held," Elliot said. "We could follow her. Did you see where she went?"

Ava nodded discreetly towards the screens. "She's sitting over there. I think she works in that corner room. It seems to be where most of the blue and green uniformed workers go," Ava said.

"I think it's some sort of research or medical area," Elliot replied. "But before we go walking in there, we need to make sure Blue Stripes are allowed access to that area," he added cautiously.

"I saw a few soldiers enter earlier," Ava mentioned, her eyes still on the group. "But we'll need a believable story in case we're questioned."

"We could say the general sent us to check on the prisoner," Elliot proposed. "Given their fear of him, it's unlikely they'll probe further."

"But what if we run into the general himself?" Ava asked with concern.

"If that happens, we'll make a quiet exit and blend back into the crowd here," Elliot said. "With these suits on, we can effectively hide in plain sight until we find an opportunity to slip away to the shuttle."

Noticing movement, Ava leaned in closer. "They're heading towards that room now," she whispered.

"Then we should follow them," Elliot said. "But let's be quick. We shouldn't linger here any longer than necessary," he added with a hint of urgency.

"Agreed."

Elliot lifted a hand, signaling Ava to pause. "One more thing, Ava."

"Yes?"

"If it is a Lunari who's being held prisoner, we can't take them back with us," Elliot cautioned. "It would reveal our presence here and put everyone in danger."

Ava's pause was brief, but it carried the gravity of Elliot's warning. "I understand," she said somberly.

They exchanged a silent nod, then rose. Blending seamlessly with the crowd, they moved with purpose, their gazes locked on the distant room shrouded in mystery.

Chapter 51

Elliot and Ava stepped into the vast room, immediately struck by its surprising depth. It seemed to stretch almost double the length of the adjacent dining areas—a detail Elliot noticed was missing from the holographic map they had reviewed at the Great Falls. This discrepancy made him wonder about potential updates or modifications since the map's last iteration.

As they ventured further, they noticed the room was bustling with workers—both male and female—clad in blue and green uniforms, diligently engaged in various tasks. The technicians' lack of reaction to Elliot and Ava's arrival suggested that soldiers were a common sight here, blending seamlessly into the base's day-to-day activities.

Adding to the room's mystery was its extension to the left, positioned behind the dining area. The full extent of this section was not immediately discernible, suggesting any holding area, if present, wasn't visible here.

Moving to the second section on the left, they entered another similar room, with technicians bustling about. The room extended back as far as the last dining room, culminating in a solid wall with a solitary door in the middle. Elliot's mind raced with questions: why were the holding cells so close to this work environment? The close quarters of prisoners and scientists within the base struck him as unsettling. As they approached the door, Elliot braced himself for whatever lay beyond, aware that their undiscovered presence was a matter of luck that shouldn't be overstretched.

A gentle touch on his forearm from Ava broke Elliot's train of thought. He looked at her, following her subtle nod towards the right. His eyes landed on a woman in a green uniform busily working at the far end of the room. She was the same one who had spoken earlier about being near the prisoner's location; they were on the right track.

Reaching the door at the end of the room, Elliot inhaled deeply before presenting his CDU to the panel. Despite no prior access issues, he feared stricter control at the holding areas. To his relief, the door slid open as easily as the others had, unveiling a corridor lined with four rooms, two flanking each side. Elliot's eyes narrowed as he surveyed the space—the holding area, he surmised.

Each room, reminiscent of the stables, was encased in transparent glass from waist height up, granting a clear view inside. While three of the rooms were vacant, the farthest one on the right emitted a faint glow. Elliot and Ava moved cautiously, quietly shutting the door to the work area behind them and peering into the empty rooms as they passed.

As they neared the occupied room, they saw that it indeed housed a figure. A solitary individual lay under the covers on a bed, turned away towards the wall. Exchanging a quick, determined glance, they decided to enter.

They stepped into the cell and gently closed the door behind them. As they did, the figure beneath the covers stirred and turned to face them, eyes wide with terror. "What now?!" the man exclaimed.

Recognition hit Elliot like a sledgehammer. "Franklin?" he uttered, his voice tinged with disbelief.

The man on the bed stirred at hearing his name. As he sat up, his face was etched with confusion. "Who are you?" he asked, voice wavering with uncertainty. "How do you know my name?"

Elliot carefully removed his helmet, revealing his face. "It's me, Franklin. It's Elliot!" he said, his voice warm with familiarity.

Franklin's eyes locked onto Elliot, his mind racing to reconcile this unexpected reunion with the harsh reality he'd been enduring. Was this real, or just another mind game?

"It's really me, buddy," Elliot assured, his tone steady and comforting.

Ava, too, slowly removed her helmet, revealing her face to Franklin. "Hi, Franklin, I'm Ava," she said gently. "I'm a friend of Elliot's."

Franklin's appearance was a stark testament to his suffering. Scars and fresh wounds marred his skin, and his eyes, once brimming with vitality, now held a haunted, distant look. Seeing Elliot, a flicker of disbelief crossed his worn face. "Elliot... I can't believe you're here. I thought... I thought you were gone," he said, his voice breaking as tears welled up in his eyes.

"It's really me, Franklin. Tell me, what happened? How did you get here?" Elliot's voice was heavy with concern.

Taking a deep, shuddering breath, Franklin's words tumbled out. "The meteor shower," he began abruptly. "I got trapped under debris when a meteor struck near us. I fought for hours to get free." His voice broke, laden with emotion. "I searched for you, Elliot, everywhere. Then, seeing Earth... the devastation... I thought all was lost."

Elliot's eyes glistened with unshed tears as he responded softly. "I know, Franklin. I saw it, too."

Franklin's story continued, his voice a blend of sorrow and resignation. "I wandered aimlessly, holding on to the slim hope of finding you alive. Then, they captured me." He looked up at Elliot. "Were you caught too?"

Elliot shook his head. "No, I got trapped beneath the lunar surface when the meteors hit. I ended up here, but I'm still trying to understand why this place exists." He paused, searching Franklin's face. "Do you know anything about it?"

Franklin spoke with caution. "They call themselves the Telvanni. The ones wearing suits like yours. They captured me, brought me here."

"The Telvanni?" Elliot echoed, trying to grasp the new information. "So, they're extraterrestrial?"

Franklin nodded. "They're human from what I understand, just not from Earth."

Elliot's gaze fell upon Franklin's bruises. "And these Telvanni did this to you?"

Franklin's features hardened. "They call him the general," he said. "Identifiable by a gold stripe on his suit," he added, pointing to the stripes on Elliot's suit. "He takes great pleasure in inflicting pain. Not to get information. He just enjoys the cruelty."

"I believe I've seen him before in Ava's village," Elliot remarked, his tone darkening. "His viciousness left a lasting impression."

"Franklin, do you know what the Telvanni's intentions are here?" Ava pressed.

"They're behind what happened to Earth," Franklin responded mournfully.

"What?" Elliot said in shock. "But the asteroid... I saw it crash. How could they be involved?"

"They have another Moon base, somewhere within our solar system," Franklin explained. "With technology that's light-years ahead of ours. They can manipulate asteroids from the belt, directing them towards targets, armed with stealth technology that makes them near invisible to radars until it's too late. They aimed one at Earth. Fired it like a missile and waited."

Ava, stunned, managed to ask, "But why would they do that?"

"Their planet was lost long ago," Franklin replied. "They want Earth. An invasion would have been too messy, so they chose extermination, planning to claim Earth once it recovers."

Elliot felt a chill run down his spine. "How do you know all this, Franklin?"

Franklin's expression twisted. "The general... he takes pleasure in telling me, reveling in my despair. He boasts about the casualties and ongoing suffering whenever he comes here," Franklin said.

"They've been planning this for years, studying humans, mapping our DNA. They've established a human settlement here on the Moon, using them as subjects for their relentless experiments. Recently, they brought in a young girl..."

"Evelyn!" Ava interrupted. "She's the girl they took!"

Franklin nodded, his eyes filled with sorrow. "I didn't know her name. She's not been back since they took her yesterday. Their primary research facility is right next door."

Elliot's expression turned grave. "But what are they testing for?"

"They're attempting to merge our DNA with theirs, driven by a distorted ambition to create a 'superior' human race. And from what I've overheard, we are not their first human subjects."

Elliot's fists clenched in anger, his voice barely suppressing the fury inside him. "A superior race? What are these Telvanni... space Nazis?"

The tension in the room was palpable, a stark contrast to the initial relief of their reunion.

Breaking the oppressive silence, Elliot spoke with renewed determination, "We have to get you out of here!"

Ava, weighed down by sorrow, recalled Elliot's caution. "We can't, Elliot. If the Telvanni realize..." She left her sentence hanging, no need to finish.

Elliot's voice faltered, torn between the urge to rescue his friend and the broader implications. "But we can't just leave Franklin with that sadist..."

"You need to leave," Franklin said, his tone resolute, locking eyes with Elliot. "The thought of endangering others just to save me... I couldn't live with that. You need to leave me here. I insist."

Elliot's eyes glistened, his resolve strengthening. "We leave now to regroup and strategize. But this isn't over, Franklin. We'll come back for you. That's a promise."

"I know you will."

After a moment of heavy silence, Elliot nodded, his mind set and now shifting to strategy. "But before we go, tell us everything you know about this base. The number of people, soldiers, and any weapons beyond these shock sticks. Anything that can help us."

Franklin gathered his thoughts before speaking. "There are about a hundred people on this base. Roughly half are soldiers, most wearing blue-striped suits like yours. There are a few, maybe four or five, with black stripes—they seem to be leaders. And then there's the general. He's in charge." His tone grew somber. "The others are mainly researchers or operate the base. As for weapons, I've only seen those shock sticks."

Elliot nodded, his mind racing with strategies. "Where's their control room? How do they access the lunar surface?"

"The control room is on the top floor, but that's all I know," Franklin replied. "I was semiconscious when they brought me in, hit by a blast from one of those sticks," he added, motioning towards Elliot's shock stick.

Ava glanced around anxiously. "We need to get moving, Elliot. We can't afford to get caught here."

Elliot squeezed Franklin's hand firmly. "Hold on, Franklin. We'll come back for you," he promised. With heavy hearts but renewed determination, he and Ava exited the room. They left Franklin to an uncertain fate but departed with the vital knowledge they had sought.

Chapter 52

Elliot and Ava hurried back through the research and medical offices, each step laden with the weight of Franklin's harrowing revelations. Relief at finding his friend alive was tempered by the guilt of leaving Franklin behind, an image that haunted Elliot with every stride.

Upon re-entering the vast mess hall, they immediately sensed an intense tension in the air. People bustled about with a sense of urgency, their hushed conversations barely audible. Something significant was unfolding, though its nature remained elusive. With a shared understanding, they used the commotion as cover, hastening towards the safety of the pump room and, ultimately, the shuttle that lay beyond.

As they entered the corridor leading to their destination, hope seemed within reach. But their plans were abruptly interrupted. The lift doors at the end of the corridor opened, revealing the formidable presence of the general, his gold stripes starkly visible under the bright lights. A worker in a black uniform, on a direct path to the lift, instantly stepped aside, standing at attention. Quick to adapt, Elliot and Ava mirrored his posture, hoping to go unnoticed.

Their ruse seemed to work; the general passed by without so much as a glance in their direction. Just as they were about to continue on their way, however, the general's commanding voice halted them. "You two," he barked, turning to face them. A chill of dread washed over them. Without waiting for a reply, he ordered, "Come with me."

Understanding the necessity to maintain their cover, Elliot and Ava complied, following the general, who cast a brief glance over his shoulder to ensure they were following. Upon approaching the mess hall again, the airlock doors suddenly opened, revealing four soldiers: three adorned with blue stripes and one, evidently the leader, with black stripes. They appeared to be pushing two gurneys, and Elliot's heart sank as he recognized the lifeless bodies of the men from the previous day's incident.

The general quickly engaged in a conversation with the black-striped leader. Terms like "bear attack" and "arm ripped off" reached Elliot's and Ava's ears. Elliot experienced a fleeting sense of relief that his cover-up had been accepted, yet the unease of the general's insistence that they follow persisted.

As the procession began, Elliot and Ava caught bits and pieces of the conversation. They followed the group as it made its way through the mess hall, moving along the side of the room where the stables were prominently visible. The gurneys, bearing the silent testimony of the recent attack, were wheeled steadily towards a destination Elliot presumed to be the research and medical offices

Upon arriving at the section beneath the large screens, the squad leader finished recounting the grisly scene they had encountered—the bear preying upon the soldiers close to their base. The general, his expression betraying dissatisfaction, stopped them in their tracks. In a voice laden with cold authority, he addressed the squad leader. "Explain to me how this happened under your supervision," he commanded, his tone demanding an immediate explanation.

The bustle of the mess hall came to an abrupt standstill, all eyes drawn to the escalating confrontation. The general's temper was well known, and as the squad leader fumbled for words, Elliot and Ava felt the weight of the dangerous situation they had inadvertently become a part of.

The air was thick with tension, each second of the squad leader's hesitation amplifying the general's growing fury. Then, in a sudden outburst of rage, the general seized the man with both hands. Displaying a startling display of strength, he hurled the squad leader several feet away. The sound of his body crashing against the transparent wall of a stable reverberated through the hall. Inside, the horses shuffled nervously, their hooves scraping the floor, while the bear cub, sensing the aggression, emitted a low, distressed growl.

"Do you know how many Telvanni soldiers have fallen during this mission?" the general seethed, his voice low but dangerous.

The man attempted to reply, but his voice was a faint murmur, choked with fear.

"Two!" the general bellowed, gesturing towards the motionless bodies on the gurneys. "These two!"

Without allowing the squad leader to respond further, the general abruptly turned towards one of the three soldiers adorned with blue stripes. "You!" he commanded, pointing at the soldier. "You are the new squad leader. Your first task is to capture the mother bear."

The general then strode towards the cub's enclosure. With a swift decisive movement, he drew his blast stick and flung open the door, delivering a vicious shock to the cub. The sound of the impact—a sharp *THWUMP* followed by a *THUD*—filled the room as the cub cried out in agony, its body slamming against the enclosure's rear wall. Subdued gasps rippled through the mess hall, the onlookers too fearful of drawing the general's anger to react loudly, yet unable to completely hide their shock and dismay.

The general's voice, cold and synthetic, echoed through the hall as he taunted, "I'll execute her cub right before her eyes." He let the cruel words hang in the air for a moment. "And then... she'll suffer the same fate." With callous indifference, he delivered another brutal shock to the cub, then slammed the stable door shut, leaving the young animal writhing in pain.

Turning his attention to the black-striped squad leader, now barely conscious on the floor, the general barked an order at Elliot and Ava. "You two, help him up and follow me."

Elliot and Ava exchanged a brief look of unease before complying. Each taking an arm, they helped the squad leader to his feet, his body trembling weakly. The general looked down at the man with contempt, remarking coldly, "The Supreme Telvarch will decide your fate." He then strode confidently out of the hall, his every step exuding authority.

Elliot and Ava, supporting the injured man, followed close behind. Their exit left a heavy, foreboding silence in the mess hall, with the remaining Telvanni exchanging worried glances, each silently contemplating the fate of their fallen comrade.

Upon reaching the lift, its doors glided open, welcoming the general's imposing figure. Elliot and Ava, still steadying the squad leader, paused momentarily before stepping inside the lift. As the doors closed, sealing them in the confined space, an oppressive silence enveloped them, broken only by the faint hum of the ascending lift.

Elliot's mind raced with thoughts and concerns. He had assumed they were heading to the command room, but as the lift ascended, doubt crept in. Would they be able to find an opportunity to escape, or had they inadvertently walked into a trap, their true identities perilously close to being unveiled?

Chapter 53

As the lift ascended quietly, a stray beam of light reflecting off the general's white suit caught Elliot's eye. In that moment, he found himself subtly sizing him up. The man had a couple of inches on Elliot's own six-foot two-inch stature and seemed somewhat leaner. The suit masked the exact contours of his build, yet it couldn't conceal the aura of authority that he exuded. Elliot recalled the general's display of strength; whether that power was natural or enhanced by the suit was unclear, but the potential threat he posed was unmistakable.

Elliot tightened his hold on the squad leader's arm, supporting his weakened state. On his other side, Ava stood steady and watchful, her posture reflecting their shared apprehension. When the lift finally came to a stop, the general, radiating authority, took the first step out. Elliot, Ava, and the ailing squad leader lined up, three abreast behind him. Their steps echoed through the sprawling, unfamiliar corridor. The only other sound was the pained breathing of the injured man, punctuating the silence as the group followed the general's lead.

The corridor stretched out before them, culminating in a massive door etched with symbols of an unknown language, the intricate patterns hinting at hidden meanings. As they approached, the general, without any sign of hesitation, made a sudden left turn, following the corridor's continued path. Bright overhead lights illuminated their way, casting long, stark shadows against the walls.

Elliot and Ava shared a brief meaningful glance. Though their faces were hidden beneath their helmets, the silent communication between them was clear, revealing their shared sense of unease amidst the unfolding mystery.

They moved swiftly down the corridor, bypassing two massive doors on the right. The sheer scale of these doors suggested the enormity of the rooms behind them, yet their purpose remained shrouded in mystery. Elliot's gaze briefly lingered, his mind racing with possibilities about what could lie within. However, an unmarked room on the left, directly across from the final room on the right they were approaching, caught his attention. This room had not appeared on the holographic map, its concealed functions intriguing Elliot.

Jolted back to the present, Elliot saw that the general had reached the final door on the right. He swiped his CDU across the panel, prompting the door to slide open smoothly. They were greeted by a technological marvel: the command room. It was a hub of activity, with monitors, screens, and holographic displays occupying every available space. Personnel clad in black uniforms worked diligently, their fingers sweeping over touchscreens and controls. They were deeply engrossed in their tasks, managing operations of a scale at which Elliot could only guess.

The general strode purposefully to a raised platform at the heart of the room, commanding a panoramic view of the entire command space. With a curt gesture, he indicated a spot near the platform, signaling Elliot and Ava to place the injured squad leader there. They did so with careful precision, ensuring the man was as comfortable as circumstances allowed.

After completing their task, Elliot and Ava subtly retreated towards the rear of the room, positioning themselves near the exit. Their eyes flickered across the space, taking in the positions and movements of the other soldiers. Every muscle in their bodies was tensed, ready for action, yet they forced themselves to appear calm and unobtrusive. Escaping unnoticed would be a formidable challenge. For now, they chose to blend in, learning what they could, whilst waiting for an opportune moment to slip away undetected.

Elliot's eyes were drawn inexorably to the sweeping array of colossal screens that dominated the room, each one a window into a different world. The rugged landscape of the Moon was rendered in striking detail, its desolate plains and towering mountains captured in live feeds that were as mesmerizing as they were chilling. His attention shifted, heart-clenching, to the monitors that bore images of Earth. The once-vibrant blue of the planet was now marred by stark, dark scars left by the asteroid impact, a sight that stirred a profound sense of loss within him. It was here, in the nerve center of the Telvanni base, that the reality of his and Ava's responsibility hit him with full force. A silent vow of retribution took root in his heart, fueled by the stark evidence displayed before him.

Amidst the orchestrated chaos of the command center, the general's presence was a force unto itself. He moved with deliberate steps, exuding a commanding aura that demanded immediate action. His sharp, authoritative gestures directed the flow of operations, a silent but potent demand for updates and reports. He would pause at a console, give a curt nod, and the operators would spring into heightened efficiency, their fingers flying over the controls to display the latest information on the massive screens.

Elliot and Ava stood motionless in this whirlwind, their presence merging into the background. They were like shadows amidst the surge of activity, observing and absorbing every detail. Surrounded by the enemy, their resolve remained firm, a quiet defiance against the frenetic energy that pulsed around them.

The general returned to his central platform, his figure commanding attention. As one of the black-uniformed operators signaled that communications were ready, a hush descended upon the room. A palpable sense of anticipation gripped the space, every gaze turning towards the front. Suddenly, the air shimmered, and a holographic image flickered into existence. Elliot couldn't help but marvel at its stunning clarity. To him, it appeared almost as real as the figures around him, a testament to just how advanced the Telvannis' technology was.

The holographic image flickering to life before them showcased a man whose commanding presence was instantly noticeable. Elliot, watching closely, noted his towering stature, which rivaled Mayto's in height. His build, lean and toned, conveyed undeniable strength; it seemed to underscore an innate authority.

Elliot's gaze then shifted from the suit he wore, all black with white stripes, to the man's face, which was helmetless. His hair was long, black, and slicked back, framing a face with a strong jawline and an olive complexion. His eyes, a deep brown with a hint of red, lent him an even more intimidating air. Elliot wondered briefly if this reddish tinge was a quirk of the holographic projection or another intimidating aspect of the man's natural appearance. The room settled into a respectful silence, every gaze transfixed on the commanding holographic figure. Anticipation hung in the air as they awaited his words.

"Greetings, General," he said, his voice cool and measured, exuding a quiet confidence that seemed to fill the space.

The general, maintaining his composure, responded with a curt nod. "Supreme Telvarch."

"Update me on the situation," the figure, now identified as the supreme telvarch, demanded. His tone was not just authoritative but carried an expectation of a detailed and prompt briefing.

"The asteroid we deployed impacted Earth two days ago, causing the level of devastation we anticipated," the general began, his voice unwavering. "Yet, our latest intelligence suggests the number of surviving inhabitants exceeds our initial estimates."

"Are their numbers beyond acceptable thresholds?" the supreme telvarch queried.

"Not currently, but the situation is still developing. I ordered a second asteroid earlier. My recommendation is to keep it on course for now. In six months, we can adjust the impact coordinates, allowing any remaining Earth inhabitants time to expose their presence."

"I agree with your approach, General. When do we expect the second asteroid to hit?"

"From our operational base on Titan, the second impact is projected in about eighteen months," replied the general.

"That's satisfactory. What are your next steps?"

"After finalizing matters here, I'll head back to Titan to supervise the terraforming and colonization preparations," the general stated.

"Very good," acknowledged the supreme telvarch. "Finally, Earth will be ours. What updates do you have on the human DNA mapping project?"

A trace of pride shone in the general's eyes. "We've successfully mapped the DNA of Earth's humans."

"And they're now sustainable?"

The general paused for effect before answering. "Conclusively."

"This is very good news indeed, General," the supreme telvarch said, barely containing his excitement. "This enhancement will significantly benefit our race. When should I expect the delivery of this new DNA strain?" he inquired.

"I will personally bring it to Titan after completing my current assignment, Supreme Telvarch," the general assured.

"The assignment concerning the Lunari, is that correct?"

"Precisely," the general confirmed. "We require a few more days at the base, four or five, before we can commence phase two."

"Phase two? You're referring to the Lunari extinction, I presume."

"Yes. The Lunari have fulfilled their purpose," the general responded nonchalantly. A small smile crossed his lips. "However, I have one final use for them," he added.

"Tell your men to savor the hunt, General," the supreme telvarch said, a knowing smile creeping across his face. "They deserve this reward."

"Your words honor us, Supreme Telvarch," the general replied, nodding in agreement.

"And what of the Earth prisoner you mentioned earlier?" the supreme telvarch asked.

The general scoffed dismissively. "He's nothing but an entertaining distraction. I intend to eliminate him alongside the others."

"Proceed as you see fit, General. I commend your efforts." The supreme telvarch paused. "Is there anything else of note?"

"There is one last issue," the general began. "Due to a squad leader's negligence, we lost two of our soldiers to an animal attack today. What are your directives on this matter?"

"Make an example of him," the supreme telvarch declared coldly. "Our people must never forget the consequences of failure."

A faint whimper emanated from the floor near the general, piercing the heavy silence. The general glanced down, his eyes reflecting scorn. "Compose yourself," he snapped sharply.

"I trust you to handle this efficiently, General. Do not disappoint me," the supreme telvarch said. With these, his final words, he terminated the communication and the holographic image faded.

The general's gaze shifted from the now-empty space to the quivering figure on the floor. He sighed, adjusted his shock stick's power setting, and pressed the trigger. THWUMP. The sound of a lifeless body hitting the floor echoed through the room.

"You two!" he barked, his voice cutting through the silence. "Dispose of this."

Chapter 54

As Elliot and Ava hastily navigated the corridor, the unsettling echo of the general's shock stick resonated in their minds. The weight of their newfound knowledge bore down on them, each step away from the command room feeling like an escape from a nightmare.

Utilizing the brief chaos that had followed the execution, they discreetly distanced themselves from the grim scene. Two guards with blue stripes had been tasked with removing the squad leader's remains. This morbid act provided the perfect distraction for their quiet exit.

Navigating the corridors with a sense of urgency, they soon found themselves at the familiar lift doors. They entered swiftly, initiating the descent to the ground floor. Upon arrival, they moved with calculated speed and stealth towards the pump room. There, under the harsh glow of artificial lights, the sleek silhouette of the shuttle promised a temporary refuge.

Wordlessly, they boarded, its familiar confines offering a brief reprieve from the chaos. Elliot quickly interfaced his CDU with the control panel and initiated the launch sequence. The shuttle hummed to life, hovering effortlessly above the tracks, and began its upward journey toward the Great Falls. As they glided away from the station, the looming presence of the Telvanni base shrank into the distance. In the relative safety of the shuttle, they removed their helmets, revealing expressions etched with concern.

The tension inside was palpable, a sharp contrast to their smooth passage through the tunnel. It was Ava who broke the ensuing silence. "Elliot, my people... they're in grave danger."

Elliot turned to face her, the shuttle's dim light illuminating his expression and casting deep shadows across his features. His eyes reflected the same mix of fear and determination that she felt. "We need to warn them right away," he said. "Their extermination plan... it's monstrous!"

Ava nodded. The flash of the tunnel lights whisking past caused her eyes to sparkle. "Time is against us. You heard the general—we have four, maybe five days at most. How do we stand against an enemy that controls our entire world?" Ava asked, her voice tinged with fear.

Elliot's face creased in concentration, the gears of his mind visibly turning. He took a deep breath, held it as he gathered his thoughts, and then released it slowly. "Knowing their plan is our edge. I have the beginnings of a strategy but convincing the chief and the rest of the Lunari... that won't be easy. They have to come to terms with a reality that they won't want to accept."

Ava made a subtle movement towards her suit pocket, indicating the hidden camera. "I think I've recorded enough to persuade the chief," she said.

"That's a good start," Elliot said. "We'll need the full support of everyone if we're to have any hope. We're not just fighting for the Lunari but for Earth too," he added with a grave tone. "You heard what they said about the second meteor."

As the shuttle continued its ascent, Elliot shared his emerging plan with Ava. By the time they reached their destination, they had agreed that while the plan was risky, it was likely their only viable option. Ava felt confident about the chief's support, but the task of convincing May-to and the rest of the Lunari community loomed large, a burden that the chief would ultimately have to shoulder.

Arriving at the Great Falls station, Elliot and Ava disembarked quickly, grabbing their packs as the shuttle began its automated return to the Forbidden Mountain. They moved efficiently along the top floor, meticulously erasing any evidence of their presence before proceeding to the lift.

Once on the ground floor, Elliot collected his original suit but opted to continue wearing the Telvanni one. He methodically closed every door they had opened earlier, ensuring their trail was covered. Approaching the exit, a quick check of his watch reassured Elliot that they were well ahead of Savage-Heart's expected return.

They crossed through the airlock and into the cave behind the Great Falls, the door opening silently. The darkness of the cave enveloped them, and Elliot realized that, unlike his suit, the Telvanni one lacked a headlamp. To his amazement, the suit adapted automatically, activating a night-vision mode that bathed their surroundings in a green hue, enhancing their visibility in the pitch-black cave.

They moved with haste, traversing the cave, swiftly passing through the den and then the waterfall room. The ambient sounds of dripping water and distant echoes filled the air as they journeyed through the last of the passage-ways before emerging safely back into the open space of Lunar.

Elliot and Ava began their descent down the two-hundred-dred-foot stone staircase carved into the mountain, finding the downward journey noticeably easier than their ascent. Ava, feeling the difference the Telvanni suit made, couldn't help but comment, "It's incredible how much stronger and lighter I feel in Lunar with this suit on."

Elliot nodded. "It does give the Telvanni an unfair edge though," he remarked with concern.

As they ventured across the Lunar landscape, retracing the path they had taken to the Great Falls earlier that day, their steps were quickened by the urgency of their mission. The pressing need to return to the village rendered the comfort of the familiar terrain almost unnoticeable.

The tranquility of the Lunar sky, previously a constant, abruptly changed as clouds gathered, darkening swiftly. Within moments, a heavy downpour enveloped them, transforming the landscape under a deluge of rain. Elliot, caught off guard, looked up, his expression one of disbe-lief. "Rain? Here on Lunar?"

Ava laughed lightly, water droplets cascading off her suit. "Of course. How did you think the plants and crops grew without it?"

Elliot furrowed his brows, lost in thought. "I suppose I never considered it. I guess it's just the thought of rain in-side the Moon!" he said. "And it's coming down so hard!" he exclaimed. "It's like a monsoon out here!"

"Lunar's weather can be unpredictable," Ava explained. "These downpours are sudden and intense, but they're usually short-lived, rarely lasting more than a couple of hours."

Before Elliot could reply, Ava abruptly pointed back to the path on which they had just traveled. "The shelter's just back there," she yelled, her voice barely rising above the relentless drumming of the rain. "With this downpour blinding us, it's going to be hard to keep moving. Better we wait it out."

Elliot nodded and gave a thumbs-up, his response lost in the roar of the rain. As they turned back, each step they took was a struggle against the unyielding wind and the sheets of rain that hammered them. They moved with urgency, aware that every moment in the open was a risk. Suddenly, as if the storm itself had manifested a physical form, an overwhelming force crashed into Elliot from behind. He hit the soaked ground with a thud, the breath knocked out of him. Scrambling to roll over, he looked up and froze—the wolf, its coat matted with rain, stood staring at him. Its eyes glowed with a predatory glint, and the unmistakable red scar on its back gleamed even in the dim light—the alpha had returned!

With a burst of speed, the wolf lunged at Elliot, drenched grass flying beneath its paws. Lying vulnerable, Elliot had mere moments to react. Muscles tensing, he harnessed his strength and used the wolf's own momentum against it. With a swift motion, he planted his feet firmly into its midsection and pushed hard. Leveraging his legs, he flipped the wolf over his body and sprung to his feet.

As the rain pelted down mercilessly, memories of his encounter with Savage-Heart and the Telvanni soldier flashed in Elliot's mind, highlighting the vulnerability of his current suit. Fueled by a surge of urgency, his eyes darted around, desperately seeking his shock stick, now lost amidst the chaos of the alpha's initial assault. The relentless downpour turned the ground into a blur, making it near impossible to spot without the time he did not have.

His attention shifted to Ava, who was positioned a few meters away, partially shielded by a gnarled tree that had seen many storms. Her stance was alert and focused, the rain cascading off her as she recovered her composure. With precise aim, she pointed her shock stick at the advancing wolf. The weapon released a resonant *THWUMP*. However, the wolf's nimbleness was unmatched; it deftly sidestepped, and the blast hit the soaked ground just behind it, sending mud and debris flying. Ava, with her back against the tree, knew that with the alpha closing in on Elliot, any further shots were too risky. She needed to wait, watchful, for the right moment to intervene without endangering Elliot.

Elliot tensed, readying himself as the wolf lunged forward again. He moved swiftly, and with a well-timed thrust of his elbow, he struck the wolf's head. The impact made the wolf stagger briefly, but the animal quickly recovered, its aggression undiminished.

"Elliot, catch!" Ava's voice cut through the sound of the rain as she threw her shock stick toward him.

In one fluid motion, Elliot caught the shock stick and aimed it at the charging wolf. *THWUMP. THUD.* The blast hit the alpha, veering him off course, yet the wolf recovered rapidly, its rage unabated.

With no time to spare, Elliot cranked the shock stick to its highest setting and fired again. *THWUMP. THUD.*

This time, the powerful blast was too much for the alpha, who collapsed, motionless on the soaked ground.

Panting heavily, Elliot bent over, hands on his knees, gasping for breath. Ava quickly ran to his side, concern etched on her face. "Are you alright?" she yelled, her voice barely audible above the pounding rain.

Elliot responded with a reassuring thumbs-up, his helmet's visor streaked with rain. "I'm fine," he said, his voice betraying signs of fatigue. "But we need to get out of this rain. Help me find my shock stick, then we'll get out of here." Together, they began a hurried search, their movements swift and focused, pushing through the exhaustion that weighed down on them like the relentless rain.

Eventually, Ava's keen eyes, aided by the helmet's enhanced vision, caught the glint of metal a few yards away. She dashed toward Elliot's shock stick, her suit's heavy boots splashing through the increasingly deep puddles. Retrieving it, she quickly rejoined Elliot, and together they made their way towards the shelter. The rain seemed to grow more intense with each step, as if actively trying to hinder them, but they persevered. Soon, they reached a large tree whose branches overhung the river, a landmark signaling their proximity to the shelter.

Ava, with the kind of deftness born of experience, located the concealed hatch in the ground. Her gloved hands worked quickly, defying the cumbersome nature of the suit, and she expertly opened it. As they slipped inside, a palpable sense of relief washed over them, contrasting starkly with the relentless downpour they had just endured. The chaos of Lunar's rugged landscape was instantly replaced by the calm, secure interior of the refuge. They could now hear only a muted patter of rain against the shelter's sturdy structure, a soothing reminder of the wild elements they had escaped.

CHAPTER 55

NOW IN THE PROTECTIVE confines of the shelter, Elliot and Ava swiftly began to shed their respective suits. Ava slipped out of hers effortlessly, but Elliot's movements were slower, more labored. With each motion, his discomfort was increasingly evident. At the sight of him wincing, concern creased Ava's features.

"Did you get hurt?" she asked, her voice tinged with worry.

"It's just a bruise from the wolf attack. Nothing serious," Elliot said, trying to downplay it.

Ava moved closer to assist him, her fingers quickly working on the clasps of his suit. With the suit removed, she leaned in to examine his bruises. As she did, the space between them suddenly lessened. Their eyes met, holding a moment longer than necessary, and in that pause, the turmoil outside faded into insignificance.

Amidst the danger they had just escaped, the relentless beating of the rain, and the rush of adrenaline still coursing through them, a different kind of urgency took hold. Overwhelmed by recent experiences and drawn to one another by the closeness of the moment, they found themselves locked into a passionate, heartfelt kiss.

In that moment, time seemed to stand still, and the world outside receded into obscurity. It was just Elliot and Ava, deeply immersed in their newfound closeness. As the storm raged on outside, its howls muffled by the shelter's sturdy walls, the minutes slipped away unnoticed. In their secluded world, only the rhythm of their breaths and the storm's distant drumming filled the silence.

When the world around them began to gain focus, they found themselves lying on the hard floor of the shelter, surrounded by their hastily discarded clothing. Their breaths, now calm and synchronized, filled the quiet space around them. Entwined in each other's arms, Elliot and Ava discovered a comforting warmth and a deep sense of connection that went beyond words, a silent recognition of the bond that had grown stronger between them.

Ava's voice was a whisper, tinged with a playful glint in her eyes. "I thought we agreed to wait until this was all over."

Elliot responded by tenderly cradling her face in his hands, his fingers lightly brushing her cheek. "With everything that's happening," he said softly, "who knows if there will be an after? Maybe we shouldn't let moments like this pass us by."

Once again, drawn by their undeniable connection, they came together in a deep, lingering embrace.

Sometime later, as they lay contentedly near each other, a contemplative look appeared on Ava's face. Breaking the comfortable silence, she began, her voice carrying a note of uncertainty. "Elliot, there's something I haven't shared with anyone before. It's about the Telvanni... and what happened to Bella's father."

Elliot's gaze locked with hers, a realization dawning. "It was Bella's father—the one who never came back, right?" he asked, his tone gentle.

Ava nodded slowly. "Yes, but there's more to it than that," she confessed, her gaze laden with concern.

Elliot intertwined his fingers with hers, bringing her hand to his lips for a gentle kiss. "I'm listening," he encouraged softly.

Ava's voice trembled as she ventured into the depths of her past, each word heavy with the sorrow of her memories. "It's true. My husband was taken by the Telvanni five years ago, and we never saw him again," she began, her voice barely above a whisper. She paused, gathering strength. "For three days, I clung to hope, certain he would be returned like the others in the past. I prayed for any news of him, but nothing came. Finally, on the fifth day, when I could take no more, I begged the chief to send out a search party. But he refused, fearing it would anger the 'gods,'" she said.

She took a steadying breath, her gaze distant. "On the sixth day, I left Bella with some friends in the village and went to the Forbidden Mountain alone, desperate for answers. I found nothing but faint tracks leading to the rocky walls of the mountain's entrance, but I couldn't find any way in. After several hours, with despair setting in, two Telvanni soldiers came upon me, returning to their base."

Elliot, sensing her pain, reached out to offer solace. "It's okay," he said softly. "You don't have to continue if it's too hard."

Ava shook her head determinedly, a tear spilling down her cheek. "No, it's important. You need to know, and I need to say it," she said, her voice quivering. She hastily wiped the tear away. "I only have fragments of memories after that. I woke up in the forest. My clothes were torn, and I felt bruised and sore." More tears followed, and Elliot gently wiped them away, his expression mirroring the anguish of her story.

In the silence that followed, a heavy air of unspoken words filled the shelter. Her story explained the contempt she held for the Telvanni and the depth of her concern for Bella, especially in light of Bella's recent experience. Elliot grappled with a tempest of emotions—anger at the Telvanni, sorrow for Ava, and a burning desire for revenge. Recognizing that Ava needed his reassurance and not his anger, he gently enveloped her in a comforting embrace, whispering words of solace. "I'm so sorry, Ava," he said softly. "I promise you, we will hold them accountable for their actions."

Tears shimmered in Ava's brown eyes as she looked up at Elliot. A vulnerability appeared in her gaze. "Does knowing this change how you feel about me?" she asked, her voice wavering with uncertainty.

Elliot's gaze met hers, and a flare of intensity burned within his green eyes. "Not even for a moment," he replied firmly. He held a deep-seated anger at the Telvanni for making Ava doubt her worth. He pulled her close, their lips meeting in a tender, affirming kiss. "If anything," he said, "it strengthens my love for you," he whispered, his words a balm to the wounds inflicted by her past.

The tears in Ava's eyes transformed into a soft smile. "I love you too, Elliot," she whispered, pulling him into another warm embrace.

They lay there in each other's arms, the comfort of their closeness a haven amid the chaos. After some time, Ava's voice gently pierced the silence once more. "Do you think our plan will work?" she asked.

Elliot's voice was firm. "I do," he said. "It's the best plan we have. But it will work because it must," he added with confidence.

There was a pause as Ava collected her thoughts. "If we succeed, what will you do? Will you return to Earth?" she asked tentatively.

Elliot considered the idea for a moment. "Probably. If there are any survivors left, they'll need all the help they can get," he said. "But I want you and Bella with me, wherever I end up... if you're okay with that," he added quickly.

Ava's face brightened into a wide smile. "Do you really mean that?"

"Absolutely," Elliot assured her. "I can't imagine a future without you both in it." His eyes sparkled with a hint of playfulness as he added, "So, how do you feel about a trip to Earth?"

"As long as we're together, I'm ready for any adventure," Ava replied.

They drew each other into a tender embrace, their bond growing stronger by the moment. Just as their closeness was about to reignite their passion, an abrupt sound shattered the moment. They pulled apart, exchanging startled glances as the unmistakable sound of a single horn blast echoed through the air.

Chapter 56

The rain had lessened to a steady rhythm on the roofs of the Lunari village. This lent a soothing backdrop to the chief's home, where he was deeply engaged in a board game with young Bella. Their lighthearted laughter echoed in the cozy room, in harmony with the rain's comforting patter.

Suddenly, the tranquility was shattered by the blaring of the horn, a sound that struck a chord of alarm in the chief's heart. His face drained of color as disbelief and fear replaced his previous calm. This was unprecedented—a taking so soon after the last, and amidst a rainstorm no less.

The door swung open abruptly, revealing Mayto, drenched and visibly shaken. "The gods approach!" he gasped, urgency in every word. "They're on the north road as we speak!"

"But we've only just heard the horn!" the chief said, struggling to comprehend. His eyes darted to Bella, protective and stern. "Stay inside, no matter what," he instructed firmly.

Outside, chaos reigned. The villagers, peering from their homes, displayed a mix of fear and confusion. The sound of hooves splashing through the wet streets grew louder, a foreboding harbinger of their approach from the north.

"To the village square! The chief shouted above the noise, assuming command. "Everyone, gather quickly!" He cast a final anxious glance towards the advancing figures before rushing back inside to Bella.

With a grave face, he conveyed the urgency. "They're here. We need to go to the square now. Stay close to me or Mayto."

Bella's eyes filled with worry. "But Mama..." she said, her voice small and fraught with concern.

The chief locked eyes with Bella. "If they ask about her, we'll say she's been held up by the rain and will return shortly," he assured her, with as much confidence as he could muster.

When they reached the square, the villagers were already gathered, their clothes clinging to them, drenched by the unrelenting rain. The chief's eyes moved over their worried faces as he tried to muster comforting words. But a heavy tension filled the air, intensifying with each echoing clop of horse hooves on the rain-slicked ground.

As before, the riders, led by the imposing figure of the general, began their intimidating patrol around the square. The general, flanked by nine blue-striped soldiers, dismounted their steeds with a sense of purpose, tethering them to a nearby post. Their presence commanded immediate attention and respect from the gathered crowd.

Without any delay, the general approached the chief. His voice was authoritative as he demanded, "Have your people ready for scanning... Now!"

"But we haven't gathered everyone yet," the chief responded, his voice tinged with desperation.

"You should always be prepared," retorted the general sharply. "If we don't find our target, everyone will face the consequences."

With a sinking heart, the chief nodded to his villagers, signaling them to prepare for the scanning. He stepped forward to be the first, but the general raised his hand, stopping him. "Not you. Not today," he said coldly. "Today, we seek a child."

The general's stark command to bring forth the children resonated with a menacing undercurrent, creating a ripple of fear through the villagers. His voice grew even more threatening as he noticed their reluctance. "I strongly advise you to present the children now, or you will all face severe consequences." At his signal, the guards stepped forward as one, their shock sticks raised, underscoring the seriousness of his warning.

With heavy hearts, parents gently pushed their children forward to face the scanning. Each beep of the device sent waves of anxiety through the crowd, only to be followed by collective sighs of relief with every negative outcome. But when it was Bella's turn, the atmosphere shifted palpably. The CDU emitted a distinct alert, signaling a positive match. The soldier's swift gesture to the general did not go unnoticed. Panic surged in Bella's eyes, a sentiment echoed in the chief's horrified gaze.

"It has to be a mistake," the chief stammered, his voice filled with desperation.

The general, silent and stoic, stepped forward and rescanned Bella with his own CDU. After a brief moment, he looked up, his expression unyielding. "There is no mistake. Take her," he ordered coldly.

As a soldier moved to take Bella, the chief, driven by raw emotion and his promise to Ava, reacted with lightning speed. In one swift motion, he freed Bella from the soldier's grasp, and using his other hand, he unleashed a powerful shove. The soldier stumbled and fell to the ground, splashing into the wet mud. The village fell into a shocked silence, the implications of the chief's defiance hanging ominously in the air.

Outraged, the general's voice seethed with fury. "You dare to lay hands on a god?!" he bellowed. In a swift, enraged motion, he brandished his shock stick and delivered a jarring blast to the chief. He fell to his knees, sinking into the muddy ground.

Mayto, witnessing the attack on his father, was overcome with a fierce protective instinct. His pent-up anger came to the forefront as he tackled the nearest soldier, picking him up and throwing him with incredible strength towards the general. He then launched himself into the fray, his powerful blows scattering the blue-striped soldiers in all directions.

Despite Mayto's formidable strength, it proved insufficient against the general's calculated and relentless use of the shock stick. Each successive shock diminished Mayto's ability to resist, eroding his strength bit by bit. Eventually, overpowered and weakened, he fell to his knees. Surrounding him, the blue-striped soldiers closed in, unleashing a barrage of kicks, their feet coming down hard on him, further subduing him into submission.

Watching his son come under attack, the chief, consumed by anger, found the strength to stand again. Ignoring his safety, he charged headlong at the soldiers attacking Mayto. With massive, powerful fists, he hammered at each man, his every blow a testament to a father's desperate need to protect his child.

Behind him, the general, unfazed by the chaos, continued to fire shock after shock at the chief's back. Each jolt coursed through him, but the chief's adrenaline-fueled rage kept him standing, allowing him to continue his protective onslaught.

However, the relentless shocks from the general eventually took their toll. The chief's strength began to wane, and his movements grew slower and more labored. With a final defiant effort to shield his son, he collapsed over Mayto, instinctively covering him, offering his body and the last of his strength as a barrier.

The general surveyed the scene with a hint of admiration. "These two have shown remarkable resilience," he remarked. Then his tone shifted to one of cold resolve. "Take the chief as well. His lesson isn't over yet," he declared ominously.

In a last-ditch effort, Mayto tried to rise, fueled by sheer willpower, but was immediately met with a barrage of shocks from three blue-striped soldiers. The villagers, witnessing this brutal display, were frozen in a state of shock and horror.

With Bella and the chief now his prisoners, the general departed the village, leaving behind an overwhelming sense of dread and helplessness. The Lunari, having just witnessed their strongest defenders overcome by the Telvanni's superior might, were painfully aware of their own vulnerability.

After the Telvanni soldiers disappeared into the distance, Mayto remained on the ground, battered and unconscious amidst the rain-soaked mud. The villagers rushed to his side, their movements quick with concern. In the background, the mournful sound of two horn blasts echoed, a chilling reminder of the recent events and the daunting challenges the Lunari now faced.

Chapter 57

The sound of the horn seemed to still resonate within the shelter as Ava and Elliot dressed quickly.

"How can there be another taking so soon?" Ava questioned anxiously. "They're never this close together."

"And why another taking at all?" Elliot added, lacing up his boots. "The general just said the Lunari are no longer needed. What could have changed in the last few hours?"

"I don't know, but I have a bad feeling about this," Ava said, her expression lined with worry.

They hurriedly finished dressing, deciding against taking the suits with them. The risk of being caught in Telvanni gear was too high, despite the inconvenience of having to retrieve them later.

As they left the shelter, Ava and Elliot made their way swiftly towards the village. Their urgent pace, however, was abruptly interrupted by the sound of two successive horn blasts. Ava stopped in her tracks, her eyes wide with alarm. "That's not possible!" she exclaimed, with a hint of fear in her voice. "It's too soon. There's usually at least a two-hour gap between those horns."

"Something must have changed with their plans," Elliot speculated.

"Do you think they found out we were at the Forbidden Mountain?" Ava asked.

Elliot dismissed Ava's concern with a shake of his head. "No, if they knew a Lunari had infiltrated their base, they would have reacted much more aggressively. It seems more likely they skipped their usual scanning protocol," he said.

"But why would they skip it?" Ava asked, confused. "They've always been so thorough, checking everyone was there."

Elliot considered their situation. "It could be because they're planning to eliminate the Lunari soon," he speculated gravely. "At this point, they might not be concerned whether someone is missing, as long as they find their specific targets. It's possible they didn't even notice your absence." His mind raced with thoughts. "Yet, the question remains: why the sudden need for another person?" Then adding with urgency, he said, "It's best we hurry back and find out!"

Ava and Elliot hastened their steps, the need for answers propelling them forward. The rain, which had been a constant companion, finally began to ease, and beams of sunlight broke through the dissipating clouds. After a determined ten-minute jog, the recognizable gates of Lunar emerged in the distance. The outskirts of the village were unusually silent, save for a faint, unsettling buzz emanating from the square ahead.

Stepping into the village, Ava felt a sense of dread weighing heavily upon her. Noticing the gathered crowd in the square, she quickened her pace, with Elliot matching her stride. The closer they got, the louder the anxious chatter of the villagers became. Driven by a need for answers, Ava reached out and grabbed the arm of a villager passing by. "What's going on? Who did they take?" she asked, her voice urgent and tinged with panic.

The villager, a middle-aged woman, spoke in a hushed, hurried tone. "They took the chief," she said, her eyes brimming with fear.

"No, not the chief," Ava responded, her mind reeling.

"Mayto tried to stop them," the villager continued hurriedly. "He fought bravely, but the gold-stripe god... he kept blasting Mayto with his shock stick. It was terrifying." Her voice trailed off, laden with shock and sorrow.

Before Ava could probe further, the villager's gaze darted away, landing on her family in the crowd. "I have to go," she said quickly, slipping away to join her loved ones, leaving Ava standing amid the worried villagers.

Pushing through the crowd to the center of the square, Ava and Elliot saw Mayto sitting on the damp ground, visibly battered but alive, encircled by a group of concerned villagers. "Mayto," Ava called out as she approached him. "Are you okay?" Her voice was filled with both relief and deep concern as she knelt beside him.

Mayto looked up at Ava, his expression one of pain and anger. "Where's Bella, Mayto?" Ava hurriedly asked, scanning the crowd for any sight of her.

"They took my father," was all that Mayto could say, his voice laden with grief.

Ava felt a tightness in her chest. "I'm so sorry, Mayto... But where's Bella?" she persisted, the fear growing in her voice.

"He fought them, he was always strong..." Mayto said. "But against those shock sticks..." His voice trailed off, haunted by the memory.

Ava's tears flowed freely. "Mayto, please," she implored, her voice cracking. "Tell me where Bella is. Where is my daughter?"

Mayto couldn't bring himself to look at her. He bowed his head, his whisper barely audible. "I'm sorry, Ava... they took her. They took both of them."

Ava's expression turned to one of utter disbelief, her tears intensifying. "No... it can't be true," she stammered, her voice shaking. In a state of panic, she scanned the crowd, calling out desperately, "Bella... Bella!"

Elliot moved to comfort her, enveloping her in his arms as her cries of "Nooo!" sobbed into his chest, each one a stab to his heart.

"We'll find her, Ava. I promise," he assured her, holding her tightly, her sobs reverberating through him.

Mayto's gaze then turned to Elliot, filled with a seething anger. "This is all your fault," he spat bitterly. "Everything was fine before you came here."

"Now is not the time for blame, Mayto," Elliot responded calmly.

Mayto's resolve was unyielding, the burden of leadership and the Lunari's future now squarely on his shoulders. With a subtle nod to his men, who had quietly positioned themselves around Elliot, he gave the order. "Seize him and bind his hands."

Before Elliot could respond, half a dozen of Mayto's men descended upon him, holding him firmly in place. With the sheer number against him, his superior strength was rendered ineffective. Recognizing the futility of his struggle, he eventually ceased resisting, understanding the need to save his strength.

Ava, frantic and desperate, lashed out at Mayto's men while pleading with Mayto. "This isn't Elliot's fault, Mayto! We have to rescue Bella! We have to rescue them both!" Yet, her cries went ignored, and her attempts to fend off the men were effortlessly thwarted.

Mayto's voice was firm, though tinged with pain. "Bella and my father are lost to us for now, Ava. I know it's hard to accept but provoking the gods further will only put us all at risk. We can only hope that they are both returned safely to us. In the meantime, I must think of the safety of my people. It's what my father would've done."

Overwhelmed by desperation, Ava screamed, "It's all a lie, Mayto! They're going to kill us all. We have to fight back!" Her voice trembled with urgency and fear.

Mayto's orders were firm, though his eyes betrayed the turmoil within. "Bind her," he instructed. "And take her to my father's house. Make sure she's unharmed."

One of the men securing Elliot looked to Mayto for further direction. "What about him?" he asked.

"Put him in the holding cells. Make sure he's constantly watched," Mayto answered decisively.

The villagers watched in a heavy, somber silence as Ava and Elliot were led away in opposite directions. Their departure cast a lingering shadow of grief and uncertainty over the crowd. Ava's desperate cries hung in the air, sowing seeds of fear and confusion. Her warning that they were all in mortal danger from the gods struck a chord, stirring an uneasy murmur among the people.

Whispers and worried glances wove through the crowd. Questions mounted. Why another taking so soon? Why the lapse in the gods' usual thorough scans? And most chillingly, what truth might Ava's warning hold?

As Ava and Elliot vanished from sight, a palpable sense of dread descended upon the village. Their collective anxiety swelled, haunted by Ava's final chilling cry: "They're going to kill us all!"

CHAPTER 58

THE QUIETNESS INSIDE THE chief's house was abruptly shattered as Ava was ushered in, her labored breaths echoing in the room. She was quickly and firmly bound to a wooden post in the center, her restraints tight and unforgiving. Once she was secured, the guards stepped outside, stationing themselves at the entrance. Their rigid postures mirrored the severity of the situation, a seriousness only heightened by the continuous, heart-wrenching cries from Ava.

Alone, Ava was engulfed by despair, her thoughts consumed by Bella. Questions tormented her. Had Bella been harmed? Was she even still alive? Her concern for Elliot compounded these worries. Mayto's eyes, burning with anger from his father's beating and capture, haunted her. That anger, born of loss and betrayal, had the potential to lead a person down a dark path. As she felt the tightness of the ropes around her wrists, her sense of desperation intensified, her cries echoing her growing fear.

As time slowly passed, the room felt like a cage, trapping her with her anxiety and fear. When Mayto finally entered, Ava's eyes, reddened by tears, met his. Her voice, now hoarse from her continuous pleading, conveyed both fear and fury. Huddled against the post, her hands still tied behind her, she looked up at him with scorn. "Where's Elliot? What have you done to him?" she raged.

Mayto paused briefly, caught off guard by Ava's fiery response. "I had hoped you would have calmed down by now," he said, trying to maintain a composed demeanor.

Ava's eyes burned with an unyielding spirit. "Calm? How can I be calm when my daughter has been taken?" she shot back, her voice trembling with anger.

"My father was also taken defending your daughter!" he spat back. "If you're searching for someone to blame, look no further than your precious Elliot."

"What have you done with him?" Ava asked, her gaze unwavering.

"He's alive," Mayto said, his voice laced with contempt. "Which is more than he deserves."

"You have to release him, Mayto. He's our only hope to save Bella and your father."

Mayto's eyes narrowed dangerously. "I'll release him... right to the gods," he hissed.

Overwhelmed by frustration, Ava's voice rose, her emotions spilling over. "We don't have time for this, Mayto! They'll kill all of us, and the blood will be on your hands!"

Mayto's face was a tempest of anger, his eyes ablaze with unchecked emotion from Ava's words. The raw intensity of her accusations hit a nerve, teetering him on the brink of restraint. He took a sharp breath and managed, "Maybe you'll see things differently by morning." Then, he turned and stormed out, leaving Ava to wrestle with her despair in the haunting silence.

Still consumed by rage and mistrusting his impulses, Mayto held off until dawn before deciding to face Elliot. Sleep had eluded him; instead, he'd spent the night pacing the village and honing his weapons. As the wait became unbearable, he headed determinedly to the holding cells, fists clenched, his intentions unclear even to himself.

Standing in the cell doorway, Mayto fixed Elliot with a contemptuous glare. "From the first moment I saw you, I knew you were trouble," he sneered, his eyes narrowing. "I just didn't realize the extent of it."

Elliot, despite his circumstances, remained composed. "How's Ava?" he asked.

"Angry," Mayto replied tersely. "But she's fine."

"What do you expect? You've tied her up and kept her from her daughter," Elliot countered.

"I'm preventing her from acting recklessly and endangering everyone else."

"She's trying to save everyone, Mayto, not endanger them. We both are!"

"You're lying!" Mayto snapped. "You might have fooled Ava, but not me."

Elliot met Mayto's stare steadily. "I haven't lied to anyone. It's not Ava or my actions that are endangering anyone, it's your foolish stubbornness that will kill us all if you don't start listening."

"Bella and my father were taken because of your actions, not mine!" Mayto spat back.

Elliot calmed himself again. He would get nowhere shouting at Mayto. "The gods didn't come today because of me, Mayto," he stated calmly. "Think about it—during

the taking, did they say anything about me or Ava?"
Elliot's question hung in the air.

"No, but that doesn't mean—"

"Did they mention any Lunari as the reason for their visit today?" Elliot followed up, not letting him finish.

"No," Mayto said grudgingly.

"They left without scanning everyone, right?" Elliot pressed.

"Yes, but—"

Elliot pressed on. "That's because they were only here for Bella. Once they had her, they didn't care about the rest of you. They only took your father because he defied Gold Stripe, right?"

Mayto hesitated, his internal conflict apparent. The truth in Elliot's words resonated with him, yet his need to direct his anger and frustration at a tangible target was overpowering.

"Mayto, listen to me," Elliot continued, his tone insistent. "They're planning to kill everyone in a few days. We discovered their plan earlier today." Elliot's words were calculated, meant to pierce through Mayto's denial.

"You're lying!" Mayto's voice rang out. Despite his conviction, an undertone of uncertainty suggested he was wrestling with the possibility that Elliot's words might hold truth.

Elliot persisted, his voice steady and convincing. "Think about it, Mayto. You've always suspected these 'gods' are lying to you. That's the root of your anger. It's why you stood up to them today, why you were willing to fight. It's the same reason your father fought them too—he shared those doubts. Deep down, you know there's truth to what I'm saying."

"Don't talk about my father," Mayto warned, his voice low and dangerous.

Elliot, undeterred, pushed on. "Your father tasked me with uncovering the truth. Today, Ava and I did that. But the truth is far worse than we imagined."

Mayto's hardened exterior showed a crack. "And what is this 'truth' then?"

"The truth is that they destroyed Earth to claim it as their own. They brought you here for testing. Now that they're done, they plan to eliminate all of you," Elliot said.

Mayto started to object, but Elliot quickly added, "We have proof, Mayto. We were on our way back to show it to your father."

Mayto grunted. "Where is this proof?" he asked, his eyes narrowing in suspicion.

"Ava has it. Go to her and see it with your own eyes," Elliot implored.

Mayto, his mind a whirlwind of doubt and conflict, left the holding cells with a last piercing look at Elliot. He moved quickly across the square and entered his father's house, steeling himself for the confrontation with Ava. As he approached her, he raised his hand, signaling for quiet. His voice was unexpectedly gentle. "Enough shouting, Ava. I've spoken with Elliot. He says you have proof. Show it to me now."

Ava, who had been prepared to confront Mayto with anger, paused, sensing a shift in him. Somehow, Elliot had managed to sow a seed of doubt. The how was irrelevant; what mattered now was convincing Mayto. The fate of

Bella, and all of the Lunari, depended on it. She nodded calmly. "Yes, I have it. Just untie me, and I'll show you."

"Don't try anything," Mayto warned her.

"Don't worry, I won't," Ava assured him. "Fighting you won't help. We need you if we're going to save everyone."

Ava, once unbound, swiftly retrieved the camera tucked into the inner pocket of her dress. She methodically showed Mayto the photographs of their expedition to the Forbidden Mountain, culminating with the incriminating video from the base. Mayto watched intently, a silent spectator until the footage concluded.

With his complexion noticeably paler, he asked in disbelief, "Is this real?"

"On Bella's life," she affirmed, her gaze meeting his firmly.

Mayto appeared lost in thought for a moment, then a resolve seemed to crystallize within him. He motioned to one of his men. "Bring Elliot to me now," he ordered.

While waiting for Elliot's arrival, Mayto studied the footage again, absorbing every detail. As Elliot was brought in, still bound, Mayto turned to face him, a newfound urgency in his demeanor. "Ava mentioned you have a plan?" he inquired.

Elliot gave a firm nod. "Yes, but it requires your men's cooperation, and trust!"

"They're at your disposal," Mayto replied without hesitation.

"How quickly can you assemble everyone in the square?" Elliot asked.

"Why?" Mayto asked, puzzled.

"Everyone must understand what's at stake," Elliot explained. "If we confront the Telvanni and fail, we all die. The village needs to know the risks."

After a brief moment of contemplation, Mayto called over one of his men and instructed them to arrange a village assembly. "It's done. We'll meet in thirty minutes," Mayto stated. "Now, tell me your plan."

Elliot turned slightly, showing his bound wrists to Mayto. "Perhaps you could start by untying these," he suggested.

Chapter 59

As Elliot concluded explaining his plan, the sun's arc had moved significantly, lengthening the shadows around them. The strategy was sound, and with Mayto's crucial input, its prospects had notably improved.

In the village square, Mayto stood on an elevated platform, much as his father had before. The villagers, gathered in an air of curiosity and concern, murmured amongst themselves, wondering about the sudden assembly so early in the morning.

Taking a deep breath and clearing his throat, Mayto began. "My fellow Lunari, you will have to forgive me, for I am not as gifted a speaker as my father. Had fate been kinder yesterday, he would have been the one talking to you now. I might not say things as well as he would have, but I'm here with the same message. Though, he probably would've told you sooner, not being as stubborn as me."

A ripple of laughter moved through the crowd. With growing confidence, Mayto continued. "I've gathered you all here because we've been deceived by the 'gods.' I, like many of you, believed their lies, too fearful to confront the truth. But the truth is, they're not gods. They are not even our saviors. They are our captors, and if we don't act—and act now—they will become our executioners." His words, stark and unvarnished, hung heavily in the air, striking a chord of urgency among the villagers.

The crowd reacted with a collective intake of breath, faces turning to one another in shock and disbelief, the weight of Mayto's revelation hitting them all at once.

The crowd listened intently as Mayto continued to unravel the deception they had been fed. "They claimed to rescue us from a dying world, promising a return once it was safe. But the harsh reality is, they abducted us from a thriving Earth and have been using us for their experiments in these so-called 'takings.'"

A sense of disbelief and confusion swept over the villagers, their faces mirroring the shock and fear that Mayto's words evoked.

Pointing towards Elliot, Mayto introduced him. "This is Elliot. He arrived from Earth, just three days ago." The crowd buzzed, a mix of disbelief and curiosity in the air.

"My father, our chief, entrusted Elliot with a mission to uncover the truth. He returned last night, burdened with revelations far more sinister than anyone could believe. Even with concrete evidence, and Ava, one of our own, testifying to everything Elliot witnessed, my anguish and stubbornness blinded me to the truth. You all saw how I acted last night." Mayto's voice faltered as he recalled his reaction the previous night, his head bowing briefly in a moment of remorse before he looked up, his resolve clear.

"The proof is undeniable. These impostors, these false gods, abducted us from our true home on Earth. They've subjected us to experiments for years, and now they seek to claim Earth, our rightful home, as their own."

Mayto paused, allowing his words to resonate with the assembled villagers. "They never intended to take us back to Earth. Instead, they've dispatched an asteroid to wipe out all remaining human life. And in just a few days, they aim to exterminate all of us too." Mayto motioned to a device in his hand, lifting it above his head. "Hear the truth for yourselves." He pressed play, and the gathered crowd leaned in, a hush falling over them as they prepared to hear the evidence.

The stillness of the village square, only disturbed by the distant chirping of birds, was abruptly shattered as the general's synthetic voice rang out from the device in Mayto's hand. His words, cold and methodical, told of asteroids and DNA mapping. It laid out their planned extinction as if it were a reward for his men. Faces in the crowd contorted in horror as they processed the stark reality of their situation.

After the message ended, Mayto played it once more, ensuring the brutal truth sunk in deeply, leaving no room for denial.

As they listened a second time, the general's words seemed even more menacing, even more real. Tears silently streaked down the faces of many, and a heavy blanket of despair descended upon the crowd.

When the recording stopped, Mayto stepped forward, his voice resonating with resolve. "Do you now understand the gravity of our situation? Our only choice is to fight."

A growing chorus of affirmative murmurs began to spread through the villagers, steadily gaining strength.

Mayto pressed on. "We possess one crucial advantage: the element of surprise. We have devised a plan, a strong one. But I must ask, with all my heart: will you stand by my side in this fight?"

A thunderous "YES!" echoed back, resonating throughout the square.

"Will you rise for your families?" Mayto's voice was filled with fervor.

The response was overwhelming, a loud, unified "YES!" echoing off the walls of the village.

"And will you fight for our survival, for every Lunari's future?" Mayto's call was impassioned, urgent.

The air crackled with their collective energy, a resounding "YES!" filling the square. Determination lit up every face, a sea of villagers united in their resolve to confront the Telvanni, no matter the cost.

As the villagers' enthusiasm reached its peak, a surreal and unexpected phenomenon occurred. In an instant, the bright daylight and clear sky were engulfed by an impenetrable darkness. The sun, the blue sky, all of it disappeared in an instant, leaving them in a world devoid of light, a moon, or stars. The abrupt transition into darkness sent a wave of shock through the crowd.

A collective gasp rippled through the villagers as they found themselves plunged into this unexpected night. Confusion and fear spread rapidly; the sudden change was disorienting, almost suffocating in its completeness. Children's voices rose in the darkness, calling out for their parents, seeking comfort in the unsettling void.

The hope and unity that had just moments ago filled the air now seemed to evaporate, replaced entirely by a sense of dread and uncertainty. The darkness that enveloped them was more than just a physical absence of light; it felt symbolic of the impending threat they faced, casting a shadow over their newfound resolve.

CHAPTER 60

AMIDST THE ENVELOPING DARKNESS, it was Elliot's quick thinking that provided the first glimmer of hope. "Mayto, tap the screen on the phone!" he called out. Mayto fumbled with the unfamiliar device for a moment until the screen emitted a faint glow. With this guiding beacon, Elliot navigated his way to Mayto. Taking the phone, he immediately turned the flashlight to its maximum setting. The beam swept across the sea of anxious faces, providing a momentary relief in the pitch black.

"Mayto, get your men to light up the torches around the square," Elliot instructed, his voice carrying a calm authority amidst the chaos. "Everyone else, stay where you are. Stay calm." His instructions, clear and composed, helped to steady the nerves of the villagers.

One by one, torches began to flicker to life, cutting through the darkness. The tension in the air began to ease slightly, though a lingering sense of apprehension remained. Using the momentary lull, Elliot huddled with Mayto and Ava to deliberate their next steps.

"It seems they've escalated their plans," Elliot stated, his tone grave.

"What do you think this means for us?" Ava asked, concern in her voice.

"It likely means they're about to begin their hunt," Elliot surmised.

"But why plunge us all into darkness?" Mayto asked, puzzled.

"To create fear," Elliot explained, glancing at the distressed villagers. "It's a psychological tactic; they're playing with us."

Mayto's anger flared. "I've never hated anyone more than these Telvanni!"

"What, more than you hated me?" Elliot quipped with a half smile. "Stay focused, Mayto. You'll have your opportunity for payback soon enough, I promise," Elliot added.

"So what are we going to do now?" Ava asked. "This changes everything."

"Not everything. We just need to adjust the plan a little," Elliot said. Noting their puzzled expressions, he continued. "Firstly, we need to get these people to safety. Ava, the shelters—you mentioned there was more than one?"

"Yes, there are seven," Ava confirmed, understanding his plan. "And the Telvanni don't know about them."

"There are four shelters between here and the Great Falls," Mayto added, seeing where Elliot was going. "It'll be tight, but we should be able to fit everyone in."

"Good," Elliot responded. "Mayto, select five of your fastest men to stay with us. The rest will follow Ava's lead." As Mayto moved to choose his men, Elliot added, "Mayto, make sure they do exactly as Ava instructs. They answer to you if they don't."

Mayto nodded, a hint of a smirk on his face as he headed off to pick his men.

Turning to Ava, Elliot continued. "I need you to divide Mayto's men into four groups, one for each shelter, and lead them there. They'll be the last line of defense if things don't go as planned."

"If you fail at what? What are you planning to do?" Ava asked.

"We're going on a hunt of our own!" Elliot stated resolutely.

"But you're outnumbered!" Ava said, her voice rising in alarm. "They could have twenty to thirty soldiers."

"I'm counting on it," he said firmly. "Ava, we're running out of time. I need you to trust me."

"I do trust you, Elliot."

"Then promise me you'll stay in our shelter. There's still one shock stick left in there," Elliot advised.

A flicker of surprise crossed Ava's face. "I thought there were two?"

Elliot reached into his pack, which he had retrieved earlier from the chief's house, producing a shock stick. "I brought one back with me," he remarked. Noticing Ava's surprised look, he flashed a mischievous smile. "What can I say? I was always taught to be prepared," he added.

Ava managed a small smile in response, just as Mayto returned with his select group. "These are the five who'll join us," Mayto announced. "The rest are under your command, Ava."

As Ava got to work organizing Mayto's men, Mayto turned to address the villagers. The crowd quieted as he spoke. "We don't have much time, so listen carefully," he began, his tone serious yet calming. The villagers fell silent, all attention on him. "Ava will divide you into groups and lead you to our hidden shelters with my men. It is vital that you move fast and stay quiet. Follow their instructions closely. We'll make sure no one is left behind."

As Mayto concluded his instructions, he stepped aside, making room for Ava to address the villagers. However, before she could speak, the sudden sound of a horn blast echoed through the air, causing a wave of panic to spread among the crowd. Murmurs and whispers intensified, but Ava stood firm, her resolve unshaken.

Raising her voice to cut through the growing fear, Ava said, "Those horns are meant to intimidate us, to make us afraid." Her words captured the villagers' attention, calming the immediate panic. "We can't afford to give in to fear or panic now. We won't be intimidated any longer!" she spoke with a commanding presence. "Quickly, everyone, line up behind these men, just like you would for the scanning!"

Motivated by Ava's encouraging words, the villagers quickly formed orderly lines, careful to stay with their family members. Ava, with a keen eye, moved through the crowd, making swift adjustments to ensure even distribution.

"Stay in your groups and follow the person ahead of you," she instructed. "The forest floor is uneven, and it will be dark, so be cautious." Guided by the torches held by Mayto's men, the villagers began their cautious journey out of the village via the southern road.

Before leaving, Ava turned to Elliot, her expression blending determination and concern. She quickly kissed him and then gave his arm a reassuring squeeze. "Be safe," she urged him.

"You too, Ava!" Elliot replied. "I'll see you soon."

"You better!" She winked at him and then turned to Mayto, offering him a small, encouraging smile. "Good luck with the hunt, Mayto," she said, her tone conveying solidarity.

Mayto returned her smile with a nod. "Be safe, Ava." His voice carried a mix of gratitude and concern as he watched her lead the villagers away to safety.

CHAPTER 61

AFTER AVA TURNED TO leave, Elliot beckoned Mayto and his men closer. "We need to make the village as bright as possible. Their helmets help them see in the dark. If we leave things as they are, they'll locate us far quicker than we can find them."

"We can light the torches around the village," Mayto suggested.

"Good, that should work," Elliot agreed, scanning the anxious faces around him. "I'm uncertain about their numbers—it could be as few as twenty-five or as many as fifty. I doubt they'll deploy their full force, so our best guess is a number between those estimates."

"That's a considerable number for just the seven of us," Mayto said, noting the concern etched on his men's faces.

"Don't worry, we're not going to take them on all at once. Plus, I have this," Elliot remarked, pulling out a shock stick from his pack. The men leaned in, their eyes reflecting the flickering torchlight.

As Elliot demonstrated the shock stick, a murmur of awe rippled through the group. He then outlined his plan, his voice firm, leaving no room for doubt.

"Do you really think this will work?" Mayto inquired, his face an unreadable mask.

"It has to," Elliot responded, with a conviction that seemed to lift the men's spirits.

"What if they don't split up as you predict?" one of Mayto's men challenged, his voice betraying his nervousness.

"Then the rest of you hang back while I go take some more shock sticks from them," Elliot replied. "After that, fight as if both your and everyone else's lives depend on it... because they do!"

"We," Mayto corrected Elliot, a hint of a smile playing on his lips.

"What?" Elliot queried, confused.

"While 'we' take more shock sticks from them," Mayto clarified. "I won't let you hog all the action. I've got a little payback to dish out for what happened yesterday," he added, the smile now fully formed on his face.

Elliot, feeling a surge of camaraderie, smiled as he observed the transformation in Mayto's men. Their earlier apprehension was replaced by a fierce determination, clearly visible in their eyes. Mayto's unyielding spirit had ignited a powerful resolve within them, uniting the group with a shared sense of purpose that seemed to fortify them against the darkness of the night ahead.

"Alright, follow your instructions, go light those torches, and meet back at the north gate once you're finished. If you hear my signal, it means they're near—come immediately!" Elliot commanded. "Off you go."

The five men dashed into the shrouding darkness, their movements swift as they ignited torches, casting dancing shadows across the village paths. Meanwhile, Elliot and Mayto departed the square and journeyed up the northern path, each torch they lit cutting through the darkness like beacons of defiance.

"Tell me honestly, Elliot," Mayto said, his voice steady as he lit a torch on the right side of the road. "Now that it is just you and I, what do you think our chances are?"

Elliot lit a torch to the left of the path, then met Mayto's gaze with an unwavering intensity. "If I have to kill every last Telvanni on my own to get back to Bella, then that is what I'll do," he said, his tone icy with resolve. "Failure is not an option for me. Something tells me that's the same for you too, Mayto."

Mayto's grin was a flash in the firelight. "You know, I liked you the moment I first saw you, Elliot."

Elliot chuckled, a brief respite from the tension. "Really... You know, I'm eager to watch you throw those massive fists at someone else for a change. You nearly took my head off the other night."

"That's merely my way of extending friendship!" Mayto joked, his laughter echoing in the night as he neared another torch.

"Feel free to show the Telvanni your 'unfriendly' side," Elliot encouraged, a smirk playing on his lips.

"Oh, don't worry," Mayto said, striking another torch to life, "I'm planning to see my father again too. Failure is not an option for me either!"

Having completed their task along the north road, Elliot and Mayto extended their efforts to the grasslands north of the village. They strategically placed torches at fifty-yard intervals, creating a glowing perimeter that would reveal the Telvanni soldiers' approach.

Their vigil at the north gate was brief yet filled with a tense anticipation. One by one, the five men returned, each adding to the growing sense of readiness. Standing there, overlooking the village bathed in the warm glow of their handiwork, Elliot couldn't suppress a feeling of satisfaction.

The group of seven took up positions within the village confines, their eyes fixed on the northern route that wound towards the Forbidden Mountain. Concealed yet vigilant, they waited in silence, the only sound the occasional crackle of a torch.

Ten minutes later, their patience paid off. The silhouettes of the first Telvanni soldiers, marching in pairs, began to materialize from the forest's edge. Elliot's eyes narrowed as he counted them—thirty-two in total. Four displayed the distinct black stripes on their armor, marking them as squad leaders. Each leader commanded a group of seven blue-striped soldiers.

Just as Elliot had predicted, the soldiers divided into their assigned groups upon reaching the village. The first two groups marched south, penetrating deep into the heart of the Lunari village. Meanwhile, the remaining two groups stayed in the north, splitting further to cover the eastern and western areas. In the flickering torchlight, their shock sticks gleamed with a menacing shimmer, held at the ready in front of them as they moved with a predatory precision.

With a silent nod to each other, Elliot and Mayto assumed their positions, melting into the shadows of the shacks in the village's northeastern area. Concealed yet alert, they watched as the soldiers methodically conducted their search. In the quiet of their hidden vantage points, Elliot's mind raced with plans. His strategy was to further divide the eight soldiers—using Mayto's men as bait. A risky move, but one that could tip the scales in their favor.

The imminent sense of confrontation deepened. With each passing moment, the atmosphere grew thick with anticipation. In the unnatural darkness of the morning, five Lunari men silently dashed off into the void, each step taking them closer to the first confrontation that lay ahead.

CHAPTER 62

THE FIVE LUNARI MEN, concealed at the end of a row of shacks, waited with bated breath for the Telvanni soldiers to approach. As the soldiers neared, the men feigned panic, scattering in different directions with convincing alarm. Their ruse worked perfectly, drawing five of the blue-striped guards into a frenzied chase and leaving three behind.

Seizing the moment, Elliot and Mayto emerged from their hiding spots behind the remaining soldiers. Elliot moved with swift precision, his shock stick set to full power. He incapacitated two soldiers in quick succession, their bodies crumpling to the ground, unaware of what had hit them.

The third soldier faced a more brutal fate. Mayto, his strength formidable, lifted the soldier effortlessly, slamming his head against the wall with a force that shattered both neck and helmet, the grim sound echoing into the night.

Satisfied that the first phase of their plan had unfolded without incident, Elliot and Mayto hurriedly dragged the fallen soldiers into a nearby shack. They emerged moments later, wearing the soldiers' suits. Elliot, now clad in the black-striped soldier's armor, hesitated momentarily before putting on his helmet. He let out a sharp whistle, piercing through the night air, a clear signal to Mayto's men.

The first of the Lunari men soon returned, having intentionally slowed down to let his pursuer close in. Tracing his steps back down the row of shacks, he encountered Elliot, now imposing in the black-striped armor of a Telvanni squad leader, with Mayto at his side in a blue-striped suit. To the weary Telvanni soldier, it appeared they had successfully cornered the fugitive.

As Elliot distracted the soldier with praise for his pursuit, Mayto, seizing the moment, struck him down with a lethal blow from his shock stick. The soldier collapsed silently and was quickly dragged into a nearby shack, with Mayto's man slipping in behind Mayto to don the fallen soldier's armor.

With another sharp whistle from Elliot, the trap was reset. One by one, the Telvanni soldiers fell into their clever ruse, each swiftly incapacitated and hidden away. Only to be replaced by a Lunari disguised in the fallen Telvanni's suit.

In just ten minutes since the initial contact, all eight soldiers had been neutralized. Mayto, unable to hide his satisfaction, declared triumphantly, "Eight down, twenty-four to go!"

Elliot, his voice synthesized by the helmet, asked, "Are you smiling under that helmet, Mayto?"

"No," Mayto replied, the mirth in his tone betraying him. After a brief pause, he nodded subtly.

Elliot chuckled to himself, shaking his head with amusement. He beckoned the men closer, ready to detail the next stage of their plan.

"Alright, now that we're disguised in their uniforms, we can infiltrate their ranks undetected. Pair up, and the one who's left can join Mayto and me. We'll each cover a corner of the village, eliminating our targets systematically. I want you to move like you're on patrol, engaging no more than two soldiers at a time. If you come across a trio, fall back and regroup with us. We'll take them together," Elliot instructed, his voice firm and clear.

He scanned the faces of his men, noting their nods of understanding. "Be smart and discreet. Hide the bodies to prevent raising any alarms. Once your area is clear, we'll meet back at the square."

As the men began forming pairs, Elliot added one crucial detail. He bent down, scooped up a handful of mud, and smeared it onto Mayto's shoulder, front and back. "Mark each other like this," he demonstrated, his fingers leaving a deliberate streak of mud. "It's our way of identifying each other. We can't afford any mistakes with friendly fire."

The men, with quiet understanding, marked each other with the same muddy insignia. This simple act, rooted in both practicality and camaraderie, seemed to reinforce their collective determination.

Elliot, with a strategic eye, quickly assigned each pair a specific sector of the village. He watched them disappear into the dark, their movements blending seamlessly with the shadows that cloaked the silent streets.

Elliot and Mayto, now accompanied by Rico, the odd man out, merged into the southern shadows of the village.

They moved with calculated precision, adeptly replicating the gait and posture of the Telvanni soldiers. Clad in the distinctive black-striped uniform, Elliot assumed the role of the squad leader with a composed authority. Mayto and Rico, in the standard blue-striped gear, followed in formation, two abreast, their steps measured and deliberate.

They hadn't been walking for long when they encountered their first targets: two blue-striped soldiers stepping out of a Lunari home. Elliot, exuding the authority of his assumed rank, approached confidently.

"Find anyone?" he asked with feigned curiosity.

"No one," the rightmost soldier responded with disappointment. "We haven't seen a single person yet. They must be hiding like the rats they are."

Elliot noticed Mayto edging forward, a hint of impatience in his stance, and quickly redirected. "I think I saw some movement over there." He pointed down the street.

As the soldiers' attention shifted, Mayto and Elliot sprang into action. Quickly and effortlessly, Mayto incapacitated one soldier while Elliot neutralized the other. They dragged their bodies into the shadowed interior of the nearby dwelling, out of sight.

Once outside, Elliot turned to Mayto, his voice low but firm. "Don't let your anger control you, Mayto. We need to stay focused. There are many more to go."

Mayto grunted in acknowledgment, his focus returning as he followed Elliot down the dimly lit path, ready for the next challenge.

The next encounter with a group of Telvanni soldiers—two in blue-striped uniforms and their black-striped leader—unfolded with surprising ease. Elliot's team ambushed them just as they stepped out of a house, quickly and silently dispatching them in a fluid, coordinated motion.

However, as they were stowing the bodies away, two more blue-striped soldiers appeared, drawn by the commotion. They rushed forward, eager to see why their comrade was being hauled into a house, but unprepared for Mayto's ambush. A few muffled thuds later, Mayto emerged, standing triumphantly beside Elliot.

"You're smiling under that helmet again, aren't you?" Elliot asked, his voice light.

"No," Mayto replied too quickly, his tone defiant. But under Elliot's knowing gaze, he eventually conceded, giving a small, reluctant nod.

Shaking his head again with a chuckle, Elliot led the way as they moved to locate the final group in their section. It didn't take long to spot them—two blue-striped soldiers methodically checking each door.

Replicating their earlier successful strategy, they concocted a story to divert the soldiers' attention. This provided the perfect opportunity to dispatch them swiftly and silently. Once the final bodies were securely hidden, they melted back into the darkness, their steps silent as they made their way toward the village square.

As Elliot and his team approached, they were met with an unexpected sight: the area teamed with soldiers. Elliot took a moment to assess their numbers—ten in total. The presence of a single black-striped uniform among the sea of blue-striped ones signaled a leader among them. Notably, two soldiers bore smears of mud on their shoulders, a discreet sign of allies in disguise. Elliot's mind raced as he quickly formulated a plan.

"I'll take the left flank," he murmured under his breath. "Rico, you take the right, Mayto, the middle. Aim to take three each. Hold until I make the first move—timing will be key!" The men nodded in silent understanding, their focus sharpened by the imminent confrontation.

Ten yards out, Elliot's voice broke the quiet, carrying across the square confidently. "You two, over here with me," he commanded, gesturing to the disguised men. Obliging, they stepped away from their group, unwittingly out of harm's way.

Elliot calculated every step, his eyes scanning the environment for the perfect diversion. As they neared the soldiers, he pointed dramatically towards a distant alleyway, exclaiming, "I see them, runners—over there!" His voice cut through the square, convincing and urgent. The soldiers reflexively turned their gazes to where Elliot pointed. Amidst the sudden shift of attention, he raised his shock stick, taking two down in an instant, Mayto and Rico joined in, their shock sticks alive with a sinister buzz, incapacitating the distracted soldiers with lethal finality. Within seconds, all had been neutralized.

"Hey," Mayto called out to Elliot, "you took down some of mine!"

"Sorry about that," Elliot replied, the amusement evident in his voice.

"Wait, are you smiling under there?" Mayto inquired.

"No." Elliot's denial came quickly, but it lacked conviction. After a moment's hesitation, he gave a small nod, conceding the point.

Inside his helmet, Mayto chuckled and gave Elliot a friendly smack on the back. "You're alright, Elliot!" he said. "You owe me some soldiers, but you're alright!"

As they surveyed the eight fallen soldiers, Mayto instructed his men to swiftly move the bodies into a nearby dwelling, ensuring they stayed hidden in case more soldiers arrived. As they worked, the final two members of their squad returned, reporting the successful disposal of their last eight Telvanni targets.

"That's thirty-two down!" Elliot declared, pride evident in his voice. "Great job, everyone," he praised, his words bolstering the group's morale. "Now, let's go get Bella and the chief back, and put an end to these Telvanni once and for all."

A wave of spirited cheers filled the air, coupled with backslapping congratulations. The team, united and resolute, exited the village through the southern gate, their steps purposeful as they headed towards the direction of the Great Falls.

Chapter 63

Under the canopy of the darkened forest, Elliot, Mayto, and their five soldiers advanced, their path faintly lit by their flickering torches. Amidst the dense undergrowth and the distant sound of nocturnal creatures, three of Mayto's men branched off, each heading towards a different concealed shelter. Elliot had tasked them with a crucial mission: to rally the rest of Mayto's men, equip them with Telvanni uniforms and shock sticks from the Lunari village, and deploy two men back to each shelter. These were precautions against any further Telvanni threats. The remaining soldiers were to gather discreetly at the Forbidden Mountain to await further instructions.

Now reduced to a group of four, Elliot and Mayto continued their trek toward the Great Falls, anticipation growing with each step. They were eager to reunite with Ava, knowing that her involvement was crucial for the next stage of their mission: the rescue of Bella, the chief, and Franklin.

When they reached the shelter, Elliot rapped on the hatch with his shock stick and softly called out for Ava. A moment later, amidst the unexpected darkness of the morning, the sound of a bolt retracting echoed sharply through the torch-lit forest, followed by the hatch swinging open. Ava appeared, her face radiating joy. She leaped out, enveloping Elliot in a warm, exuberant embrace.

"Did you get them all?" Ava asked, stepping back to examine Elliot for injuries.

"All thirty-two of them," Elliot replied, his grin mirroring her enthusiasm.

"Thirty-two!" Ava echoed in shock. "Did anyone get hurt?" Her eyes quickly scanned the group, a flicker of concern crossing her face as she noted some missing faces.

"Not on our side," Mayto added, his voice laced with a cold satisfaction.

"The rest of Mayto's men are securing the other shelters," Elliot added.

Ava's expression brightened at the news. "That's wonderful," she said. "What's next?"

He quickly briefed Ava on their next move, echoing the instructions given to Mayto's men earlier. "We'll leave two men here for security, while you, Mayto, and I make for the shuttle. Our plan is straightforward: take control of the base and rescue Bella, the chief, and Franklin."

Without a moment's delay, Ava slipped into one of the Telvanni suits left in the shelter. Brief, solemn farewells were exchanged with the Lunari taking refuge there, each word heavy with the unspoken recognition of the daunting task ahead.

Then, united by a shared sense of purpose, Ava, Mayto, and Elliot set out toward the Great Falls, a pivotal location for the next phase of their plan.

As they approached the iconic waterfall, an eerie silence enveloped the area, contrasting sharply with its usual vibrant state. The thunderous roar of cascading water, a hallmark of the falls, had vanished, leaving behind an unsettling quiet. The customary mist that lingered in the air, giving the scene a mystical quality, was conspicuously absent, rendering the landscape hauntingly desolate.

Elliot hesitated, his gaze sweeping over the eerily calm falls. "They didn't just turn out the lights; they've turned off the power," he observed, a note of disbelief creeping into his voice. The implications occurred to him quickly. "If they've escalated to turning off the power, we should assume they've also cut off Lunar's oxygen supply," he said.

A heavy realization dawned upon the group, and the weight of their task became even more apparent. "If the oxygen has been shut off, how much time do we have?" Ava asked, urgency sharpening her words.

"I can't be certain," Elliot said. "But what I do know is that taking control of the Forbidden Mountain has just become our top priority. Once we've secured the command center, we'll have the leverage to force them to reactivate both the power and the oxygen supply."

"That means no killing everyone, Mayto!" she cautioned.

Mayto let out a grunt, his disapproval barely masked. "Not you too, Ava," he grumbled, shaking his head. "Fine, I'll spare those without a weapon."

With the mission's stakes heightened, they quickened their pace. This was no longer merely a confrontation with the Telvanni; they were now racing against time to restore Lunar's vital power supply. The silence that had befallen the once-vibrant Great Falls stood as a stark reminder of the urgency of their quest. The fate of every living creature on Lunar, both human and beast, hinged on their success.

As they ascended the mountain, navigating the shadowy passages beyond the falls, Elliot's eyes briefly settled on the empty den of Savage-Heart. "She didn't return," he murmured, sadness creeping into his tone. "They must have captured her, following the general's orders."

Ava's expression reflected Elliot's concern. "Most likely," she agreed. "I just hope she gave them a fight first."

Their trek through the cave unfolded in hushed silence, each step drawing them deeper into the mountain's heart. Upon reaching the airlock, a palpable sense of anticipation gripped them as the door slid open, ushering them into the alien world beyond. Mayto, who had only ever glimpsed these corridors in photographs, found himself in awe. The smooth walls, bathed in ambient lighting, and the surprisingly confined space of the corridors were stark contrasts to the forests and open skies of his known world. He proceeded with a cautious step, his eyes wide, absorbing the surreal surroundings with a blend of curiosity and wonder.

Upon reaching the Great Falls station, the group was met with an unsettling quiet. The silence of the pump room, so starkly contrasting with the once-busy hum of machinery from just a day earlier, lent a surreal quality to their mission.

Then came the shuttle ride, an experience that completely captivated Mayto. The sensation of hovering just above the tracks, traveling at an incredible speed, was nothing short of extraordinary. As they sped through the encapsulating darkness of the tunnel, the lights flickering past in a rhythmic blur, Mayto felt an overwhelming sense of awe. He was part of something far greater than his past experiences had ever allowed him to imagine, a witness to the technological wonders of a world beyond his wildest dreams.

Finally, they arrived at the Forbidden Mountain station. The shuttle doors smoothly slid open, and they stepped out onto the platform. Like the station above, this one and the adjoining pump room stood deserted, with silence echoing the stillness.

"I know we all want to head straight for the holding cells," Elliot began, "but a hasty attack could spell disaster. If the enemy sends just one alert to their other base, it could jeopardize not only today's rescue but also the future safety of all our people," he warned.

Leaning against the wall, Ava felt the faint hum of machinery as she wrestled with her emotions. The fierce desire to rush to her daughter's aid conflicted with the logic of Elliot's words. "We need to reach the airlock quietly and bring our people in," she suggested, her tone betraying a hint of internal conflict.

Mayto agreed, adding his perspective to the strategy. "With more of us to secure the ground floor, we reduce the chance of any alerts being sent out. Plus, having extra hands increases the likelihood of a successful rescue."

Elliot nodded thoughtfully, his mind calculating the odds. "Their forces include about eighteen soldiers, plus the general. If we bring in additional support, we'll likely outnumber them. But our numbers alone won't ensure victory if they manage to send out a single warning. We need to be smart and use the element of surprise to our advantage."

The plan was agreed upon: Elliot, Ava, and Mayto would stealthily head to the airlock to gather reinforcements. They exited the pump room, turning right into a corridor that stretched silently ahead, leading them toward the airlock and the promise of strengthened numbers.

Barely had they distanced themselves from the pump room when the muted sound of footsteps approached. Two Telvanni soldiers, identifiable by their stark uniforms, rounded the corner. Confusion flickered across their faces at the sight of the closing pump room door.

"What's your business here?" the soldier with a black stripe challenged, his hand instinctively nearing the shock stick at his belt. "The general has strictly forbidden unauthorized access."

Elliot's mind whirred into action, his reply smooth and convincing. "The general sent us to check on a system anomaly," he lied with a confidence he barely felt. "But there's a problem. We could use your help."

The soldiers exchanged a glance, then nodded. Protocol was protocol, and the general's name carried weight.

"Very well," one of them said, gesturing for Elliot and Mayto to step aside.

Exchanging a quick, knowing look, Elliot and Mayto stepped back, allowing the soldiers to move past them toward the pump room door. As it slid open to the unremarkable interior, the soldiers' alertness waned momentarily—a fatal mistake.

With the precision of a well-rehearsed play, Elliot and Mayto lunged, their shock sticks alive with charged anticipation. The soldiers crumpled without a sound, and in a swift motion, they were dragged into the room while Ava sealed the door shut behind them.

Mayto cast a glance at the fallen soldiers, his eyes crinkling in a semblance of a smile beneath his helmet. "Well, that's two less to worry about," he commented, their precarious situation not overshadowing the small victory.

Focused on the next steps, Elliot nodded in agreement. "That brings our count down to sixteen," he observed, surveying the area. "Let's move them further inside, just in case we have more unexpected company."

After repositioning the bodies in a more concealed part of the shuttle station, they ventured back into the corridor. The hall was quiet this time, save for the faint, distant clamor from the mess hall. With calculated speed, they moved towards the airlock at the corridor's end.

As they passed the mess hall entrance, Elliot's gaze flicked to the left. His quick assessment tallied four soldiers interspersed with a group of maybe fifteen to twenty individuals garbed in workers' attire. He memorized the scene, a tactical map forming in his mind for what might come next.

As they reached the airlock, Elliot abruptly signaled a halt, his expression serious. "Change of plans," he declared. "There are only four more soldiers in the mess hall. Mayto and I will lure them to the pump room for a quiet takedown. Ava, you take this opportunity to bring the rest of our team through to the airlock. We'll meet you there in five minutes."

Ava nodded in understanding and swiftly disappeared into the airlock, leaving Elliot and Mayto in the brightly lit corridor. Elliot turned to Mayto, determination in his gaze. "Ready for this?" he asked, giving Mayto's shoulder a firm pat. "We'll take them down in pairs, just like we did earlier."

"I was born ready. Though, I thought we might try for all four this time?" Mayto asked hopefully.

Elliot let out a soft chuckle. "Let's stick to the plan. And remember, I'll do the talking."

"Yeah yeah, I know, I'm just the muscle!" Mayto said, falling into step with Elliot as they made their way towards the mess hall.

CHAPTER 64

THE MESS HALL BUZZED with activity and low conversation. Personnel clad in uniforms of various colors—blue, green, and black—filled the space, engaging in animated discussions or focusing on their duties. Elliot's gaze swept over the crowd, quickly counting eighteen individuals, not including the four soldiers marked by blue stripes. He knew additional personnel would likely be stationed in the rooms adjacent to the holding cells.

Elliot and Mayto moved with deliberate purpose, seamlessly blending into the crowd without attracting undue attention. Their target was two Telvanni soldiers, seated somewhat apart from a larger group.

Approaching confidently, Elliot addressed them in a clear, authoritative tone. "I need you two to come with me. There's been an incident in the pump room. The general requires an immediate investigation."

The urgency in Elliot's voice prompted the soldiers to spring into action, abandoning their conversation to swiftly follow his lead.

As they started to exit, two other soldiers from a nearby table called out.

"Sir, if it's a matter concerning the general, we'd like to help as well," one of them offered.

Elliot exchanged a quick, understanding glance with Mayto before nodding decisively. "Your assistance would be valuable," he agreed. Turning, he led the group of four soldiers out of the room.

The pump room stood in quiet contrast to the bustling mess hall, its stillness punctuated only by the low hum of machinery at rest. As they entered, one of the soldiers, trying to be helpful, asked, "Sir, what exactly are we looking for?"

With the door shut firmly behind them, Elliot faced the group. "We've received reports of unauthorized activity near the shuttle docks," he fabricated with ease. "And get those weapons down!" he admonished. "The general would not take kindly to an accidental discharge around this equipment."

The soldiers, looking abashed, swiftly offered their apologies and lowered their weapons, their alertness waning.

Elliot and Mayto then led them deeper into the room, directing them through a door into the adjacent shuttle station. The sight that greeted the soldiers was unexpected—the bodies of their two fellow soldiers, motionless on the ground.

The confrontation was as efficient as it was brutal, leaving four more soldiers lying inert on the station floor.

"You see, I told you taking all four at once would be better," Mayto said with a hint of satisfaction in his voice.

Elliot couldn't help but laugh; Mayto was certainly starting to grow on him. "Well, it was certainly more efficient, I'll give you that," he acknowledged. Shifting back to the task at hand, he added, "Let's sweep the mess hall one more time. I want to be sure there are no surprises before we return to the airlock."

The room, once filled with the chatter and movement of numerous Telvanni, now seemed somewhat less populated. Elliot's quick count confirmed his initial impression: there were two fewer people present. This observation led them to surmise that some had likely retreated to their offices.

Elliot and Mayto moved discreetly through the mess hall and its adjoining offices, their eyes scanning every corner with meticulous attention. Elliot's mental tally was precise: twelve people remained in the hall, while five more could be seen in the offices. Notably, there were no more soldiers in sight.

With their intelligence gathered, they carefully navigated back to the airlock. There, Ava and a contingent of twenty Lunari soldiers huddled together, their posture and expressions radiating a sharp sense of readiness.

"How did it go?" Ava asked as they entered.

"Like a dream," Mayto boasted, unable to hide his pride. "We took down all four at once!"

"We've successfully removed six Telvanni soldiers, leaving twelve more and the general yet to be accounted for," Elliot announced. His words bolstered the confidence among Mayto's men within the airlock; they now held the numerical advantage. However, Elliot remained cautiously focused. "But this is far from over. We still need to find the prisoners, and most importantly, secure control of this base without raising any alarms." Nods of agreement echoed in the confined space, each one a silent acknowl-edgment of the task's complexity.

Elliot swiftly explained the next phase of their strategy. The Lunari soldiers would be deployed in small, incon-spicuous groups throughout the ground floor, taking po-sitions near offices, exits, and the elevator. This strategic placement was designed to ensure they could seize control at the critical moment without triggering any alarms.

Once the Lunari were in place, Elliot, Mayto, and Ava would focus on the base's more secluded sections—the offices and holding cells. Hidden from the main paths, these were the crucial areas for their rescue mission.

Having given the last of their orders, the trio took up po-sitions near the offices. They remained vigilant, observing the Lunari soldiers as they silently filed out of the airlock and dispersed into their prearranged posts on the ground floor.

Seeing that the last group was in place, they sprang into action. With a shared sense of resolve, they made their way into the research and medical offices. The area was a clinical space marked by the quiet beeping of machines and sporadic murmurs of conversation. They stealthily entered the first room, observing five personnel deeply en-grossed in their work, seemingly unaware of their presence. With careful steps, they slipped through the door on the far left, entering the second chamber. Here, a further ten staff members in blue and green uniforms were scattered about, each absorbed in their individual tasks. The three of them passed through with barely a glance in their di-rection. Their thoughts were laser-focused on the holding cells ahead of them.

Upon reaching the final barrier, Elliot presented his CDU to the access panel of the holding cells. A wave of anticipation mixed with foreboding swept through them. The chance of reunion was tantalizingly close, yet the uncertainty of what lay ahead loomed large.

Silently, the door slid open, revealing a startling scene. The cells, meant to hold Bella, the chief, and Franklin, were hauntingly empty. Until this moment, their plan had been unfolding smoothly. Now, it was starting to unravel.

Ava's voice shattered the stunned silence. "Where are they? Why aren't they here?"

"Could we be too late?" Mayto said, his voice edged with rising anger.

"I don't know," Elliot confessed, his expression briefly clouded by doubt. Then, steeling himself with resolve, he instructed, "Wait here, I have an idea." Without further explanation, he turned briskly and headed back towards the main office area.

Ava and Mayto observed Elliot as he strode toward three uniformed workers, his demeanor unwavering. "Follow me!" he demanded, the synthetic tone of his voice leaving no room for challenge. The workers, though visibly confused, complied without question, and trailed behind him.

Back in the confines of the holding cells, Elliot turned to face the workers squarely. "Where have the prisoners been taken?" he demanded, his voice cutting through the silence.

A woman in a green uniform, one of the workers, broke the silence. "The general moved them about an hour ago," she disclosed.

Unable to hold back her impatience, Ava cut in sharply. "Where to?"

The workers shared uncertain glances, their expressions marked by sincere ignorance. "We don't know, we swear," another worker stammered, fear tingeing his voice.

"Does anyone here have access to these cells?" Mayto interjected, shifting the direction of the conversation.

The woman in the green uniform, furrowing her brow in bewilderment, replied, "No, only soldiers and the general have access."

Elliot gave Mayto a subtle, almost-undetectable nod. "Then you'll stay here for now," he stated firmly. Both he and Mayto raised their shock sticks, an ominous gesture that left no room for argument. The workers, their faces showing both fear and confusion, hesitantly moved into the cell. They couldn't comprehend why they were being detained; they hadn't done anything wrong.

"Stay quiet in here or we'll inform the general," Elliot commanded, his voice stern and allowing no room for argument. His warning was met with immediate compliance, quelling any further resistance.

Elliot, Ava, and Mayto made their way back to the offices, embarking on the systematic task of detaining the remaining workers. They led each person, sometimes in small clusters, to the holding cells that had, until recently, imprisoned their loved ones. With each Telvanni worker they secured, their control over the facility steadily grew stronger.

After securing the last Telvanni worker, they gathered at the mess hall entrance for an essential, but brief, strategy session. Elliot chose ten Lunari soldiers to accompany them in the advance. The rest were ordered to fortify the ground floor, a maneuver set to start five minutes post their departure, aiming for a discreet approach to the command room without drawing attention.

With their plan established, the goals were unmistakable and vital: take control of the command center, locate the general, and rescue Bella, the chief, and Franklin. The success of their mission hinged on the perfect execution of each of these tasks.

CHAPTER 65

THE LIFT COMMENCED ITS silent journey upwards, carrying Elliot, Mayto, Ava, and the ten Lunari soldiers towards the top floor. In the confined space, a turbulent blend of fear and anger swirled among them. Ava's mind was a whirlwind of worry for her daughter Bella. She agonized over the questions that haunted her: what did the general want with her? Was she still unharmed? And why had they all been moved from the holding cells?

Beside her, Mayto's thoughts were equally tumultuous, dominated by concern for his father. He yearned for the chance to reconcile, to express his remorse for years of stubborn defiance, and for not heeding his father's wisdom.

Elliot, meanwhile, radiated a steely determination. His concern encompassed everyone's safety, but his thoughts were particularly focused on Bella. He had vowed to protect her, a promise he intended to keep at all costs.

The Lunari soldiers accompanying them were gripped by apprehension for their families' safety and a deep-seated desire to restore their dignity. For too long, they had been misled by the Telvanni, who had proclaimed themselves as deities. Now, the Lunari were ready to stand up and challenge the lies and fight for their future.

The lift eventually came to a stop, the doors smoothly opening, revealing the top floor. They stepped into a desolate corridor, ominously quiet and seemingly unguarded. Cautiously, the group filed out.

Elliot, with Ava by his side, took the lead. Silently, they approached the first turn on the left, eyes vigilantly scanning the corridor for any hint of movement. Yet, it remained eerily vacant, its stillness only adding to the tension of their mission.

At Ava's quick, silent hand gesture, the group advanced. Their target, the command center, loomed at the end of the passageway—a stronghold brimming with secrets and power, critical to their mission's success.

The corridor, flanked by a series of rooms, appeared to extend infinitely ahead. Ignoring every door that did not align with their mission, they proceeded with stealth, almost like shadows. Driven by a sole purpose, they advanced toward the facility's core. The command center, pivotal not only to their mission but also to Earth's fate, was their sole objective.

As they drew closer, the silence grew more profound, heavy with the weight of impending confrontation. Their strategy was straightforward. Elliot and Mayto would spearhead the entry into the room. Following in pairs, the team planned to quickly surround the area, systematically neutralizing all guards in a coordinated assault. Once they secured the room, their focus would immediately shift to those at the terminals, offering them a single opportunity to step back. Hesitation was not a luxury they could afford;

triggering an alarm or allowing any communications to slip through was out of the question.

Elliot and Mayto discussed their roles: Elliot would deal with the general while Mayto would handle any guards marked with black stripes. Standing at the entrance to the command room, they shared a silent countdown, a mutual understanding passing between them. With a coordinated movement, they breached the room. Elliot, his shock stick primed, quickly moved to the left, while Mayto headed right. Elliot scanned the area for the general, but to his surprise, he was absent; the room's sole security had been left in the hands of two soldiers, each with blue stripes on their uniforms.

In a swift and decisive motion, Elliot fired upon the leftmost guard while Mayto blasted the other. Chaos erupted in the command room as the Lunari soldiers poured in, swiftly encircling the room. With their shock sticks raised, they shouted orders at the technicians to step away from their consoles. Ava, entering last, closed the door behind them, sealing the room.

The technicians, dressed in their stark black uniforms, complied instantly, hands raised and faces marked by fear. They stood immobilized, encircled by the intimidating figures of the disguised Lunari soldiers.

Abruptly, a technician, his gaze locked on a red button on the wall—likely an alarm—bolted towards it in a frantic attempt. However, before he could get there, a sharp *THWUMP* resounded in the room. He crumpled to the ground instantly, incapacitated by Ava's swift intervention. Every eye in the room shifted to the downed Telvanni worker, and a tense stillness prevailed; no one else dared to move.

Elliot stepped into the center of the room, his voice firm and authoritative, commanding their attention. "Who's in charge here?" he demanded.

A middle-aged man, among the technicians and marked by fear, hesitantly acknowledged his role. Elliot quickly approached, his presence intimidating. "Answer my questions and no harm will come to you. Understand?"

The man's nod, shaky and uncertain, was accompanied by a weak, "Yes."

"Where's the general?" Elliot asked.

"He's... in the hangar," stammered the technician.

"And where exactly is this hangar?" Elliot asked.

"Opposite... opposite the command room." He pointed at the door.

"What about the prisoners? What did he do with them?"

"I don't know. The general took them with him."

"What's he doing with them?" Elliot asked, his voice hardening.

The technician swallowed hard, his Adam's apple bobbing. "I... I don't know."

"His men. Are they with him?" Elliot asked.

"Yes, most went with him. The rest are either in the mess or on the hunt."

Elliot leaned in, his presence imposing like an impending storm. "I've already dealt with your 'hunting party,'" he stated icily, "and your friends in the mess hall!" His voice was a cold ultimatum. "If you don't want to join them, tell me how many more accompanied him. And don't even think about lying!"

"I don't know for sure... no more than ten," the technician replied nervously.

A heavy silence filled the room, the air thick with tension. Elliot's next words emerged softly, yet resonated with an ominous undertone. "Can you restore the power?"

The technician's face drained of color, turning ghostly pale in the harsh lighting. His eyes, wide and filled with a deep, instinctual fear, remained fixed on Elliot. The unexpected shift in questioning, contradicting what he knew of the general's orders, clearly unsettled him.

"The power, in Lunar," Elliot pressed, his voice firm and commanding. "Can you turn it back on?"

The technician responded with a jerky, anxious nod. "Yes, but it must be initiated from the pump room."

"Then that's what you're going to do!" Elliot's tone was uncompromising. "Choose someone now to go with my men to the pump room who can do this. Any tricks, and you know what will happen." The hum of his shock stick underscored his words, a silent yet potent threat.

"We won't try anything foolish. I promise," the technician quickly assured.

Elliot instructed two of the Lunari soldiers to escort the chosen technician to the pump room and return him unharmed once he was finished. He then turned his attention to the remaining Telvanni staff. "You're all going to be taken to the holding cells. As long as you do as you're told, no one will be harmed. Don't, and... well, look at your friend over there!" Elliot said, drawing their attention to the man who had tried to sound the alarm.

"Everyone, except for you!" Elliot said, fixing his gaze back on the technician. "You'll stay here and ensure the power comes back on... I'll be holding you personally responsible for it. Do you understand?"

The man nodded quickly.

Elliot turned his attention to Ava. "Ensure everyone is taken to the holding cells without harm and confirm that the power is restored. Begin securing the base. Stay sharp, especially on the first floor—there's likely to be more Telvanni there."

Ava gave a short nod, then asked, "What will you be doing?"

"Mayto and I will head into the hangar and scout the area. We'll try to locate the prisoners," Elliot replied. "By the time you've secured the base, we'll have a plan to confront the general and his men. Meet us outside the hangar doors in five minutes. Then we'll go in for Bella and the rest, together."

Ava's voice carried a note of steel as she added, "But if there's any indication they're in danger..."

"I won't hesitate to act if lives are on the line," he stated with conviction.

"Neither will I!" Mayto added.

Elliot swept his gaze across the command room, every soldier and technician acutely aware of the tension hanging in the air. With a subtle nod to Mayto, they edged towards the exit, their movements measured and silent. As they slipped out, the room remained in a deliberate pause, granting them the cover of stillness to ensure an unnoticed entry across the corridor to the hangar. Moments later, under Ava's efficient directives, the room buzzed back to life, the Lunari forces moving with purpose as they secured their captives, ready for transport.

Chapter 66

As Elliot entered the hangar, he was struck by its immense scale. The ceilings stretched high above, fading into the dim light, a stark contrast to the confined corridors he had traversed. Subtle lighting from above cast vast shadows that danced across walls and floors, intertwining with rows of silent machinery and spacecraft. These towering craft, each an intricate marvel, stood as testaments to the Telvanni's advanced engineering. The air, laden with the scent of lubricants and metal, filled his senses and brought the surrounding machinery to vivid life. In this expansive space, he felt like an interloper among slumbering metal giants, each harboring secrets and power beyond his understanding.

Mayto's hushed voice interrupted his thoughts. "What are all these?"

"Spacecraft, I think," Elliot responded in awe, his voice low. "But they're unlike anything I've ever seen."

The hangar's quiet was punctuated only by distant, indistinct sounds of commotion and the faint echo of footsteps close by—Telvanni soldiers on their rounds. Elliot and Mayto exchanged a glance of understanding and stealthily blended into the shadows of the spacecraft. Their movements were a whisper in the vast space. Using hand signals to communicate, they positioned themselves for an ambush, the nature of the distant uproar still unknown to them.

Mayto moved with smooth and efficient grace, a fluid dance of shadows. He emerged from his hiding place, swiftly overpowering the guards without a sound. The soft thuds of their bodies hitting the ground were the only indicators of his actions.

Elliot, emerging from his concealment, observed the scene. "We were meant to take one each," he said.

"Consider this payback for earlier," Mayto shot back, his voice tinged with quiet satisfaction.

Quickly, Elliot and Mayto concealed the Telvanni soldiers' bodies within the deep shadows of the stationary spacecraft, tucking them away amidst crates and machinery. As they delved deeper into the hangar, the previously indistinct commotion sharpened into clear, discordant sounds. Jeers and the harsh echoes of cruelty intensified with each step they took, casting a dark shadow over their resolve. With thoughts of their captive loved ones burdening their hearts, the growing cacophony heightened their unease. Navigating the labyrinth of colossal machinery, they stumbled upon a secluded corner turned makeshift arena, where a raw, brutal spectacle was unfolding.

They came upon a clearing encircled by towering stacks of equipment, where the general stood at its heart, orchestrating a horrifying spectacle. With each cruel jab he delivered to a bear cub, his men erupted in raucous cheers. The sharp, relentless *THWUMP* of his shock stick broke the hangar's stillness, a jarring contrast to the agonized howls of the cub's mother, Savage-Heart. Confined in a transparent cage, she paced in frantic desperation, her claws scraping in vain against the unyielding walls. Her mounting distress reached a fever pitch, fueling a monstrous crescendo of delight and applause from the Telvanni soldiers encircling the scene.

On either side of the general, two soldiers stood guard, their vigilance unwavering as they held Bella and the chief captive. Fear and defiance intermingled on their faces, resembling scars from unseen battles. Despite the evident distress in their eyes, the lack of physical injuries provided Elliot and Mayto a fleeting, somber respite amidst their mounting rage.

This brief calm was abruptly destroyed when the general inflicted another shock on the cub. The small animal collapsed, its breathing weak, its struggles ceasing. Savage-Heart, the mother bear, released a heartrending roar of anguish that resonated throughout the hangar, met only by the cruel laughter of the soldiers.

"We shall return to our entertainment with the cub and its mother later," the general declared, his voice dripping with icy amusement as he signaled a temporary halt to the bear's torment. His cold, smirking gaze swept over the ranks of entertained soldiers. "But let us not overlook our other more... earthly entertainment," he added, his hand gesturing towards the center of a circle formed by eight soldiers. In the midst of them, Franklin knelt, embodying both defeat and unyielding spirit, his face etched with the marks of the brutal treatment he had already suffered.

At the sight of his friend, so broken yet resilient, among the Telvanni soldiers, a wave of cold fury washed over

Elliot. This was no longer just a mission; it had evolved into a deeply personal battle. His eyes met Mayto's, and in them, he saw his own determination reflected. They both realized there was no time to wait for reinforcements. Immediate action was imperative.

The air in the hangar was thick with a suffocating mix of tension and malevolence. The sounds of the Telvanni soldiers' brutal assault on Franklin echoed, their blows landing with sickening thuds. Despite his resilience, the strain of the relentless onslaught was evident.

From the shadows, Elliot and Mayto emerged, tense and ready, their bodies a tight spring of contained fury. Witnessing Franklin in such a vulnerable and battered state propelled them past the brink of restraint. Overtaken by a wave of anger and desperation, they could no longer stand idle in the face of such cruelty. Compelled to act, they stepped forward, prepared to end the torment.

Elliot's and Mayto's weapons discharged in rapid succession, their muted sounds quickly downing the four Telvanni soldiers in mid-assault. Their sudden intervention momentarily ceased the savagery, drawing astonished stares from all around.

The general's voice cut through the ensuing chaos, exuding commanding authority. "Drop your weapons!" he ordered icily. In that instant, Bella and the chief were thrust forward, the ominous buzz of shock sticks pressed threateningly against their skin. Elliot and Mayto, caught in a whirlwind of emotions, hesitated, but the grips on their weapons did not loosen.

With a chilling nonchalance, the general turned towards Franklin. In one swift, brutal motion, he fired his shock stick. The impact was devastating and unequivocal. Franklin's body crumpled to the ground, lifeless, as his final breath escaped him. The finality of the act sent a shock wave through Elliot and Mayto, freezing them in a moment of profound horror and disbelief.

Elliot stepped forward, his voice instinctively crying out, "NO!" as though he could somehow reverse what had happened. But both he and Mayto were abruptly stopped in their tracks as the general swung his shock stick toward Bella and the chief, threateningly redirecting their focus.

The general chuckled, a cold, synthetic sound echoing eerily through his helmet, as he turned back to Elliot and Mayto. "These two will be next unless you comply," he threatened, his voice dripping with malice.

Faced with this grim ultimatum, grief and concern weighed heavily on Elliot and Mayto. They slowly lowered their weapons to the ground, their gaze lingering on Franklin's motionless body.

"Take their weapons," the general ordered. His men promptly obeyed. "Now, remove your helmets!" he commanded, eyeing Elliot and Mayto. "You may be wearing Telvanni suits, but you're clearly not one of us!" he spat.

Upon removing their helmets, Bella's voice shattered the tense silence, "Elliot!" she exclaimed, her eyes alight with recognition. Elliot's gaze instantly shifted from Franklin's lifeless body to Bella's worried face.

"Silence, child!" the general barked, his voice cutting through the air with harsh authority.

Mayto exchanged a glance with his father after removing his helmet. The chief's face reflected astonishment and pride at him.

"Well well, if it isn't the chief's son," the general mused with a hint of mockery. "I must admit, I underestimated you. Thought you were just all muscle with no brains, but here you are, proving me wrong." His gaze then shifted to Elliot. "Or perhaps the true mastermind is you, Elliot," he observed, his tone laced with curiosity. "Tell me, why haven't you crossed my path until now?"

Elliot remained silent, his gaze shifting between Bella and Franklin.

"Ahh, he's your friend, isn't he?" the general pressed, his tone amused. "I always wondered why the Earthman was alone."

His name was Franklin," Elliot shot back, his voice cold, his eyes firmly locked on the general."

"His name is irrelevant!" the general dismissed with a wave of his hand. "He's dead, and soon, so will you be.

"But before that, you might be useful. I seem to have cut short my men's fun by killing your friend there. They were just starting to enjoy themselves." Playing to his audience, the general then addressed his soldiers. "What do you think, men? Should we let these two provide some replacement entertainment?"

Excitement crackled in the air as a chorus of cheers erupted from the Telvanni soldiers. They swiftly formed a ring around Elliot and Mayto, their faces alight with eager anticipation. The four soldiers Elliot and Mayto had downed were now stirring, gradually regaining consciousness. Their shots, though at full power, had been less effective due to the distance.

Bella and the chief watched, horrified, as the Telvanni soldiers looked at Elliot and Mayto like predators eyeing their next prey.

"Just one more thing," the general added with a malicious chuckle. "Strip off those suits. We can't have you gaining any advantages, can we!"

Chapter 67

Elliot and Mayto, now stripped of their suits, stood back-to-back. They braced for the looming clash against the circle of eight Telvanni soldiers. Born on the harsher gravity of Earth, Elliot's strength was easily double that of any Telvanni, a fact amplified by his superior combat training. Mayto, standing beside him, presented an equally daunting figure. Deprived of his suit's gravity assist, he was expected to be weaker under the base's oppressive gravity, yet his extraordinary natural strength compensated for this disadvantage. Having seen Mayto's formidable strength and combat skills firsthand, Elliot knew there was no better ally for this uneven battle.

"You remember when I told you not to kill everyone?" Elliot asked.

Mayto grunted. "Yeah."

"Forget that. No rules."

Mayto's low chuckle momentarily lightened the heavy air. "Finally, some real action!"

"Keep an eye on those shock sticks," Elliot cautioned, his gaze sweeping over the soldiers circling. "They won't be set to lethal, but they'll still pack a punch."

"We need to neutralize them quickly," Mayto replied. After a brief pause, he added firmly, "I've got you covered, Elliot. If you get a shot at rescuing Bella and my father, go for it. Don't hesitate!"

Elliot returned a resolute nod. "The same goes for you."

Mayto's muscles tensed, his focus laser-sharp on their opponents. "Get ready," he whispered, his voice carrying a fierce determination. A moment later, he surged forward. His large frame moved with surprising speed, delivering a powerful blow to the nearest guard, who crumpled to the ground. Quickly, Mayto seized another, locking him in a choke hold from behind. Using the disoriented soldier as a human shield, he steadily advanced on the next target, his movements a perfect blend of raw power and strategic acumen.

Like a flash, Elliot sprang into action, a mere heartbeat behind Mayto. He lunged towards one of the soldiers, his actions a blend of precision and speed. With one fluid movement, Elliot seized the soldier's shock stick in an iron grip while his other hand delivered a crushing blow to the man's solar plexus with the force of a battering ram. Gasping for air, the soldier crumpled, overwhelmed by the impact.

As Elliot turned to check on Mayto, he caught sight of another soldier aiming a shock stick at Mayto's back. Without a moment's delay, Elliot used the seized weapon to fire a powerful blast. The soldier was hit squarely, the impact sending him flying off his feet, depositing him hard on the ground.

As soon as the soldier targeting Mayto hit the ground, Mayto executed a rapid pivot, his movements fluid in the midst of chaos. He raised a massive foot and brought it down with ruthless finality onto the chest of the fallen soldier. The thud resounded through the hangar as the battle continued unabated, but the soldier lay still, no longer a participant.

Still gripping the now-unconscious soldier in a choke hold, Mayto quickly assessed the evolving battle. With a calculated step, he mustered his impressive strength and flung the soldier towards the two nearest to Elliot. The soldier, transformed into an unexpected missile, collided with his comrades, the impact sending all three scattering in disarray.

Mayto's quick thinking did more than just neutralize an additional threat: it provided a crucial pause in the onslaught. This brief respite allowed both him and Elliot to momentarily regroup, bracing themselves for the next surge of attackers.

Watching the tide of battle turn unexpectedly in favor of Mayto and Elliot, the general realized he needed to act. His authority, perhaps even his safety, hinged on the performance of his soldiers. With a shrewd look, he discreetly dialed down his shock stick's power, aiming for incapacitation rather than the lethal force used on Franklin. Resolved to subdue Mayto and Elliot, he advanced with deliberate purpose, intent on tilting the balance back to his soldiers.

The chief's eyes were locked on Mayto and Elliot as they valiantly fought against the eight Telvanni soldiers. A wave of pride swelled within him, watching them overpower their adversaries with such formidable strength, tossing them around as if they were mere playthings. The urge to jump into the fray and fight alongside them was almost irresistible. Yet, bound by his captor and under the stern gaze of the general, who wielded his menacing shock stick, the chief was gripped by a profound sense of helplessness.

The moment the general advanced with his recalibrated shock stick, intent on intervening, a fierce fury erupted within the chief. Driven by fear for his son and Elliot, and recognizing a pivotal moment, he summoned every ounce of his strength for a swift, decisive strike. The guard, his attention momentarily diverted by the general's approach, was utterly unprepared for what followed. Seizing the moment, the chief unleashed a powerful punch. His fist, driven by a surge of protective rage, connected with the guard's jaw with a thunderous impact. The force of the blow was so immense that the guard was sent reeling backward, collapsing to the ground in a disordered heap. If not for his helmet, it would surely have been fatal.

Instantly seizing the moment, the chief charged at the general, his approach reminiscent of a bull bearing down on a matador. The general, caught off guard by the abrupt turmoil, turned just in time to see the chief hurtling towards him, but it was too late to dodge the inevitable clash. The impact sent the general tumbling to the ground, his breath forced out by the sheer magnitude of the collision. The chief, landing heavily atop the general, used his weight to pin him down, rendering him momentarily defenseless.

However, the moment of triumph was short-lived. The guard overseeing Bella, snapping out of his initial stupor from the chief's audacious assault, leaped into action. He aimed his shock stick at the back of the chief, who was relentlessly attacking the general on the ground. With a pressing of the trigger, a loud THWUMP echoed in the hangar, soon followed by a heavy THUD as the shock stick's charge hit the chief. The abrupt shock disrupted his momentum, forcing him to relinquish his upper hand. The general, quick to capitalize on this opportunity, rolled out from under the chief, freeing himself.

With his freedom swiftly reclaimed, the general sprang to his feet, his expression burning with rage. He wasted no time in aiming his shock stick at the chief, who was still reeling from the initial shock. As the chief appeared to shout something, the general discharged his weapon: THWUMP. The charge collided with the chief's body with a resounding THUD, knocking him to his knees. A third THWUMP echoed in the hangar, followed by another thunderous THUD as the shock stick's charge hit the chief once more. Succumbing to the successive shocks, the chief fell face forward onto the ground, motionless.

Bella, initially stunned by the chief's bold confrontation with the general, was jolted back to reality when she saw her guard shoot the chief. As the guard readied for another shot, Bella's instincts surged into action. In a swift move, she stomped down hard on his foot. He grimaced in pain, his hold on the shock stick faltering. Bella quickly wrested the stick from his loosened grip. With no hesitation, she jammed it against his abdomen and pressed the trigger. The guard convulsed under the direct, intense shock, then staggered back and collapsed to the ground, rendered utterly motionless.

Bella, intent on rushing to the chief's aid, froze as his voice cut through the tumult. "Run!" he implored, even as another jolt from the general's shock stick wracked his body. Her heart hammering, Bella was torn between desperation and duty. Casting a final tormented glance at the chief, now forced to his knees, she made her choice. Bella spun on her heels and sprinted towards the deeper shadows of the hangar. Her footsteps made muted thuds in the sprawling, dimly lit expanse.

"General, the girl's escaping!" shouted the guard, recently floored by the chief, his voice still groggy.

The general, quickly redirecting his focus, caught just a glimpse of Bella as she darted behind a stack of crates. Her figure, determined and swift, faded into the shadows of the hangar, the commandeered shock stick clutched in her hand. A surge of urgency overtook the general.

"You, come with me," he barked, his voice cutting through the air as he signaled to the fallen guard. With a look of steely determination, they set off in hot pursuit of Bella, their footsteps resonating with a foreboding echo across the vast hangar.

Engulfed by the unfolding chaos, Mayto, witnessing his father's brutal takedown, was driven into a whirlwind of rage. His attacks grew more ferocious, his considerable strength seemingly magnified by the storm of his emotions. Each blow he delivered was charged with a raw, unbridled fury.

Elliot, too, was gripped by a heightened sense of urgency, driven not only by the brutal treatment of the chief but also by the sight of the general in pursuit of Bella. There was no time to lose; this confrontation needed to end, and end now.

Mayto's imposing figure transformed into an unstoppable force, his powerful strikes sending Telvanni soldiers flying. Each of his punches and kicks landed with the impact of a sledgehammer, his adversaries overwhelmed by his raw physical prowess.

Elliot's strategic precision perfectly complemented Mayto's ferocious onslaught. Together, they formed a relentless storm of destruction. In the heat of battle, a Telvanni soldier charged at Elliot, brandishing a shock stick. Elliot, reacting swiftly, disarmed him and turned the weapon on its owner. The shock stick discharged with a resounding crack, the jolt sending the soldier sprawling to the ground, convulsing.

Mayto, following Elliot's lead, snatched up a shock stick from a downed soldier. The hangar reverberated with the chaos of their conflict—the dull thumps of bodies slamming into the deck, the fierce crack of shock sticks at work, and the guttural sounds of exertion.

Finally, as the last Telvanni soldier fell, a profound silence fell over the hangar. It was a stark, haunting contrast, broken only by the labored breathing of Elliot and Mayto, both visibly worn from the struggle. Mayto, with a look of fear etching his features, hurried towards where his father lay motionless. Each step he took was driven by concern for his father's well-being.

Elliot, driven by unwavering determination, spun and sprinted deeper into the hangar's expanse in search of Bella. The vast space unfurled before him, a maze of shadows and hidden threats. Yet, undeterred, he pressed on, driven by an unwavering promise to protect Bella, whatever the cost.

CHAPTER 68

Bella's heart raced as she weaved her way through the maze of colossal machinery and towering crates in the hangar. She became a shadow herself, her movements silent and swift, allowing her to remain unseen by the general and his accompanying soldier. Each careful step she took was accompanied by the loud beating of her heart, resounding in her ears, while her heightened senses remained acutely alert to her surroundings.

She eventually found a moment's respite, crouching beneath the vast shadow cast by a parked spacecraft. The distant echoing footsteps of the general and his guard were the only disturbances in the otherwise oppressive stillness. In the comparative safety of her hideout, she attempted to calm her frantic heartbeat, drawing deep, steadying breaths.

Her thoughts inevitably drifted towards Elliot and Mayto and the daunting odds they faced—a stark eight against two. A surge of guilt washed over her as she thought of the chief, left alone to bear the brunt of the general's wrath. Doubts plagued her—was he still alive? The burden of regret weighed heavily on her conscience. She berated herself for giving in to fear, for running away when she was needed the most. This self-recrimination was a bitter pill; she despised herself for fleeing in their darkest hour.

But then, a sudden cessation in the footsteps of the general and his soldier snapped Bella back to the present. The abrupt halt in their pursuit was as disconcerting as it was unexpected, but it provided her with a vital opportunity to collect her thoughts and strategize her next step. She couldn't keep evading them indefinitely. Her current situation, hidden amongst the hangar's vast array of machinery, felt alien yet strangely familiar, echoing the days of hunting in the forests of Lunar with her mother. This fleeting reminiscence grounded her, infusing her with a sense of purpose and determination. Bella knew she needed to act—and act soon.

Hidden beneath the spacecraft, Bella cautiously peered out, ensuring the shadows continued to conceal her. Her eyes methodically scanned the hangar's expansive interior, alert for any sign of activity. Time seemed to elongate, with each minute marked by a growing tension.

Then, a subtle disturbance caught her eye—a shifting shadow in a nearby row. Her heart skipped a beat, but she quickly reined in her fear, steadying her grip on the shock stick. It felt reassuringly solid in her hand, a tangible reminder of her newfound resolve.

Bella's intense focus zeroed in on the emerging figure, its details gradually becoming clearer amidst the shadows. The uniform, stark white and accented with a distinctive gold stripe, unmistakably belonged to the general. He moved between the crates with calculated precision, his strides deliberate as he searched the rows of equipment, clearly hunting for her. Bella's breathing became controlled and even; she understood what she had to do. Drawing upon the lessons ingrained into by her mother, she prepared herself for the imminent confrontation.

Holding the shock stick firmly, Bella recalled her mother's guidance—the importance of maintaining composure, the art of striking with precision from concealment. Her plan was simple: to target and fire silently from her hideout. The simplicity of the act gave her a renewed sense of determination.

Inhaling deeply, Bella fine-tuned her hold on the shock stick, readying it for use. She waited with bated breath for the opportune moment, her eyes intently tracking the general's progress as he neared her position. In her mind, she rehearsed the action: wait for him to pass, then swiftly aim and shoot, just like her mother had shown her. The time had come to reverse the roles in this deadly game of cat and mouse.

Bella, seizing this moment of opportunity, held her breath as the general passed by, a mere few steps away. His back was turned towards her, his focus on the area ahead. Clutching the shock stick with a firm grip, she cautiously began to rise from her crouched position under the spacecraft. It was crucial to be silent, to avoid alerting the general to her presence.

With the shock stick poised and ready, Bella carefully aligned it towards where the general stood. She slowly raised her foot, intending to step out from the shadows for a clear shot. But, in that pivotal moment, a flicker of doubt halted her. Her mother's lessons resonated in her mind: *When you move, you need to move with control... and you need to move with patience.*

Glancing down, Bella noticed for the first time the cables snaking across the floor from the spacecraft. With deliberate care, she gingerly placed her foot back on the ground, ensuring she avoided the cables. Her movements were slow and precise, mirroring the stealth and caution her mother had ingrained in her.

As she stepped forward again, shock stick still trained on the general, she remained acutely aware of her surroundings. In her peripheral vision, she meticulously watched where she placed each foot. Lining up her target, Bella took a deep breath and held it, steadying herself. Then, with a resolute squeeze of her hand, she pressed the trigger on the shock stick.

THWUMP. THUD. Bella's shot found its target. The electric charge hit the general's back with such momentum that it momentarily lifted him off the ground, propelling him several feet forward before he collapsed onto the hangar floor. As Bella approached, a newfound sense of empowerment washed over her, replacing the fear that had gripped her earlier. She stood over the general, her mind briefly flashing back to the merciless fate he had meted out to Franklin, Elliot's friend.

With determined resolve, Bella adjusted the shock stick to its highest setting. She aimed the weapon directly at the general's head, her hand remaining steady despite the swirling storm of emotions within her. Inhaling deeply, she briefly closed her eyes, confronting the weight of her impending action. Then, steeling herself, she exhaled, opened her eyes, and pressed the trigger once more.

In that critical moment before the shot, the general's soldier, attracted by the noise, burst onto the scene. He moved quickly and forcefully, knocking the shock stick upward just as Bella pressed the trigger. The blast, diverted from its intended target, struck a nearby container instead. The impact shattered the container's fragile equilibrium, spilling its contents—a jumble of wires and tools—across the hangar floor in a clattering cascade.

Reeling from the soldier's sudden intervention, Bella had only a fraction of a second to brace herself. As she turned towards him, he struck ruthlessly. With a swift, merciless backhand, he delivered a powerful blow across her face. The impact was staggering, overwhelming her senses and sending her tumbling to the side. She crashed to the ground, a sharp pain radiating across her cheek. Her vision blurred, and for a moment, the hangar seemed to spin around her.

The soldier, with his shock stick primed for a decisive strike, was abruptly disrupted by a noise behind him. Whirling around, he faced a scene that struck instant terror in his heart. Elliot, his green eyes ablaze with wild fury, was barreling towards him. His roar reverberated through the hangar, thunderous and fierce. He charged like a relentless bull, driven by raw anger and seemingly unstoppable momentum.

Despite his fear, the soldier's training kicked in. He aimed his shock stick at the oncoming man and fired. *THWUMP. THUD.* The weapon's shock hit its mark, but astonishingly, this did little to slow Elliot's charge. Driven by an unyielding rage, he closed the distance rapidly.

Before the soldier could react or discharge his shock stick a second time, he found himself completely overpowered.

The charging man, propelled by a fury that seemed almost inhuman, had closed the gap in the blink of an eye. Exerting a strength that defied belief, he lifted the soldier off the ground, even as he continued his relentless forward momentum.

Elliot launched the soldier into the air. The force of the throw sent the soldier spinning end over end in a dizzying arc. His flight was abruptly cut short as he collided with a stack of containers. The impact was catastrophic, sending the containers tumbling down in a cacophonous cascade, scattering in all directions.

The soldier's body came to a gruesome halt amid the scattered debris, the brutal force of the collision arresting his motion instantly. He landed with a sickening crack, his form crumpling into an unnatural position at the foot of a transparent cage. Inside the cage, a mother bear paced restlessly, her agitation heightening the sense of chaos that now permeated the hangar.

The soldier lay eerily motionless amidst the wreckage, his neck contorted in a grotesque manner that starkly illustrated the fatal nature of his injuries. The harsh, reverberating echo of his collision hung in the air, a chilling testament to the violence that had just unfolded. Nearby, Elliot, who had caused the destruction, paused to assess the soldier. Seeing no further threat, he turned, his attention shifting as he sought out Bella.

"Bella!" he called out, his voice echoing throughout the expansive hangar.

At the sound of her name, Bella cautiously emerged through the gaping hole in the container wall, her eyes sweeping over the area. Spotting Elliot, a wave of relief flooded her features. "Elliot!" she exclaimed, her voice filled with both happiness and relief. She immediately ran towards him.

Elliot enveloped Bella in his arms, a surge of relief flooding through him as they found solace in each other's embrace amidst the turmoil. For a fleeting moment, they remained locked like this, the chaos encircling them momentarily receding into the background. As Elliot drew back slightly, his attention was drawn to the vivid red mark on Bella's cheek, a painful reminder of the violence she had faced. With a gentleness that stood in stark contrast to their harsh surroundings, he brushed his fingers lightly over the bruise. "Are you okay?" he asked, his voice laden with concern.

Bella met his gaze, a hint of resilience shining through despite the ordeal. "I am now," she responded, her voice steady, her arms tightening around him once more. After a moment, her tone tinged with worry, she inquired, "Where's Mama?"

"She's safe. She's just outside the hangar. You'll see her soon," Elliot reassured her.

Their brief respite was abruptly disrupted as the general emerged from the ruins of the shattered container wall. Gone was his helmet, revealing a face marred by scars, a clear indicator of countless battles faced. A mane of greasy long black hair cascaded over his shoulders, adding to his intimidating presence.

Without delay, he raised his shock stick, aiming it directly at them. In that critical split second, Elliot's reflexes sprang into action. He swiftly turned, putting his body between the blast and Bella. The shock stick discharged with a resounding *THWUMP*. The force of the blast slammed into his back, sending both of them crashing to the ground. They collapsed into a heap, the searing pain of the shock radiating through Elliot's body, a harsh reminder of the danger they were still in.

CHAPTER 69

THE DUST SLOWLY SETTLED in the hangar. Elliot, despite the excruciating pain coursing through his body from multiple shock blasts, lay protectively over Bella, who was unconscious. His body acted as a shield, safeguarding her in her vulnerable state. Beneath him, Bella's gentle breaths were a subtle but reassuring sign of life, their steady rhythm a small comfort amidst the chaos.

However, the sense of danger was far from over. The air was thick with the threat of more violence, a tension that Elliot could almost touch. Despite his aching muscles and throbbing head, his determination did not waver. Bella's safety was still his primary focus.

Summoning every ounce of willpower and pushing through the agonizing pain, Elliot managed to lift his head just enough to survey his surroundings. Through blurred vision, he focused on the imminent danger approaching. His gaze locked onto the general, who was advancing with a menacing stride, his eyes burning with cold, ruthless intent. The general, shock stick at the ready, was unmistakably intent on finishing this conflict once and for all. His steps, measured and deliberate, brought him ever closer to Elliot, who appeared vulnerable and defenseless on the ground.

Elliot, feigning greater injury, remained still, his body tensed in anticipation. He was wounded, yes, but far from defeated. As the general neared, thinking Elliot incapacitated, a window of opportunity opened.

As the distance closed, Elliot's survival instincts intensified. Fueled by a rush of adrenaline, he unleashed a swift sideways kick from his position on the ground. His foot connected with the general, delivering a powerful strike. The force of the kick took the general by surprise, causing his shock stick to clatter to the ground while he doubled over, gasping for air from the unforeseen attack.

Elliot, propelled by sheer willpower, rose to his feet. His instincts for self-preservation were now in full control. With a deliberate kick, he sent the shock stick skittering across the ground, away from the general's reach. Pain surged through his body, a piercing ache in his ribs hinting at possible fractures, but he dismissed it. Clenching his teeth, he stood upright, bracing himself for the final fight.

Enraged beyond measure, the general lunged at Elliot, his voice filled with murderous intent as he bellowed, "I'll kill you!" He charged with the fierce determination of a linebacker hunting down a quarterback, his shoulder colliding into Elliot's midsection with brutal force. The impact drove Elliot backward and slammed him up against the transparent cage that imprisoned Savage-Heart.

Within her enclosure, Savage-Heart was engulfed in a storm of her own making, her agitation amplified by the sounds of conflict just beyond her reach. Each roar she unleashed was a thunderous cry of maternal fury, resonating through the hangar. Her powerful claws, capable of immense destruction, scraped and pounded against the barrier in a frantic effort to reach the man responsible for her cub's suffering.

The impact against Savage-Heart's enclosure had left Elliot breathless, his ribs aching sharply with each inhalation. His energy was almost spent, his body stretched to its breaking point.

Mustered with great effort, Elliot grunted determinedly and delivered a forceful double-fisted blow to the general's back. The impact of the strike forced the general downward, clearly diminishing his strength. Seizing the opportunity, Elliot then thrust his knee with force into the general's head, snapping him upright.

With a final surge of exertion, Elliot unleashed a devastating uppercut. The power of the blow was sufficient to launch the general into the air, sending him several yards away. He crashed heavily onto the ground, lying still among the scattered debris of the containers.

Elliot stood, his chest heaving with labored breaths from the exertion of their battle, his gaze unwavering, fixed on the general lying defeated on the ground. The hangar resonated with the roars of Savage-Heart and the echoes of their fierce battle. He took a step towards the general, intent on ensuring the fight was truly over. But in a cruel twist, the general's arm shot out, snatching the shock stick, previously kicked away but now lying beside him. He aimed quickly at Elliot and fired. The blast struck Elliot directly in the chest, slamming him backward against Savage-Heart's enclosure.

Dazed, Elliot looked up to see the general, with laboring effort, rising to his feet, the shock stick pointed steadily at him. "You were a worthy adversary, Elliot," the general sneered, advancing. "But just like all the other inferior humans, you Earthlings let your emotions cloud your judgment as well." Another blast—THWUMP, THUD—hit Elliot, sliding him down the cage wall, each breath a battle against scorching agony.

The general's mocking laughter echoed through the hangar, laden with contempt. Elliot, driven by an indomitable will, fought to stand again. "You never know when you're beaten, do you?" the general taunted, his lips curling into a cruel smirk. "Not the brightest species," he sneered, his voice dripping with disdain for Earth's version of humanity.

The general's gaze shifted to the shock stick in his hand, his smirk evolving into something more sinister. "But even your stubborn friend back there couldn't withstand a shock at full power... could he?" the general taunted, his fingers deftly adjusting the device to its maximum setting. The growing hum of the shock stick filled the air with an ominous tone.

Elliot, wrestling with the agony coursing through his body, locked eyes with the general, defiance burning in his gaze. He shot back a final biting retort. "Perhaps if your species had a little more emotion, you'd have had someone watching your back too!"

As suspicion flickered in the general's eyes and his attention wavered, Ava emerged silently behind him like a shadow. Unnoticed until the decisive moment, she now stepped forward. Just as the general turned, sensing the presence behind him, she struck. The blast caught the general off guard, sending him hurtling forward from the force of the impact. He stumbled directly into Elliot's path.

Capitalizing on this moment, Elliot, using the last reserves of his energy, stepped forward to meet the off-balance general. He grabbed him by the scruff of his suit and, with a forceful spin, slammed him against the wall of Savage-Heart's enclosure. "You should know better than to come between a mother and her child," Elliot stated, his eyes piercing into the general's.

The general's eyes darted between Ava and Bella's still figure on the ground. In his eyes, a flash of understanding sparked, but the realization came too late.

"And it's an even graver error to come between a mother bear and her cub," Elliot asserted, his voice imbued with a sense of finality. Grasping the general's arm, Elliot thrust it towards the control panel of the cage. The door opened with a mechanical hiss. Seizing the moment, Elliot delivered a powerful front kick, sending the general reeling into the cage with Savage-Heart, his fate sealed.

Ava dashed to the control panel with swift reflexes, sealing the door using her CDU. As the door slid shut, entrapping the general with the enraged bear, his screams echoed through the hangar, starkly contrasting the ensuing silence. Elliot, having pushed his body past its limit, crumpled to the floor, completely drained. The magnitude of his exhaustion, coupled with the extensive damage he had endured, was overpowering.

Ava looked down at him, her expression one of compassion, witnessing the extent of his ordeal. Elliot, gasping for air, whispered a single word: "Bella!" His voice, almost lost amidst the diminishing screams of the general, was as frail as his battered body. Each breath was a painful, laborious effort. Lying there, with the full weight of their harrowing ordeal bearing down upon him, Elliot's eyes fluttered closed, his breathing becoming increasingly faint. A profound stillness settled over him and his body finally yielded to the overwhelming strain.

Chapter 70

In the silence and darkness, a faint sense of awareness began to stir within Elliot. It was difficult to discern whether this was an awakening from a deep slumber or a transition to a different plane of existence. The lines were blurred, the boundaries between the two states indistinct. In this place, there was no pain, no physical burden, only a tranquil, otherworldly existence.

Gradually, the all-encompassing void began to dissolve into a soft light, gently piercing the peaceful oblivion. Sounds filtered into his consciousness, muffled and distant at first, but slowly growing in clarity. The sensation of solid ground beneath him, the softness of a pillow under his head, and the texture of linen against his skin began to draw his awareness back to the tangible world.

Elliot's eyelids flickered open to an unrecognizable ceiling. Confusion swirled in his mind as he tried to decipher his surroundings. He lay in a room that exuded warmth and character, yet felt completely alien. His body throbbed with a deep, persistent ache and each breath brought a sharp stab of pain in his ribs—a harsh reminder of the physical reality he had re-entered.

As he tried to sit up, the room spun around him, forcing him back onto the pillow. He shut his eyes tightly, grappling with fragmented memories. The last clear images in his mind were of the hangar, the confrontation with the general, and the brutal fight that ensued.

His efforts to piece together the sequence of events were abruptly interrupted as a door swung open. Bella's voice, vibrant with relief and excitement, pierced through his fog of pain and confusion. "Mama, come quick! Elliot's awake now!" she exclaimed, calling over her shoulder. The sound of her voice anchored him back to reality.

He opened his eyes once more, this time more slowly, adjusting to the light. Bella rushed to his side, her face filled with joy. "Finally, you're awake! I thought you were going to sleep forever! Mama said we had to leave you to rest," she said.

A pained but grateful smile creased Elliot's lips as Bella's evident excitement provided a brief respite from his discomfort. "Where am I?" he asked, his gaze drifting around the unfamiliar room.

"You're in the chief's house," Bella responded. "It's a lot fancier than ours. They thought you'd be more comfortable recovering here," she added, seeing his confused expression.

As Bella's words settled in, Elliot's mind began to piece together the fragments of his scattered memories. He surmised he must have been brought to the chief's home following the skirmish with the Telvanni. Vivid images surged through his mind: the intricate game of cat and mouse played in the shadowy lanes of the Lunari village, the bold capture of the Forbidden Mountain base, the intense battle with Telvanni soldiers, Mayto bravely fighting at his side, and the grisly moment when Savage-Heart, the formidable bear, delivered the fatal blow to the general.

A wave of deep sorrow washed over Elliot as he remembered Franklin, so brutally killed by the general. Bella, perceptive to the subtle shift in his expression, asked, "Why so sad?"

"It's nothing, I was just thinking about how badly you were injured," he said, redirecting his focus to Bella. His tone softened as he asked, "How are you? The last time I saw you, you were lying unconscious." His gaze tenderly swept over her face, searching for any residual signs of the harm inflicted by one of the general's soldiers. Much to his profound relief, the angry red mark that had once marred her features was nowhere to be seen.

Bella caught his observant gaze and offered a smile of reassurance. "I'm okay, all thanks to you," she replied, her voice carrying a resilience that seemed beyond her years. "I don't remember much about the blast, just you shielding me from it." She rolled her eyes playfully, her tone laced with mock annoyance. "Looks like I owe you one again, I guess," she added, her laughter lightening the atmosphere.

"How about a hug and we'll call it even?" he proposed warmly.

At his suggestion, Bella's face brightened with a joyous smile. She leaned in eagerly for a hug, enveloping Elliot in her arms.

"Owww!" Elliot suddenly cried out. Bella pulled back immediately, her expression morphing into one of alarmed concern. Elliot's smile widened mischievously. "Got ya!" he chuckled.

A wave of relief and amusement washed over Bella's face at Elliot's jest. She leaned in once more, this time embracing him more carefully. Just as they were sharing this tender moment, Ava entered the room, pausing to watch the heartwarming scene. The deep bond that had developed between Bella and Elliot filled her heart.

As their embrace concluded, Ava made her presence known with a lighthearted comment. "I do hope you're not planning on making a three-day nap a regular thing," she remarked, her grin wide and infectious.

Elliot turned to face Ava, his expression brightening further. She approached the bed and leaned down, enveloping him in a cautious hug and planting a tender kiss on his lips.

Bella, her face lighting up with a look of surprise, remarked, "Well, this is new!"

Drawing back from their embrace, both wearing matching smiles, Elliot let out a soft chuckle, while Ava seemed slightly bashful. "I'm sorry, Bella, I meant to tell you," she said.

Bella dismissed the apology with a playful grin. "Don't worry about it," she said. "It was pretty clear what was going on between you two anyway!" she added.

Ava's cheeks turned a shade rosier as she smiled warmly. "How long have you known?"

Bella's smile widened. "You remember that time we saw that strange man screaming at Savage-Heart on top of the Great Falls? About then!" she replied, her eyes sparkling with amusement.

"Speaking of Savage-Heart..." Elliot interjected, deftly steering the conversation to a different topic, "What happened to her after... you know, with the general?"

Bella's face brightened at the mention. "She was re-united with her cub!" she exclaimed.

Ava nodded in agreement. "That's right. Some of Mayto's men temporarily placed her cub in the prison with her while we figured out a safe way to transport them back to Lunari."

"And they managed to do that?" Elliot asked, curious about the logistics.

"Yes, both Savage-Heart and her cub were released yesterday," Ava confirmed. "She's been seen around the Great Falls area since then."

"But how did they manage to get her out safely?" Elliot queried.

"With assistance from some of the Telvanni workers we captured," Ava explained. Elliot's eyebrows raised. "There's a lot to catch you up on." She smiled at him before continuing. "I don't want to overload you all at once though. If you're feeling up to it later, we could take a stroll around the village and discuss more then."

Elliot nodded. "That sounds good! But first, tell me, how's the chief doing?"

Ava's face softened with a reassuring smile. "He was pretty banged up, just like you. But he woke up yesterday and is already starting to get better. He's strong, Elliot. He's going to be okay."

"And Mayto?" Elliot inquired further.

Bella gave a playful eye roll. "So annoying! He's here every five minutes checking on you!"

Ava chuckled. "Yeah, it's kind of weird. When did you two become best friends?" she added.

Elliot cracked a smile, reflecting on the recent events. "I guess we just found something in common."

"And that was?" Ava asked curiously.

"It turns out we both enjoy fighting Telvanni soldiers. Though, I think Mayto might enjoy it a bit more than I do!" Elliot said, his grin broadening.

The room was filled with lighthearted laughter, a welcome sound after the tension and turmoil they had all endured.

Ava glanced towards the window, where soft sunlight filtered in. "We'll let you get ready," she said, rising from her seat beside the bed. "Take your time, Elliot. We'll be waiting outside when you're ready to join us."

Bella sprang off the bed, her energy seemingly endless. "I can't wait to show you around," she said with a burst of excitement. "My friends are dying to meet the man from Earth who saved Lunar!" Her smile was radiant as she exited the room.

Elliot returned their smiles. "Thank you... both of you. I'll be out shortly," he responded, watching them depart.

Alone now, Elliot hesitated, his thoughts swirling. The conversation left him with much to contemplate—from the comforting news of the chief's recovery and Savage-Heart's joyful reunion to the myriad of questions that lingered after they triumphed over the Telvanni. It was a lot to take in, but for the moment, he focused on the task at hand—rising to face the new day that lay ahead.

CHAPTER 71

BENEATH THE AZURE EXPANSE of a mid-afternoon sky, Elliot, Ava, and Bella meandered through the Lunari village. The village hummed with activity, the inhabitants animated by a newfound zest for life. Smiles as bright as the sun above warmly greeted them, each one a silent expression of gratitude for their pivotal role in the village's liberation. Elliot's presence among them was particularly heartwarming, his heroic deeds already becoming a part of the village's rich lore.

Bella, radiant with youthful enthusiasm, eagerly introduced Elliot to her friends. She proudly heralded him as the hero from Earth, the savior of Lunar. Elliot, ever humble, tried to deflect the accolades, insisting it was a group effort. Yet, in his modesty, he skillfully shone a light on Bella's own courage, elevating her in the eyes of her friends. After promising to spend the day playing with them, Bella excused herself, leaving Ava and Elliot to stroll on.

The tranquil ambiance of their walk provided the perfect backdrop for a sincere conversation. Elliot, with genuine concern, inquired about Bella's well-being following her recent ordeal. Ava shared that Bella had a tough first night, waking up in tears. "But a moment with the photo we took on your phone seemed to soothe her," Ava explained. "Since then, she's slept peacefully, no more disturbances."

Elliot smiled at Ava's recounting and tenderly clasped her hand in his as they walked on. "She's an incredible girl," he remarked, "very much like her mother." As he gently squeezed Ava's hand, their eyes met in a glance brimming with mutual longing.

Their conversation gradually shifted to a more somber topic—Franklin. The mention of his name cast a heavy pall over them, a weight of unspoken sorrow filling the air. Ava's voice, softened with regret, broke the silence. "I'm so sorry about Franklin," she whispered, her words met with a silent nod from Elliot, his face marked by deep loss.

"If I had the chance to kill the general again, I wouldn't hesitate," Elliot confessed, his words edged with a raw, barely restrained anger. A fleeting glimmer of rage in his eyes revealed the turmoil beneath his calm exterior.

Ava gently shook her head, her face set with determination. "No more talk of the general. No amount of vengeance will ever take back what he's done, and we shouldn't honor him by speaking of him anymore," she suggested, steering the conversation away from darker paths.

"You're right," Elliot acknowledged. "What happened to Franklin's body?"

Ava's voice carried a solemn note. "We brought him back from the Forbidden Mountain and laid him to rest here, on Lunar soil," she said. "I'll take you to visit his grave later, if you'd like."

"I'd appreciate that. And thank you for taking care of him," Elliot replied, his gratitude evident. "What about the Telvanni soldiers?"

"We burned all the bodies," Ava responded, her tone icy.

Elliot nodded in agreement. "No more than they deserved."

As their stroll around the village circled back to the chief's house, they were met with open arms and familiar faces. The chief, standing at the doorway, embodied a comforting mix of authority and warmth. Mayto, unable to contain his excitement, darted forward, his grin widening as he neared Elliot. In a burst of exuberant affection, he heartily clapped Elliot on the back. The well-meaning but robust thud sharply reminded Elliot of his still-mending wounds, drawing a wince and a brief flash of pain across his face.

"Easy there, big man," Elliot chuckled, trying to hide his discomfort.

"Sorry, Elliot!" Mayto exclaimed, his eyes widening with brief concern. "I forget you Earth humans are built softer than us Lunari," he said, his smile playful.

Elliot responded with a grin. "A rock is built softer than you, Mayto!" He then turned to the chief, his tone sincere. "It's great to see you too, Chief. We wouldn't be here without that diversion in the hangar."

"Speak for yourself!" Mayto retorted. "I was barely breaking a sweat against those soldiers!"

The chief, wearing a look of relief, then addressed Elliot. "It's good to see you up and about, Elliot," he said. "Come inside, we have a lot to talk about." He motioned towards his home. "And I bet you're hungry too."

"Starving," Elliot agreed with a smile, stepping up towards the house.

Upon entering the chief's home, a wave of tranquility washed over them. The interior was a showcase of Lunari heritage, adorned with artifacts and symbols that spoke of a history rich with tradition. They were led to the main room, where a lavish dining area awaited, meticulously set for lunch.

The chief, embodying the essence of gracious hospitality, invited them to be seated. Quiet, efficient servants appeared, bearing trays heaped with an array of dishes. The mingling aromas, both familiar and unfamiliar, filled the air, teasing their senses and heralding a feast of culinary delight.

As they settled in, the chief turned to Elliot with a respectful nod. "We are honored to have you dine with us, Elliot. Your bravery has brought new hope to our people," he said, his voice imbued with gratitude and respect.

"Thank you, Chief, for your kind words and this warm welcome," Elliot began, his voice rich with sincerity. "It's an honor to be here among friends and family."

He picked up his cup, the liquid within catching and reflecting the light. "To the Lunari people," he said, his gaze sweeping across the faces around the table and pausing on the chief, "for their resilience and their courage."

Elliot's eyes shone with sincerity as he turned to face Mayto. "To good friends, who stand back-to-back with us in the darkest of times." Mayto's chest swelled with pride at Elliot's words. He raised his cup higher, nodding in acknowledgment.

Turning towards Ava, Elliot continued. "And to our loved ones, who remain our anchor through every storm." Ava's eyes shimmered, tears beginning to form at the corners of her eyes.

Raising his cup higher, Elliot concluded, "And here's to the bright future that lies ahead for the Lunari people."

"Here here!" Mayto bellowed, raising his cup high, prompting everyone else to follow suit in a unison of clinking cups and shared sentiments.

As they settled into their lunch, the atmosphere around the table was one of familial ease and joy. Each person took a turn to share stories. The sound of laughter echoed through the chief's home, a testament to the resilience and enduring spirit of those gathered.

As the laughter subsided and the final remnants of the meal were cleared away, the chief leaned forward, his expression turning more serious. The room quieted, filling with a sense of anticipation.

"We have all enjoyed good food and good conversation," the chief began, his voice steady, capturing the attention of everyone around the table. "But now, we must address our future. If we wish for it to be as bright as Elliot suggests, then we must be proactive in ensuring that."

The chief began to update Elliot about the latest developments since their triumph at the Forbidden Mountain. Mayto and Ava contributed with additional insights and details, where they had firsthand experiences.

Elliot sat attentively, interjecting only occasionally with follow-up questions. He learned of Ava's successful role in leading the Lunari team inside the Forbidden Mountain while he and Mayto were engaged at the hangar. She had skillfully ensured the restoration of power and life support systems in Lunar, all while securing the Telvanni workers. Only after completing these tasks and noticing Elliot and Mayto's absence at the hangar entrance did she sense something amiss. Accompanied by some Lunari soldiers, she had ventured into the hangar, eventually encountering Mayto and the chief. Following Mayto's direction, Ava quickly made her way to the location where Elliot and Bella had last been seen. Beyond this point, Elliot was familiar with the events, his own experiences filling in the narrative.

Following the ordeal, both Elliot and the chief had been brought back to the Lunari village. In the chief's home, they received the essential care needed for their recuperation. During this time, Mayto and his team assumed control at the Forbidden Mountain, overseeing the prisoners and maintaining order until the chief had recovered sufficiently to resume his duties.

The chief, Mayto, and Ava delved into in-depth discussions about their next steps. They decided to work with the cooperative Telvanni workers, enlisting their help to operate the base and improve the Lunar systems in exchange for better living conditions. Under Mayto's supervision, his team closely monitored these workers, guaranteeing fair treatment while maintaining security.

One of the first tasks for the cooperative Telvanni workers was safely returning Savage-Heart and her cub to Lunar. This was achieved by carefully sedating the animals in captivity, ensuring a tranquil and secure journey back to the Great Falls. The Telvanni's skilled management of this task proved essential. In recognition of the Telvanni workers' efforts, they were permitted to return to their original living quarters. However, to ensure continued security and order, Mayto's team maintained control over their movement and access within the base.

In the ensuing days, a deeper understanding of the Telvanni people emerged. They discovered that many lived under the oppressive shadow of fear cast by the supreme telvarch and, by extension, the general. The Telvanni workers' compliance was driven more by self-preservation than loyalty, and they adamantly distanced themselves from any violent acts, attributing such deeds solely to the general and his soldiers. However, a faction among the Telvanni workers staunchly adhered to their traditional ways. This division came to a head on the second day when these loyalists assaulted their own people, signaling the need for their segregation. These hard-liners were now confined to separate holding cells, prohibited from interacting with those Telvanni who had expressed sympathy with the Lunari cause.

"And that's where we are now," the chief concluded. "Everyone is trying to return to some sense of normality."

Elliot nodded in agreement. "And that's not a bad thing," he said. "The Lunari have lived under the shadow of the Telvanni their entire lives. This conflict isn't over, as we all know. It's probably just starting. But we've bought ourselves some time, and it's crucial that we use it wisely."

"What are you suggesting, Elliot?" Ava asked.

"We start by learning everything we can about the Telvanni," Elliot responded, his gaze moving thoughtfully from one face to another. "Luckily, we have about forty or fifty of their people as prisoners, plus a base full of their technology to study. We need to understand what we're up against if we're to be the first species of humanity to survive them."

Mayto grunted. "You know I'm always ready to fight, but we have to be smart about this. They've conquered entire worlds, many with far more advanced technology than ours, and none could withstand them. So, what odds do we really have with just our spears, arrows, and a handful of their shock sticks?"

"And what were our odds here with those same weapons?" Elliot countered confidently.

"That was different; they weren't expecting us."

Elliot responded with a broad, confident smile, his green eyes alight with determination. His reply, simple yet filled with astonishing resolve, left no room for doubt about his intentions. "Then let's ensure they don't expect us this time either!"

EPILOGUE

THE MASSIVE HANGAR DOOR groaned into motion, its heavy panels retracting to unveil the stark, desolate expanse of the Moon. Beyond the threshold of the hangar, the lunar landscape stretched out, a vast canvas of shadows and light. The blackness of space enveloped this alien terrain, stars twinkling like distant beacons in the vastness. Craters, each a testament to the Moon's ageless history, pockmarked the surface, their edges sharply defined under the unfiltered sunlight.

As the door completed its majestic sweep, a sleek hover rover embarked on its odyssey across this unforgiving landscape. The vehicle, a pinnacle of contemporary engineering, appeared almost spectral against the rugged lunar backdrop. Its design, both light and sturdy, was crafted to withstand the harsh lunar conditions. Beneath its frame, the advanced hover technology hummed to life, a seamless blend of magnetic levitation and ion propulsion.

The rover glided across the Moon's surface with a fluidity that masked its intricate technology. Its sensors and AI systems continuously surveyed the terrain, piloting with an intelligence that seemed almost sentient. Inside, a plethora of scientific tools relayed data from the rover's extensive external sensors. Subtly integrated into its exterior, solar panels soaked in the relentless solar energy, powering the rover's silent, vigilant exploration of the Moon.

As the rover accelerated, its silhouette glided smoothly over the lunar terrain, effortlessly navigating craters and rocky outcrops. Behind them, the airlock door of the hangar began its slow, inexorable closure, sealing off the last remnants of the base, leaving behind no trace of its presence. The rover, now a solitary voyager in this immense wilderness, continued steadfastly toward its predetermined destination.

The interior of the rover hummed with quiet energy, its five passengers each cloaked in sleek white suits adorned with a striking blue stripe down each side. Their helmets, featuring wide black visors, provided an expansive view of the lunar landscape while shielding their faces from view.

Up front, a noticeably large man turned to the driver, his voice laced with awe. "I can't believe after all these years I'm finally going to see the sun with my own eyes," he said. "Thanks for bringing me along, Elliot."

Elliot, focused on the controls, responded without taking his eyes off the path ahead. "I needed to see the damage done to Earth for myself, and I couldn't think of a better place for you to see your first sunrise from, Chief."

Behind him, a substantial hand belonging to a figure of similar stature as the man up front reached out, resting reassuringly on Elliot's shoulder. This silent gesture of gratitude, a wordless *thank you*, resonated deeply in the confined space of the hover rover.

"How's everyone doing back there?" Elliot called back, his voice coming through clearly, a result of an upgrade to the suit's communication system by a helpful Telvanni technician earlier.

"This is the best adventure ever!" exclaimed Bella, her excitement evident as she kept switching views from one window to another. "You wait till I tell my friends what I did today!"

"Just look at all those stars, darling," Ava said, gazing through the rover's panoramic roof. "Have you ever seen anything so incredible?"

"If you think that's impressive, wait until you see Earth alongside the sun from here," Elliot replied. "It's a real game changer, even though Earth might look a bit battered right now."

Mayto's hand returned to Elliot's shoulder, offering another comforting squeeze. "She's bruised, buddy, but still standing strong."

As the hover rover continued its journey, each passenger was immersed in their own thoughts and emotions, united by the anticipation of witnessing a sight few had ever seen. The comfortable silence that followed was filled with shared understanding and unspoken bonds forged by their common purpose.

Advancing, the lunar landscape revealed a new vista—the silhouette of Earth's lunar base, now a stark emblem of devastation, rose into view. This place resonated deeply with Elliot; here, one chapter of his life had closed and an unexpected one had begun.

"There's the site ahead," Elliot announced. "You should see Earth in a minute."

As the hover rover neared the base site, the stark remnants of what once was stood bathed in the unyielding lunar light, a poignant reminder of the past. But it was the sight beyond that captured their collective breaths. Earth, hanging like a fragile marble in the vastness of space, was visible in its full, tragic glory.

Once a vibrant blue-and-green jewel, Earth now bore the deep scars of the catastrophic asteroid impact that had occurred less than a month prior. Huge swathes of the planet were enveloped in a veil of dust and debris, obscuring the once-familiar continents. The blues of the oceans were muted and the greens of the landmasses dulled—a stark visual testament to the devastating event that had nearly obliterated all life.

Amidst this solemn backdrop, the rover slowed, its hover engines emitting a soft hum as it approached an evocative landmark: an upturned lunar rover. This was no ordinary relic; it was the very rover that Elliot and Franklin had used, now lying in a state of silent abandonment. Its once-gleaming surface, marred by the lunar environment, stood as a testament to the unforgiving nature of space and the fragility of human endeavors.

Elliot's gaze lingered on the upturned vehicle, a flood of memories and emotions visible even behind his helmet's visor. The sight of Earth's wounded state, alongside the rover's silent testimony, fostered a shared understanding among the passengers—a reflection on the enormity of their loss and the resilience of the human spirit against overwhelming odds.

For the other passengers, witnessing Earth for the first time was a moment of profound amazement tinged with sorrow. They had only known of Earth through stories and images, and seeing it now, scarred and fragile, was both awe-inspiring and heartbreaking. The sight of the once-thriving planet, now a shadow of its former self, elicited a mix of wonder and grief. They were seeing history, a pivotal moment in the story of humanity, and it was both incredible and tragic.

For Elliot, the view of Earth was a stark, painful reminder of all that had been lost. The planet he once called home, now marred by the catastrophic actions of the Telvanni race, stirred a deep-seated anger within him. This anger, intermingled with profound grief, reflected not just personal loss but also the ruthless devastation of an enemy bent on dominance.

As Elliot gazed at the damaged Earth, his resolve hardened. The sight of the battered planet, coupled with memories of what had transpired, ignited his determination to seek retribution and honor those needlessly lost. He felt a duty to past victims and future generations inheriting this scarred world. In that moment, he made a solemn vow to himself and to the lives that had been extinguished: he would relentlessly pursue those responsible for this genocide.

Elliot's grip on the rover's controls tightened, a tangible sign of his resolute spirit. He closed his eyes briefly, inhaling deeply to steady himself. In that pause, he embraced the full weight of his emotions—the anger and grief for Earth. Exhaling slowly, he allowed the tension to ebb away. When his eyes opened again, a serene calm enveloped him. Turning to his companions, a subtle smile touched his lips.

"There's about twenty minutes to sunrise," he announced, his voice now imbued with calm steadiness. "Who fancies a walk on the Moon?"

Excitement rippled through the cabin at his suggestion. The idea of a moonwalk, combined with the awe-inspiring sight of a sunrise, offered a brief yet powerful respite from the weight of their circumstances. As they prepared for the excursion, the lunar landscape outside beckoned—a realm of tranquility and enigma beneath the timeless night sky, offering a stark contrast to the strife they had endured.

As they took their first steps onto the Moon's surface, the crunch of regolith under their boots resonated in the silence of the vacuum. Around them, the stark, barren landscape was bathed in the faint, ethereal glow of Earth's light on the horizon—a sight of profound beauty and solemnity that quickened their hearts.

The chief, though his face was obscured by the visor of his helmet, exuded a quiet sense of contentment as he gazed toward the emerging sunrise. Beside him, Mayto, equally captivated, sat observing the celestial display. For the chief, this sunrise was more than a beautiful spectacle: it symbolized hope for his people.

The sun's first rays began to creep over the lunar horizon, casting long, ghostly shadows across the Moon's surface. The light, diffused and delicate, bathed the landscape in a gentle glow. The sight was breathtaking, momentarily eclipsing the memories of hardship and loss.

As the sun climbed higher, its beams spread across the lunar landscape, illuminating the derelict site and scattered debris in a soft, otherworldly light. The celestial dawn reached the lunar rover, highlighting its massive idle wheels. Sunlight streamed through the windshield and side windows of the overturned rover, filling its interior with a warm glow, contrasting the cool lunar morning.

Inside the rover, the once-orderly space was now a tableau of chaos. Equipment and personal items lay scattered, indicative of a sudden violent disturbance. The cockpit, formerly a hub of activity, had become a jumbled mess of controls and screens, some flickering weakly in the dawning light.

Amidst the rover's turmoil, its communication console, surprisingly intact, began to crackle to life. A faint, static-filled message cut through the silence, emerging from the speakers. The distant, intermittent voice offered a jarring contrast to the tranquility outside, reminding them of the rover's troubled past amidst the serene lunar dawn.

[Static crackles; the sound is faint, interspersed with bursts of clearer audio.] "This is an SOS call for any and all survivors. If anyone can hear this, please respond. We're a group of forty-three, men, women, and children, sheltered in Government Bunker Delta-4. The asteroid impact—[static interference]—we thought all was lost, but we somehow managed to find our way here."

[The voice is strained, yet hopeful.] "We have a lot of scared people here, unsure of what to do next... [An audible sigh is heard.] We're seeking any information, any signs of other survivors. We're just looking for some hope. If anyone else is out there, please, respond."

[Static crackles; the transmission ends.]

Outside the window, five figures sat together on the lunar surface, absorbed in a collective silence as they watched the sun rise over the ravaged Earth. The dawn cast its light over the desolate Moon, ushering in a new day filled with an unspoken promise of hope.

Thank You! Please Read.

Thank you for joining me on this journey and reaching the end of this adventure. I sincerely hope you found as much joy in reading it as I did in writing it. Your support means the world to me and plays a pivotal role in bringing stories like this to life.

It would mean the world to me if you could share your thoughts on this novel and leave an honest review on Amazon and/or Goodreads (link on next page). Your reviews and feedback are invaluable, helping to introduce these stories to more readers and allowing me to continue my passion for storytelling.

For those who wish to stay connected and dive deeper into the worlds I create, I invite you to visit my website, ht tps://bradleyjamesauthor.com/ , and join the mailing list. Members of my community are always the first to know about upcoming books, the progress of current projects, and exclusive sneak peeks, including short stories, sample chapters, and cover reveals before they are made public.

Your engagement and enthusiasm fuel my creativity, and I look forward to sharing more adventures with you soon.

Thank you once again for your support. Until our paths cross again in the pages of my next book, happy reading!

Bradley James

How to leave a review on Amazon

Step 1. Point your phone's camera at the QR Code below.

Step 2. Press the link displayed on your phone's screen.
Step 3. Leave an honest review on Amazon

THE AFTERMATH: TITAN

BOOK 2

TITAN'S CALLING...

The Telvanni have grown suspicious from Titan, not everyone can be trusted on Lunar, and there's something deadly lurking in the void—join Elliot Adams in a brand new adventure as he steps deeper into the aftermath.

Suspicious of Lunar's silence, the Telvanni have begun asking questions from their moon base on Titan. But Elliot's troubles run deeper. Before his death, the General unleashed the Telvanni's deadliest weapon—the Death Shepherd—on a mission to wipe out the last remnants of humanity on Earth. But how can they stop something they cannot even see?

With time running out and those closest to him in danger, Elliot and his friends must embark on a perilous mission to Titan. But the Telvanni moonbase harbors its own dark secrets, and the Supreme Telvarch will stop at nothing to achieve his goals.

As the lines between friend and foe blur, Elliot must confront more than just a relentless enemy if he's to save more than one world.

Packed with action, intrigue, and unexpected twists, The Aftermath: Titan delivers an unforgettable sci-fi adventure where survival depends not just on strength—but on making impossible choices.

GRAB YOUR COPY NOW!

To find all the platforms this book is currently available on, you can either scan the QR code below, click the following link, or enter it into your web browser:

https://books.bradleyjamesauthor.com/the_aftmath_titan